THE SECRET OF
the Journal

ROPE OF SAND

C. F. Dunn

LION FICTION

Published by Lion Fiction
an imprint of
Lion Hudson plc
Wilkinson House, Jordan Hill Road,
Oxford OX2 8DR, England
www.lionhudson.com/fiction

ISBN 978 1 78264 087 5
e-ISBN 978 1 78264 088 2

This edition 2014

Acknowledgments
Cover images: Woman © Maja Topcagic / Trevillion Images; Man ©
Robert Recker/Corbis; Books © iStockphoto/Diane Diederich.

Internal background images: p. 10 © iStockphoto/Kim Sohee

A catalogue record for this book is available from the British Library.

Printed and bound in the UK, March 2014, LH26

ROPE OF
SAND

BY THE SAME AUTHOR
Mortal Fire
Death Be Not Proud

"An addictive mix of suspense, romance, and the supernatural. C. F. Dunn has a voice that makes you want to read on."
Jane Bidder, author of *Guilty*

"A triumph of storytelling draws us into an electrifying climax. A true tour de force."
Eric Delve, author of *To Boldly Go*

Contents

To my girls, for their inspiration and forbearance.

Acknowledgments

This is my opportunity to thank all those involved in bringing *Rope of Sand* out of my imagination and on to the shelves. So, to start with, I owe grateful thanks to my publisher and editor in the UK, Tony Collins, and the Lion Fiction team with editors Jess Tinker and Sheila Jacobs, designers Jude May and Jen Stephens, and Simon Cox, who have helped bring Emma and Matthew to life, and to Sarah Krueger of Kregel Publishing in the USA.

I am indebted to authors Jane Bidder (aka Janey Fraser/ Sophie King) and Revd Eric Delve for their timely and invaluable comments, and to the many people who, in their professional capacity, have generously given their time and advice, especially: Hon William Mahoney, District Court Judge, for explaining the intricacies of the legal system; for her insight into psychological conditions, consultant psychiatrist Dr Kiki O'Neill-Byrne MB, BCH, BAO, Dip Clin Psych, MRCPsych; and the medical advice of Dr Catherine Handy MB, BAO, BCh, MRCGP.

Thanks, also, to author Sue Russell and colleagues Dee Prewer and Lisa Lewin for their invaluable feedback and support, and to the staff at Cobham Hall School for providing an appropriately historic setting in which to hold my launch events. Michelle Jimerson Morris – many thanks for helping me with your contact – you know who it is – and thanks to Norm Forgey of Maine Day Trip, who once again answered my plea for help and provided vital local information.

Everlasting gratitude to my husband and daughters, my mother and father, and my brother and his family, whose love and tireless encouragement keep me going, step by step, along the road.

Characters

ACADEMIC & RESEARCH STAFF AT HOWARD'S LAKE COLLEGE, MAINE

Emma D'Eresby, Department of History (Medieval and Early Modern)

Elena Smalova, Department of History (Post-Revolutionary Soviet Society)

Matias Lidström, Faculty of Bio-medicine (Genetics)

Matthew Lynes, surgeon, Faculty of Bio-medicine (Mutagenesis)

Sam Wiesner, Department of Mathematics (Metamathematics)

Madge Makepeace, Faculty of Social Sciences (Anthropology)

Siggie Gerhard, Faculty of Social Sciences (Psychology)

Saul Abrahms, Faculty of Social Sciences (Psychology of Functional Governance)

Colin Eckhart, Department of History (Renaissance and Reformation Art)

Kort Staahl, Department of English (Early Modern Literature)

Megan, research assistant, Bio-medicine

Sung, research assistant, Bio-medicine

The Dean, Stephen Shotter

MA STUDENTS

Holly Stanhope; Josh Feitel; Hannah Graham; Aydin Yilmaz; Leo Hamell

IN CAMBRIDGE

Guy Hilliard, Emma's former tutor
Tom Falconer, Emma's friend

EMMA'S FAMILY

Hugh D'Eresby, her father
Penny D'Eresby, her mother
Beth Marshall, her sister
Rob Marshall, her brother-in-law
Alex & Flora, her twin nephew and niece
Archie, her nephew
Nanna, her grandmother

Mike Taylor, friend of the family
Joan Seaton, friend of the family

MATTHEW'S FAMILY

Ellen Lynes, his wife
Henry Lynes, his son
Patricia (Pat) Lynes, Henry's wife
Margaret (Maggie) Lynes, his granddaughter
Daniel (Dan) Lynes, his grandson
Jeanette (Jeannie) Rathbone – Dan's wife, and their children:
Ellie Lynes
Joel Lynes
Harry Lynes

Monica – Henry's first wife

THE LYNES FAMILY TREE

Eliz'beth b. 1575
m
M'tthw Monfort

Henry b. 1577
d. ?
m
Marg'rt Fielding

W'llm b. 1586
d. 1643

M'tthw b. 1609
m
Ellen b. 1914

infant d. 1611

Monica
m [1]

Henry
m [2]

Patricia

Ellen
(Little Ellen)

Marg'rt
(Maggie)

Daniel
m
Jeanette

Ellie   Joel   Harry

The Story So Far

Independent and self-contained British historian Emma D'Eresby has taken up a year-long research post in an exclusive American university in Maine, fulfilling her ambition (and that of her grandfather) to study the Richardson Journal – the diary of a seventeenth-century Englishman – housed in the library there.

Single-minded and determined, Emma is wary of relationships, but she quickly attracts the unwelcome attention of seductive colleague, Sam Weisner, and the disturbing professor of English, Kort Staahl. Despite her best intentions to remain focused on her work, and encouraged by her vivacious Russian friend, Elena Smalova, Emma becomes increasingly attracted to medical research scientist and surgeon Matthew Lynes, whose old-fashioned courtesy she finds both disarming and curious.

Widowed and living quietly with his family, Matthew is reluctant to let her into his life, despite his clear interest in her, and Emma suspects there is more to his past than the little he tells her. The familiarity of his English-sounding name and the distinctive colour of his hair intrigues her, and Emma believes there is a link between Matthew and the very journal she came to the United States to study. Against her nature, she smuggles the historic document from the library to investigate further.

Events take a sinister turn as a series of savage assaults on women sends ripples of fear through the campus. Emma is convinced she is being followed, and during the prestigious

All Saints' dinner at Halloween, she is viciously attacked by psychotic Professor Staahl, leaving her on the edge of death. Only Matthew's timely intervention saves her and, as he cares for her in his college rooms, their relationship deepens and Emma finds herself battling between her growing love and her need to learn more about him.

A near-fatal encounter with a bear raises questions about Matthew she can no longer ignore.

Frustrated by the mystery surrounding his past and his refusal to tell her who he really is, Emma reluctantly flees Maine to her claustrophobic family home in England. Hidden from sight, but not her conscience, she has also taken the journal.

Years of acrimony with her family and a bruising affair a decade before with her tutor, Guy Hilliard – a married man – have left their scars. Now broken both physically and emotionally, and facing a crisis, Emma drifts, until a chance meeting refocuses her attention on the unanswered questions she had left behind. Using her historical training to trace Matthew's family to an almost extinct hamlet in the tiny county of Rutland, she makes a startling discovery. Her instinct had been right: Matthew is a relic of the past.

Born in the early years of the seventeenth century, Matthew had been betrayed during the English Civil War when a clash with his uncle left him fighting for his life. He not only lived, but *persisted*, growing steadily in strength and surviving events that would have killed any other man. Diary entries by the family steward in the same journal now in Emma's possession reveal that in the overheated atmosphere of seventeenth-century England – where rumours were rife and accusations of witchcraft frequent – Matthew faced persecution because of his differences, and he fled to the American colonies.

Coming to terms with Matthew's past, Emma is all too aware that she possesses knowledge that could destroy his future and, when she learns he has disappeared from the college, sinks further into desolation. But as winter descends on the old stone walls of her family home, Matthew, unable to remain separated from her, comes to find Emma and takes her back to America.

Looking forward to the future, Emma believes she has all the answers, but Matthew has one more revelation that could end their relationship once and for all. In a fraught confrontation in a remote snowbound cabin high in the mountains, Matthew tells her that he is still married. Over a harrowing few days with their relationship hanging in the balance, Matthew recounts his story, and Emma learns that his wife, Ellen, is a 96-year-old paraplegic, and the man she thought was his father is, in fact, his son. Emma is faced with a stark choice: cut all ties with Matthew as she once did with Guy, or face an uncertain future with the only man she has ever really loved. Emma believes that her life is inextricably linked with Matthew's and makes the decision to stay with him with all the complications it will entail.

As she prepares to meet Matthew's family at Christmas, the last thing on Emma's mind is college professor Sam Wiesner, but it becomes apparent that she has been very much on his. After a brief but unpleasant encounter in which Sam acquires a broken jaw, Emma is forced to warn Sam off. But, despite her best efforts to protect Matthew's identity, wheels have been set in motion that one day could expose him to the world.

Secure in their bonds of faith and love and now approaching the threshold of his home, Emma faces far more than just meeting Matthew's family for the first time; but what she does not know cannot hurt her, surely?

1

Future Perfect

When had curiosity become fascination? At what point had fascination become love? How could I have let it happen after everything I have been through, after all the promises I made myself? After all the years spent reined in so tight that I hadn't let my guard down – not once, not ever – and now this; stealthily and without declaration and without any shadow of doubt.

Riding compacted snow, the car drew in front of the classical house and came to a standstill. Emphatic silence replaced the sound of the engine.

"Do I *have* to do this?" I asked Matthew, knowing the answer before he came around to my side of the car and offered me his hand. Reluctantly stepping onto the snow, I looked up, and an unexpected movement caught my eye as a face appeared at a first-floor window. Ghost-pale and with silver-white hair, hollow eyes punctuated its skull. The disembodied face hovered momentarily before retreating into the darkness. I stared. I blinked. "Matthew, is your house haunted?"

The tall, distinguished man who greeted us had one of those faces you couldn't help but like straightaway. Well-cut hair of a distinctive aluminium framed his face with a neat, trimmed moustache and beard. Eyes of an indeterminate blue gleamed behind silver-framed glasses, and he was already smiling, a habit evident in the uplifted corners of his mouth and the deep lines either side of his eyes that crinkled on seeing me. There was good humour and kindliness in this face, patience and wisdom.

"Dr D'Eresby, you are welcome. Please, come in." He opened the door wide and I stepped across the threshold of Matthew's home, finding reassurance in the steady pressure of his arm around my waist.

"Henry, thank you." Matthew indicated the older man in front of him. "Emma, this is my son, Henry, and his wife, Patricia."

I held out my hand to the man old enough to be my father, although the quality of his skin was that of a much younger man than his hair suggested. With a slight bow of his head he took my hand within his firm handshake. "We're so glad you can join us for Christmas, Dr D'Eresby."

"Thank you. How do you do?" I said shyly.

"Pat's been looking forward to quizzing you about traditional English fare. I think she's hoping to ring the changes with Christmas dinner, and experiment on you."

"I'm probably not the best person to ask," I said apologetically, turning to a woman in her sixties, my height, and with fashionably short hair coloured soft greys and gold, the colour of late summer, and returning her smile.

Pat tutted. "There now, don't listen to him! He's a terrible tease. We can do with some more female company around here, can't we, Ellie?" I recognized the slim figure of Matthew's great-granddaughter from the hazy days I had spent recovering in the medical centre, and noted she didn't reply.

Matthew interjected before her silence became too obvious. "Emma – you've already met Ellie and Harry." Leaning on one of the elegantly curved banister rails of the wide wood staircase, Harry beamed cheerfully at me over his sister's head. "Dr D'Eresby, *ma'am!*"

I suppressed the urge to respond with something pithy; Ellie threw him a sharp sideways look and smiled stiffly, but I saw the way she glanced at Matthew's hand on my hip, and the slight pout of her mouth.

Pat left Henry's side. "Oh, just look at us all standing around here when I'm sure you would like to come on in and have a cup of tea. I've been just dying to meet you, sweetie, and I want you to tell me all about where you come from. Matthew has been so secretive that getting him to say anything is like drawing rope through a needle."

Matthew held on to me firmly. "Before I relinquish you to Pat's interrogation, I'll show you around. Where is Maggie?"

Henry's briefest hesitancy said it all. "I... don't think she knows you've arrived. I'll find her and let her know." *That must be Ghost-face*, I thought; *and therein lies a problem.*

"Thank you, if you would. Pat, we won't be long. Harry, will you fetch Dr D'Eresby's bags from the car, please – they're in the back." Matthew guided me towards the stairs, and I could feel four pairs of eyes watching us. He didn't take his arm from around my waist until we reached the galleried landing and were out of sight; then he enfolded me in both. "That's the worst bit over; have you survived?" he asked, his mouth against my ear. I held on to him, my head tucked under his chin.

"I will now, but I didn't expect to meet your family so soon."

"They wanted to be here to help you feel at home."

"That was kind. Pat and Henry are so welcoming, and it

must be as strange for them as it is for me. They live next door in the long building at right angles to this one, don't they?"

"Yes, in the barn conversion, and Ellie and her brothers live with their parents in The Stables across the courtyard. You'll meet Dan and Jeannie later, I expect."

He'd left out one other member of the family: his granddaughter, Margaret.

"And does Maggie have a problem with me being here?"

He nuzzled the top of my head with his cheek. "Oh, you caught that, did you? Maggie has a few issues to work through. It's not you so much as her internal demons. But whatever her problems, you are here with me and that won't change, so don't let it worry you." That was easier said than done and I suspected that it was more straightforward than he let on: Maggie didn't want me there. Full stop. End of discussion. He took me by the hand, not letting me dwell on it. "Come on, I'll show you where everything is."

A central window above the front door, and one either side, made the broad horseshoe of the landing immensely light despite the overcast day. Doors led off the landing.

"That's Maggie's room when she stays here – she has a place of her own in town – another couple of guest rooms, then yours, and then mine next to it. Come and have a look at your room and make sure you have everything you need."

A fire had been lit in the fireplace of a room much bigger than my bedroom at home. Matthew led me past the rosy polished wood of the bed to where a wingback chair overlooked the sheltered courtyard and the mountains roaming the skyline beyond. On a slender-stemmed table, a crystal vase of pale pink and cream blooms lent an unseasonal fragrance. It felt a comfortable, inviting room and someone had gone to a great deal of trouble to make it feel so.

I turned to Matthew. "It's lovely, and I'll have everything I need – but you."

He gave me a roguish grin. "Who says you won't have me – or most of me, at the very least?"

"Well, in that case, I have everything." I glanced around the room at the pretty antique bed with its floral quilted covers, and the glossy women's magazines on the table. "Who stays here normally?"

He frowned. "Normally? No one. Only Maggie stays in this part of the house. Why?"

"It almost feels as if someone does, that's all."

He nodded slowly, "Good, that's how it's supposed to seem. Would you like to see my room?"

He took me out onto the landing and through the next door. I didn't know what I expected to find. Bedrooms are so intensely personal that entering one without invitation is tantamount to a violation. Even being there with him made me feel a little awkward. Larger again than mine, the windows threw cold, snow-reflected light against sombre grey-green walls. Classic it might have been, and in keeping with the fine, restrained antiques that simply furnished the room, but it lacked heart.

He led me past his plain bed, lying forlornly against the left wall, and to the far windows, where a gleam of sunlight struck the richly polished floor, casting a strip of light across my feet. Almost enclosed by the heavy curtains, we were alone again in our own world as we looked out on his. As he stood behind me, I pushed back against his solidity, feeling safe.

"This is what I wanted you to see," he said quietly.

A vast snowscape of foothills, rising to meet the distant mountains, flowed from the house, velvet-gloved and rolling away to where clusters of trees marked the course of the river.

Trees stood more thickly beyond the thin ribbon of water, crowding along the embankment as if queuing to cross. The attraction of the land derived from its simple beauty, and the sense of total peace and freedom that lay upon the open spaces and big, wide sky.

"It's so different to what I'm used to…"

"But do you like it?"

"I *love* it," I breathed.

His arms tightened about me. "In spring, the new leaves on those trees look like early morning sun, even when it's cloudy, and those dips and bumps down there…" he pointed at the white undulations, "… are covered in flowers, just… just as I remember the Meadows down by the river at home after the winter floods." I heard a note of longing in his voice and gave him a moment. "When we first came here and the children were younger, we taught them to fish in the river – not rod and line fishing – we caught them by hand…"

"You tickled trout!"

"Mmm, well, they didn't catch much but that wasn't the point; they loved to have a go, and it was great when they succeeded. Have you ever tried?"

I remembered my one and only attempt to tickle a fish. "Yes – and no. I tried to catch a wounded pike and it didn't like it."

He shook his head, and held out my hands, spreading my fingers, a tiny white scar at the base of my thumb all that remained of my encounter. "No bits missing. What were you doing trying to catch a pike by hand, you strange creature?"

"Well, Grandad – my father's father, that is – had managed to hook a monster, but it had become caught in a bit of submerged fence so he sent me in to get it."

Matthew peered at me incredulously. "And how old were you?"

"Ten-ish, I think."

"What did he think he was doing? You could have lost a hand!"

"Um, well, I don't think he thought about it that much. He said, 'Don't let it see you're frightened, girl; show it who's in command,' or something like that. Anyway, it tried to bite me…"

"Oddly enough," Matthew muttered.

"… and I fell in and managed to dislodge the fencing and it escaped – thankfully. I didn't want to see it stuffed and mounted on the wall."

"What did your grandfather say to that?"

"He wasn't very pleased. I managed to avoid going fishing with him after that."

"I'm glad to hear it." He wrapped his fingers through mine and stroked my palm with his thumb as we took pleasure in our solitude.

"Will you show me how to tickle trout?"

"If you would like me to," he laughed. "I promise I won't use you as bait. On another note, what do you think of this room?"

I looked around it again. "Why?"

"I would value your opinion."

"You don't spend very much time here, do you?"

"No, not really. I don't need to."

"That's what it looks like – empty; there's nothing of *you* in here. Lovely furniture, wonderful room, of course, but it's like it's staged: no photos, no books, no – oh, I don't know – dressing gown. It's unlived in."

He sighed. "That's probably because it is. I was afraid of that. I try to make everything look as normal as I can, in case… let's just say so that it doesn't invite unwelcome questions, but I can't seem to get this room right. Perhaps you could help me change that in the future?" His voice softened, and I noticed that he had slipped that bit in as if he were testing the waters, and my heart tumbled haphazardly. I bent my head back to look at him upside down and he kissed the tip of my nose.

"That sounds good. That sounds *very* good. How long do you think you will have here before you have to move on?"

"Another three years or so, perhaps a little longer, before we – before *I* – become obvious. I'll be sorry to leave; we all will." I wondered whether by then I would be leaving with him. "Like to see the rest?" he asked, interrupting my thoughts.

We were halfway down the stairs when Henry came into the hall with a sheaf of papers in his hand. He looked up as he heard us. "I was coming to find you. When you have a minute I have something I think you'll want to see." He raised the papers and an eyebrow, in that instance looking just like Matthew. There was an undercurrent of excitement in his voice, and I saw the query on Matthew's face, and the sudden light in his eyes.

"Any chance I could have that cup of tea now and see the rest of the house later?" I suggested.

Matthew squeezed my hand. "Thank you for that. This is work-related, I'm afraid. I'll find you as soon as Henry's shown me these." He showed me a door on the far right of the hall beyond the staircase and kissed me, not attempting to hide it from his son. "I won't be long."

As they moved across to a door diagonally opposite to where I still stood, Henry was saying something quietly to Matthew about Maggie. I didn't catch his reply.

The kitchen had fabulous views looking towards the river on one side and into the sheltered courtyard on the other. Broad, pale wood planks made up the floor, and where the black iron stove would have been, a modern range sat radiating heat. This homely room of light painted wood and glass-fronted cupboards had a disarming simplicity – the finish bespoke – and I wondered if all the family used it or whether this represented part of the stage upon which Matthew acted out a normal life.

Pat sat reading a newspaper at the old farmhouse table, frameless glasses perched on her nose. A large crate of mixed vegetables bulged on the floor next to her. She looked up when she heard me come in. "There you are!" she greeted me, putting the paper down, rising from the table and kissing me on both cheeks. "Come on in. I'm just about to sort things out for this evening. Are you ready for that cup of tea now, or would you like something to eat? Did you get lunch? Matthew does remember you need to eat, doesn't he?" She had a clear, down-to-earth voice, gently accented. I nodded before she could force-feed me.

"Yes, he does – constantly – and no, thank you, I had lunch. I'd love a cup of tea, though. If you show me where everything is, I'll make it and then give you a hand, if you would like?"

Pat looked at me over her glasses making her appear like a schoolteacher. "You just sit on down there and let me look after you." She moved across to the kettle and switched it on, evidently at home in Matthew's kitchen. I frowned, tried really hard to get my head around the fact that she was his *daughter*-in-law, found it too much at this stage in the game, and gave up. I settled for sitting on the edge of a chair at the end of the table, trying to look more relaxed than I felt.

"My son, Dan, and his wife, Jeannie, will be back soon. I don't know if Matthew's told you, but they work in pharmaceuticals and they've been on some sort of conference these last few days. And Joel… that's their oldest boy…" Pat took an elegant teapot out of one of the cupboards and lifted the lid, peering into it doubtfully. I wondered if she had used it before, "… will be back on leave tomorrow. We're fortunate to have him home for Christmas this year." She opened a narrow door and disappeared, returning a moment later with a small packet. "Won't your family be missing you this Christmas, Emma?"

"Yes, I suppose so, but… well, I'm here."

She took a moment to assess me, then said, "Yes, you are, and very welcome you are too." She peered at the packet, then opened it and sniffed the contents, frowning.

"Pat – may I call you Pat?" I ventured.

"Why, of course, that's my name."

"I wasn't sure. Matthew can be quite, er, formal and I don't know what's expected in your family."

She took me by surprise with a sudden hoot of laughter, reminding me of my mother on sunny days. "He *can* be very old-fashioned, can't he? But he's making sure that… oh my, I suppose I can only explain it in this way: Matthew is just making sure that we understand your *position*, so that there's no misunderstanding."

"I'm afraid you've lost me."

"He's making certain we recognize your status. What you mean to him. That you're not just a casual… acquaintance."

"Yes, I think I've got the picture," I said hurriedly so that she didn't have to embarrass us both with further explanations. "Even so, Pat, I'd prefer that everyone called me by my name. It could get quite awkward otherwise. It'll be much less like a college faculty meeting – all titles and no respect." I found Pat very easy to talk to, a little like my mother in some respects, but without the burden of prior knowledge and family responsibility. And she appeared far more relaxed, despite the fact she tried to look as if she knew what to do with the tea, but clearly hadn't a clue.

"I'll make the tea if you like." Pat handed me the packet of loose-leaf tea gratefully. "Can I make you a cup?"

She hid her involuntary grimace well. "I'll have coffee, and *I'll* make it. I'm afraid we're a family of coffee drinkers – except for Matthew, of course, but then he doesn't drink anything. I expect you find that strange?"

I smiled. "I'm getting used to it," I said, and took the teapot. Boiling water released aromatic bergamot, taking me straight back home in an instant. Loose-leaf Earl Grey: a considerable amount of care had gone into making me feel welcome, even though my presence must have been difficult, whatever Matthew would wish me to believe. "Pat, you wouldn't happen to have a tea-strainer by any chance?"

"A *tea*-strainer?" She glanced dubiously towards a colander hanging on a hook by the sink. "No, I don't think we do. Can you use anything else?"

She accepted my offer to help sort vegetables for tomorrow's evening meal and we gradually emptied the crate into piles of green and brown and orange, until it stood empty. "Enough to feed an army," I commented.

"Sure, it'll take this and then some, especially with Joel home." She produced stout paper sacks of the sort provided by supermarkets, and we started putting the piles into separate bags.

"Pat, how does Christmas work here? What's the normal routine – apart from the vegetables?"

She laughed. "I reckon that's the same in all families. Well, we start the celebration on Christmas Eve with a big meal. My grandfather came over from Norway, and it's been the way we do things in the family since Ellen was crippled."

Her directness quite disarmed me, but she eased off her stool and carried a bulky bag of potatoes over to the wood kitchen counter, so didn't see my reaction at the casual mention of Matthew's wife. She came back to the table. "After the meal we gather together and each have one gift from around the tree – that's traditional in Norway – but we have most of our gifts on Christmas Day, as I expect you do?" I must have appeared a little subdued because Pat put a reassuring hand on my arm. "You mustn't worry, nobody expects anything from you – you're the guest." How could I tell her that the whole idea of being trapped around a table making conversation and eating brought me out in a sweat of cold, clawing horror, when my instinct told me to slide away into obscurity and escape? I felt a little better when she added, "And you'll be next to Matthew, not that he'll let you sit anywhere else. And then on Christmas Day, we all do our own family things straight off – presents and church and such – and then…" she wavered, seemingly unsure whether to tell me something.

"What?"

"Then we all go and see Ellen," she finished, looking away from me for the first time.

"Yes, and…?"

"So Matthew told you?"

"It's fine, of course it's fine – it's what I'd expect," I said as if I had known all along, and briefly wondered when Matthew had planned to tell me about this part of the proceedings.

Pat appeared relieved. "Well, that's just dandy. I wasn't sure if you knew. I'm not sure if Jeannie's going this year anyhow.

She's had a bit of a cold and doesn't want to risk passing it on to Ellen. Then, when we come back, we have our Christmas dinner, and that takes just for-*ever.*" She sounded as if she loved every minute of it.

"You said 'church' a moment ago," I said, moving the conversation away from food.

"Sure. Henry and I always go to my Lutheran church in the morning – although Henry's Episcopal – and Harry goes to his church in town."

The potatoes had seeded granules of earth on the table and I used the soft edge of my hand to gather them in a pile. "What about the rest of the family?"

"Oh, they do their own thing, you know?"

I concentrated on scraping the grains over the precipice and into my other hand. "And Matthew?"

She knew I was going to ask; I could tell by the way she hesitated, looking uncomfortable.

"I don't feel I can say. You'd better ask him yourself."

Light seeped from the overcast sky and Pat switched on the low-slung lamp over the kitchen table. In the time it took for her to avoid answering my question and me to find something to fill the awkward silence that followed, she persuaded me to eat and we sat opposite each other – I with my toast and a preserve of some kind, she with her coffee and a bucket-load of questions about my family that she had held back out of politeness.

I took the opportunity to clear up one or two queries of my own, and I thought that the only approach to take with Pat would be a direct one.

"I don't know how this works and, quite frankly, I'm finding it all a bit scary. Joining you for Christmas when you don't know me or I you is one thing, but our particular set of circumstances makes it downright bizarre. I know Matthew says everything's fine, but I'm acutely aware of treading on toes – especially Henry's, given the situation with his mother – and I really need to know from someone less… *biased*, I suppose, what the real situation is." I had begun to spread the jam on my toast, but now stopped, knife still in my hand, waiting.

She set her mug down on the table and looked at me directly. "I can't pretend this is easy, Emma, but then, as you said, this isn't a normal situation we find ourselves in. But you can rest easy about Henry – and about me, if it's any comfort. Matthew's been very upfront with us, and we've known about you for some time." She picked up her mug and put it to her lips, then put it down again without drinking. "Look, Henry's realistic. He knows Ellen will die sooner or later, and sure, it would have been simpler if she had already gone when Matthew met you, but then that's just the way the cookie crumbles. Henry wants his father to be happy. Matthew's been pretty lonely for a long time – ever since I first met him, and that's longer than I care to remember – and you've…" she halted as she heard voices outside the kitchen door, "… you've brought him back to *life*," she finished rapidly, and then picked up her mug and looked towards the door as it opened.

"Mom! We thought you might be in here." The tall, grey-suited man bent to embrace his mother, kissing her on the cheek she offered. He turned to me, holding out his hand. "Hi there, you must be Dr D'Eresby – good to meet you. I'm Dan, and this is my wife, Jeanette." He indicated the earnest-looking woman next to him.

Instantly warming to his open manner, I stood up and shook his hand. "Hello, yes, I'm Emma." And turning to

Jeanette, I held out my hand. She took it and I realized with a rush how different it felt to her husband's: hard, thin, bony, but with little pressure as she shook my hand, as if her heart wasn't in it. She didn't say anything, but looked at me inquisitively. Dan loosened his tie and inspected the level of coffee in the pot, muttering cheerfully about the appalling standard of the catering at the conference.

"I understand you work in the pharmaceutical industry?" I ventured, trying to engage Jeanette.

"Yes, sure, we both do," Dan answered, handing a mug of black coffee to his wife and then pouring milk into his own. "We've just been to a conference in Ohio. Not much of interest, Mom, but there was one contact we made. Dad and Grand... Matthew'll be interested." He directed a sideways look at me to see if I'd caught his slip, but I sat down again and spread the rest of the preserve on my toast, assiduously oblivious. He must be in his forties, but he appeared much younger, whereas Jeanette was clearly middle-aged with her untidy brown hair greying in streaks. Skinny, medium height and slightly olive-skinned, her dark eyes narrow and lined beneath, she carried her years wearily. Her features lacked the refined elegance of the Lynes: her nose ended in a rounded blob and her lips were too thin to be attractive, and when she smiled I thought her chin would wrinkle unevenly. But she had a well-meaning face, if rather serious, and the lack of malice more than made up for her want of beauty. She must have been aware of her appearance of age next to her husband, even if she clearly wasn't concerned with how she looked. Or was it that she had given up trying? She sat down in the chair next to me. Dan finished his coffee in a gulp. "Where's Dad, by the way? And I haven't seen the kids. Joel's not back yet, is he?"

The door from the courtyard slammed open in answer, and Harry came in with a mass of cold air and darkness, followed by Ellie, each carrying a huge box stuffed full of packets and foodstuffs, which they dumped on the table. Ellie gave her parents a hug, lingering longest with her mother. I felt as if I were intruding on something unvoiced, but understood, and wondered if I should leave. Harry had no such reserve. "I've put your bags in your room, Dr D'Eresby." He grinned.

"Thanks, and you *can* call me Emma – unless you would like me to call you *Master Lynes*, that is?"

"Aw shucks, Dr D'Eresby, ma'am, that would be just *great.*"

I pulled a face at him, which he thought very funny. Ellie watched us, unsmiling, and I wondered if she thought I should act my age, whatever *that* meant.

Jeanette broke her silence. "You're a lecturer at the University of Cambridge?" I detected a note of respect in the way she said it.

"Yes, I'm here on a research project."

"Is that a fixed-term position? Is it held for you, or do you have to reapply for your post? It must be a senior lectureship you hold."

I cut my toast into quarters, wondering what lay behind her questions. "It is a permanent position, but it isn't that senior. I don't hold a Chair, or anything like that."

She looked disappointed. "Never mind. You must be glad you've a position to go back to, and there must be opportunities for advancement, I expect."

I wasn't quite sure how to answer that. I didn't know whether Matthew had said anything to them about the possible future we might have together. It seemed unlikely as we had only just agreed it ourselves.

Ellie hovered behind her mother, her hands gripping the top rail of her chair. "So, you *are* supposed to go back at the end of the year?"

"Yes…" I said.

"Then you'll be leaving, won't you?"

"Ellie!" her grandmother said sharply. "That's none of your business."

Ellie flicked her long toffee-coloured hair over her shoulder, giving me an arch look, blatantly unrepentant.

"We'll see," I said noncommittally, taken aback by the aggressive stance the young doctor had adopted since our first meeting, when she cared for me after Staahl's attack. She had been cool then, but this bordered on ice age. Dan shuffled his feet looking embarrassed as Pat briskly collected mugs from the table. "Time we were thinking about dinner. Ellie, you can help me. I think we'll eat in here tonight. Dan, if you're looking for your father, he's in the study. Perhaps you'll take Emma through so she knows where it is."

I followed him back through the hall. He stopped at the bottom of the stairs, solemnly surveying me with dark blue eyes from behind glasses. His suit emphasized the heavier set of his shoulders, and he carried a little more weight around his waist and face than either his father or Matthew although, for all of that, he moved as easily as they did. He was not as fair-skinned either, having a more naturally bronzed complexion as if he tanned easily, but he smiled in a similar way, and his eyes creased with the same humour. At this moment, though, he looked confused, and he scratched behind one ear.

"I'm sorry about that; Ellie's not normally rude. I don't know what got into her. I'll have a word with her later on."

I shook my head. "It's all right. It must be a bit strange with me being here. I'm sure she didn't mean it." I thought about the look she gave me, and wasn't persuaded by my own argument.

"Well, now, I hope not," her father said, equally unconvinced, but he smiled readily and changed the subject. "The study's through here…" He had his hand on the door handle when it opened suddenly.

"… I'll see what I can do," Henry was saying over his shoulder as he almost stepped into him. "Dan, you're back! How'd it go? Any news? Come and tell me over a beer, son." He gave him a bear hug in greeting, then saw me hanging back. "Dr D'Eresby, we're just coming through."

"*Please* call me Emma – everyone else is," I urged him.

"Emma it is, then, thank you. I'm going in search of food if my brood have returned."

Matthew joined them on the threshold of the room, smiling at me over Henry's shoulder and making me feel better instantly. Standing together, the resemblance became more striking than ever.

"It's good to see you safe back, Daniel. We'll catch up later," Matthew said as he took my hand in his.

They were barely out of sight when I turned on Matthew. "Don't ever leave me alone that long again," I rushed.

"Why? What's happened?"

I took a breath; he didn't need to know about Ellie. "Nothing, it was just too long not to see you. I missed you, that's all."

"That's all?" he queried. I reached up and kissed him to make my point. "Mmm." He caressed my face, his eyes suspicious. "I suppose I'll have to believe you. Have you been given the third degree by Pat?"

I shook my head. "No, we've been making polite conversation over tea. You promised to show me the rest of the house."

"I did indeed. Have you met Maggie yet?" he asked almost casually as he led me through to a room opposite the kitchen where a fire burned low in the grate.

"No, is she avoiding me?"

He didn't answer but the familiar tightening of his mouth was a bit of a giveaway. "This is the drawing room," he said needlessly.

"Why?"

"Because it's one of the principal reception rooms…"

I poked him in the ribs, remembering not to do it so hard that I risked breaking my finger. "Don't be facetious. *Why* is Maggie avoiding me?"

He looked as if he were weighing up whether to tell me. "I don't think she's come to terms with me seeing you." That didn't seem enough to justify the tension that surrounded this woman.

"And?"

"And… nothing. Do you like this room?" He turned me around so that I could see it.

"It's fine, very nice," I said huffily, not doing it justice. Cushions on the sofa had been dimpled by someone who had recently sat there, and a book lay open on a table where a reading lamp spread light in the darkening room. I craned my neck to read the spine: *In the Mind of a Killer*. "What does Maggie do?" I asked.

He lifted my hand and kissed my palm. "She heads up the psychiatric unit of the hospital in town."

I remembered the stark, masculine face staring at me. "Is she married, or seeing anyone, or anything?"

He pushed up the sleeve of my sweater and planted a series of tiny kisses along my wrist that tickled, making me giggle. "You're doing that on purpose; I was just asking."

He sighed and pulled my jumper back over my wrist. "I didn't think I needed a reason to kiss you, but since you ask, no, she's single. It's just her in her flat with her cats. I don't think she's ever been interested in relationships of any kind other than with the family – and even those are limited."

"And I'm a relationship too far for her?"

"That's one way of looking at it, yes."

Since I didn't know any better, it seemed the only way I *could* look at it. He was beginning to look twitchy so I brought the subject back onto safer ground. "This *is* a lovely room; it has beautiful proportions. Do you choose all the furniture? And what happens when you move? Do you take it with you?"

He touched the golden satinwood surface of the table and ran his finger along the thin line of inlaid ebony. "I choose the furniture and, yes, when I can, I take it with me depending on the circumstances. This piece I haven't had for very long, but this…" he went to a handsome display cabinet and opened the glass door, "… I've had since I watched it being made." He picked out a fragile-looking glass object from among a group of pieces. About eight inches high, it resembled a finely wrought winged glass horse, with a dragon's tail curling up its back to where the broken end must once have formed a narrow fluted cup at the top, held above the animal's head. Its translucent apricot body shimmered with flecks of gold, its wide, wild eyes, tail, and clawed feet coloured a deeper, richer salmon.

"It's a candlestick?" I turned it over in my hands gingerly, feeling its fragility.

"Yes, a hippocampus – a winged water horse – made by a master craftsman. It must be nearly two hundred years old now."

I gave it back to him in case I dropped it and compounded the damage. "Why did you buy it?"

He held it out in front of him, a faint smile just evident. "I chose it… why did I choose it? It's such a long time ago." He drew his eyebrows together as he tried to remember. "I bought it because it's a fantastical creature, like me. Neither of us should exist, but we do." He placed it carefully back in the cabinet and closed the door.

"For which I am grateful," I whispered.

He looked at me. "Are you?"

"Of course I am!"

"To whom? My uncle for his betrayal, which led to this, or to God, for allowing it to happen?"

He had caught me off guard, and I took a while to answer. "Not your uncle, no – betrayal can never be good – but God? Yes, I am thankful you are here, for whatever reason, or purpose – or none."

He grunted. "Do you think I might have a *purpose*, then?"

"Of course – don't we all have a part to play? You're already fulfilling a purpose in what you do, aren't you?"

"*Can* there be a purpose in living for ever?" He wasn't really asking me, but searching for an answer that had been eluding him for all of his existence. I put my hand tentatively on his arm and he glanced down at it, then placed his over mine, finding reassurance in my touch.

"I'm not sure if we necessarily know what path we tread, Matthew, or why, until we are already on it. Even then, sometimes we don't find out until we get to the end. I wouldn't have known that I would be here with you six months ago when I booked my flight to America. I knew I was coming to find something, but I didn't know it would be *you*."

He lifted his hand and gently splayed my fingers on his arm, running his index finger in and out of the indentations they made before answering. "I think I knew you were coming

– not *you* exactly – but someone. I can't explain the feeling. It was like waiting for an electrical storm: you know it's coming long before you see it; you feel it in the air."

"*Spoo*-ky," I shivered.

"And I'm not?" he said, more lightly this time.

"No, you're not in the least bit sinister, and I should know."

"Of course, you being an expert on monsters," he smiled, all darkness gone. "Hmm, you're chilly."

I went and sat down while he built up the fire before joining me, and I curled up next to him in the hook of his arm.

"But then, you're not a monster, Matthew, so you wouldn't spook me."

"So if you had a choice, what would I be? A zombie, a vampire – what?"

I shrugged under his arm. "I don't know; that's all Gothic novel stuff. I suppose you could describe your life as being rather Gothic, though…" I stifled a laugh. "How about Shelley's monster?"

He fingered his chin, pulling a face. "I would rather you suggested Dr Frankenstein. That would be a little more flattering."

"Yes, and a little more dead. *He* didn't get a second chance."

"If not him, how about a vampire? They've gained more kudos over the last century. Quite popular again now, I believe." He pretended to bite my neck and kissed it instead, sending a shiver of pleasure through me.

"Mmm, and there's a certain attraction associated with them, of course. Definitely a possibility, but for one thing…"

He had reached the base of my throat, becoming absorbed in his task. "What's that?"

"You're not, are you?"

He sat up. "No."

"Alien?"

"Certainly not."

"Elf?"

He laughed.

"Mutation?"

"Probably closer."

"You don't know what made you the way you are, do you?"

"No, not for certain, but I'm working on it." The fire popped and a blue tongue of flame flared before it became green and died. He stared into the heart of it, the light in his dark pupils subtly changing as I watched.

"Matthew, is that what all this research is about?"

"Mmm."

"And when you've cracked it, what then? Is it just a question of gaining a deeper understanding of what you are or *why* you are, or are you looking for something else?" He didn't answer. I turned around in the circle of his arm. "Matthew?" He looked away so that I could no longer see his eyes. "You're not looking to change yourself, are you?"

"Would that be such a bad thing?"

"Yes!"

"Why?"

I put both my hands around his face, making him look at me. "Because you're you. I love you as you are. I don't want you to change."

"Do you want me condemned to this shadow life forever, when *you* can leave it and find peace?"

I slowly shook my head. "Is that how you see it? A life of nothing but shadows? But surely where there are shadows there has to be light?"

"Would you seek immortality, Emma, if you were given a choice?"

"But you weren't given a choice were you? Your uncle took that away from you!"

"Are you saying that I should accept this life because I wasn't given a choice in the first place, is that it? *Fait accompli* – no going back." The darkness filling him spilled into his voice, and I couldn't look at him any more in case I disappeared into it.

"No..."

"So, would you choose to live forever?" I couldn't answer him. "You wouldn't, would you?" He put his fingers under my chin and raised my face so that I looked into his. "Even though we could be together."

I thought of being with him, inseparable by death, ready to take the plunge into the unknown if he asked me. I swallowed, pulling back from the brink. "I don't know, Matthew. I've never had to think about it and there are so many issues to consider. It would be easier if that decision were to be taken away from me, but then, immortality is not an option, is it?" It was his turn to look away. "*Is* it?"

He took a very long time to answer. "No, it isn't," he said eventually, "and I wouldn't wish it on you." He smiled suddenly, a tight, drawn smile. "Not a vampire or a monster, then, just an anomalous entity waiting to be resolved. And you, Emma – still willing to wait with me? What does that make you?"

"Patient. And hungry."

He laughed, hugging me close and lifting the atmosphere in an instant. "Well, that's something we can sort out at least. We'd better see what's on offer that will tempt you, even if I can't."

I put my fingers over his mouth. "Don't say that, please, Matthew. *Temptation* doesn't even come close."

He put his lips against my brow. "I'm sorry, sweetheart, I

know. I was trying to make a joke, but obviously not a very funny one." He stood up and I joined him, finding my legs unexpectedly shaky. He put out a hand to steady me. "Low blood sugar," he said. Food would undoubtedly help, but it wouldn't ease the inexplicable trembling that unsettled me – but then, I didn't know what would.

Dinner proved interesting. We all sat around the big family table in the warm kitchen looking like an episode from *The Waltons*. I say *all*, but one chair remained stubbornly vacant until it was removed and the setting taken away. Matthew and I sat at one end of the table, our legs touching, tension stretching across my shoulders like the string of a bow. In full view of everyone, he took my hand and, to my surprise, said grace. Not a modern version, but straight out of the mid-seventeenth century. Pat then took over and the bewildering array of food was passed around until our plates were piled high. Matthew had a setting laid in front of him, and a token of each food arrived before him on a plate.

"Normality, just in case," he murmured, "and in celebration of what I once was," he said even more quietly. I nodded and looked despairingly at my own full plate.

I did pretty well, all things considered. I remained quiet for most of the meal, and the family left me alone to gather information about each of them from the rapid scattering of banter that tattooed the conversation. As a result, I made considerable inroads on the food, and avoided the usual comments my lack of appetite inevitably caused. Nonetheless I felt relief when the end of the meal came, and I stood up with everyone else to help clear away.

"No, you're the guest. You go and sit back down, this won't take long."

I put my foot down at that. "Pat, I really would like to help." She took one look at the set of my jaw and at the grinning Matthew – whom I tried to ignore in case he made me laugh – and gave in.

There is such relief in having something practical to do, especially when among strangers; it takes the searchlight of their interest off you. At home, I couldn't wait to escape the cramped, damp kitchen space with its walls dripping condensation from the old gas stove and the Belfast sink. How anyone cooked for the family in there was a bit of a mystery. I dreaded Nanna's attempts to teach me to cook and Mum didn't have much success either, although she would rather have been on a tennis court than in the kitchen with me. I took as little pleasure in combining the ingredients and cooking them as I did in their consumption. Nanna persevered until even she relinquished her obdurate granddaughter to the all-embracing arms of history. It would have helped my cause had Beth had a similar outlook, but my sister loved food, and spent many happy hours ensconced in the kitchen with Dad. As I couldn't see the point in trying to compete, I didn't, and retreated to the less contentious issue of cleaning and tidying.

Hailing from a family where the production of food had been ritualized to something resembling a military operation overlaid with an almost religious mysticism, to me the Lynes were a revelation. Everyone joined in and, out of the seemingly chaotic process, produced order amid much laughter and jostling, jibes and wet tea towels that were used more for flicking unsuspecting victims than for drying anything. By the end of the process, I became adept at darting between the flying elbows and comments to retrieve a plate or glass, drying it and giving it to whoever was putting things away at the time. Chaos it might have been, but it made it all so much more *fun*.

"Is it normally like this?" I asked Matthew as the family began to disperse to their different homes.

He wiped a bunch of soapsuds off my cheek. "Yes, although that was pretty tame. Wait until Joel arrives tomorrow – that'll liven things up a bit. Doesn't your family do this sort of thing?"

"You've met them! The most interesting thing that I can remember happening recently was Flora's Barbie getting stuck in the gravy."

"Point taken; you had a deprived childhood for which we must endeavour to make amends."

My mind boggled, especially as he had that look on his face that suggested he was scheming. "It wasn't *that* deprived," I said, backing away from him.

"Indeed," he said, eyes glinting, "but there's always room for improvement." He glanced around the empty kitchen. "Now, which will it be tonight, your bed or mine?" He picked me up before I could respond and flung me over his shoulder, my hair falling out of its loose plait and swinging as he spun around and headed for the door.

"Matthew! Propriety please!" I gasped, although all I could do was hang on to his sweater.

"I reckon I have the best view in the house," he said, patting my behind. I squeaked, kicking my legs in token gesture of protest.

"This one's not bad either," I pointed out, laughing. His strong legs carrying me easily, we were already halfway up the stairs, my protests undermined by fits of giggles, when he suddenly stopped, his head whipping up.

"What's the matter?" I tried to look around, but he slid

me off his shoulder, guiding my feet to the broad steps. He listened intently. I could hear nothing. "What is it?"

He put his finger to his lips, eyebrows pulled together in concentration. Just as suddenly, he took my hand. "Come on, let's go." As we reached the landing, a door on the left opened and Henry came out with his head down, a look of concerned displeasure on his face. He looked up as he heard our footsteps. He said nothing as he came towards us but gave a slight nod of his head as he passed to go downstairs.

"I'll see you in the morning, Henry," Matthew said, as if in answer.

"Goodnight," his son replied.

"That was Maggie's room," I prompted, as my bedroom door shut with a reassuringly solid *click*.

"Yes, it was." He walked over to the fire and began placing logs in the raised grate. "Your room or mine?" he asked, without offering any further information. I took the hint.

"Yours needs to look more lived in," I suggested.

"True, but yours is warmer. How about yours tonight, mine tomorrow?"

I pursed my lips and tried to look as if it were a really hard decision until he tickled me around my waist and I writhed to escape. "OK, OK, you win, but give me half an hour's head start."

He squinted unnecessarily at his watch. "Twenty-nine minutes and forty-six seconds and counting. Forty-five, forty-four, forty-three, forty... what are you waiting for?"

I waved him towards the door, laughing. "For you to leave. Go – now – *shoo*."

"I know what's missing." I spluttered around my toothbrush, coming out of the bathroom to speak to Matthew, who lay, ankles crossed and fully clothed on my bed, waiting for me to finish. He had given me exactly the half hour in which to shower and get ready for bed. He had his hands behind his head as he contemplated the ceiling. "What's that?" He turned to regard me, a smile hovering around his lips as he took in the toothbrush I brandished like a conductor's baton.

I retreated to the bathroom to rinse the mouthful of toothpaste. I returned to the doorway, brush still in hand. "Christmas decorations. Why don't you have any? You don't have anything against them, do you, any religious objections, or anything like that? Without them, it makes the house look sort of… forlorn."

Light from the bedside lamp glinted off the face of his watch as he adjusted his position on the bed. "Does it? I hadn't thought about it. I don't have any reservations about having them, and certainly not religious ones. There didn't seem to be much point before now – not just with me here – and this year… well, it might surprise you to learn I've been preoccupied." He slipped off the bed and sauntered over, running the palm of his hand down the length of my hair and then the long revers of my dressing gown. "Can't think why that might be… mm, you have toothpaste just… *there*…" I tried to lick at the remnants at the same moment he used the side of his thumb to wipe the corner of my mouth, and my tongue brushed inadvertently against his skin. Our eyes met, an unspoken current running between us. "It's being *very* resistant." He leaned down slowly, eyes locked, mesmerizing, and drew the tip of his tongue in a line along my bottom lip, lingering at the corner. My lips burned as I stretched towards him, feeling his mouth smile beneath mine at my response.

"That's better," he murmured. "I've been waiting to do this all day."

I breathed him in, my cheek against his. "Do what – exactly?"

"Be alone with you in my own home, in our own time, no interruptions." His voice became low and gruff and laden, and the room swam out of focus. His mouth travelled under my jaw and down my neck, sending goosebumps along my arms and across the top of my shoulders.

"*Almost* alone," I managed to remind him as my breaths shallowed and shortened, and my heart battered against my ribs. And then it didn't matter anyway because he picked me up and took me to my bed and showed no sign of stopping, and I didn't care because this is what I wanted and had wanted for so long that it hurt to remember.

But it was wrong.

"No, Matthew, no. Please, don't…" I twisted my head away and tried to push him from me but, encased in his arms, I had no room to break away – although every corpuscle of my body yearned to be with him. "Matthew – no, this is *wrong!*" His arms opened abruptly. I wriggled out from under him, curling my legs up tight on the far edge of the bed, and pulling my dressing gown around me. He looked bewildered, his honey hair dishevelled, his blue eyes wild. "You wouldn't forgive yourself," I whispered.

He ran his hand slowly across his eyes and down his face, then rolled over and sat with his back to me for what seemed like an age. "You're right, of course," he said, at last. "I'm sorry, I shouldn't put you in such a position. That was stupid, no – selfish – of me. It's just that sometimes…" he shook his head, "… sometimes it feels so right – *we* feel so right – that I forget. God forgive me, but I *do* forget, Emma." He turned and looked at me so despondently that it was all I could do to resist throwing my arms around him. I grabbed a plump pillow and hugged it instead.

"Don't be sorry for me, I'll survive. And you're not being selfish, and if you are, then so am I, so don't go and do a guilt trip on me. Although," I said ruefully, "I think we both deserve medals for our restraint."

He managed a half-hearted smile. "As I said, that was selfish of me…"

"But utterly tantalizing," I interrupted, clasping the pillow more firmly and burying the lower part of my face in it so that all he could see were my eyes peeping out over the top.

He leaned over and stroked my bare feet, which I hadn't realized were wiggling feverishly. "So I see." He kissed my toes and my skin warmed at his touch. He drew the counterpane resolutely but regretfully over them. "I think we'd better think pure thoughts for a while. So you would like some Christmas decorations, would you?"

"Can I ask one thing first, before we change the subject?"

"What's that?"

"Do your family think we are sleeping together as in *not* sleeping together, if you see what I mean?" I flushed, embarrassing myself with my ridiculous ambiguity.

He held back a laugh. "Well, I think I do. Let me see… I haven't said anything directly other than to Henry, and he won't have said anything to the others – except perhaps to Pat – so I would have to say that the rest of the family have probably drawn their own conclusions. Why, does it matter what other people think?"

I gazed at him over the pillow, thinking it through. "Normally, I would have said not, because it is our business and our consciences, but I wonder if it does matter to them, or to some of them at least, especially Maggie and perhaps Ellie. It's not a usual situation as it is."

His brow puckered. "Are you saying I should tell them?"

I cringed at the thought, my toes curling correspondingly under the covers. "No! Well… *blow it*, I don't know, Matthew, but you know as well as I do that where there is room for doubt and speculation people fill it with all sorts of nonsense and, sometimes, it's better to give them the information straight rather than let them make it up – or let it fester." I shook my head slowly. "I don't envy you this one."

He stared blankly at the floor. "I'm not sure what's for the best. I'll think about it. Now, decorations."

I welcomed the change of topic. "I wasn't asking, so much as saying the house looks a bit bleak without them."

He smiled. "But you would like them all the same?"

"Can we – please? It would make it more Christmassy. Just a few; we don't need to go over the top."

He patted my feet beneath the counterpane. "I think we can do something. In the meantime, you need your sleep, and I need a distraction." He rose from the bed and I felt my face fall as he made for the door.

"You're not leaving, are you?"

He stopped and looked back. "I won't leave you. I'm just going to get a book. I'll return in a minute." And he smiled his half-smile, thin with restraint and thick with longing.

2

Christmas Eve

By the time I woke next morning, Matthew had changed, and the dark blue sweater contrasting with his full, fair hair did nothing to reduce the memories of the night before that had dogged my sleep. He saw me awake and watching, and drew the curtains back to reveal a sun-laden sky, before coming over and kissing my forehead. "Good morning. Sleep well?"

I grunted and he grinned, making me wonder what he knew that I didn't. "How about breakfast first, then decorations?" he suggested, looking immensely cheerful, and infecting me with his good humour.

Once I had showered and dressed, we walked downstairs and through to the kitchen holding hands.

"It won't upset anyone having decorations up, will it?"

Matthew filled the kettle. "No, not at all. Why should it?"

I took the teapot from the cupboard. "It won't be seen as muscling in on Ellen's territory, or anything like that?"

He put down the bread he had taken from the larder, regarding me with that earnest look he adopted when he wanted to get something important across to me. "Emma, you have to remember that Ellen has never lived here, and that only Henry and Maggie remember Christmases when we were all together. As much as I respect Ellen, this is *my* home and I choose who lives here and what happens within these walls." At a slight disturbance in the air, he raised his head and his tone changed, becoming resolute. I puzzled at the alteration, but he held my eyes steadily with his, as he continued. "While you are my guest here, you treat my home as your own. I will expect you to receive the respect and acceptance of *all* my family, irrespective of any misgivings anyone might have. As far as I am concerned, I have made my choice and the rest of my family will have to abide by it." He released me from his rigid gaze and looked over my shoulder. "Good morning, Maggie."

My back stiffened, feeling her rancour before I turned around to see it, and mentally shook my head out of the stupor in which his voice had left me. Given the conversation of the evening before, I guessed that Matthew had thought about our discussion, and had come to a decision. "Maggie, this is Dr D'Eresby. Emma, this is my granddaughter, Margaret." I turned resignedly to greet her, my nerves in knots. A tall, handsome woman of an indeterminate age stared down at me, her beauty masculine, her manner haughty. "Maggie…" Matthew's voice held a threat in it.

The sharp line her mouth formed made a mockery of her greeting. "Dr D'Eresby, you are welcome." *Blow*, you could have fooled me – her tone dripped acid. I did a rough calculation and guessed that she must be fifty or thereabouts.

"Dr Lynes," I replied equally coolly. We kept our hands to ourselves. She regarded me with intensely blue, intelligent eyes – as blue as Matthew's – but without any hint of his warmth or humour. Her platinum hair had been cut short and inflexible around her square jaw, but her eyebrows made dark, harsh lines across her brow. I sensed no softness in her, no forgiving nature. She might have the unreal beauty of a Lynes, but it lay shrouded in a soul of concrete and steel.

With a grace that belied the rigidity of her manner, she went over to a cupboard and took out a mug. I thought about making tea, but Maggie was brewing coffee with her back to us and I decided my tea could wait.

Matthew ignored her. "Joel should be home today," he said to no one in particular. "You'll remember me mentioning him, Emma?"

"Yes, of course, it'll be good to meet him." Joel would need to have horns and a tail to outdo the evils Maggie exuded towards me at the moment.

She finished making coffee that smelled as noxious as her manner, and left the kitchen without giving me another glance. My shoulders relaxed. Matthew leaned his knuckles on the kitchen table. "Well, that went better than I expected."

"It did! What on earth did you expect?"

"Not that," he dodged, coming around to where I stood at the end of the table. "What I said wasn't just for Maggie's benefit, Emma, I meant it. You treat this house as your home. You go where you want and do what you want, and don't be intimidated by anyone." His eyes glanced to where Maggie had been moments before.

"Thank you," I mumbled. Then more strongly: "I'll get my tea now, in that case."

He chortled and slid the toast out of the toaster before I heard it pop.

"This wasn't what I had in mind for you." Matthew surveyed the kitchen table and its multicoloured contents.

"But it has to be done and I don't mind in the least bit; it makes me feel useful. Have a knife." He took the vegetable knife from me and proceeded to chop the potatoes I had peeled into neat, even chunks before I had picked up the next one. He looked expectantly at me. "Don't be so impatient. I can't work at your pace. Here, peel some potatoes or go and entertain yourself for a bit."

He picked up the knife again and started to take thin parings off the rough-skinned potatoes faster than I could blink. "You really know how to make a girl feel inadequate, don't you?" I said. He smiled to himself as he reached out for another. "Matthew, Pat and I were talking yesterday…"

"Uh-oh."

"Wait, it's not that bad. Pat said that she goes to church on Christmas morning, and I wondered whether you do. I mean, it's not something we have talked about much, is it? You did say grace yesterday – I haven't heard that version before, by the way – and I just wondered where you stand religiously, given your… unique… viewpoint."

A slow smile had crept across his face as he listened to me struggle to outline what I knew could be a potentially explosive subject. He tossed another potato on the pile and then retrieved it as a second thought and dissected it expertly. "How long have you been wanting to ask me that?"

"Since this morni…"

He fixed me with one of his interrogative looks. "Emma, I know you better than *that*."

I pouted. "Oh, all right, then. Since I read the journal in Stamford."

"Ah."

"Well, it must have been an issue for you in the seventeenth century, so I wanted to know how it influences you now."

"Hence the question about Christmas decorations?"

"Well, perhaps, ye-es."

"I would say that's a definite *yes*."

I flicked a potato paring at him. He moved and it passed inoffensively, landing on the floor.

"So…?" I pushed.

"So… yes, my faith is very important to me, it always has been. And that wasn't just because of when I was born, either. My father was a deeply religious man, not dogmatic in the sense he didn't impose his belief on me – or the household servants, for that matter – but he led by example. I think that's why he found the war so difficult: it left no room to manoeuvre for those who had a less well-defined faith, and it forced them to take sides when they hadn't yet fully understood the implications of it. I think it was why what happened to me all but broke him."

The half-peeled potato sat forgotten in my hand, browning by stages in the air.

"Why? Because he didn't understand what had happened to you? Did it make him question his faith?"

"No, not at all. You would have thought so, wouldn't you? But then neither of us knew that I would *persist*, as you so aptly put it, so I don't know how he would have coped with that. He was convinced salvation can be secured by all, and that included me, and he continued to believe in me despite everything, and long past when I had ceased to believe in myself. What shook him more than anything was how quickly people we had known for years – who had known my grandparents – turned against us. He never understood how fickle people can be…"

"Like his brother?"

At the reminder of the betrayal, Matthew's mouth skewed briefly, and he stabbed at a nearby carrot, severing its knotty head from its shoulders. "Yes," he said finally, "like his brother. William's treachery almost destroyed my father, but not his faith, nor his belief that what had happened formed part of

God's plan for me. For all of his naïvety about the frailty of our neighbours, my father believed in people's innate goodness, and that their faults and failures were just the mistakes they made on their way to finding oneness and healing with God." Pausing, he looked up. "He had such insight, Emma. Sometimes I wondered if he could see right inside people, past all their shortcomings, right into the very heart of them where their true nature – devoid of sin – lay. That's why he always seemed surprised when someone did something that he believed to be out of character for them, but also why he was so quick to forgive: he knew what they *could* be if they had time on their side."

"So where does that leave you?" I asked. *Confused*, I would have thought, not that I said so.

Matthew started chopping and slicing again and I had to hurry to keep up with him. "Emma, I've seen what people do to each other in the name of religion all over this world – as you are all too aware from your own studies – and I have to say that in four centuries, nothing much has changed. We cloak our justifications and motivations in different words, but the meanings are just the same."

"That makes it sound so depressing, as if there is no hope that people will ever change."

He looked surprised. "Do you think so? I find it quite comforting in some respects. Just consider: despite people's propensity to harm one another, there is still that bedrock of humanity that comes through even in the worst atrocity or natural disaster as if, despite our tendency to do otherwise, most of us can't help but do good."

"Yes, but Matthew, where does that leave *you*?"

He balanced the tip of the knife on the end of his finger, the blade bouncing light as he moved it to keep it upright –

an unconscious act that made his differences all too apparent – as he thought about my question. He flipped it into the air and caught it.

"Well, as you know," he started slowly, "sometimes I find it difficult to accept my place in the great scheme of things and, for a long time, was all but lost to my faith. But, on a good day, I'm in agreement with my father. He continued to believe in my validity in the eyes of God – that forgiveness is mine despite all that I was, or am, or might be – and that's what I hang on to. So, to answer your question, I continue to hold my faith in salvation through Christ as I was brought up to believe, but my faith is mine, and I pass judgment on no one, and expect no one to pass judgment on me."

I took a moment to consider the finer points of his explanation, relieved, but not surprised, that we shared the same tenets of faith without having needed to say so before now. "Okey-dokey," I chirped brightly. "So, basically, Christmas decorations are fine…"

"Ye-es," he said, patiently, "as are carols, wassailing, and dancing. We weren't Puritans, Emma, nor was I a Digger or a Ranter. What mattered to us was what went on inside our heads, not the trappings of religious observance. Anyone can don a black hat and a long face." An involuntary giggle broke from me. "What now?" he asked.

"I just had an image of you in a black hat with long hair. It wasn't pretty, or rather it was, which is worse."

He arched his eyebrows and I tried not to laugh again. "For your information, I never grew my hair long, and as for…"

"Why?"

"Why what?"

"Why didn't you wear your hair long? It was the fashion, after all."

He looked exasperated. "Because it used to curl when it grew any length, and because those of us in the…"

That did it. Perhaps the sheer relief of surviving meeting his family, or the insane normality of discussing his youth four centuries before while preparing vegetables, finally got to me, but the result was that I bent over, my forehead almost touching the table, and howled with laughter – so much so that I missed the tea towel flying through the air until it hit me damply. I saw that as a challenge and returned fire, but he anticipated the move and leaned back slightly so that the cloth sailed harmlessly past him.

"Whilst you may find me a source of easy amusement, madam, I would remind you that some of us regarded long hair as a sign of lassitude and cut our hair short as a demonstration of our serious demeanour and godly intent."

Bother, I should have remembered that, but I chucked a small potato at him regardless of the facts. He speared it on the end of his knife, removed its skin, and added it to the pile of naked spuds.

I slammed my peeler down. "Stop being right all the time, and so… *quick*… it's infuriating. And you're smirking – that's unforgivable. At least have the decency to appear chastened."

Without replying, he put his knife down carefully and stood up with exaggerated slowness. I watched him from the corner of my eye, wondering what was coming next. He came around and stood behind my chair, and I could feel his cool breath on the back of my neck raising the tiny hairs down my spine.

"So, I'm *always* right, am I?"

"Yes, you wretch," I squeaked, my voice thin, not sure if I wanted to laugh or not.

"And you want to hurl *missiles* at me, do you?"

"Only a little bit."

"Only a bit, mmm. And how do you propose to do that, might I ask?" His voice had taken on a velvety texture that I didn't trust. I swallowed. "Perhaps you were considering more vegetable peelings or something a little colder... snow, perhaps?" He placed his hands on the top of my shoulders.

"Um..."

"But then..." his hands slid down the length of my arms, sending shivers through me, "... you would have to catch me first. Do you think you could do that?"

I began to tremble. "Matthew..."

He plucked me off the chair before I had time to draw breath and I was over his shoulder again as he headed for the door to the courtyard, thumping on his back to put me down, and squirming as hard as I could in between fits of crying giggles. And then we were outside in the sunshine – shamelessly, jubilantly, *outrageously* – laughing as he ducked me in the snow.

I fought to throw as much of it as I could at him before turning over and trying to escape, clawing at the friable crystals, being dragged back towards him by my ankles, my jersey filling with snow around my stomach, making me yelp.

"Yield," he growled.

"Not a chance," I said into the snow.

He rolled me over, standing above me. "Yield," he demanded.

"Never," I defied, sticking my chin out stubbornly.

He bent closer, until his mouth hovered just above mine. "Yield," he said, very, very softly.

"What are you going to do about it?" I challenged, although even as I said it, I began to feel my resolve weaken and fade under his burning gaze. His eyes flashed wide, and I made a last-ditch attempt to escape from between his straddled legs before he whipped around and caught me again, and I squealed like a piglet.

"*Hm-mm.*"

Matthew stopped and looked up, suspending me like an overgrown salmon by my waist, my loosened hair trailing in the snow.

Harry cleared his throat again. "I've been sent to help prepare vegetables," he mumbled, obviously embarrassed by our antics.

Matthew straightened, putting me the right way up on my feet and helping to brush me down as my face flared crimson from my exertions and self-consciousness.

"Excellent," he grinned, taking me by the hand and leading me back towards the house. Harry trailed behind.

"Nothing in your religious code about frolicking in snow, then?" I muttered.

"Not that I can remember, no," he murmured back.

I settled down to some serious peeling, this time with Harry's help as well. He seemed abnormally subdued and he avoided my eyes whenever I looked at him. I know Matthew noticed too, but he said nothing, and we kept up a trivial banter that could offend no one. At one point, Matthew pivoted on his chair abruptly, facing the courtyard. Harry stopped and listened too. I strained my ears, and just made out the sound of a car's engine. "Joel?" Harry said.

Matthew shook his head. "Diesel. I'll go and see. Stay here." It was the way he said it. Not a "*don't bother to get up, I'll go and have a look*" type of "stay here", but more of a "stay here and keep *safe*". He moved swiftly to the door and out of my line of sight. Harry remained tense and alert until, minutes later, Matthew returned. "Delivery," he said and looked at me.

"Delivery?" I mouthed back.

He crooked his finger for me to join him by the door, and led me to the garage block. "Is this anything to do with you?"

"It got here – *yes!*" I whooped. A large wicker basket with *F & M* painted on the side sat solidly on the floor of the garage. "I didn't know if it would get here on time."

"What is it for?" Matthew asked, his brow furrowed.

I gave him a withering look. "In case you don't feed me and I need a snack. What do you *think* it's for?"

He tapped a foot impatiently. "You don't have to do this, Emma; we don't need presents."

"Well, tough, it's here now, and yes, I do need to do this. There's no way I could come and stay and not bring something, now could I?" I stood on tiptoes and kissed him chastely on his cheek, just where it would crease into a smile. "*Could* I, Matthew?"

"I suppose not, but…"

"But me no buts." I danced away from him, pulling him along with me back outside into the snow-filled courtyard. "Will you help me bring it in? It's for Pat really."

He shook his head, laughing. "I didn't think it was for me."

CHAPTER

3

Insight and Intuition

Joel arrived home on leave before lunch. We knew he was back because the roar of a car's engine in the courtyard filled the silence, followed by the back door to the kitchen crashing open. "Where's my baby brother?" he shouted, accustomed to the noise of the engine.

Harry leapt out of his chair and they whacked each other convivially on the arms, hard enough, it seemed to me, to break them.

"What'ya been doin', squirt?" Joel thumped Harry again, this time on his back.

Harry indicated the pile of vegetables with his thumb. "Hah, kitchen duties for Grams. Always know I'm home when there's chores to be done." Joel flung his kitbag on the floor where it slithered into a corner, sat down without pausing to take off his coat, and picked up the peeler. "Hi, you must be Dr D'Eresby. How's things? Grams been making you work too?"

"Hello, and you must be Joel. It's good to meet you and no, Pat didn't impose peeling vegetables as a punishment – I offered."

Shaking his head, he pulled a face, and I smiled at his comical expression. I had recognized him instantly as the young man standing outside the deli in town, talking on his mobile as the sun glanced off his wheat-stubble hair the day Elena and I shopped for our All Saints' outfits. Matthew had told me recently – amongst other, more weighty, confessions – that he and his family had kept a watch over me in the lead up to Staahl's attack. That he had been unable to prevent it was something I knew played on his conscience. I shuddered slightly, and suppressed the memory of the aftermath of that otherwise happy day.

Joel reached for another carrot. "Where's everyone else, bro'?"

"Ellie's out with Dad, collecting stuff from town. Mom's doing Christmas things. Grams is next door and Grump is with Matthew taking a phone call. Anyone else? Oh, yeah," he hesitated, "and Maggie's around… someplace." Both boys' eyes swivelled in my direction and away again.

"So you're left *do-in'* the *cook-in'*, hey, ma'am?" Joel grinned at me.

"Not a chance," I said rapidly. "Strictly unskilled labour unless you don't want to eat this Christmas."

He chucked a carrot on the pile; he had already peeled three in the time it had taken me to peel one. I watched him surreptitiously. His hands flew faster than I thought possible, a scattering of vivid orange shavings appearing on the table in front of him. It wasn't just the looks the boys had inherited.

"So, you've joined us for Christmas, huh? Should be in-*te-res-ting*." He rolled his eyes and shuffled in his chair. More heavily built than his brother, broad, and strong, he made the chair squeak as he moved.

Harry shot him a warning look. "Yeah, it's good to have you here, Emma; the more the merrier."

"Thanks, Harry."

"Yeah – *grr-eat!*" Joel grinned at me. Apart from the length of their hair and Joel's built-up frame, the boys might have been identical twins.

Voices filtered through the kitchen door and Matthew came in followed by Henry, both still talking rapidly. He saw Joel and broke into a smile, elongating his stride so that they met halfway across the room. To my astonishment Joel lashed out, throwing a double punch with all the weight his hefty shoulders could bring to bear. Matthew didn't break step, neatly parrying the blows and planting a punch against Joel's ribcage. "Have to be quicker than that," he grinned at his great-grandson, who tried to scowl at him but failed totally, breaking into a beam.

"I'll get you one day, *old man,*" Joel replied, rubbing his ribs ruefully and playing up his feigned injuries shamelessly.

"I'm sure you will," Matthew responded amiably. "Keep on trying – you never know, you might get lucky one day." He dodged a left hook to his head. "Glad to have you home anyway, we need some more free labour. Come to mention it, I've a job for you two later on."

The boys groaned in unison: "It's supposed to be a holiday."

"Welcome to the real world, boys." We all laughed and Matthew added, "Go and get something to eat, there's time enough for chores later. Now, have you introduced yourself to Dr D'Eresby?"

"He did *this* time," I said.

"I certainly hope so…" Matthew looked at Joel sideways and he bolted for the door, picking up his kitbag on the way.

Three large packing boxes sat on the hall floor. I peeked in the first one as Matthew hovered uncertainly behind me. "It's all we could find. There's not much and I don't know if it's what you had in mind. Some of it is pretty old."

I held up a long, heavy string of silver tinsel and peered at him through it. "Not as old as you, though."

He took it off me and wrapped it around my neck like a muffler. "Do I have to put up with barbed comments about my age?"

I opened the lid of another box. "Ooo, baubles." I held one up to the light. "You're as young as you feel," I smiled sweetly at him. "There's plenty here, by the way. But," I chewed the side of my lip, "we could do with a tree."

He had that self-satisfied look on his face again. "All sorted."

"Is it? Where?"

"Not where, just when. This afternoon, after lunch – *if* you can wait that long."

"I'm learning patience," I said ruefully.

"It's good for your soul," he said, opening the third box, "and for mine."

Thin, high cloud weakened the sun, adding a halo to the yellow disk, and the air held a promise of snow. After lunch, Joel and Harry attached the trailer to the beetle-black 4x4 and, taking a hefty-looking axe, went in search of a tree.

Pat didn't have any more jobs for me to do and I retreated to the drawing room to read in front of the fire. Matthew had been looking decidedly twitchy, and asked if I minded him completing something with Henry, and the two of them were now ensconced in his study. I fought the desire to hide in my room and decided I would stake my claim as Matthew wanted, first poking my head around the drawing room door to check the coast was clear. I put more wood on the fire and settled on the sofa with a copy of Antony Burridge's *Man and Monsters in Medieval Europe*, which he had just brought out. Intrigued, I wanted to see how close to my own research he sailed given our extended discussions in recent years, and I admitted feeling slightly piqued that he had already distilled his theories into the book I should have written. There's nothing quite like professional jealousy to get under an academic's skin, and I was not immune.

I slid my shoes off and wriggled comfortably in the warmth of the fire. I had delayed starting the book I planned to write for ages, concentrating instead on preparation for transcribing the journal once my proposal to spend the year in Maine, where it resided barely known, had been agreed. Now I felt stumped. I hadn't given a great deal of thought to what I would do work-wise since my change in circumstance. Obviously I wouldn't be asking for a sabbatical, so New Zealand would have to wait, perhaps forever. I had made my choice to stay with Matthew and with that decision came a number of certainties that would shape my future. First, that his welfare mattered more to me than anything else. Secondly, that living with him inevitably meant that I would have to accept a semi-nomadic existence. Thirdly, I would always have to guard against any slip that might reveal his true identity. Fourthly – ah, yes, the one thing I would perhaps find the hardest of all – that I would have to sacrifice the journal in order to protect him, because if *I* had been able to work out who he was, it would only be a matter of time before somebody else did. And even if that wasn't in m lifetime, it would be in his.

That left me with a quandary, one that I had s around but against which I kept on bumping like a flotsam: I always meant to put it back where it I

I never really intended to take it – but now that time had slipped without revealing me as a thief, the temptation was to keep it. To keep it would be wrong. On the other hand, if I was caught putting it back, it would draw attention to its existence. No matter what angle I looked at it, I kept going around and around in circles until it became clear that the angles were an illusion, and I remained as trapped by the dilemma as a spider in a glass. I considered discussing it with Matthew as he had the most to lose, but the journal also represented *my* life, as meaningful to me as his work to him. And, willing though I found myself to give Matthew my future, could I also let go of my past any more than he could his? The journal had shaped me, had largely made me who I was, but its very existence threatened the future we could have together. Could I destroy it and put it beyond the clutch of an ill fate that would lead someone to him? Could I, as a historian, destroy a priceless original document that to anyone else contained the mundane thoughts of an ordinary servant of a modest English gentleman? My sigh filled the empty room. I could as much destroy the journal as I could have lit the torch that incinerated the library at Alexandria. I could not destroy it, and my conscience dictated that I could not keep it. I would have to return it and hope that, for now at least, the safest course lay in its obscurity until another solution could be found.

The drawing room was quiet and the house beyond silent. w, dense text made a crazy paving of references fully annotated, leaving me yawning after the ected a fair amount of our discussion and one d lifted directly from my own work. Three ld have been steaming; now, I had to ask ough to do anything about it?

I flicked through the volume to see if he had given me any credit for my work. He hadn't, but there, leering out at me, I saw a name I hadn't expected. Guy Hilliard had been referenced numerous times, not only from familiar works, but from a new book as well. So, he still took an active role in research, still grubbing around and no doubt slavering over some poor, hapless, innocent, stupid, naïve, hopeful undergrad. Despite the time and distance between us, cool sweat dampened my neck and I passed my hand over it, wiping it away along with my memories.

As the sun gave way to thick cloud, the room darkened, bringing a sudden chill. The air moved. Maggie emerged abruptly from the gloom by the door as if she had been waiting there all this time. In the light of the lamp, her eyes became hard, sharp points in the pale square of her face and she said nothing, but let her gaze fall first on the book in my hand, and then to my chest and face – as if she knew what I had been thinking – as if she knew the very heart of me. I started at the thought and her corresponding look of satisfaction lingered for no more than the few seconds that it took for me to register it before she drew the mask of icy passivity over her features once more.

She walked deliberately towards me right up to the sofa, and I thought at first that she meant to speak. She leaned forward and I felt myself involuntarily flinch from her. In one movement, without taking her eyes from mine, she scooped her book from the table, turned her back, and retreated into the darkness whence she had come. I stared after her until I could be sure she was no longer in the room.

It happened so quickly that it was almost as if it hadn't happened at all, except that the frantic beating of my heart bore witness to it. I knew I shouldn't let her get to me. Matthew had made it very clear that he would take no nonsense from her and neither should I, but I had nothing on Maggie, and she seemed to have everything on me.

I gave up on Burridge's turgid gleanings and considered seeking out Matthew but decided that he would take one look at me and know that something had happened. Something and nothing. Instead I distracted myself by surveying the contents of the display cabinet where the hippocampus subtly glittered.

Display cabinets are curious because they reveal more about their owner than perhaps they realize, whether they be an avid collector, an amasser of trivia, or use it as an ostentatious display of wealth or taste to impress the observer. Matthew's cabinet formed a collection entirely privy to him, with no obvious meaning to the eclectic mix of ephemera – no theme in the way of date, or style, region, or subject – just a random assortment of objects whose meanings were known only to him. I frowned, trying to figure out the small, round, nut-brown object that lay next to an exquisite piece of jade-green porcelain. Opening the door, I picked it up gingerly between two fingers to have a closer look.

"You've found the nutmeg." Matthew's voice sounded soft in my ear, and the nut spun out of my fingers as I jumped. His hand shot out and caught it before I could react, placing it back in my outstretched hand.

"Don't *do* that!"

"It's a good thing it wasn't the Lung-Ch'uan bowl; I might not have caught it." He grinned at my shocked face.

"*Why* do you have a nutmeg among treasures, may I ask?" I held it in my open hand: an ordinary nutmeg, if a little larger than usually found, rattling in a slightly withered shell like the skin of a sun-blown sailor, but a nutmeg for all of that.

Matthew rolled the spice around my palm with his index finger, making my hand tickle. "You're familiar with the idea of a cabinet of curios?"

"Yes, of course."

"Of course. Well, this is mine. I've had more things over the years; some I've had to leave behind if I've had to move quickly, but these I've managed to keep together and, although the cabinets change, the content doesn't. They're souvenirs, some more precious than others, but all remnants of my travels, nonetheless."

I cast my eyes across the shelves, beginning to see a geographical pattern in the pieces. "So these represent the places you have been to?"

"More or less. I suppose you could say that I'm carrying my history with me, if I could put it in such crude terms. I used to collect things when I was a boy – oh, birds' eggs and feathers, interesting stones, finds from the battlefield…"

"The sword from Losecoat Field," I murmured.

"Yes, that sort of thing. I think that I tried to capture the beauty of an object, or its vitality, or its past, and keep it with me always. The value of it was – is – irrelevant, but its association is everything."

I held up the spice. "And the nutmeg?"

He took it from me. "Ah, this is one of a handful I had and, at the time, they were worth more than the entire contents of this cabinet now. I think that you could say that they were part of the foundation of everything that I have today."

"You went to the Spice Islands back then!"

He laughed quietly. "Trust you to know what I'm referring to! Yes, I went to the Banda Islands when a small bag of these could make a man's fortune. The islands had been taken by the Dutch then and my presence wasn't entirely welcome.

I traded the spices – keeping this one, of course – and went on to other parts of what we now call Indonesia, to China..." he lightly touched the Lung-Ch'uan bowl, beauty conjured in its simplicity, "... and India. A rajah tried to cut my throat with this." He paused, smiling slightly as he lifted an ornate knife in a heavily jewelled sheath next to the candlestick. "The dagger was his peace offering to make amends for his breach of courtesy."

The skin of his throat bore no evidence of a blade, but I stroked it delicately with my fingertips to make sure, and he bent his head to kiss them. "But I thought you came to America early on?"

"I did, but I came and went over the decades. It helped me avoid detection, but I also searched for anything that might explain what had happened to me, at the same time learning more about medicine than any single institution could teach me today."

"And amassing a fortune on the way," I said, wryly, removing the nutmeg from his fingers and placing it carefully next to the bowl. "Let's hope Pat never finds herself short of spice."

"Indeed! I think I might miss it almost more than any other piece. Anyway, with my certain peculiarities it meant that I could take risks that other men couldn't. I didn't do it solely for the money, although I quickly came to understand that it was a way I could help protect myself. Have you any idea how much good false documentation costs?"

"I'm not sure if I want to," I joked.

But he was serious. "You might need to one day, Emma. The money enables us to have a means of escaping detection using fake passports, birth certificates – even the physical means of escape using planes, fast cars. Wealth is a means to an end. I've lived too long to see it as an end in itself. I just hope that we don't have to use it for that purpose." He looked so worried for a moment, his brow drawn together, that I felt fear pressing in around us from the unlit corners of the room.

I inched closer to him. "You said that you took risks for a reason other than for money?"

"Risks? Oh… yes, well, I took risks because I wanted to see how far I could go before I… succeeded."

"In killing yourself?" I said a little crossly, remembering Richardson's account in his diary of Matthew pushing the boundaries. "I trust you don't do *that* any more."

He looked sheepish. "No, I don't need to. There's not much point, and anyway I have additional responsibilities that far outweigh the inconvenience of long life." He caressed my cheek briefly, his face brightening, then lifted his head as if listening. "The boys are back; ready for your tree?"

"Math sucks." Joel pushed his hat to the back of his head, giving himself a halo of cropped gold hair, as he surveyed the length of the tree. Harry gave him a *I told you so* look and Ellie snickered, her hands on her hips. "What did Mom always tell you?" she said, and all three intoned, "'*Math is the sum of all knowledge.*'"

Joel groaned, kicking snow with the toe of his boot. "Geesh, don't let Mom know I messed up."

"Yeah, *sure* we won't," Harry smirked, dodging the loose snowball that narrowly missed his head.

I walked down the length of the tree as it lay in the snow of the courtyard. It represented a very fine specimen. "It really isn't a problem. I could do with those lower branches for decorating anyway, and then it's only a question of taking an inch or two – or perhaps twenty – off the bottom and it'll be fine. And I totally agree with you, Joel – maths is a foreign language intent on confusing us lateral thinkers. Don't listen to anyone who tries to tell you otherwise."

Joel nodded appreciatively. "Gee, thanks, Doc, it's like I've been telling these *freak geeks* for years: math squares your brain – think outside the box."

Ellie looked as if she couldn't decide which of us deserved her derision more. She had returned from town with Dan shortly after the boys trundled in with the fir strapped to the trailer, the tip nodding its head in agreement as the vehicle rode every bump of hardened snow. She had been told by her father to give us a hand with the tree and she made it quite clear she did so under duress. The boys ignored her, shaking the snow and loose needles off the branches. They proceeded to manoeuvre it through the double doors of the drawing room into place in one corner where it had room to spread its boughs. They made it look all so easy, hoisting the heavy trunk on their shoulders as if it were made of nothing but air. It wobbled slightly before settling into its makeshift stand, the soft point skimming the high ceiling.

I clapped my hands in triumph. "There, you see? Perfect, thanks."

Joel high-fived his brother. "I gotta shift, Doctor D, I've been summoned by Mom and Dad." He went off whistling with his hands in his pockets, a little too nonchalant for it to be natural. I wondered what it was about his parents that worried him.

I turned back to Harry, who had undertaken the removal of the lower branches, putting them to one side for me. "I don't suppose you could spare me a few minutes' help getting the lights and decorations on, could you, Harry, please?"

There were few enough and I didn't need his help, which he probably knew, but he was gracious enough not to let it show. His smile was minimal but he bothered to make the attempt anyway. We each unravelled a long string of tiny lights in little clear hoods like icy snowdrops and started to intertwine them near the trunk, unleashing the resinous scent of childhood when Christmas trees smelt of pine. In all that time, Harry kept his comments to monosyllabic questions or answers, always polite, but reserved.

I took out the first of the baubles and handed it to him with an expectant look, knowing he would have to stay to finish the task and couldn't avoid the conversation I had been cooking up. "Harry," I began, "do you get to see much of your great-grandmother? She lives quite a way away, doesn't she?" I handed him another silver ball, the harsh metallic colour softened by age so it gleamed rather than shone.

"Yeah, sure, I see her regularly – we all do – it's not that far."

I straightened a hook on a red bauble and handed it to him. "That's good, because I know Matthew thinks it important to keep in touch and how much she means to him." Harry declined to comment, and his mouth formed a single line, making his resemblance to Matthew when he avoided something even more striking. This was delicate territory, and had he turned around and told me to mind my own business, I wouldn't have been surprised. I went on. "It must be pretty lonely for Matthew without his wife for all these years."

Harry gave me a tight look. "He has his family."

"Yes," I said, evenly. "He has, and his family are everything to him, but he also has me now, and I mean a lot to him too." I don't know where I found the nerve to talk to him so directly or why I felt it necessary that he understand the nature of our relationship.

He sucked air over his teeth, building himself up to reply. "Look, Dr... Emma. I don't mind you being here and I'm really glad if Matthew's happy – OK, I know he's happy – but he's *married*. I didn't want to say anything because it's up to him what he does, and I guess he's old enough to know what he's doing, but there's things I believe in so please don't ask me to go against my conscience and say it's all right."

I bent down to select another ball from the box and to give myself time to think. "I understand, Harry; we both do, perhaps more than you might think. Matthew would not – *will* not – be disloyal to his wife and, for that matter, whether you choose to believe it, neither would I." I looked at him straight without wavering, without blinking.

For a clear minute he regarded me with his bluer-than-blue eyes before he swallowed, and gave a quick nod of his head. "Right then, Emma, how many of these do we have, 'cos this tree is *sure* gonna look mighty nak'd wit'out 'dem balls." He threw me a wicked sideways glance as he slewed his language, and I burst out laughing.

The sun had not long set behind the dense blanket of cloud, but outside the blank windows the darkness became intense. Harry left the tree and began closing the shutters rapidly in a well-rehearsed routine.

"Are the shutters always closed at night, Harry?"

He clunked one of the heavy iron bars into place. "Yep – always." *Clunk*, the next one fell into its socket. He pulled the lined curtains in front of it.

"They're more for security than heat conservation, aren't they?"

He looked at me over his shoulder, then continued battening down the room. "They do the job for both. Less light pollution too," he added, though I wasn't convinced by *that* argument. He closed the double shutters over the doors to the courtyard, and secured them with bars top and bottom.

He leaned against them without turning around. "Do you mind if I ask you a question, Emma?"

I continued hanging the fragile baubles around the tree, the occasional needle pricking my skin. "No, not at all – go ahead."

"You wear a cross, right?" He turned now and looked at me steadily. "Does it mean something to you? I mean, is it *significant* to you, or just a piece of jewellery?"

I ceased what I was doing, feeling the weight behind his question. "Yes, it is important to me as a symbol of my faith. Why?"

He ran his hand through his hair making the tidy spikes stick haphazardly in all directions. "You know about Matthew, right?"

I chose my reply carefully, guarding my words, remembering that only I knew how old Matthew really was. "If you are talking about his longevity, yes, I know about it."

"And you're OK with that? I mean, it's not natural, it isn't how things should be, how they're *meant* to be." He stalked the length of the room and back again checking each of the shutters in turn needlessly. Clearly this was something which had been on his mind for some time.

"Harry, what's worrying you?"

He stopped and stuck his hands in his pockets, making him look younger than his nineteen years. "I don't know who else I can talk to about this. You're the only person outside the family who knows about Matthew, and I can't talk to Grams or Henry because… well, you know… and Ellie and Joel don't believe in anything so they can't see why it matters *what* Matthew is. And I can't talk to anyone at church for obvious reasons. I don't know what to think because his being as he is goes against everything I believe." He ruffled his hair again and hunched his shoulders, looking miserable. "If Matthew doesn't die or can't die, what does that make him? Where does that place him with God? If he can't die, how can he ever *find* God? I don't know whether I can even *accept* him as he is, and…"

"Whoa," I cut in. "Hold on, Harry – there are several questions here. Don't confuse the issues and bundle them together. First, don't for one moment think that Matthew hasn't been through all of this over the last… countless years. He's as much in search of answers as you are," I paused. "Haven't you discussed this with him directly? Of all the family, I would have thought he is the one person you can talk to."

Harry shrugged. "Yeah, he's always been easy to talk to, and we've talked about loads of things, but I don't want him to know that I have doubts about… you know… about his soul. He's done everything for me, he trusts me. I don't want to let him down. Gee, that sounds weird. I've talked over things generally with him, but not specifically *about* him."

An uncomfortable clawing sensation was having a go at my gut, the one that warned me that all was not well. "Do you think he's damned? Is that what you're saying?"

He flinched. "I'm saying I don't know."

I draped a string of tinsel on a broad bough, and abandoned the tree. "Whatever happened to make Matthew this way – and he was born like the rest of us, Harry – God allowed in His wisdom. We might never know what caused it, but we can't second-guess God, we don't have that right. And if Matthew is wrong, what does that make the rest of you, who have seemingly inherited some of his traits?"

Harry sat on the sofa and buried his head in his hands, and it was then that I realized the full extent of what he had been putting himself through in his own silent agony of faith. "Harry, if there is one thing I do know, that is that this is a question that is too big for any of us to tackle and, talking from my own point of view, whatever the answer is, I have to believe that Matthew is *right*, and that makes *you* right as well. In the end we all have a choice, don't we? It's what we have been given, the gift of free will – the *yes* or the *no*, the right or the wrong, to believe or not to believe – and that is more important than the whys and the wherefores. In your heart of hearts, do you feel that Matthew is *wrong*?" He took a big, shuddering breath and shook his head. "No, and neither do I. So I have to believe that whatever or *why*-ever Matthew is as he is, God has a purpose and a place for him."

"I would like to believe that," Harry whispered, leaning his elbows on his knees and putting his hands behind his neck. I rubbed my hand across the upper part of his back the way Nanna used to do when I was a tormented teenager. "The thing is, Harry, we are all that Matthew has in this world, and one day we will leave it – and him – behind, and he will have to face it alone again. So all he has is his faith, and it would be wrong of anyone to take that away from him with doubt."

He sat upright, and took another deep breath. "Right – so you're saying we should support him whether he's *damned* or not?"

"How does it hurt our souls to love and support him in any way we can? And there is one other aspect we can't overlook that is central to our faith…" he gave me a puzzled glance, "… that Matthew himself has the right to choose his soul's path and that doesn't depend on his death but what he chooses in this life, however long that might be. The question that torments him is how will he find peace on this earth, not how he will find God. He already has his faith, and God has always had him here…" I held out my hand, face up, forming a cup, "… in the palm of His hand. What happens next is between them both."

Harry pinched the bridge of his nose with his thumb and forefinger and squeezed his eyes shut for a second. "I wish," he said, "I just wish he would come to church…"

"Why?" I intercepted, remembering what had happened to Matthew at the little church in Martinsthorpe nearly four hundred years before that had led to him fleeing his home for fear of persecution.

"It would show he has faith, I suppose, and give him a spiritual community…" he trailed off.

"Then he wouldn't be doing it for himself, or for God, but for you, and that isn't the right reason. There are many ways of demonstrating your faith, and Matthew's found his own way in the work he does and the family he protects. *You* are his community, Harry, you and your family. It's the only community he can trust." I had to remember that Harry hadn't known about Matthew for very long, and that this sensitive, deep-thinking boy was still trying to work out his own faith as well as tackle someone else's. "Do you think we had better finish this tree while we can? I'll have nightmares if it's not done by morning and, from what Pat told me, this evening is going to be taken up with food."

Harry stood up, still a bit pale but happier than before. "Yeah, Grams' roast pork. We wait all year for this – *great*." He rubbed his stomach in token appreciation and I forced a smile. "Mmm, great," I echoed.

I found Matthew alone in his study. I knocked tentatively on the door and he opened it almost instantly, and I wondered if he had been waiting for me. A familiar choral work flowed from a hidden sound system. It was the first time I had heard him listen to music.

"So this is where you are, I won…" He silenced me with his mouth, warm and insistent on mine, feeding me through his touch. But he had forgotten I needed to breathe occasionally.

"I missed you," he murmured into my hair as I drew oxygen into my lungs and remembered what Harry and I had discussed only minutes before. I put my hand to his face and traced each contour, absorbing every little detail through my fingers as if it were my last chance. He took my hand and put it against his face. "So how did it go with Harry? Did you say what you wanted?"

I leaned against his chest and felt the human rise and fall as he breathed in and out – even and steady, neither too quick nor too slow, a never-changing rhythm. Human – so human – not a monster at all.

He caressed my hair. "What's the matter, sweetheart?" I shook my head, not trusting my voice, fighting the tears that stood behind my eyes, willing my heart to calm. "Emma – what is it?" He grasped my upper arms and tried to see into my face, his eyes at once concerned and kind.

"Nothing's the matter. I love you, that's all. Sometimes it becomes too much to bear. Don't take any notice, I'm just being silly."

"Did Harry say something to upset you?"

"No – no, not at all; he's a lovely boy. We talked things through and he understands about you and me now, so everything's fine. And the tree's finished, more to the point. I love all the old decorations, they're not at all gaudy."

"You mean they're shabby."

"No, I don't, I mean they are subtle and I much prefer them to all the tawdry tat you get nowadays. You should come and see what we've done between us."

"I will, in a moment. When you came in and said, '*This* is where you are,' what did you mean?"

"Oh," I smiled. "I meant that this is the first room where I can feel your presence, your personality – the real *you* – not something put together for the rest of the world to see. I feel comfortable here, more at home."

The smile faded from his eyes. "I had hoped you would feel comfortable in the rest of the house as well, not only in here." He glanced at the room, densely lined with books, paintings in between the bookcases, photographs, a desk filled with papers, and the odds and ends of an existence that breathed life into the walls and surfaces.

It was my turn to be concerned. "I didn't mean that I don't like your home; I do, but I'm a stranger to it, whereas in here I feel I already know it, and it knows me – we're old friends."

"Then you come in here whenever you want to, whether I'm here or not, if this is where you feel most comfortable."

"Are you planning on going away?" I hardly dared ask.

"No, of course not, I'm not planning on going anywhere, but I might be at work, or in town – who knows." He glanced at his watch. "Time for dinner. We usually get changed for Christmas Eve – it makes it more of an occasion. Shall we go?"

I narrowed my eyes but didn't say anything, because for once it wasn't the thought of a table laden with food that worried me.

I showered quickly and changed into a slender black skirt that skimmed my ankles, and a classic Liberty print silk shirt in auburns and blues with long, tight-buttoned cuffs and a deep plunge neck made entirely decent by a blue silk camisole. For once I wore high heels in black patent leather, and I practised a few steps to make sure I wouldn't trip over my skirt and make a total idiot of myself.

I donned my cross as usual, and then reached without thinking to my earlobes, only to remember with a pang that Nanna's earrings had yet to be returned from the jewellers. I missed them. I missed the comforting association they brought, and I missed her with a sudden twist of longing for home and familiarity. I drew my brush resolutely through my hair and frowned at the mirror: pulled back off my face, my hair seemed too businesslike, but let loose, almost wayward and wanton. I settled on something inbetween and forgot about it.

Matthew surveyed me from the door. "Now, you look quite…" He shook his head, for once at a loss for words.

"Quite – *what?*" I demanded.

"Let's just say, it shouldn't be allowed. It places too great a burden of responsibility on the male of the species. You're missing something though." He wandered over to me, all long limbed and agile. He wore a suit and tie and I missed the little "v" of skin at the base of his neck that always beguiled.

"Am I?" I checked myself over but I seemed all in place. "Is this not suitable?" I asked anxiously.

His eyes drifted over my throat, the scallop of my collarbone, the plunge of my blouse. "Oh, absolutely; however, you have a little too much skin on display."

"I don't… I can't have!" I spluttered in alarm, knowing that changing now would make me late.

His smile broadened into a grin. "It's nothing that can't be easily fixed." He produced a little domed black leather box. It took me a second to cotton on to what it was, and another before I reached out and took the box from his outstretched palm. "I know they are not your grandmother's, but I hope you'll accept these as a token of my love."

I released the tiny catch. A pair of earrings – rich blue sapphires shaped like polished tears suspended from simple diamond studs – lay on the bed of dark silk.

"Matthew, they're *beautiful*," I breathed, watching them catch the light. "Thank you." I put them on and he turned me around so that I could see in the mirror on the wall above the fireplace. His expression softened. "They're quite old – perhaps a hundred years or so – and they came from the estate of an émigré Russian countess." He wavered for a split second. "Does that bother you, or would you have preferred something new?"

"Bother me? They're *lovely*, and their history makes them all the more intriguing. Thank you so much."

The stones were almost the exact colour of my eyes. As I looked at them, I saw him standing behind me with his hands on my shoulders, and I saw us – not him and me – but *us*. Our eyes met in the mirror, and we were one, except that we remained separated by law and loyalty and conscience.

"I never really noticed before," I murmured, resting my head back against him, "but our eyes are almost the same colour."

"They are," he agreed; "but the sapphires suit *you* better."

CHAPTER

4

Wassail

Awake, glad heart! get up and sing!
It is the birth-day of thy King.
HENRY VAUGHAN (1621–95)

The rest of the family were already gathered in Pat and Henry's home when Matthew showed me through a door at the back of the drawing room behind the Christmas tree. It led into a narrow no-man's land of passage between the two houses. "I'll join you in a minute," he said, squeezing my arm in encouragement when he saw the flash of nerves in my face.

"Welcome, honey." Pat put her arm around me as I entered an open-plan kitchen, heady with the smells of roasting meat and cooking vegetables. "I have you to thank for this, I think." The large Fortnum's hamper sat on the kitchen surface, its lid thrown open and a portion of the contents already gathered by its side.

I smiled, shy. "I didn't know what you would like so I had to go for a bit of everything."

Pat squeezed me warmly. "That's so thoughtful of you. I love it – it's so very English." She removed her glasses and wiped steam from the lenses. "Come on through and have some eggnog, if the boys have left any. I'm just finishing putting things together." An assortment of dishes waited on the sides, but she declined my offer of help and instead showed me past the open framework of great wood beams that represented a partition, and into a dining area.

A gentle hubbub filled the beautifully converted space of the old barn, made bright with a homely ruggedness and comfy, chunky furniture sitting on hewn plank floors worn smooth by centuries of feet and polished to a wax shine. Candles scented the air and the long room glittered with lanterns and with strings of white lights on a tree. A log burner threw a shifting radiance against the plain, pale walls. Henry's cabin in the mountains, where Matthew had revealed his life to me, had been a pared-down version of this home: all Scandinavian hues and Shaker simplicity.

"Matthew won't be long," I said in explanation as Henry looked up from laying serving spoons on a substantial table, and saw me alone.

He embraced me affably, and ladled a glass of a pale, creamy liquid from a large bowl. "I imagine you must find us all a bit overwhelming, but this might help. We always start the celebrations with a glass or two of Pat's eggnog, and it seems to do the trick. While we are on the subject of drinks, I must say that I was particularly impressed with the whisky in the hamper – single malt; couldn't be better. Thank you, Emma – it is much appreciated."

I took the glass from him. "Matthew said you like Scotch. I had to take advice on which one though; I hope you enjoy it."

"We sure will," Joel's voice drawled from where he slouched on the sofa at the other end of the room.

His grandfather shot him a look of pseudo severity. "I'll be sure to lock it away while you're at home, young man; it's far too good for you."

Lounging against the chimney breast with his hair in neat disarray, Harry called out, "He worked out how to pick the lock on your alcohol cupboard last year, Gramps." He caught the cushion that had sailed perilously close to the glass in his hand and chucked it back at his brother.

Jeannie cut across the banter, her voice a little sharper than it needed to be. "Boys, I'm sure Dr D'Eresby doesn't want to know about what you've been up to."

Joel stretched. "Sure she does, Ma – don't you, Emma?" He slid a look towards me accompanied by a lazy grin, and I recognized a wind-up when I saw it.

His mother bristled and I took a taste of the drink for something to do. It had a bite I couldn't place. I took another couple of sips; it was really very good and a little wouldn't hurt. "This is lovely, Pat," I commented as she joined us.

"I'm glad you like it," she said, pleased. "I'm sure you must be hungry – there's not an ounce of flesh on you. Matthew's bringing in the meat now."

A murmur of appreciation ran around the table as Matthew brought in the pork, the glazed crackling bursting with boiling fat and spitting furiously in all directions.

My stomach constricted, but I put on the enthusiastic look I usually adopted at home when Dad or Beth produced something that required special recognition. An air of expectant tension reigned as Henry carved thick slices of meat onto each plate.

"Everybody go ahead and help yourselves before it gets cold," Pat urged, giving me free rein to take as little as I could get away with without appearing rude. Then the room hushed expectantly and everyone looked at Pat. She bowed her head and said a less antique version of grace. Looking up, she paused, then broke into a smile. "What are you all waiting for?" she beamed, and the room immediately resounded to the sound of animated chatter and of food being consumed with relish.

She leaned towards me. "In *my* family, my momma ruled the roost and she *always* said grace. Papa wouldn't have dared speak out of turn."

"I heard that," Henry called out from the other end.

Matthew grinned genially. "In *your* family, Pat, I could well believe it."

She laughed, patting his arm, and then addressed me as a faint waft of cinnamon and cloves rose as she spooned fragrant apple sauce on to the side of her plate. "So, Emma, what do your family do at Christmas? Do you celebrate on the twenty-fourth or twenty-fifth?"

I cut a tiny sliver of meat. "We get together as a family as you do, and the twenty-fifth is traditional in England. We don't do much on Christmas Eve except panic and prepare for the next day. It's pretty manic and there are always things that need to be finished at the last minute. We stop to hear Carols from King's, though; it sets the right mood and reminds us what it's all about." In the warm room, I began to feel light-headed and took another sip of eggnog.

Her forehead creased with a question. "You have kings sing carols in the UK?"

Dan called out from across the table, breaking through the noise his sons were making. "Keep it down, boys. I think Emma means King's College, Mom. It's one of the Cambridge colleges, isn't it, Emma?"

"Yes, it has a particularly fine choir and there's a service of carols and readings from the chapel every Christmas. It's very traditional and very beautiful."

"So you're missing it this year, huh?" Joel said, cramming his mouth full of food, his plate half-cleared already. Jeannie gave him a reproving glare, which he seemed not to notice but more likely chose to ignore.

I attempted to calculate the time difference without much success, and winged it instead. "Well and truly missed it, by about – ooh – I don't know, quite a few hours."

Ellie poured gravy over her vegetables. "Never mind, Emma, you'll be able to catch it *next* year... ow!" She bent down to rub her ankle where one of her brothers must have kicked her, judging by the way she scowled at them. She glanced up at Matthew and then away again, her face colouring under his cool stare.

"Wine, Emma?" Henry held up the bottle.

"No, thank you."

Joel leaned forward. "Teetotaller?"

"No, I just don't really drink." I smiled at the look on his face as he worked out the contradiction.

Dan leaned an elbow on the table. "Do you come from a large family?"

"Not really. Apart from my parents it's just my sister, her husband, and their three children. My grandmother is ill, so she's not at home."

Pat invited us all to help ourselves to more food. "So, I'm curious, are you a traditional English family?"

"In what way *traditional*, Pat?"

Harry grinned. "I think Grams means do you live in a castle and take afternoon tea?" A rumble of laughter rolled around the table.

"I do not," she protested. "Well – do you?" she asked.

"Only the castle," I said earnestly, "and then only on Sundays." Joel and Harry cracked up and even Ellie raised a smile while their father laughed into his glass. Pat tried to silence them with a reproving look, but that didn't work so she turned back to me. "Sorry, I do know what you mean, Pat. I think we would be considered fairly traditional of our type of family, yes, but it is a long time since we lived in castles, and afternoon tea disappeared with my grandparents' generation. I think women going out to work put paid to that. But I can still just about remember my great-aunts and the rattling of teacups when I was very little."

"And cucumber sandwiches?" Pat asked with a smidgeon of hope.

"Yes – and tea from a silver teapot set on tables between herbaceous borders, and the vicar, and croquet on the lawn. All very Jane Austen – without Mr Darcy. But we abandoned all that along with the petit fours and the shooting parties years ago."

Pat looked triumphantly at her grandsons.

"What's petit fours?" Joel asked.

"Little fancy cakes, dummy," Ellie hissed at him.

"But that was a long time ago," I reiterated, "and nobody has time for afternoon tea any more, and if we did we'd go to the supermarket to buy the cake – if you allowed yourself to eat it at all, that is – and the tea comes in bags, and the vicar serves so many churches that she spends all her time in the car travelling to them." I hadn't meant the note of regret to creep into my voice, and it surprised me how much I cared about the loss of something so simple that it had been taken for granted by my spinster great-aunts.

"Well, that *is* a shame," Pat exclaimed. "At least you can uphold the tradition if *you* wanted to. You can bake, can't you, Emma?"

No matter what I did to avoid it, the subject of food always seemed to crop up. Matthew shifted in his chair and stroked the stem of his wine glass, ready to intercede if need be.

Joel chortled. "Emma can't cook, Grams – she said so."

I shot him a look. 'It's not that I *can't* cook…" I began.

"Naw, it's just that you *won't* cook, right?" Joel finished.

"Something like that," I said.

"How *sad*. Didn't anyone ever teach you?"

"Uh-oh, watch out, Grams has got her charity face on. You'll be adopted if you're not careful," Harry grinned.

With all eyes turned in my direction, I had that closed-in feeling creeping up and smothering me. I took another drink. "My family tried their best, but I'm afraid I'm a hopeless case where food and cooking are concerned. I'm just not *interested*," I said firmly, in the hope that Pat wouldn't pursue me as a project.

At the other end of the long table, Maggie had stopped talking to Henry and was now listening intently to the conversation.

Jeannie leaned around Harry so that she could see me. "I'm not particularly interested either," she sympathized.

Joel snorted. "Yeah, we noticed."

"Mom's not *that* bad," Ellie said. "She managed to feed us well enough."

Harry pulled hamster cheeks and smirked at his older brother across the table. "Yeah, just look at *you*."

"Can it, you three," Dan said. "Your mother did a pretty good job considering what she had to put up with. I'm surprised she didn't put you all up for adoption. I bet your family don't behave like this, Emma." It was well meant, of course, and perhaps he thought that well brought-up English girls didn't argue, but it struck a raw nerve, made more tender by Pat's kindly probing and the alcohol in the eggnog. The familiar knot tightened in my stomach, and I felt Matthew's leg press against my own. I stared at the intricately embroidered tablecloth where a tiny splash of gravy stained it, unable to formulate an answer.

Matthew lifted the jug and filled my glass with water. "I thought that the twins get on remarkably well – they're what, eight years old, aren't they, Emma? And the baby is teething – which needs no explanation, *does* it, Harry?"

The rest of the family groaned as one, except Maggie, who continued to watch me.

"I couldn't help it, I was only a baby," Harry wailed.

"Yeah, but it went on for *years*, bro'," Joel snorted, "and I had to share a room with you. I didn't get enough sleep."

"Stunted your growth, retard," Ellie snickered at him, and the siblings exchanged good-natured insults until Pat intercepted them with an offer of more food.

Under the table, his diversionary tactic working admirably, Matthew held my hand, his thumb stroking my palm in slow, soothing movements until the tension dissolved and I became an adult again and not a het-up, confused, and defensive teenager at war with her family.

Pat wiped her hands on a damp tea towel as she made an announcement. "Gifts time with *kaffe og kake*."

"Coffee and cake – very Scandinavian," Matthew said quietly at my quizzical look. Pat overheard him. "I have tea for you, Emma, don't you worry. Ellie will make it." It wasn't a request and Ellie smiled stiffly but went to do as asked.

"Can I help?" I offered hopefully.

Matthew took the drying cloth from my hands. "No, you can't, you've done enough. Come and sit down." He led me through to a deep, wide armchair near the fire and pulled me next to him.

"I only wanted to help," I objected.

"Really? And I thought it might be because you want to avoid being the focus of attention."

My mouth turned down in a moue of protest but he snuck a finger between my shirt and the waistband of my skirt just above my hip where his hand couldn't be seen, and began gently caressing a square inch of skin, his face a mask of innocence. I found it immensely distracting and tried to elbow him to stop but he just slid his hand around towards the centre of my back where I couldn't reach and continued to stroke softly.

Having organized her grandchildren into serving the cake and coffee, Pat settled comfortably in a chair next to ours, looking a tad tired and glad to be off her feet. At home across the Atlantic, my parents would be thinking about putting the turkey in the oven for the long, slow roast towards dinner, and my mother would be looking just the same: a little time-worn and frayed around the edges.

Pat strained towards me, peering at my earrings. "I couldn't help but notice your earrings – did you inherit them? They look old and they are just *so* pretty!"

"Thank you. No – they were a gift, but you're quite right, they are old. I like *old* things." I nudged Matthew's arm and, mercifully, he ceased stroking my back. "Tell me about the beautiful embroidered tablecloth, Pat – it looks very complicated."

Pat's face warmed with pleasure. "My Grandmother Andersen made it. It's called *Hardangersøm*, like the fjord, you know? It's very difficult to do and it must have ruined her eyes. We use it for every special occasion we can: Christmas, Easter, weddings, christenings."

"It's very lovely," I agreed. Matthew resumed his stealthy

embrace; I clenched my teeth against the delicious sensation and was only saved when Harry brought a tray over and set it on the low table in front of Pat. It bore a darkly rich, moist cake on a wavy-edged plate. I took the opportunity to remove Matthew's hand and brought his arm around in front of me, where it remained fully visible and under my control.

"Spoilsport," he breathed in my ear.

Pat turned to me; "Cake, Emma?"

"Thank you," I said, keeping a straight face, although he was trying to make me laugh by tickling my stomach with his little finger.

Ellie brought a tray around with tiny white coffee cups on little saucers, and placed a dainty cup in front of me. The heady aroma of strong, black coffee seared my senses and in the same instant, Matthew's hand tightened around my middle and his eyes hardened. He opened his mouth but I made a hushing face, willing him to silence and she moved away, unaware of his annoyance.

"It doesn't matter, she probably just forgot," I soothed. "Anyway, it'll help wake me up a bit." The pressure around my waist relented a little, but he continued to scrutinize his great-granddaughter as she took her own cup from the tray and settled next to Maggie on the other side of the room.

With Ellie's indiscretion unobserved by the others, and my desire to forget it lest it spoil the festivities, I joined in raising my cup as Pat lifted hers, singing out *"God Jul,"* in her strong, clear voice, echoed by her family.

When the first bite of the bitter liquid burned my throat I gave Ellie nothing – she could have derived not even the slightest iota of satisfaction from my response – and I replaced the empty cup in the saucer as if it had been entirely to my liking. She exchanged looks with Maggie, and the older woman shrugged. At least it looked like a shrug, but the minute movement of her shoulders might have been a nervous twitch – it was hard to tell.

The room spun, then steadied. I complimented Pat on her cake. It had been soaked in what tasted like an infusion of coffee and chocolate – very rich and very sweet but quite delectable – and it managed to douse the aftertaste of the coffee, enough at least so that I could smile and accept another cup from Harry, who had taken over drinks duty.

I cleared the second cup and had another mouthful of cake, feeling increasingly reckless. Caffeine coursed through my body, the unfamiliar sensation both exhilarating and alarming as my pulse became a staccato beat. I could feel Matthew's anger simmering as clearly as he could feel my racing blood. The room brightened, throbbed. I shook my head to clear it.

Henry began handing out the presents that had been left under the tree, each person receiving one present as a token gift to welcome the Christ-child.

Now, sitting among the family with my body in a state of hyper-alertness, I became aware of an energy flowing between them. I attempted to reach out and touch the air but my arm remained static. My heart flustered.

Matthew sensed the change, pulling me close to him, a casual embrace to anyone watching. "Emma?" His voice echoed, remote. I tried to answer but became distracted by colours made brighter, the room sharper, as if a fog had been lifted from my eyes, and I could hear and see things that I hadn't noticed before: the hum of the reading light on its stand as the current ran through the wires, and the *tik, tik* of needles dropping from the branches of the fir tree. I heard the whisper of snow falling ever faster beyond the shutters, and the room pulsed and glowed as I had never noticed before. I even fancied that I could hear the hidden conversation in the mind of the girl across the room from me, but in colours, as if I could read her heart. I turned my head to look at her, following the trail of orange and brown and green she left as she moved across the room… and I saw her fear, I *felt* her jealousy.

I understood. I smiled.

Ellie's face froze in realization that I knew her thoughts, and it was seconds – but the fleeting moment in which my heart stopped – when everything became *knowledge*.

"Emma!" Matthew's voice pierced the veil between us, sharp beside me. I opened my eyes. Still encased by his arms, I rested against him, but Henry now crouched in front of me, his fingers on my wrist although I couldn't feel them, his brow deeply furrowed. Shocked white, Pat still sat beside us and the boys were unnaturally silent. Only Ellie displayed any other emotion, and that was of disbelief.

I hadn't imagined it.

I became aware of my body as it roared back to life, the pressure of Henry's fingers on my wrist almost unbearable although he held it lightly. He shook his head slowly, counting silently. "She's fine – pulse is fast, but it's strong and regular. I don't know what happened there."

I sensed Matthew's shock, but his voice came low and dark. "I do."

"That was *fantastic*," I purred, still between worlds. "So bright."

He spoke quietly, words thunderous in my head. "What was, sweetheart?"

I tried to hang on to the neon-bright images, but they were fading fast as voices intruded on my dream world. "She's on something; she's *wired*," I thought I heard Harry say. Or did I just sense his disappointment?

Joel's voice cut through the haze. "Happens all the time in the corps – guys off their heads. Crap, didn't take her for a dope-head."

"*Joel!*" Jeannie whipped at him.

My hand flapped weakly against Matthew's chest. "Tel'you later," I whispered to him, my words slurring unnaturally.

Pat craned forward. "What's she saying? I can't hear what she's saying."

Henry squinted at each of my eyes in turn. "What do you think it was?"

"Coffee," Matthew said, engaging Ellie in a hard stare. She blanched.

Pat gasped. "Ellie, you were asked to give Emma tea – what were you *thinking*?"

My disembodied hand found Pat's arm, negotiating the complicated stitch work of the knitted jacket, feeling her worry in waves. "Pat, leave her, she didn't know how I would react…" *She wouldn't dose me with caffeine again, that was for certain.* "*I* didn't know how I'd react."

"Caffeine junkie!" Joel whooped, relieved. "Great!"

Henry frowned. "Anaphylaxis?"

Matthew shook his head. "No. No, I don't think so. Emma, have you had any problems with your heart? Or has anyone in your family?"

"Not that I know of. I'm fine, really I am." I felt a little sick, but then I wasn't used to drinking coffee.

Releasing my wrist and rising, Henry slowly stood up. "What about allergic reactions, food intolerances, medications?"

"I don't think so. Coffee doesn't suit me but it's never done that before. Is that what you think it was?" I looked at Matthew, at his eyebrows drawn into a deep frown as he considered the options.

"Twenty-four hour heart monitor?" Dan joined in, coming to stand next to Henry and rubbing his earlobe thoughtfully.

"No," Matthew and I said almost simultaneously, his response measured and calm, mine coming out as an anxious squeak as I looked from one to the other. Matthew gave a reassuring squeeze with his arm around my waist. "That won't be necessary. It was probably just a reaction to the coffee, but," he continued, his forehead smoothing as he made a decision, "I think we'll have some of your blood and run a few tests just to be sure."

I wasn't supposed to have seen the look that passed between the two men, but the after-effects of the coffee or whatever it was that had sharpened my senses until they lacerated my being were enough that I caught the tiniest movement between eye and the responding mouth. "Ugh," I pulled a face, "is that really necessary?"

"Humour me," Matthew replied, but I saw none in his eyes.

"But if it was just the coffee…" I began.

Harry shifted the tray over to make enough room on the coffee table for him to perch, a trapped sugar crystal grating painfully across the surface setting my teeth on edge. "Hey, Emma, your heart stopped; we've got to find out why, just in case."

"Just in case you drop dead, he means," Joel stretched out on the sofa, seemingly unconcerned except for the edgy glint in his eyes.

"Shut up, you idiot," Ellie snapped at him. "I'm really sorry, Emma. I didn't know, I just thought you didn't like it, that's all. I was being stupid…"

"Yeah, right…" Joel drawled.

"*Shut up!*" she rounded on him, teeth clenching as her temper flared.

Matthew cut across the disorder of voices. "Enough!" Hush fell abruptly. "This needs to be done *now*. Harry, my bag is in my car, fetch it please. Henry, I'd appreciate your assistance. Ellie, you and Joel run the bloods back to the lab; I'll make out a list of what I want covered. Ellie, you get them done tonight…"

"Wait," I interrupted him. "It's snowing heavily; they won't get through. It's too dangerous."

Joel waved a hand towards the darkened windows to the courtyard. "Nah, it wasn't snowing that much earlier. Don't worry about it, Dr D, we'll be OK."

Matthew fixed me with a steady gaze I found hard to break. "These can't wait, Emma, every minute counts." And he rose immediately, lifting me with him. "We'll go next door to my study."

I looked back over my shoulder. "Pat, I'm *really* sorry…" She dismissed my apology with a wave. "Don't worry about it. You just get those tests done and I'll save the washing-up for you."

"Thanks," I managed with a passing attempt at being caustic before we were through the door to the next building.

"You're welcome," I heard her reply.

Matthew's study was blissfully quiet after the cacophony of the other room. He sat me in his big armed chair behind his desk and began to undo my cuffs.

"The snow's really bad out there; I didn't realize how deep it's got." Harry shook the broad bag he carried of the snow gathered in the folds of the leather, and put it on the desk. He knocked his shoulders free of ice.

"Deep, is it?" Henry gave me an appraising stare. "Harry, go warn Ellie and Joel. Is it passable, do you think?"

"If Joel's driving, they should make it in the 4x4, Gramps, yeah."

I looked at him anxiously, but a sudden intake of breath from Matthew diverted me. He was running his thumb over the inside of my arm, but I couldn't see what he looked at. He started to unbutton my other sleeve, rolling it up and out of the way, his thumb tracing the silver-pink line of my scar. "Strap," he muttered, and Henry fished in the bag and handed him a thick, rubberized band, which he wrapped around the top part of my arm, pulling it tight. I hated that sensation – the constriction – the squeezing just before the needle would go in and suck out my blood.

"There's nothing there." Henry straightened, rubbing his chin. "Is she usually this bad?"

Matthew shook his head. "No, she isn't," he said slowly. "We'll have to go for a modified cut-down."

Irritation and unease prickled at my patience. "Gentlemen, excuse me, but I am here and I am conscious – can you please tell me what's wrong? And will you *please* get this thing off me, it's hurting like mad."

Matthew came to. "Henry, if you would…?" The strap was unwound and removed. "You seem to be lacking veins this evening. It's going to make it somewhat more difficult getting blood from you."

I looked for the familiar blue lines like the tributaries of a river that were usually quite evident in the crease of my elbow and running down my inner arm, but my skin looked smooth and clear. Even my freckles were less clearly defined than usual.

"Oh. Is that so strange?"

Matthew couldn't disguise the dry smile. "For you, yes. You're normally quite generous with your blood. We'll have to use alternative means."

"Normally? But... but I don't remember you taking blood before..."

"You wouldn't, you weren't conscious at the time."

"What if you can't get any now?" I wondered what they were planning, getting more and more jittery as the initial elation of the coffee was rapidly replaced by the negative side-effects.

"Matthew's never failed yet," Henry said kindly, but that only made it sound more ominous. Matthew held out his hand and Henry gave him a scalpel. I swallowed nervously as Matthew swabbed my skin, the cold sterile wipe raising goose pimples on my exposed arm, and sprayed something even colder on the area. It began to numb immediately.

Henry took the goosebumps for fear and put a comforting hand on my shoulder.

"This is Matthew's version of a cut-down. It's quicker and less invasive, and it's the only way we can get enough of the red stuff quickly. Look away if you don't like blood, Emma. This won't take long but it's not pleasant."

"I'm OK with blood, Henry, it's the needle part I'm not so sure about."

Matthew had a look of intense absorption as if selecting an area to pierce was a matter of divining. He angled the scalpel against my arm above my scar but below the crease of my elbow. A sudden revulsion filled me and I jerked my arm away. He looked at me, concentration broken. "Matthew, please not *that* arm."

He didn't hesitate, moving to the other side, repeating the process of selection and swabbing, followed by the anaesthetic spray with quick, confident movements.

Despite what I had said to Henry, I couldn't bring myself to look and focused on the way Matthew's dark eyelashes and the fine black line around his iris defined the blue of his eyes. I barely felt the tiny incision the blade made but I certainly felt what followed because it wasn't like a needle at all: not the sharp jab of the inoculation, nor the stab of a blood sample being taken for medical insurance, but a cut and slice of my skin and the sensation of tearing and drawing as if he were pulling a vein out through the incision he had made. I bit the sides of my tongue to prevent an involuntary cry escaping. He raised his eyes to mine and anchored them while he continued the procedure, seemingly not needing to look. But I wanted to, I wanted to see what caused my blood to flow sickeningly through the needle like glue. He wouldn't let me, intensifying his gaze until whatever he did became irrelevant, siphoning the overwhelming discomfort along with my blood.

With a sudden realization, I understood what he was doing. *Stop it, Matthew*, I pleaded in my head, because I couldn't find the words to say it out loud. *It's my pain, let me deal with it.* I tried to move my eyes away from his, but an invisible line stretched between us as unbreakable as a steel hawser. *I don't want you to have this. Let – me – go,* I silently implored, but he held on to me, sucking all sensation as surely as if drawing poison from a wound. And an answer, so faint that I didn't know if it represented an echo of my imagination or a whispered thought: *No.*

"Nearly done," Henry said, his voice beyond my comprehension, close but a thousand miles away. "That should do it. Good job."

I felt a shift inside my head and a release that brought me back to my body. Matthew put a small wad over the incision, holding it firmly with his thumb.

"How did you *do* that?"

"Matthew could get blood from a proverbial stone," Henry said, his back to us as he rapidly sealed small, plastic bottles containing my blood.

Matthew took his thumb away from my arm, immediately replacing it with what looked like a glorified plaster, avoiding my eyes. He took my hand and placed it firmly over the patch. "Keep the pressure on it; you'll be fine in a minute." He rose and began writing indecipherably on a sheet of paper, with Henry next to him, penning corresponding numbers on the little bottles as the list on the paper grew to about a dozen lines. As each bottle received its number, Henry put it carefully in a padded bag the size of a child's large lunch bag and, when the last one went in, zipped it securely shut.

Completing the list, Matthew held it out to Ellie. "Take these for analysis without delay, and when that's done I want you to run the results through Eve."

I hadn't seen her come in. Now she stood by the unlit fire staring at Matthew as if he had asked her to walk across coals. She sounded uncertain. "Sure, but *Eve?*"

"*Now*, please, Ellie. Send the results through to me here immediately you have them. Phone me when you have the first one." She nodded dumbly, taking the bag from his outstretched hand, glancing at me with a subdued apology, before leaving and shutting the door behind her. "Harry, retrieve the coffee cup Emma used from your grandmother before she washes it, and keep a sample of the coffee as well. And tell Joel to drive carefully," Matthew added, before the boy left to follow his sister.

"Eve?" Henry asked, casting a sideways look at me. "Do you think there's a connection? Why would there be?"

Curiosity gnawed as Matthew studiously avoided me as he packed items away in his bag. "I have to explore all possibilities, Henry, however remote they might seem." He turned back to me, lifting the edge of the plaster. "That's going to be fine. How are you feeling?"

"Puzzled."

"Apart from your insatiable curiosity that is, how do you feel?"

"Buzzing. Fizzing. I'm not sure. A bit sick I suppose, and light-headed… definitely light-headed."

Matthew put a hand under my jaw and turned my head so that the light from the desk lamp shone full on my face. I blinked in the strong light and brought up a hand to shield my eyes.

"No problem there," Henry commented.

"No, none," Matthew agreed. "Tell me *exactly* what happened – right from the moment before you drank the coffee – every detail, and I mean *every* detail, Emma, whether you think it relevant or not."

His eyes were earnest and dark and I knew that what he asked must be important, but my head had begun to thump and, if I closed my eyes, I could see snow falling and tyre tracks disappearing flake by flake but it wasn't falling as heavily now and it would stop soon and *what a ridiculous way to spend Christmas Eve*, I thought, *and even worse, to ruin everyone else's, making this whole episode doubly embarrassing. And I'm thirsty – very thirsty – and my tummy is grating and frankly, I've had enough and if it weren't for the audience I would be very tempted to have a good howl about it all like I did when Emily Carter stole the stone hand-axe Grandpa had given to me to take in to school. She never did that again, the sneaky moo.*

A soft touch against my neck brought me back to the present as Matthew brushed a wisp of hair behind my ear. "Emma, are you finding it difficult to concentrate?" I nodded. "Henry, if you wouldn't mind getting Emma some water and a piece of dry toast, please, I think that might help."

And I felt ratty. "You took blood without my consent," I grumbled, referring to my earlier comments about my willingness or otherwise to be tapped for blood like a maple for its sap.

Matthew breathed out but it was more like a sigh. I marvelled at the way he kept up with my erratic thought processes, although at the moment, *process* was too precise a word to place on the acrobatics my mind was playing.

"You were unconscious, Emma, and anyway, would you have withheld your consent if I had asked?"

"Probably not. But I thought there was plenty washing about without you taking more."

He crouched down next to my chair so that our eyes were level. "Remember Staahl?" I felt my face screw at the memory. "Indeed, how could you not. Well, you said he licked you when he cut you with the knife – you had an open wound on your neck as well as your arm." I felt disgust contort my face. "So I ran a few tests to make sure he hadn't infected you – hepatitis – that sort of thing."

"I see. I can't really complain, can I? It would be a bit ungracious of me in the circumstances."

He smiled. "Yes, it would," and kissed my forehead.

We both looked towards the door a second before it opened and Henry came in with a small tray in one hand, which he placed on the desk in front of me. "This should help settle you. It's stopped snowing, by the way. It's not too bad out there now."

I nodded in agreement, picking up the glass and drinking deeply. I had already drunk a third of the ice-cold water when I remembered to thank him.

Matthew regarded me closely. "You heard Henry *before* he opened the door, Emma?"

I finished the water, placing the glass carefully on the tray and already feeling better. I looked at him in surprise. "Yes, of course, didn't you?"

"Yes, I did, that's my point – *you* shouldn't have done. What did you hear?"

I thought about it. "I can't say what I heard exactly, I just knew he was there, if that makes sense."

"Not really, no. Tell me what happened earlier."

Henry settled into a chair he had drawn up opposite the desk, placing his hands in an arch as he listened.

"I drank the coffee. I'd felt fine before, just a bit cross when I realized what Ellie was up to. That's all sorted now; she and I have come to an unspoken understanding, so don't make an issue of it – please?" Neither father nor son said a word. "After the first few mouthfuls I had the same reaction I had the last time I drank coffee…"

"Which was when?" Matthew asked.

"When I was last in Stamford. It was very weak – a latte – nowhere near as strong or as good as Pat's, but I had the same rapid pulse, that feeling of… euphoria, I suppose you could call it. Not exactly a pleasant sensation, but I can see why people get hooked. And disorientation – I'd forgotten that, almost like being drunk – but that didn't last very long. Anyway, this time everything changed after the second cup I drank: everything became accentuated, came more into focus. I could hear and see things I hadn't noticed before. It was as if this fog had lifted that I had lived with all my life – a veil

– like mist over the Meadows at home when the sun breaks through and you can see clearly again."

"And you've never had an experience like this before?" Henry asked.

I shook my head. "Only a hint of that clarity, just the one time, in Stamford."

Henry looked down over the edge of his glasses at me and I could imagine him questioning a patient. "Forgive me for asking, Emma, but have you ever taken any recreational substances, especially hallucinates?"

I shot him a reproving look. "Absolutely *not*. I've enough rubbish in my head without adding to it."

Matthew's eyes tipped upwards in amusement for the first time since we had entered the study. "So you saw and heard things more clearly within the room?" he prompted.

"Yes, but not just in the room. What I thought so odd was that I could hear – see – *sense* – the snow falling, and how fast it fell. And the weirdest thing of all…" I hesitated, not sure how, or even whether, I should mention it at all. Matthew read my reluctance.

"It's fine to speak in front of Henry, Emma."

"The weirdest thing…" I repeated slowly, "… I saw what Ellie was feeling, and I understood why she gave me the coffee. I knew what she was feeling and *she* knew that I knew. It lasted only seconds though."

"The amount of time Emma's heart stopped, but not enough time for anoxia to set in?" Henry asked Matthew. I had forgotten that Matthew would have felt the beat of my heart cease as he held me close to him.

"Perhaps. Did you have any pain at all, any discomfort anywhere, not just around your heart?"

I tore a strip off the now cold toast. "None; if anything,

I felt great." But he already knew that; he would have felt it. "This isn't just a question of my heart stopping, is it? I didn't imagine what Ellie was feeling and nor was it a lack of oxygen, and…" I said severely, "… it *certainly* wasn't drugs." Henry held his hands up in a gesture of surrender. "So, who's Eve?" I bit a corner off the toast in the hope it would absorb some of the caffeine still running races around my system.

The corner of Matthew's mouth twitched. "E-V-E. It's a computer program we've developed through which we run data. It saves a lot of time in analysis. You saw it when you visited the lab." I caught the hint of something else in his voice but I couldn't work it out. I wondered vaguely if I could have done so half an hour ago as the edges of my mind seemed to be closing in again, a shadow of what they had been, leaving me bereft of clarity. I mourned its loss.

"Does it take long to run these tests?" I asked, remembering with a niggle of guilt that Ellie and Joel were stuck in the lab at the college and that they both might very well be harbouring a growing resentment towards me for putting them there.

Henry stood up, stretching. "Don't worry about the kids, Emma. Ellie deserves to make up for what she did to you, and it'll teach Joel a bit of filial duty. As for me, I'm too old to stay up into the wee small hours, so if you'll excuse me… Do you need anything else, Dad?"

I choked on the last piece of toast and Matthew patted and rubbed my back until I stopped coughing. "Sorry," I spluttered, my eyes watering.

"Don't mention it." Henry's eyes crinkled. "It takes a bit of getting used to. It took Jeannie a decade."

5

Christmas

I shuffled around in bed trying to get comfortable, the area from which blood had been taken still sore and intermittently stabbing, and the caffeine potent enough to keep me wide awake despite the sleep for which I yearned.

I sat up, dumping a pillow behind my back, surveying his room as I waited for Matthew to return from wherever he had disappeared to ten minutes earlier. He had ensured that the radiator was switched on and had lit the fire before he left, both making inroads on the long-chilled air, but the room was otherwise neither loved nor lived in, and it had an air of abandonment despite the wealth of the furnishings. I sighed, and reached for the journal to pass the time.

I had tucked it into my bag for quiet moments like these. The zip had made a buzzing sound like bees in a chimney as I lifted it out of my luggage and took the book from its protective bag. The last time I had seen it was in Matthew's hands as he read through the night in Grandpa's chair. We hadn't discussed it since. This was the first opportunity I had found to read beyond his father's death and before Nathaniel Richardson had taken his family to the New World.

Making myself comfortable, I opened the journal, turning pages until I found the last entry that had referred to Matthew's disappearance. I read on. Richardson had been concerned with the management of the estate as Henry Lynes' health deteriorated and he sank towards despair. Matthew had been the sole heir and, without him, the estate should have been disposed of to the next surviving relative, which was his aunt – Elizabeth. The house and land did indeed go to her and her heirs, but there was a reference to some dispute over *divers goodes* that had not been resolved. Nathaniel said neither what had happened to them nor what they were. I blinked and stifled a yawn. Reading between the lines, Richardson didn't have much respect for Elizabeth Montfort, who in turn had little regard for the estate, and she had broken it up soon after acquiring it. This had been one of the main reasons why Nathaniel had left Rutland and sought a life elsewhere.

Holding the journal open at that angle nipped the skin of my arm and, hearing soft steps on the landing, I put the book carefully on the table beside the bed for reading later.

I was pulling the duvet over me as Matthew came back in, and I inched over so that he could lie on the bed with the covers chastely between us. He raised his arms and I snuggled into them.

"Happy Christmas, Emma."

"Is it already? Happy Christmas. If I don't spoil it," I added. He poked me gently and I laughed. My arm twinged.

"I'm sorry I can't give you anything for your arm. I know it hurts, but we have to wait until the results are back." He laid his hand over the tender area and it soothed under his touch. I nestled into him, listening for the comforting rhythm of his heart, and felt him tighten his hold as if he were afraid I would melt away and disappear.

"It doesn't matter, it doesn't hurt that much anyway. So, tell me, how did you do it?

"Do what?"

"You know what I'm talking about. How did you take away that revolting sensation when you were extracting blood from me? It felt like you were… absorbing it somehow."

Matthew caressed the top of my head with his chin, not answering for a moment.

"I don't know," he said finally. "I've never been able to do that before."

I pushed away from him so that I could study his face and he gazed back at me, solemnly. "Why not? Why now? Why *me*?"

"I can't say."

"You heard me tell you to stop though, didn't you, Matthew?"

"Yes."

"And you know that I heard your reply?"

"I guessed you did – I wasn't entirely sure."

I recalled the remote yet certain resonance. "It was very faint. How did you get inside my head?"

He cocked a brow. "How did you get inside *mine*?"

We lay like that, each within our own thoughts for a time, the gentle cadence of his breath almost lulling me to sleep. "I suppose," I said sleepily, "that there has to be a connection between your ability to feel other people's pain and what you did tonight."

He had obviously been thinking along the same lines. "Very possibly. The question is, why could I go a step further with you and take away your pain, and why tonight? I suspect the link was latent and that whatever happened to you made you more responsive or… receptive." He drifted into a reverie, and I waited, perfectly content as long as we were together. Content, that is, until a thought struck me. "You don't think that you will become more sensitive to everyone's pain, do you?"

"I hadn't thought about it – it is possible. I'll have to see when I'm next at the hospital."

I sat up as the implication sank in. There was so little I knew about him and, just like climbing a range of hills, every time I thought that I had reached a peak of understanding, there in front of me would be yet another summit to climb.

"Matthew, I don't want you to suffer. I don't want you to be hurt *at all*. It's bad enough you feeling my pain, but everyone else's? You can't carry that as well."

An air of resigned acceptance had settled over him, and he put his hands behind his head as he watched firelight dance on the ceiling.

"You think that you might be able to take their pain away as well as feel it, don't you?" I challenged. "Don't you dare start that game! What right have you to take people's pain from them without asking?"

His eyes slid away from mine. "I took yours away from you tonight…"

"Yes, and I told you not to. You stole it from me, I didn't want to have it. You can't go around assuming people don't want their hurt."

"Have you ever seen someone die of stomach cancer?" he asked softly. I shook my head, angry that he would try to undermine my valid, but feeble, argument. "They can suffer terribly, Emma. If I can help them, shouldn't I do so?"

"Not if it means you suffer too," I said, mournfully, on a losing wicket but defiant to the last. "You shouldn't, without asking their permission. You can't assume consent, even if you think they would give it; that would be like playing God."

"I see," he said slowly, "and don't you think I would look good in a long white beard, then?"

"Blasphemy!" I squeaked and launched at him, the sudden release of tension making me impetuous. He caught me and rolled me onto my back. I became serious. "Matthew, please, *please* promise me you'll try to protect yourself. You don't have to save everybody. You wouldn't let me if our roles were reversed, would you?"

"That's below the belt," he complained.

"Maybe, but it's true nonetheless. Promise me."

"I promise," he said reluctantly.

I smiled up at him. "And gentlemen always keep their promises."

He suddenly grinned – a wicked, impish grin – as his hand ran up the outside of my thigh, making me squeal and smack his hand away. "And who says I'm a gentleman?"

"*A History of the Gentry of Rutland 1461 to 1660*," by J. M. Standing. You get a mention."

Matthew groaned, collapsing next to me and shaking with laughter. "You wait…" he threatened. "I'll show you how much of a gentleman I am."

I squirmed up to him until our noses were touching. "Is that a promise too?"

He grabbed a pillow, stuffing it between us. His eyes burned hot but not from anger.

"Hen's teeth, woman, there's only so much I can take. It was *you* cautioning *me* yesterday, remember?"

"Sorry, but it's your own fault, Matthew. You only have yourself to blame."

"What's that supposed to mean?"

"Well, look at you. What's a girl supposed to do when faced with *that* day in, day out?" I cast my eyes up and down the length of his body, which his clothes only served to enhance, and melted internally.

"Why, what's wrong?"

"I bet Ellie doesn't have a boyfriend, does she?"

"You've lost me. What has Ellie to do with anything?"

"She adores you, silly, that's why she's been so odd with me. She's jealous." His eyes opened wide with horror. "No, not like that – nothing incestuous or anything. It's just she measures everyone against you, and you're a hard act to follow. Other men don't have a chance with you around – not with her, or Megan… or the nurses come to think of it. Haven't you noticed? It must have been going on for centuries. In fact, Nathaniel mentions it in the journal."

He lay on his back again. "Megan's always been attentive, it's true, but Ellie? It explains something, though…"

I rested my chin on the pillow he held to his chest. "What?"

"She's had several boyfriends, but they don't seem to last. She won't even let us meet them." He paused. "And you think that's because of me?"

"Oh, yes," I said, "I told you that I could feel what she was thinking. It was very peculiar, but I'm quite sure about it. Don't say anything and don't change the way you treat her – that wouldn't be fair and she would suss you anyway, which would be humiliating for her. Just let time take its course; she'll be OK."

I rested my cheek on the pillow and he pulled the covers over me, putting his arms around the bundle we made. He stroked my hair. "What made you so insightful all of a sudden?"

"Coffee," I said.

By the time I woke, light crept around the edges of the shutters and burnished the dark wood of the floor. The absence of a clock made guessing the hour futile, but Matthew had risen so there was no point staying put.

I extended my limbs into a stretch like a kitten and yawned, disturbing something that softly crackled on the end of the bed. Tentatively pushing with my foot, I felt it engage with an object too hard to be a pillow. Clasping it, I slipped out of bed, tiptoeing across the thick rug to open the heavy shutters and blinking in the sudden sunlight that saturated the room. About a foot long and like a thin plank of wood, the package had been wrapped in a rich glossy paper and tied with a bronze silk ribbon off which a toning tassel hung. Tucked under the intersection of the ribbon was a matching card. On the front of it, Matthew had written in his beautiful flowing script:

> *And still she slept an azure-lidded sleep,*
> *In blanched linen, smooth, and lavender'd,*
> *While he from forth the closet brought a heap*
> *Of candied apple, quince, and plum, and gourd...*

I slid it out and turned it over. On the cream reverse, he had added:

> *Not to be consumed before breakfast.*

Which gave the game away even if I hadn't already caught the heady, dry scent of a very expensive chocolate. I whooped with delight, wondering if I could extricate a sliver without Matthew knowing, then realizing that he would be able to smell it on me a mile off like a lunchtime drinker returning to work after an overindulgent booze-up. There was nothing for it but to follow orders and have breakfast.

Keeping a weather eye on Maggie's room as I passed, I padded downstairs, my winter socks absorbing the sound of my footfall. The murmur of low voices came from the study as I reached the bottom step, and I stood outside deciding whether to knock and go in. I leaned my forehead against the cool surface of the wall, trying to choose, and knew instinctively that I was being discussed. It wasn't that I could hear what they were talking about, nor even that I caught any mention of my name. I could just *feel* it – in colours – a fleeting murmur inside my head like a half-remembered conversation heard through a closed door.

Stunned that this new-found facility lingered long after the obvious effects of the caffeine had faded, I swivelled to leave. From above, I heard what sounded like a tut.

On the landing, her hand resting on the polished banister rail, Maggie regarded me with unmoving eyes. She must have seen me by the door and thought I was listening.

I flushed without cause and reddened again as she acknowledged my discomfort with a trace of a smile. I felt like the Girl in *Rebecca*, with Mrs Danvers – draped in the vestiges of hate and oozing resentment – looking down on me, a silent assassin slipping killer words from between unmoving lips. I found her sort difficult to deal with, not least because my crime was either uncommitted or unidentified, and how can you apologize for something you haven't done? I couldn't bring myself to wish her a merry Christmas.

"Good morning, Maggie," I said stiffly.

Danvers continued to peer down at me using the height of the stairwell as an effective vantage point. "Good morning, Dr D'Eresby. I trust that you had an enjoyable night?"

I sucked my teeth wondering whether she intended a double entendre or if I misjudged her. Although not unfriendly, nor did she wave a white flag. I erred on the side of caution. "I did, thank you." Had she been Pat, I would have been throwing apologies at her for ruining her evening so fast it would have made her head spin; as it was, I thought that my untimely episode had probably made Maggie's day. I supposed she was en route somewhere, but she made no move to leave. Instead she continued to spit icicles.

"I'm afraid you will be alone this morning. Although the rest of the family are understandably tired after yesterday's excitement, they will be eager to visit my grandmother. She plays an important part in our lives, as I am certain you will have realized by now." The arctic plane of her face almost cracked before resuming its previous expression. "I'm sure you will be wanting breakfast. My grandfather will have left something for you in the kitchen, no doubt."

"Thank you, I'm sure you are right," I replied. I could not be faulted for my civility as long as no one could read *my* mind.

Quietly seething, I stalked across the hall to the kitchen door and was safely beyond her line of fire before she could let off a further volley, and found she had been right in one respect, at least. Waiting on the table in the clear, weak winter sun, Matthew had left me breakfast: a jug of something strongly red like cranberry juice (*exceedingly* red, like blood), a bowl of fresh fruit exquisitely prepared with his surgeon's precision, and a crisply fresh croissant still warm to the touch.

As I ate, ruminating on Maggie's remarks and surprising myself by my hunger, my eyes occasionally strayed to the luxurious bar of chocolate whose warmed scent the sunlight lifted towards me. Despite the intervening hours, remnants of the coffee had left my senses heightened, tingling as if magnetized. I pulled the tassel on the ribbon through my fingers, feeling each silky fibre, then reached out to pour the ruby juice into the glass left for me. Tied to the handle of the jug dangled a tag matching the one on the chocolate. I turned it so that I could read the inscription:

> *Have ye tippled drink more fine*
> *Than thine host's Cranb'ry wine?*

It sounded like something Keats would write. I smiled to myself: I wasn't the only one to misquote when it suited.

I finished the juice and ate the last of the fruit, went to wash up and found another tag propped against the tap, where I couldn't miss it:

> *The moderate consumption of chocolate is to be recommended on the advice of your physician.*

I laughed out loud and kissed the label, and heard a quiet cough behind me. Matthew sat on the table swinging a leg, the slab of chocolate in one hand while he watched me with a glint in his eye. "Careful, I might get jealous." I danced over to him, no longer surprised by his sudden appearances, and flung my arms around his neck. "That's more like it," he chortled, his arms about me.

"Thank you, thank you, *thank* you!"

He smiled, bemused. "Had I known I could get this response with a bar of chocolate, I would have bought you dozens by now."

"Not just for the chocolate, but for breakfast and the messages as well. Thank you for *bothering!*"

He swung me up onto the table next to him. "You are most welcome. I take it you would like this now?" He held up the bar just out of reach.

"Don't tease – I did as I was told."

"Yes, you did and you are to be commended for your temperance. However, I want to tell you one thing before I let you loose on the chocolate: this contains a serious amount of caffeine…"

I saw immediately where he was going with this. "Yes, but…"

"Wait. Some of the test results are back and the very odd thing is that you are *not* intolerant of caffeine."

I stopped bouncing. "I'm *not*?"

"That's right. You can eat as much chocolate as you like – you'll feel sick of course, but it won't kill you. However, you'll have to avoid coffee like the plague until we can work out what it was you did react to, and that is going to take time."

"And you, of course, know all about plague, don't you?"

He arched an eyebrow in response. "Oh yes, indeed I do."

"So those messages weren't because of the caffeine in the chocolate that you wanted me to avoid?"

"No, they were because a diet solely based upon the consumption of chocolate is not thought to be beneficial in the long term."

I pulled a face at him, wrinkling my nose, whose tip he kissed, making me laugh again. He coasted off the table and lifted me down. He let his hands linger around my waist. "You'd better get ready if you're going with Pat and Henry to church. Henry will look after you while you're there, but I think it would be a good idea if I stayed at home with you later, just in case."

I viewed him suspiciously. "You said there was nothing wrong with me."

"No, I did not. I said that you can tolerate caffeine. I still don't know what happened last night and until I do, I'm not leaving you alone."

"Matthew, you *have* to go and see Ellen. You can't not see her, today of all days. I'll be fine here – look, I won't even touch the chocolate until you get back." I put it resolutely on the table and turned my back on it.

"I admire your self-restraint, really I do, but that's not the point. I can't risk leaving you here, Emma. I don't know what would happen if your heart stopped again. It might not start spontaneously next time."

"But I'm not going near coffee and it was coffee that caused it, wasn't it? And you left me alone this morning, didn't you? Anything could have happened in that time. Be reasonable, Matthew; you can't stand watch over me all the time – you'll make me feel like a prisoner. Anyway, think how Ellen will feel if her husband doesn't turn up because he chooses to stay with his *girlfriend* on Christmas Day rather than with his *wife*."

He winced. "Ouch, you certainly know how to punch low. That's the second time in the last twelve hours, but," he shook his head earnestly, "I'm still not risking it." His jaw had adopted a stubborn line in a way that made me want to kiss the blunt end of his chin to make him smile again. Or just want to kiss him.

"I tell you what, how about a compromise? I'm sure Pat mentioned something about Jeannie not going to see Ellen today; can't I stay with her? I bet there's lots to do before this evening, and I could be getting on with that. And how long are you going to be, anyway? What's the likelihood of anything happening that Jeannie couldn't handle?"

I could see him compiling the list in his mind. "Well, for a start, she's not medically qualified to deal with…"

"She doesn't have to be because nothing – is – going – to – happen." I kissed him between each word and a smile crept over his lips.

"Well, it better not," he rumbled, pulling me close to him, "or you'll have me to deal with when I get back."

Matthew had left me with an air of resignation and worry stalking his eyes. He also left a list of instructions for Jeannie should I do anything as foolish as let my heart stop beating.

Before he reversed the car out of the garage, I leaned through the window in the privacy the garage briefly afforded us, and kissed him with a mixture of longing and apprehension. "Just drive carefully and don't put your immortality to the test," I told him.

He gave a strained smile. "I'll be back as soon as I can."

I touched my hand to the tense lines between his eyes. "That's what I'm afraid of. I'd rather you were late than I be sorry." A dark shape intercepted the sun as it seeped into the garage and I didn't need to turn around to know that Maggie stood behind me.

"Be safe," I implored him quietly, before stepping back out of the car's way.

6

"Divers Goodes"

Light from the east windows saturated Matthew's study, where no trees or buildings impeded its passage. I inhaled the warm scent of leather-bound books and the polished wood of the desk, of the silver of the photograph frames gently oxidizing in the air, and the fresh-sawn resins of the logs in the fireplace. I took in his choice of ornaments, and the lute-like cittern sitting propped against one wall. I felt Matthew's presence in every particle of the room. Like a blanket in which I could wrap myself, he would be there with me for as long as it took for him to return.

I hovered uncertainly beside his desk. He had told me that no part of the house was barred to me and that I could wander at will through every room, but without him, I still felt like I intruded in the one place where I could be closest to him.

This is ridiculous, I thought, and sat a little too rapidly behind his desk, knocking one of the smaller photographs, its silver frame *tinging* as it hit the ornate handle of a silver and ivory letter opener. I resurrected the frame, carefully checking the corner for dents, before looking at the photograph itself.

The picture was old, creased, and foxed with age. Ellen knelt on one knee smiling at the person behind the camera, with a small Henry, aged about three and bright blond in front of her, one pudgy hand on his mother's leg, the other clasping a small hunting horn. They were in a front garden and behind them the bonnet of a car dated the photo to the late thirties. It was one of those touching, domestic photographs that litter the memories of most families. That it must be a loved and treasured picture was borne out by the years of passage with its keeper, worn into the edges of the leather back, and beaten into the dents of the frame.

I put it back where it belonged. I hadn't looked at what lay on Matthew's desk yesterday, having been preoccupied at the time, but now that I was alone and time not an issue, I felt increasingly like a guest whose eyes prod and probe relentlessly, seeking the source of their hosts' secrets while all the time being in receipt of their hospitality. I couldn't bring myself to look any further.

I picked up the telephone and dialled my home number. Beth answered. "Hi, happy Christmas," I said as I heard her familiar voice. "How's it going?"

"You've missed the washing-up."

I laughed. "Don't worry, I've plenty enough here. How are the children; managed to wear them out yet?"

She groaned in exasperation. "Alex and Flora are happy as Larry with their presents. They'll want to tell you themselves, I expect. By the way, that was very extravagant of you, and it's your own fault if they expect the same next year. Flora hasn't stopped talking about it and Alex hasn't said a word since he opened his. In fact…" I heard her twist away from the phone, her voice fading momentarily, "… Alex is under the table with it now."

I was gratified, if somewhat surprised, that my presents had been received so enthusiastically. "I'm glad they like them…" I said, but Beth was already part-way through her next sentence.

"Rob and I looked at something similar, but we just couldn't stretch to it this year." I had a sneaking suspicion that we weren't talking about the same things. "And the postage must have cost a *fortune*, Emma, as well as the combined effect of all that plastic upon the petrochemical industry."

"What on earth are you talking about, Beth? You've lost me." Silence on the end of the phone. In the background, Flora held a one-sided conversation, while further off still, I could just hear Archie's intermittent wail.

"The children's presents, of course – the Barbie castle and the Inter-Galactic Space Station. And Archie's ride-on dog – he's been chewing the ear since he got it. What did you think I meant?"

I sighed. "Beth, in all the years we have known each other, when have I ever succumbed to the temptation of mass-produced plastic toys?"

She hummed down the phone. "Never."

"So why would I do so now?"

"Er, I thought you might have had a complete personality transplant or alternatively that you… so, *you* didn't give them the toys?"

"No, it wasn't me."

"So, who did?" I let her think about it for a moment. "You don't mean…? He didn't! Golly, that's very generous. Wow, Emma, and you didn't prompt him?"

"Hardly – not when it comes to plastic, you know me: wood, stone, or metal – and educational."

"Wow."

"Yeah, wow," I muttered, slightly irritated that Matthew had known exactly what my nephew and niece would like and had no qualms about giving them what they wanted rather than what he thought they should have.

Beth had a note of awe in her voice. "He didn't say they were from him."

"No, he wouldn't, and he didn't tell me, either. You were saying the twins are fine – so who isn't? Are Mum and Dad OK? What about Nanna?"

"It's Arch and his teeth, it's non-stop at the moment." Archie gave a particularly piercing wail in the background, emphasizing his plight. "See what I mean? Can you send Matthew back? We've still got that spare room he can stay in. Nanna's fine, by the way, we saw her this morning. You know she had a bad turn just after you left? She seems a bit better now, more like her old self. We gave her your love."

I bit my lip as I thought about her lying there on the edge of life, so very far away.

"Go and see her whenever you can, won't you, Beth?"

"Oh, we are. Dad's been brilliant. He's taking Mum up there most days and he's even looked after Archie so that I can get to see her when Rob's at the café. He seems so much better – Dad, I mean, not Arch. And Rob's fine, too. How about you, Emma – what've you been up to, or shouldn't I ask?" She tittered down the phone, sounding more like a sixteen-year-old than an exhausted mother of three.

"Nothing I shouldn't, I assure you." I left out the drama of last night. "I went to church first thing, but it's still morning here and we've lots to get done. Tell the children we have loads of snow and it's very cold and the sun's shining."

"Ooo, it sounds lovely. What about Matthew's family? What are his parents like? Isn't it a bit scary meeting them all?"

I traced the edge of the desk with my finger while I tried to remember who was supposed to be related to whom, and resorted to generalities instead. "They're lovely – most of them. Very welcoming."

"Has he given you any presents yet? Mum'll want to know."

"He gave me lovely earrings last night," I fingered them, feeling the elongated stones; it seemed like an age ago, "and this morning he left me a *huge* bar of chocolate. It looks fab and it smells... *won-der-ful*." I dragged the word out longingly.

I could hear Beth whispering to someone, and shared laughter. "He certainly knows the way to *your* heart. So, what have you given him?"

The ivory and silver letter-opener in the shape of a dagger and almost as sharp lay at an angle on the leather-topped desk. I pushed it idly with the tip of my finger and the heavy object spun slowly on the carved ivory hilt and stopped. "Nothing yet, I'm saving that for later."

"Emma, you wicked girl! What would Nanna say if she heard you talking like that?"

I rolled my eyes and tutted in a spinsterly way. "Is that what having children does for you, Beth – give you a one-track mind?" I picked up the letter-opener, feeling its perfect balance.

"It's all I've got at the moment with Archie keeping me awake at night. I'm too shattered most of the time to do anything other than *think* about it. It's all right for you, unfettered with offspring and with no other encumbrances than a rich, handsome boyfriend – or whatever you want to call him. Those were the days," she sighed, "though Rob was never rich. We don't need any contraception, I can tell you; Arch's seen to that."

"OK, too much information, thanks. I don't need the details," I laughed, imagining a pout dimpling her chin at the other end of the phone. I leaned my free elbow on the desk, feeling the pinch in the crook of my elbow where the plaster stuck to my skin. "Send Mum and Dad my love – and Rob and the children, too – especially Archie if he's suffering."

Beth gave a short *humph*. "*He's* suffering… I'll give him suffering," she muttered. "Mum's with him now – she's a saint, really she is. She cried when she unwrapped the knitting wool you gave her. I think she's missing you, but Arch is keeping her busy. Dad's in the potting shed fiddling with whatever you gave him for Christmas. He's been out there for ages, he must love it. Thanks for our presents by the way, oh, and I've yours here, do you want me to send them, or will you be back sometime soon?" My sister had mastered the loaded question long ago.

"Hang on to them and save on postage," I evaded with equal skill. "They'll be something to look forward to when I do see you. Say happy Christmas to everyone from me, won't you?"

I put the phone down with a combination of relief that we were getting on so much better now and a hint of homesickness. I placed the letter-opener back where I had found it and considered it high time I broached the chocolate.

I almost stumbled into Jeannie when I opened the door of the study.

"I was just coming to find you," she stammered. I suspected that Matthew had asked her to check up on me at regular intervals.

"And I have a bar of chocolate that needs eating – care to join me?" I offered.

Jeannie had a sharp face with a tendency towards seriousness that demanded that someone try to inject some levity into her. Chocolate – as I always attest – is the pan-global cure for all ills and the means by which world peace will be achieved. Unfortunately for the world, not enough men eat it – hence women, by rights, should rule the planet.

She broke into a smile, which warmed her face. "I'll put the kettle on, you supply the chocolate. Do you know your way to my place?" I shook my head. "Through the store cupboard in the kitchen. The door's built into the rear wall; it looks like panelling – slide it open. I'll see you in a minute." She left without waiting for an answer. I supposed there must a good reason why there should be a door concealed in the larder between the two buildings, and one day I would get around to asking Matthew about it.

I retrieved the chocolate and went into the larder. The shelves of grey-veined marble were not as full as they should have been, even for a man living by himself. The packets were unopened and some, by the looks of it, were out of date. For all the care Matthew took to protect himself and his family, the subtle details were lacking, which would lead anyone who knew what they were looking for straight to the questions that would begin to unlock his secret. I took the only open packet – my tea – from the shelf, and slid the back panel of the wall. I walked straight into Jeannie's kitchen.

Jeannie and Dan lived in the converted stables opposite Henry and Pat and whereas Pat mothered her home, Jeannie disciplined hers. It made an inspiring space. Open to the rafters along the long, windowed wall of the open-plan room, the skeleton of the old building stood out like the bleached bones of a whale. Two-thirds of the huge area had been floored as a mezzanine to create bedrooms, I assumed. The room was sparsely furnished in white and black, with accents of natural wood. It reminded me of Sam's designer furniture, except that this seemed minimalist with a capital M. There were no Christmas decorations, but huge modern canvases in shocking, vivid colours were mounted between each window. There were three of them – a series on a theme that eluded me. I curled my toes in abject pleasure on the heated polished stone floor.

"Hi," Jeannie said, briskly, "the kettle's just boiled. Is that tea?" She held out her hand.

"Yup, but I'll do it, if you like," I offered, to avoid the confusion Pat had faced.

Jeannie gave me a severed smile. "No need," and held out her hand again.

I tried to think of a topic of conversation which would help us break the thin sheet of ice that separated us. "This is an amazing space, Jeannie – did you design it?"

"Daniel did, yes. He drew up the plans and had an architect oversee the building works. Daniel wanted to be an architect." I waited for the *but* that she left hanging off the end of the sentence, but she didn't supply it. I wondered what had prevented Dan from pursuing his choice of career.

Proffering a handleless cup, she indicated a seating area and I perched tentatively on the edge of a large white leather cube with a curved seat for my bottom. It was perfectly comfortable as long as I didn't want to lean back. I looked for somewhere to put my cup, and ended up resting it on my hankie.

"I have a request to make, Emma, if I may."

I shifted my behind so that it found the gentle curve of the cube. "Of course, Jeannie."

"I prefer to be called *Jeanette*."

I opened my mouth, then shut it again. "Right. Jeanette."

"Everyone calls me Jeannie, but that's not my name."

"I understand. Jeanette it is, then."

"Thank you," she said.

"Chocolate?" I suggested.

Thankful for something to do, I broke the wax seal that secured the thick tassel to the bar with a reverence second only to the opening of a papal bull. The aroma – spicy, sharp, intense – was equalled by the smooth, bitter-dry flavour with all the whack of a high caffeine-content chocolate. I hoped Matthew would be proved right and I could take the caffeine because I sure as anything didn't want Jeanni... Jeanette trying to resuscitate me from what I could only describe as chocolate heaven. I let the tiny square melt slowly on my tongue, speechless as the full essence engulfed my senses.

"I prefer milk chocolate," Jeanette remarked, her piece already consumed, corrupting the exquisite flavour with a slug of coffee. *Pearls before swine; pearls and swine...* I folded the bronze foil around the open end of the chocolate, and put the bar down beside me on the cube. "Matthew said that you're not a doctor, but he didn't say what area you do specialize in?" I asked politely.

Her pale face brightened a little. "I've two doctorates: one in chemistry and one in pharmacodynamics. I'm considered an expert in my field."

"Gosh, *another* Dr Lynes – is there anyone who isn't? It's very confusing."

Jeanette's face became stony. "Actually, I've kept my maiden name for professional purposes. I'm Dr Rathbone."

"Right. Dr Rathbone. Twice." I couldn't help it, there was something about her that just made me want to be flippant. Or perhaps it was the exhilarating effects of the chocolate kicking in.

"Yes, twice," she said, missing the joke. "My parents are both academics and my brother is a professor in a nuclear physics department in Europe. We are a very intellectual family. You must come from a similarly academic background." She made it a statement of fact rather than a question.

"No, not really. Apart from my grandfather, who also held a post at Cambridge, I'm the only academic. The D'Eresbys were all land, military, or the church. I was a bit of a disappointment." I laughed.

Jeanette stared, nonplussed. "Oh – I see." I heard the note of disillusionment. We both struggled to find something to say in the gulf between us.

"I don't understand," she said at last, daubs of red the colour of rose hips rising on her neck, "when you have achieved so much, why would you want to stay here in Maine when you could return to Cambridge? It would be such a sacrifice. You won't be able to achieve anything like the recognition you have now. Why would you want to do that?"

For a brief moment, I stared at her dumbfounded before I found my voice. "Why would I be sacrificing anything? I can work just as well from the States as I can from home, and what I can't access remotely, I can always travel to."

The red patches faded and flared again, making her look feverish. "Why should you give up your position? You won't be able to retain your post at Cambridge, will you?"

"No, probably not, but there are compensations."

"There are?" she said flatly.

I thought they were obvious, but Jeannie – sitting on the edge of the her X-frame chair, her hands clasped in front of her, her pinched face even sharper than usual – waited for an explanation.

"Well, yes – Matthew's here."

She leaned forward. "And…?"

Perhaps *I* missed the point. "And he's not in Cambridge."

I frowned. "I'm not sure if I understand. You live here and you have a successful career; I can't see what the difference is."

Jeannie bristled. "I could have done so much better. I had the opportunity to work for an international pharmaceutical group but Daniel didn't want to leave. We decided to stay here, but you have a choice."

I picked up the square cup awkwardly, and sipped out of one side, taking care not to let the liquid spill either side of my lips. "And you blame Matthew for that?" I asked, not sure how I would react if she said "yes".

She shrugged. "It's true Daniel wouldn't stay if it weren't for Matthew and his… peculiarities. He won't leave Matthew and I won't leave Daniel. I can see why, of course; Matthew has a brilliant mind, although it's wasted *here*." She screwed her face, making the word ugly. "And he has helped us, I accept that. But you – you don't have to make the same mistake I did. You have everything ahead of you, Emma. I don't know why you would want to lose what you have."

I repositioned the scalding cup, giving myself time to collect my thoughts. "I think," I said slowly, carefully selecting my words, "that we have a different perspective on what we might deem to be priorities, Jeanette. My career is – was – important to me, or at least my subject was. Meeting Matthew has changed the way I look at things; my priorities have altered. I still love history and my work and Cambridge, but they are no longer the be-all and end-all of my life, it's as simple as that. I choose to stay because of Matthew in the same way as you choose to stay for Daniel. It's not so very different." Except that it was, of course. She had been coerced to a degree by circumstance, whereas I had made my choice freely. Had I been ten years younger, about nineteen, the age she had been when she met Daniel, would I have come to the same decision as I did now, when history was all I desired? I had chosen it over Guy, after all. I looked into the eye of the cup, at the tar-black depths of my milk-less tea, and thought that probably – given the man – I would.

"Hey-ho," I said cheerfully. "What needs to be done for dinner this evening?"

I found it a relief to escape to Matthew's kitchen perhaps as much as she felt relieved of the burden of responsibility for me. It wasn't that I didn't like Jeannie, just that we were completely different people, and being near her sometimes made me feel as if I were sitting under a black cloud, devoid of all hope. I concluded, as I made myself another cup of tea and snaffled a square of chocolate, that she sounded depressed, or at least, that the compensations of living the life she did – with her doting husband, three children, and a great job all wrapped up in a very comfortable lifestyle – made no impression on her psyche. It would be bad enough sitting under a cloud, but it must be so much worse *being* it, because how could she escape? Four months ago, would I have said the same thing? After nearly twenty-five years of being with the same man in the same situation would I, too, feel trapped like a flightless bird on a rock in the middle of the ocean? I thought of my particular rock and, given his *peculiarities*, as Jeannie put it, considered myself blessed.

After completing the simple tasks I had been set by Pat, chosen, I suspected, with the intention of turning me into a competent cook one day, I retreated once more to the study. Engrossed by both the book I had found and by the intoxicating music playing on the superb system, I didn't know that the family had returned until I heard the faint slamming of car doors and, by then, Matthew had found me.

"Mmm, you smell of cold air and mountains," I said between kisses, "and you taste of them too."

"Which do you prefer: mountain or chocolate?" he asked, with just enough space between our lips for me to answer.

"No contest," I mumbled, leaving him none the wiser. "How's Ellen?"

"She's fine and she said for me to say 'Happy Christmas' to you, and she looks forward to meeting you."

"Bizarre," I said. "Perverse. I hope you returned the greeting from me to her."

"I did, as I promised. Now, what have you been up to left to your own devices – apart from eating chocolate and listening to The Lark Ascending and…" he turned his head so that he could see the book I had been reading, "… raiding my books for Culpeper's *Herbal*."

"I've never seen an original edition before," I mused. "It's beautiful – oh, and so is the chocolate – a masterpiece of confection. And before I forget, can you explain what is so educational about a plastic castle and a fantasy space station?"

He grinned. "Ah, so you've spoken with the twins, have you? Did they like their presents?"

"No, I haven't spoken to the twins because they were too busy playing with their *favourite* Christmas presents to speak to their aunt, but no doubt they'll want to speak to *you*. Archie's already started chewing the dog's ear, apparently, so that was a hit, too."

"Excellent," he beamed, "and the educational value is in the imagination of the child, not of the giver."

I stuck my tongue out at him. "Stop being so reasonable, it's galling."

He rolled his hands down my waist making me giggle so that I had to try very hard to look stern. "Would you rather I were *un*reasonable?" he asked, raising one eyebrow. His hands moved an inch lower. "Have you had your lunch?"

I found it increasingly difficult to concentrate. "Lunch? What lunch?" His eyes were remarkably blue today, the irises wide, inviting pools.

"The lunch I left for you in the fridge, Emma – didn't you find it?"

"Mmm?"

He withdrew his hands and stood with them on his hips instead; I felt their absence. "So you haven't eaten since breakfast. I despair of you sometimes. Come on." He took me by the hand and led me towards the kitchen.

"I had chocolate; it's full of iron."

He didn't credit my comment with a reply.

Joel deposited another heavy box on the kitchen table. "Grams says we'll need these for dinner, and she said for me to ask you if you've put the oven on, Emma?"

I confirmed that I had once Matthew had shown me how. "And she says have you put the fat she left out in the big roasting trays?"

"Uh huh. And I've cut up the potatoes as she said and boiled them for exactly five minutes, drained them, and let them dry – for whatever reason, she *did* say – can't remember. Anyway, they're done."

Joel shook his head sorrowfully, "Gee, Emma, she'll try to make a cook of you; you gotta watch her every move."

I grinned. "I'm pretty resilient; I wouldn't worry."

"I can confirm that," Matthew said as he unpacked the contents of the box onto the table. Jars of different coloured jams and jellies glowed under the late afternoon sun. I scanned the gathering collection, ignoring his remark.

"Where are we eating? There won't be enough room in here, not with all this."

"Despair not, Dr D, we have a dining room – all very formal – tux and tiaras for dinner. Only the *best* for the *guest*."

I looked in horror at Matthew, who was smiling. "Emma, he's joking. Joel, stop making trouble and fetch the trunk for me, please. You know where the key is."

Joel sauntered out, hands in his pockets, whistling "There May Be Trouble Ahead".

"It won't be too formal, will it?" I asked anxiously, when he had gone.

"No, not at all, he's only teasing you because he knows he can. You haven't seen the dining room yet, have you? Come and help me get it set up. It's not used the rest of the year; it's a pity."

He took me to a room the same size as his study, but here the furniture was older – much older. I stood transfixed. Before me was the closest thing I had seen to a seventeenth-century dining hall outside of a museum or country house, and I inspected the room with a historian's sense of awe. I stroked the wood of the long elm table dominating the centre of the room, feeling the slight drag of wax, and let my fingers negotiate the carved backs of the tall chairs ranged around it, noting the tiny indentations where they had been nibbled by worm. Wax had gathered over the centuries in the thick split planks of an oak sideboard between the two windows, and large pewter chargers and two Delft bowls sat on the surface. Around the walls, early landscapes and Dutch still-life injected colour, echoed by the stronger reds and blues of the Turkish rug, and, above the fireplace, two swords hung: the one heavy and designed to cleave, the other a rapier – svelte, elegant, and every bit as lethal. The room felt as if it had been there forever, solid and enduring, comforting in its great age.

I turned back to Matthew, who watched for my reaction, his smile now reticent as he repeatedly rotated his signet ring on his little finger.

"Matthew, it's *beautiful*. It feels like home should."

He crossed the floor, his face becoming animated and bright, taking both my hands in his. "Do you like it? It's as close to how I remember my home was. The rug isn't an original of course, but everything else is English or Dutch and is more or less what we had. My father always grew bulbs every spring in a bowl like that one," he indicated the blue and white bowl on the left hand side of the sideboard, "in memory of my mother. He said she loved flowers. The first spring bulbs were in bud when she and my brother died…" He stood looking at the bowl for a few seconds longer, giving me time to snatch my hand away from his, and quickly wipe my eyes. He gazed back down at me, his smile soft and his eyes warm. "In all the lifetimes I have been on this earth, you are the only person I have ever been able to share this with who understands."

"Oh…" I clasped my hand to my mouth, my voice breaking along with my heart with the rending poignancy of it all.

"My love, I'm sorry, I didn't mean to upset you."

I shook my head, laughing shakily at my own stupidity. "You haven't. This is so *right*, and I love you so *much*." I flung my arms around his neck, taking him by surprise. He lifted me up and held me close to him, burying his face in my hair, emotion rendering us both speechless.

"I didn't know if you would like it," he said finally. "My family think it's too old-fashioned, though they wouldn't say so to my face."

I rubbed my cheek against his. "You know I like *old* things."

"Well, thank God for that," he said, meaning it, his jaw moving against my face as he grinned.

"I do, every day."

In the kitchen, a door slammed back against the wall and the sound of someone struggling with something heavy resonated through the walls. Matthew looked up.

"I'd better give Joel a hand. Are you any good at polishing?"

"A good sight better than at cooking."

"Well, we have plenty to do before we can lay the table," he said mysteriously, pushing the door open for me.

Joel wrestled with a large, domed metal trunk of the sort you often see battered and rejected in flea markets. Matthew relieved him of the weight and put the trunk down under the west window, where the sunlight leached from the sky towards gloaming. He thumped Joel's back good-naturedly. "Way to go there yet, Joel. Perhaps I should fetch it next year?"

"Not – a – chance, old man. I'll be a year older and a year stronger by then. Just don't tell Mom or she'll freak," the boy panted, holding out a key, which Matthew took and pocketed. "Grams says, 'Can you put the oven trays in the oven to heat up now, please, Emma?'" He dawdled as I did as asked.

"Don't bother waiting, Joel, and you can tell Pat that I know what the oven looks like and anyway, Matthew'll tell me if I get it wrong."

Joel chuckled as he went back the way he had come. I closed the heavy oven door on the trays. "Is it just Joel who's getting stronger, or does it seem to be happening to all of your... er, descendants?"

Matthew smiled at my use of the word. "It's not yet clear exactly what my *descendants* have inherited, but they all seem to have enhanced strength, among other things. Why?"

"Just wondering. So there is a genetic element to what you are? There must be if your offspring show similar traits."

He took another key and unlocked the padlock holding the trunk's hasp in place.

"Obviously, but it couldn't have originated from my parents as there was no sign of any of these abilities or longevity in them of which I'm aware. It must have been the result of a spontaneous genetic mutation caused when I was stabbed by that..." he muttered something under his breath, which I might have heard except that the lid of the trunk fell back with a crash against the kitchen surface.

"Is that likely or even possible?" I asked.

"Am *I* either likely or possible? I'll keep looking for an answer until I find one, if not for me, at least for the family." He took a bulky item in a soft cream bag out of the trunk, and peered into it. "Not too bad," he said, putting it to one side.

"And when you've found the answer, what then? How will that affect the children? Will you tell them you've found a cure – because that's what you're looking for, isn't it? A *cure*." Try as I might, I couldn't keep the raw edge from my voice.

His hand stopped mid-way to lifting another object from the trunk and he viewed me soberly. "We've had this conversation before, Emma. There's no likelihood I will find anything like an answer in the near future."

"In my lifetime, do you mean?"

A muscle worked in his cheek. "Yes, in your lifetime – and probably that of my great-grandchildren."

Crossing my arms, I leaned against the side of the worktop. "And if you did, what then? If it meant that the effects could be reversed, would you?"

He turned so that he faced me squarely. "I don't want to be left behind. It's hard enough watching Henry age, even though it's slower than normal. I know I will see my son die and his children and theirs. And then there's you." He brushed the back of his fingers up the side of my cheek. "And then there's you," he repeated softly, pressing his lips against my forehead.

"Matthew, you will tell me if you discover anything – anything at all – that will affect you or the family, won't you?"

"Yes, of course," he said, a little too easily for me to believe him. He carefully lifted a series of similar-looking bundles out of the trunk and handed them to me. They were heavy. "Please would you put these on the table; I've made space for them." He made it clear that he didn't want to discuss it any further. There was too much emotion, too much of his history bound up in all of this, and I was only at the tail end and beginning to unravel it inch by inch.

He finished emptying the trunk, and then went to fetch some bottles and cloths from a cupboard under the sink. I took the first object out of its small cloth bag. Dull silver in colour and round – more like a shallow bowl than a plate – it had a finely rolled edge for a rim. It weighed heavy for its size and had a faint coat of arms engraved on one side.

"*Bloody hell!*" I exclaimed before I could stop myself.

"I hope not," Matthew said dryly, smiling nonetheless at the look on my face. I turned it over as if it were made of glass, not silver. I peered more closely at the coat of arms.

"But this is…" I stammered, looking first at the salver, then at Matthew and back again. He looked more amused by the second. "It's… it's a… *good grief*, Matthew… *and* it has your coat of arms on it!"

He nodded towards the similar-shaped bags in front of me. One by one I divested them of the contents, each being a similar dish, until twenty-three sat in front of me, reflecting the light from the lamp above the table. My heart beat unevenly.

"*Divers goodes*," I muttered, fanning my face with my hand as it suddenly flared with heat. "Is this what Nathaniel referred to in the journal as the 'divers goodes' that went missing?"

"Probably," he said, quietly.

I shook my head to clear some space for my brain cells to start working again. "But that was *after* you had left. There was some sort of a wrangle about it with your aunt Elizabeth."

"Was there? I'm sorry to hear that. She always did like them. I would be disappointed to think that they were the cause of any dissension." He picked one up and regarded it, far away in the distant past.

"How did you… how come you have them?"

"Mmm?" He looked up. "Oh, I went back to see my father shortly before he died. I couldn't leave the country without saying goodbye. I couldn't leave him with so much… unsaid."

"But Nathaniel didn't mention you coming back."

"No, he wouldn't, and nobody else knew that I came to see him in the autumn – around Michaelmas, I recall. Perhaps the dogs recognized me, because they didn't bark for some reason. It wasn't hard to get in the house; we had a small postern gate by the moat and I knew where the key was kept." He smiled. "Nat and I used it when we were younger when we wanted to leave undetected." The look he threw me had a touch of something about it – guilt perhaps – leaving me to come to my own conclusions about what they had been up to. "Anyway, I managed to get past the household servants. The hour was late and there were fewer than I had been accustomed to – as there *should* have been. Things were looking more rundown, the fires unlit, the furniture dusty, unkempt. It had the air of decay, of lost… hope." Fleetingly, his face creased with painful memories.

"I think Nathaniel did his best, Matthew," I said gently, "but how could they have carried on the same way without you? They didn't know what had happened any more than you did." *And some of the servants wouldn't have wanted to work in a household tainted by suspicion of witchcraft, no matter how respected it had been.* I recalled Matthew's broken image on his parents' tomb, of his name expunged from the parish records. No, he didn't need to know that; he didn't need to carry the burden of the knowledge as well as everything else.

"Emma, I'm not blaming Nathaniel. I brought it upon my family no matter how unwittingly. It was pitiful to see, that's all. My father was ill, and I didn't know how he would receive me. It broke my heart to see him so grateful when I returned. I feared for him when I told him I couldn't stay, but he accepted it; I think he already knew." As he spoke, the language he used slipped back and forth in time as if, with each moment drawn from his memory, came the words he had used to frame the image of it. He rubbed his hand across his forehead, where lines betrayed his distress. "He had heard the rumours, of course, although he said that Nathaniel had tried to protect him from the scandal. He knew that to stay would endanger me, but he needed to see me, to see that I hadn't become a… monster." He looked at his hands, then turned them over as if he might find traces of his father's fear sprouting from the palms. "That was important to him. He had to know before he died that I had some hope of salvation. Neither of us knew then that I wouldn't die, and he had been so fearful for my eternal soul. But he was comforted when at last we spake… spoke."

He looked me straight in the eye as if he had to convince me that he had no other choice. "I *had* to leave, Emma, not just because of the gossip or what I feared might happen if I stayed, but because I didn't know what was happening to me. I had to leave to *sort my head out*, as you said once." He smiled thinly. "My father knew he was dying – *I* knew he was dying, although it was only a feeling then and I didn't know how to interpret it." Matthew held one of the silver bowls under the light as he rotated it between his hands. "He told me to take the family plate, take anything of value. My aunt didn't need it and I was still his heir even if I couldn't take the house and land. He said he would say that it had been taken in the night – that amused him – and he had no further need of it."

"So you did," I whispered, looking at the array in front of me.

"Yes, I did," he confirmed. "I still felt like a thief, but I needed it to live off until I found some other way of making a living, so I sold some of it – as little as I could get away with – just enough for passage to new lands and somewhere to hide."

"How much more of it was there?"

"There were twenty-four plates originally. I sold five of them initially and over the years I've bought them back one by one. It's just the last one I can't find. Perhaps it didn't survive, who knows. I would like to get it back if I can; it belongs with the others. Somebody probably has it in a private collection. It's not in any museum as far as I know."

The silver discs showed their history in the little scratches and dints on the surface of some of them as he lifted them into the light.

"How old are they?" I asked.

"My grandfather was given them by the young queen for his loyalty to her in the last years of her sister Mary's reign, when her future was uncertain. He was particularly handsome, apparently, and very brave. He helped her secure the throne, and the queen was rather fond of him as a result, as you can see."

"A princely gift."

"Indeed." He grinned, looking more like himself again. "We always used them at Christmas – all the way through to Epiphany – that's why I like to use them now; there's no point in having them otherwise."

"But the family don't know what they are, do they?"

"No, they don't – they just think they are part of a collection."

"Priceless."

"A very valuable one, yes."

"And you keep them for old time's sake?"

He hesitated. "Mostly, yes."

"And as portable wealth in case you need to leave in a hurry?"

Matthew sat back in his chair and regarded me. "Yes, that as well, but I hope never to have to resort to using it as such."

"I hope *not*," I echoed emphatically. "At least using them once a year means they are kept in remarkable condition. Except this one." I picked up a plate next to me whose coat of arms had been worn away. "Someone's been overenthusiastic with the polish."

"I reckon they only need washing this year, that's all. These, however, do need a good clean." He pulled one of a pair of tall candlesticks from a cloth bag, the silver smoked with oxidization. He inspected it, turning it around. "This hasn't been cleaned for some time."

"Hand it over, then, and I'll make a start. It's filthy. When was it last used?"

"Pat and Henry's wedding, I think. Look, are you sure you don't mind doing this?"

"Not in the least bit; it's one of my favourite jobs at home. Why don't you use these more often?"

Matthew was already finishing the central section of the other one, his hands moving swiftly and delicately over the surface. "Ellen didn't li… we just never did."

"They take a lot of work," I suggested.

"Yes, but some things are worth it. If you like them."

"Ah, I see. Well, they're not to everyone's taste, I suppose."

Pat came bustling into the kitchen with intent. "I came to see how the potatoes are getting on." Matthew and I exchanged glances. "You haven't forgotten to put them on, Emma, have you? How do you manage to look after yourself? And you can stop smiling, Matthew, you're just as much to blame." She wrenched the oven door open, standing back to let the wave of heat out before taking the trays and rolling the cold potatoes into the sizzling fat and putting them back in the oven. "What have you been doing?" She came over to the table, squinting at the piles of silver. "Not cleaning these old things? Far too fussy, I don't know why you bother." She hurried out of the door without waiting for an answer and we burst out laughing.

"I rest my case," I said. "Do you think she'll forgive me?"

"She'll forgive you, Pat forgives everyone, but whether she'll *trust* you with vegetables again is another matter," he chortled, buffing a large silver tray until it reflected his face.

"Mission accomplished," I said, triumphantly.

"That's amazing, Grams," Harry declared, eyes popping at the sight of the enormous turkey. "It makes a change to have turkey at Christmas." Joel put it on the sideboard lit by tall cream candles, flames licking and kicking in the draught from the open door.

"What do you normally have?" I asked no one in particular. Apparently keen to make amends, Ellie answered. "Venison or beef. We had goose one year, but I didn't like that – too rich."

Joel leaned around his mother. "Yeah, and we needed three of them to get enough meat."

"Sure, only because you had a *whole* one to yourself." Harry rounded his stomach at him and the three of them laughed.

Pat spooned steaming swede, fragrant with nutmeg, onto the first plate. "This is so you feel at home, chickadee. Dan, pass this to Emma, please. Help yourself to the jellies, won't you?" Arranged around the nearest candlestick were three pretty stemmed glass dishes with vibrant jellies that shone orange and red in the glow of the candles. I took a little of each, the translucent colours pooling on the side of my plate.

"Pat, what are these? They look wonderful." I passed them to Harry.

Pat peered at the dishes. "The one on the left is cranberry, the one in the middle sour apple, and the one on the right is cloudberry. I made them this fall. Do you have jelly with meat?"

Eager to make up for my earlier kitchen misdemeanour, I nodded enthusiastically. "We use crab apples for the same purpose, and believe it or not, it is the one bit of cooking I do get involved with every year without fail. We used to go to someone's orchard years ago – I loved that – but now we go into the Wolds and collect them from the copses. I make bramble jelly as well."

Pat flourished a spoon. "You see, there *is* hope for you yet."

"I wouldn't hold out for much else though, Pat," I rushed. "I only like making them because it brings out the hunter-gatherer in me and doesn't involve having to sit around a table with people more than a couple of times a year." It was neither a tactful nor a wise comment to make and I didn't need to hear the just audible groan from Matthew to be aware of my blunder the second it left my mouth. A hush fell, the searchlight of Maggie's eyes trained upon me along with everyone else's.

"OK," I said slowly, "that didn't come out the way it was supposed to. I meant…" I hesitated because the trouble was, that was *exactly* what I did mean. "What I *didn't* mean to imply," I tried again, "was that I don't like eating with people… with you, just that I don't…"

Henry said soberly from across the table. "Emma, you don't need to explain."

"Yes, but I *do*," I said with a note of desperation. "I'm sorry, I know I'm a pain when it comes to food. I don't mean to be, it's just that it's such a big deal for families, and it's not for me."

Pat's sympathy made me feel even worse. "It's fine, sweetie, all families are different. Not every family has to eat together. I know some who never get around a table at *all*."

I stared in turmoil at the nut-brown surface of the table. Matthew bent close to me. "It doesn't matter, Emma, let it go."

I looked at him, and then at the rest of them, and realized that, as much as I would have liked to have crawled under the table at that moment, *letting it go* was the one thing I couldn't do.

"It *is* a big thing in my family though, Pat. My family *make* a big deal of it. It was always important: the gathering of the family, the formality, the *ritual* of it. We had huge family meals that went on and on with endless… questions."

"Then you're saying you don't like formal meals?" Harry said, frowning as he tried to work out what I meant.

"Yes – no… no, not really. I'm fine with formality to a degree, I have to be – Cambridge just about invented it. And I'm fine *here*. It's not the place, it's the people." I sighed. "It's my family I have problems with." Even from where I was sitting I could see the gleam in Maggie's eyes. Goodness only knew what she would make of this, and why she always made me feel as if she was compiling a dossier on me.

Joel raised his eyebrows in disbelief. "So you don't eat because of your family? *Gee*-sh, and I thought *this* family was strange."

"Joel!" Jeannie snapped.

"Well, he's right," I smiled apologetically, "not entirely, of course. I do eat, but my family… let's just say mealtimes were not as relaxed as they are here; not for me, anyway. I think I associate food with tension."

Henry picked up his glass and inspected the contents. "Our asking you a lot of questions isn't going to help you much, then, is it? I'm sorry, Emma – this must be very difficult for you."

I considered what he had said for a moment. "It isn't so much the questions, Henry, as who's asking them, and what lies behind them, and the implications that prompted them in the first place. You can't escape so easily when you're sitting around a table being… er… interrogated."

"Does this feel like an interrogation to you?" Henry asked gently, placing his glass back on the table.

I smiled suddenly. "No, and even if it did, I think I'm glad you asked because now you know, I hope that you won't think I'm so rude or downright… odd."

Joel guffawed. "Odd? You? Sure you are – you're here with us, aren't you?"

Matthew interposed as Jeannie opened her mouth to reprimand him again. "Quite, thank you, Joel. I doubt whether

Emma needs much reminding of the peculiarities of the family with you to help her." Laughter ruffled the warm air and Joel grinned cheerfully, and now that my secret was out, the muscles in my stomach relaxed, and I began to taste the food I ate. It was the first time that I had ever fully identified and voiced the complex issues surrounding my hang-up with food. Now that I had, it felt as if a huge burden had been lifted from me. It didn't improve my appetite as such, but what I ate I enjoyed for the first time in so many years that I had lost count.

I successfully avoided most of the soapsuds flying around the kitchen until Harry and Ellie decided I had managed to get away with too much, and pinned my arms while Joel deposited a large handful on the top of my head. I wiped the bubbles from my hair as they drooled down my cheek, and flicked the suds off my hands in his direction, managing to keep a very straight face.

"Oops, you've gone too far, bro'," Harry smirked at us, backing away just in case I turned on him.

I set my jaw, my eyes steel. "Vengeance *will* be mine," I growled at Joel, his scalped blond hair dotted with bubbles from Harry's latest attempt to duck him in the sink.

"Ooohhh, I'm scared," he mocked. Walking behind him, Matthew deftly flicked at the back of his head with a tea towel. "So you should be," he uttered quietly in his ear, as Joel spun around and tried to *whop* him back, missing him.

"You can't take Emma's side – it's not fair," Joel complained, rubbing his head although it looked perfectly all right to me.

"I don't need to – Emma's quite capable of looking after herself," Matthew said, drying one of the Regency glass dishes and placing it with the other dry things on a large tray.

He took them through to the dining room for putting away. I thought that his faith in my attempts at self-preservation might be somewhat optimistic – or misplaced, even – but I still glowed quietly at his praise and took the next glass dish from Pat.

Dan looked over his shoulder. "If you three get on with your chores, we can get to our presents before the night's through. At the rate we're going, it'll be tomorrow and we might as well put them away until next year and save ourselves a fortune." He smiled at Jeannie, standing with her hands immersed in the soapy water, and she returned his smile with a softened expression, handing the glass she was washing to him for rinsing.

"And we didn't get to give the Christmas Eve gifts, either," Pat reminded us all.

"Yeah, sis', and whose fault was *that*?" Joel taunted.

Ellie pushed a hand past her mother into the sink, scooped up some suds, and threw them at him.

"Cut it out, you kids!" Dan said more sharply, but Joel was already retaliating, shoving his hand into the sink as Jeannie turned away to fetch another load of dirty dishes.

Crunch. Even muffled by the depth of water, we all heard the sound as the brittle glass exploded in the sink.

"Joel!" I cried as his face went from white to scarlet and back again, his eyes wide with surprise. Nobody moved. "Joel... *Matthew!*" I looked around in desperation but he wasn't there, while the rest of the family remained standing exactly where they were, exchanging looks. I couldn't understand why nobody did anything. "For goodness' sake!" I exclaimed in exasperation, grabbing a clean tea towel. "Joel, give me your hand."

Obediently, he took his hand out of the blood-reddened water, eyes fixed on my face, and held it out for me to see.

Glass shards pierced his skin, his palm lacerated by a dozen slivers of fine, lead crystal sharper than scalpels, blood oozing around each puncture. I stared at it in dismay and he turned it slowly in front of my eyes, a grin seeping across his face. He made tweezers out of two fingers of his uninjured hand and pulled a piece of glass from his skin, watching for my reaction. No further blood, no sudden gush, followed the splinter of glass as it fell with a *chink* on the stone draining board. Ellie tittered nervously. He repeated the action, then again and again until his palm was clear. Where the glass had penetrated, hardly a mark remained, only the faintest red bruising under the already healing skin. Barely aware that Matthew had come back into the kitchen, I took Joel's hand in both of mine examining it back and front. "You could have told me!" I accused anyone and everyone.

"And spoil the fun, right? No way! You should have seen your face," Joel grinned down at me.

I felt Matthew's hands on my shoulders. "All right, that's enough, Joel. I'm sorry, Emma – I didn't think to tell you and I didn't think it would be necessary to tell you quite like this." He shot a look at Joel.

"Klutz," Ellie snuck in. "Sorry," she muttered, as Matthew cautioned her with a glance.

Still spellbound, I asked, "Are you *all* able to heal like that?"

"I can't," said Jeannie, picking the pieces of glass off the draining board with due deference to their sharpness. Pat came over to help her. "Neither can I, more's the pity. It was such a shock when I found out, too."

I wasn't sure whether I felt shocked or miffed at being duped so effectively. I wondered if she had suffered the same con. "How did you find out, Pat?"

She turned away. "I… don't remember. It was a long time ago. I'll put the kettle on, shall I?"

I was about to say something but Matthew squeezed the top of my shoulders to warn me not to pursue it. Dan and Jeanette exchanged looks, equally puzzled. Out of the corner of my eye, I saw the door close behind Maggie as she left the room.

Henry picked up the kettle before Pat reached it. "You go and organize the presents, Pat – I'll see to this. Kids, go help your grandmother."

The kitchen emptied. I looked at Matthew. "Later," he said, and I started to pick up the remaining shards of glass from the side. He put out a hand to stop me. "I think I'd better do that." He finished the task, draining the sink and scraping out the remains of the glass as if they were petals. I couldn't help wincing until he showed me his hands.

"OK," I acknowledged. "I get the message; you're indestructible."

He smiled. "Pretty much."

"Good," I said, kissing the palm of each of his hands. "Long may you remain so."

7

The Gift

In the quiet of the drawing room, the Christmas tree lights gave the impression of warmth. We were the first there. I dislodged one of the baubles where its cotton caught on a branch, making it hang askew. It swung lazily back and forth, its faded red surface reflecting a moving miniature of my face, before settling plumb-straight.

Matthew admired it. "Thank you for decorating the tree." He touched a green bauble, its silvered dimples like tummy buttons, making it spin gently. "I had almost forgotten what they looked like. They haven't been used for forty-six years or so. You've made it feel more like home again."

I linked my arm with his. "You can't have Christmas without a tree; there would be nowhere to daydream without it."

He slipped his arm around my waist. "Is that what you do when left to your own devices – daydream?"

"When I was little, if I could escape from the table before everyone else, I would lie under the branches and watch the lights against the trunk and the baubles, and pretend I was alone in my own forest. You should try it – it's very contemplative. Did you ever do something like that when you were young?"

I watched his eyes wander back in time and a wistful smile draw across his face.

"When I wanted to be by myself, I would go down to the river to a small spinney of hawthorn by the bank where I couldn't be seen. It was sheltered and I made a den when I was about six or seven years old, where I used to sit for hours and watch the water. It was never the same – always changing, depending on the weather, or the time of day, or how much rain we'd had. I fell in once, trying to catch trout. I didn't do that again. I nearly drowned but it wasn't as bad as the beating I was given when I went home dripping." He laughed softly at the memory.

I pulled a face. "You were beaten for nearly drowning?"

"Ah well, you see, my father was away and Nathaniel's father was steward then, and he didn't want me killing myself while in his charge. So, yes, I had a thorough thrashing, but I didn't try to catch trout by myself again, and I didn't tell my father or I might have had another one." I sensed no resentment in his voice, and he seemed to accept that the punishment meted out to him was probably justified, but to my modern sentiments it still seemed harsh.

"Were you beaten often?" I must have sounded unduly anxious because his eyes creased with mirth.

"No, I wasn't, and I probably should have been, but my father was a very mild man who believed he should lead by example and that you couldn't beat righteousness into a child. Just occasionally, however, if I did something dangerous – like trying to ride the bullocks in Long Acre field during a thunderstorm – I'd get a beating for it. I think that the fear of losing me overcame his natural reserve."

"I can't see you as a reckless youth, somehow."

He grinned, making it much easier to visualize him fifteen years old and intent on self-destruction.

"Imagine a mix of Harry and Joel and then take away all caution. I'm afraid my uncle wasn't the best influence. He was younger than my father and didn't have his responsibilities or the burden of my mother's death, and he had a reputation as a bit of a hellraiser. As a teenager, I didn't have the maturity to understand that, so…" He paused, listening for any sounds outside the room, then dropped his voice. "… I was sent to Cambridge to channel my energy and natural curiosity into something more positive, and to put a safe distance between William and me." He finished and turned just as the drawing room door opened and Jeannie and Dan came through, followed by Ellie and Joel with trays of cups and two porcelain pots.

I was still miles away when I realized that Ellie hovered in front of me, holding out a cup with a thin, pale liquid in it. "It *is* tea – Grams showed me how to make it. I hope it's OK."

"Thanks, Ellie, it looks great." I took the cup from her. I found a chair to one side and perched on it, watching and waiting to see what everyone did next.

Matthew looked around, puzzled. "What are you doing over here?"

"Drinking tea?" I suggested, proffering the cup as evidence.

"Come and sit by the fire. One of the children can rough it on the chair."

I glanced back at the handsome chair with its curved and scrolled arms and thought if he considered that *roughing* it, I would like to see what Matthew's idea of luxury might be. I noted, as I followed him to the heart of the room, that Maggie took possession of my newly vacated position, from which she proceeded to observe us all with that unnaturally calm exterior of hers. We had exchanged barely two words since this morning's encounter, although she talked quite freely with the rest of her family. Towards me, she maintained a glacial reserve, and I found myself cogitating on what I could do to melt it when Pat and Henry emerged from the door to the passage between the two homes carrying a variety of objects.

Holding aloft a small pink animal shape, a little larger than a kiwi fruit, Henry said, "Now, you all know what this is…" A chorus of voices rang out. "Pat's Pink Pigs!" followed by laughter.

"Happy Christmas, Emma – I don't expect you have these in England." Pat deposited a pig-shaped object in my hand. Wrapped around its neck like a shiny collar was a piece of curling ribbon off which hung a soft, squishy package much larger than the pig, dangling in bright, rainbow-coloured tissue paper.

"Thank you. What is it made of?"

"You're welcome," she smiled and sat next to me in a companionable, motherly sort of way. "It's a marzipan pig. I don't know whether Norwegians still give them, but they were a traditional Christmas gift in my family to wish health, wealth, and happiness for the next year."

I turned the little fat pig with his blush-pink cheeks, black eyes, and snout wrinkled in a piggy smile and thought it a shame to eat him. "I think it's a lovely custom. Thank you for including me."

She rubbed my arm, her kindly face creased in a heartfelt smile. "Well, of course you're included." She leaned in close. "I've never seen Matthew so happy, and I mean *never*, in all the time I've known him. He has spent so much time helping others that he deserves a little happiness of his own. And I wanted to say," she went on, raising her voice so that her husband could hear, "that Henry and I loved our present."

She clapped her hands. "Mercy, I couldn't stop laughing this morning when I opened your gift and told him you had given us a herd of goats for Christmas; his face made such a picture! It took him quite a minute before he realized a family in Africa would be getting the benefit, and we wouldn't have to build a goat shed."

From a few feet away, Henry shook his head and winked. "It's all too much for a man of my age," he said, holding up a pig. "First it's goats, and now pigs. We'll end up with a veritable farm."

Pat accepted a cup of coffee from her grandson. "I'd better not sit next to you with this. Matthew would never forgive me if anything happened to you." She eased herself off the sofa and went to sit in one of the armchairs.

I felt less and less like a stranger, as if, gradually, the barriers I had put up over my lifetime to protect me were being dismantled by the consistent show of warmth and acceptance from the majority of the family.

Matthew pulled me closer to him. "That was a well-considered gift, my love," he murmured into my hair in his old-fashioned way. "Are you going to open your pig present?"

"Is that what it's called!" I smiled and slid the ribbon off the parcel, pulling a tasselled soft scarf in a delicate blue from the paper. I wrapped its length around my neck. "Pat, Henry – it's lovely; thank you so much!"

"Perhaps Dad can have his scarf back now?" Henry chuckled.

The younger members of the family were opening their presents. Joel had already bitten the head off his pig, and he waved the decapitated creature in the same hand that clasped a lethal-looking hunting knife. "This is the best, Gramps, it's exactly the right one – it'll do the job great. Hey, Emma, pity the bear, right?"

Matthew leaned towards his great-grandson. "Joel, may I have a look?" The boy handed the knife to him and he took the blade out of its sheath.

"Merry Christmas," Maggie's silky voice, as hard as carbon, said softly in my ear, making me jump. She laid something on the arm of the sofa next to me. It slipped heavily down between my thigh and the seat cushion. She went to sit next to Jeannie and Dan, who were reading the blurb on the back of a book Ellie had been given. I hadn't had time to thank her, and although she pretended not to watch me, every few seconds her eyes cast in my direction.

I fished the object from where it lodged and turned it over in my hands, feeling the unmistakable weight and shape of a book. She had wrapped it in a plain, matt paper, as red as ox blood, on which she had written in a tight, controlled hand: *Dr E. D'Eresby*, as if I didn't know my name. I slid my finger under the tape holding the paper and slipped the book from its anonymity. Where it lay, face downwards, I was clueless, for the back was completely blank – black and blank – the only marks on the cover the faint fingerprints where the acid from her fingers had scorched the chalky surface. I turned it over and felt the colour drain from my face. Across the front in bold, red letters, was written:

The Devil's Whore
The Role of Women in Medieval & Early Modern
Literature
By
Professor Kort Staahl

My throat turned to dust as I swallowed, and my heart heaved and lurched in my chest. *Crump*. I felt it, and so did Matthew. He spun around. "What is it? What's the matter?"

My eyes stole to where Maggie, seemingly deep in conversation with Dan, wore an arch look of triumph on her spectral face. I wouldn't give her the satisfaction.

I turned the book over in my lap, presenting its void façade, looking back at him as if surprised he asked. "Nothing. Nothing's the matter – just a bit of indigestion, that's all."

Harry called to him over his parents' heads. Matthew reluctantly took his gaze from mine and turned away. I quickly folded the paper over the book and tucked it down the side of the sofa, not caring if Maggie saw the act of rejection or not. It was irrelevant now. She had made it abundantly clear that she would not tolerate me and, worse still, seemed prepared to do so in front of Matthew. Perhaps she believed he wouldn't act, or maybe she didn't care. Now that I understood Ellie, her behaviour towards me made sense. With Maggie, however, her motives remained opaque even if her antagonism did not. Her actions could be interpreted as that of a mind intent on some path as yet unclear to anyone else – irrational, but whose lucidity would become apparent in time. That she had an agenda was now evident, and the very thought of it shook me to the core.

The hard edge of the book dug insistently into my thigh, nagging like toothache. Her choice of book must be purposeful… no, not so much the *book* – although that in itself was relevant – but the *author*. Revulsion turned my stomach. She had probably learned of Staahl through Matthew's endeavours to protect me and his subsequent involvement in my rescue when his vigilance had, in his eyes, failed. In giving me this book she would realize that it amounted to a deliberate act of provocation and a source of distress for me. The interesting question was, what did she think I would do about it?

I knew what I wanted to do – I wanted to go up to her and shake her by her thick, meaty throat and tell her to get off my case. That, however, would neither be wise nor diplomatic. I could ignore her, as you would an attention-seeking child, or I could tell Matthew and let him sort her out; but I didn't want him put in an invidious position where he might find his loyalties divided – he had enough of that to contend with as it was. I could, on the other hand, talk to Henry about his daughter, and that, I considered, was a decidedly more attractive option.

I found that I had been staring at her all the while I had been thinking, and now I saw her consciously, she looked at me with equal curiosity. Perhaps I wasn't reacting the way she expected.

Ellie stepped light-footed over to the sofa and squeezed between Matthew and me so that she could show us the book she had been given. I felt relief, first because she wanted to share something with me other than her scorn, and secondly, so that Maggie could see that Ellie was one little puppet she could no longer manipulate.

By half-eleven, Ellie had become ensconced with her book as I talked quietly with Dan about his love of architecture and his children's ideas for the future. Ellie wanted to stay with the family and work principally with Matthew, although he had been encouraging her to look at furthering her studies in one of the major hospitals. Harry had been thinking about studying abroad, and Dan wanted to run a few ideas past me concerning Cambridge.

"And Joel?" I asked, whose muscular form draped over an armchair, his exuberance tamed at last after his long night in the laboratory.

"Joel's happy in the Army." He glanced over his shoulder at Jeannie as she gathered wrapping paper, watching her smooth it out, fold it precisely, and deposit it in a bin bag. "Jeanette's not so sure, but it's what he wants to do and he's good at his job. I think he could have gone off the rails if we tried to push him in any other direction. He's settled down now and he comes home, which was more than he was doing. No, Joel's OK."

I looked at the boy, dark rings under his eyes. "He looks ready for bed," I smiled.

Dan grunted, stretching. "As are we all. I think we'd better say goodnight, if you don't mind?"

"No, of course not," I said, a little surprised because it sounded as if he were asking me. Then I remembered that this was Matthew's house and I his "friend", which sort of made me the hostess, and that felt odd – but odd in a good way.

As the door closed on the last of the family, I collapsed on the sofa.

"Tired?" Matthew stood looking down at me. I nodded. "Too tired for your present?"

I shook my head, yawning, and went to fetch his gift from behind the tree, where I had hidden it before dinner.

He switched off all the side lamps, leaving just the tree lights and the remnants of the fire to light the room, and we sat side by side with our heads touching, looking at the spiky branches speckled light and dark. We stayed like that forever, each comfortable with our own thoughts, until Matthew turned to face me. He picked a pine needle off my hair.

"Hello," he said.

I wriggled closer. "Hi."

He brushed my hair out of my eyes and I wondered if mine were reflecting the lights of the tree as his did, the multiple points fluctuating brightly in his dark pupils. I reached out an index finger and traced the long line of his nose down to his lips. He smiled under my fingertip and I followed the quirky up-tilting crease as it grew broader. "What are you thinking?" he asked, his voice all honey.

"I was thinking of *Some Like It Hot*. Have you seen it?"

"We are all alone and you are thinking of a *film*?"

"Uh huh." My fingers found my favourite place in the hollow of his neck, where I had managed to loosen his tie. "It is relevant." I stroked into the hollow and heard him catch his breath.

"It is?"

I started humming "I Want to be Loved by You" but stopped when I needed all my concentration to prevent me from doing something rash. I drew away. Matthew breathed in, linking his hands behind his head and then, after a minute of examining the star on top of the tree, exhaled, slowly. "Sorry. I'm a little susceptible at the moment. This is getting more difficult, isn't it?"

"Yes, but I don't *want* to stop, Matthew. I like us being together like this, whether it's difficult or not, although it still feels…"

"What?" When I didn't answer, he prompted, "Emma, what does it feel?"

"It still feels… adulterous."

He did the unnerving thing he had a tendency to do when confronted with something requiring his full attention – he didn't blink. Then he simply stated, "Yes," echoing the guilt I experienced in quieter moments.

Without thinking, he gathered more pine needles from my hair where they tried to cling stubbornly with their residual resin, his fingers sending waves of electricity through me although I could hardly feel their touch.

"Matthew…"

His smile coloured with regret as he stopped and took his hand away. "I know, sweetheart, I feel it too."

And yet neither of us would voice it – neither of us would say what we both thought and must not dare to think: that only through his wife's death would he be free. This roller-coaster ride of emotions was taking its toll, wearing me down, unravelling my resolve to protect him from himself and from my own desire. Although I could not deny his physical attraction, the need to be joined in every way possible – physically, emotionally, spiritually – played a greater role in my longing, and every moment spent apart from him represented another grain of the sand of time lost to me. I drew a deep, shuddering lungful of air, and strengthened my resolve once more. I forced a smile. "Presents, then."

Matthew switched on the lamp on the sofa table, piled small logs on the fire so that the quick flames soon warmed the hearth with light, and turned to face me. He held out a book-shaped object whose lightness meant it wasn't for reading. I gave him the present I had managed to acquire only just in time for Christmas, and we sat on the sofa, close, but without touching.

Freeing my present of the heavy cream and gilt paper, I revealed a plain box in a dark-grained wood like rosewood, with a hinged lid and a small gilt hook for a catch. I turned the box over and something shifted inside. I slid the hook out of its clasp and opened the lid. Lined in aged plum velvet, the box had been padded and shaped to receive an item of great value to its owner. I gently eased the contents out and cradled it in my hands. It looked old – much, much older than the box – a gilded and blue-painted wooden arch in the shape of a gothic window, pointed at the top, two doors held shut in the middle by an ornate hook like the one on the box. I undid the hook and carefully folded the doors back – and gasped.

"Hah!" Matthew exclaimed, breaking through my awestruck silence as he unwrapped my present to him.

"Oh, *wow!*" I managed seconds later. The doors protected a scene as vibrant as the day it had been painted. Christ stood in white within the central panel in an idyllic rural landscape, the Lamb at his feet, the Dove in an aura of light near his head. On the left panel, John dressed in browns and reds, on one knee in adoration, a castle in the background on a hill. On the right panel, Mary in royal blue robes, her hand held out towards her son, a tree hung with fruit behind her. An intimate scene, not oozing sentimentality like so many painted several centuries later, but touching in its honest simplicity. This was no Christ woebegone and betrayed, haunted by the responsibility placed upon him, but a live, living Christ gazing out and inviting the onlooker to join him. I saw an optimistic scene full of hope and promise of renewal. I had seen triptychs in museums and continental churches all over Europe: it wasn't unique, but it was rare.

"Where did you find it?" I uttered, finally finding my voice.

Matthew shifted a little closer so that we could look at it together. "Do you like it?" Like it? I didn't know whether to laugh or cry, I thought it so beautiful. I nodded mutely, which seemed the safest thing to do. "It's late fourteenth century – probably one of the northern Italian states by the look of the castle – and it was designed to be a portable altar. The box is old but is not the original, obviously, though everything else about it is."

I followed the line of the gilded and carved tracery of the arch with my finger, feeling the tiny irregularities in the surface, absorbing the essence of its past.

"Thank you, it's wonderful…"

He frowned. "But?"

"But? There are no buts – except…" I hesitated. "I wouldn't have thought you would approve of images like these given your background, and when you were born – iconoclasts and idolatry, and all that."

He threw back his head and laughed, but I must have looked a little put out because he quickly restrained himself, although his eyes were still full of amusement.

"No one's ever accused me of being an iconoclast before. I loathed that sort of behaviour: urinating in fonts and smashing statues is indefensible and one of the reasons why I left the Parliamentary Army and returned home. Remember what I said before? If it's the one thing all my years have given me, it is a sense of perspective and an appreciation that others might represent their beliefs in ways in which I might not agree or understand, but it doesn't make their faith any less valid. The expression of faith through violence is never acceptable, however; there I will draw the line. Anyway." He tapped the triptych lightly. "I thought you might appreciate this as a visual counterpoint to all the images of magic and monsters with which you surround yourself."

It was my turn to laugh. "You mean, you wanted to remind me of whose side I'm on?"

He quirked an eyebrow. "You *could* put it like that, I suppose. It doesn't hurt once in a while."

I heard the earnest concern for my spiritual well-being in his tone and risked reaching up to kiss him. "Don't worry. Dealing with my subject day in, day out, I tend not to forget."

He smiled. "Quite. I wasn't trying to preach to you, I just thought that you would like it."

"I *love* it – and I'm already converted, so preach away, I don't mind. I'm grateful that you would even think about it."

"It's never far from my mind," he said gravely. "Talking of which, where did you find this?" He held up the book I had found for him on a website specializing in fine and rare books. It had taken every spare penny I had to buy it.

"You don't have a book of George Herbert's poetry already, do you? I couldn't see it on your shelves if you have. I saw works by Donne, Marvell, and Crashaw, but not one by Herbert."

He opened the book to the title page and then to an engraving of the poet. "No, I certainly don't, but I've been looking for a copy of this quality for a long time. Thank you."

"I remembered shortly after we first met you saying how much you liked metaphysical poetry. I didn't understand why, then, of course; I just thought that you did for the same reason I do, rather than because they were your contemporaries. And I'm sorry it's not strictly contemporaneous, but it's the closest in date I could find."

He held the fragile book open. "I wonder sometimes," he said, looking thoughtfully at me, "whether we follow some predetermined path, you and I. You seem to know me so well, yet we only met a few months ago." He let the thought hang in the air between us for a moment before shaking his head, smiling at the idea. "I must be getting fanciful in my old age. Look, this is one of my favourites. '*I struck the board and cried no more…*'"

"'… *I will abroad*,'" I finished softly. "Yes, I like 'The Collar' too; it suits you somehow."

"Mmm, does it indeed? I especially like the last few lines:

> *'But as I rav'd and grew more fierce and wilde*
> *At every word,*
> *Me thought I heard one calling, Childe:*
> *And I reply'd, My Lord.'"*

I tried to imagine him in the early years before he came to terms with what happened to him. "Were you very fierce and wild?"

"Yes, I was, quite – for a time. When I realized I would outlive my own generation – and perhaps the next – it was as if everything I had ever believed or understood was turned on its head. Life wasn't a fragile rope of sand, but a chain of steel keeping me bound to this earth with no hope of eternal reward." He studied the poem in the little book for a while, then handed it to me. "Which one do you like?"

I took it and carefully leafed through the pages. "This is my *absolute* favourite." I gave it back to him.

"'Life'?"

"Yes. I always thought that, when I die, I would like it read at my funeral." I meant to be matter of fact about it, so Matthew's reaction took me by surprise. His eyes spat fire.

"In Heaven's sweet name, Emma, I don't need to be reminded of your mortality – or my lack of it!"

"Sorry," I whispered, taken aback.

"No, *I* am, you caught me unawares. Just… well, just don't expect me to be there to recite it." He shuddered, then regained his composure. "Will you read it to me?"

I didn't need to because I knew it by heart.

> *'I made a posie, while the day ran by:*
> *Here will I smell my remnant out, and tie*
> *My life within this band.*

But time did beckon to the flowers, and they
By noon most cunningly did steal away,
And wither'd in my hand.

My hand was next to them, and then my heart:
I took, without more thinking, in good part
Times gentle admonition:
Who did so sweetly deaths sad taste convey,
Making my minde to smell my fatall day;
Yet sugring the suspicion.

Farewell deare flowers, sweetly your time ye spent,
Fit, while ye liv'd, for smell or ornament,
And after death for cures.
I follow straight without complaints or grief,
Since if my scent be good, I care not, if
It be as short as yours."

He remained without moving or commenting as the last words resonated, his eyes closed, the slightest puckering of the skin between them as he concentrated. Then he opened them and smiled at me. "You recite beautifully and yes, it is poignant, isn't it? I think I had forgotten. But there's hope there, too, and that's what we hang on for – especially in my case."

"I understand," I said softly.

He put his arm around me and I cuddled into him. "Yes, I know you do," he said.

I didn't want to spoil the moment and remind him that he actively searched for a way to undo the creation I so admired. We were warm and at peace together, and there should be time enough in the future in which to pursue that conflict of interests, and that time was not now.

8

Boxing Day

On the little table in the window of my bedroom, the two marzipan pigs touched noses in the sunshine. Matthew had bound them together, nose-to-nose, with a strand of curling ribbon from my parcel, so that to separate them I would have to cut the ribbon like an umbilical cord between mother and child.

"Good morning!" Matthew was where he had been when I had fallen asleep next to him, the duvet tucked between us so that I could only feel him when he moved. I turned over. He lay on his side, watching me, his book of poetry closed in his hand. I wondered if I would always be so fortunate to wake with him beside me, and felt the familiar grope of doubt in my heart. "I'll get you some breakfast. Get up when you're ready."

"I could do with some exercise," I said after breakfast when we were in his study, feeling the stiffness in my limbs and distinctly pudgy around my tummy. Matthew looked up from the computer screen.

"Would a walk by the river do?"

"Admirably."

"Good. I think we can rustle up ample exercise for you later on."

That sounded oddly portentous and I could swear he was hiding a smile behind his hand. No matter, music would have to do for now. Selecting Mozart's Requiem Mass, I settled back onto the pile of cushions on the floor in front of the fire with a book.

Matthew leaned back in his chair and put his fingers together in the way Henry sometimes did, looking at nothing in particular.

"I heard Mozart play once when in Vienna; a quite remarkable young man." He said it as he remembered it, not for effect.

"*Don't* think you can say things like that and get away with it," I said, nonetheless impressed.

"Sorry, I forget sometimes. But I can with you – who else can I tell?" He had a point.

"You can tell me anything, but you have to expect a full interrogation if you come out with stuff like that, otherwise it would be like putting a child in a sweet shop and telling them not to touch. Torture."

"Understood – I'll try to remember."

"I won't let you forget."

He grinned and turned back to his computer screen, which he was finding more absorbing than the book I was failing to read. I suddenly remembered something I had forgotten to do the evening before. "I'll be back in a minute," I said, and made for the drawing room before he could ask.

I stuffed my hand down the side of the sofa, but the book wasn't there. I searched along the sides of the cushions all the way round in case it had somehow migrated of its own accord. "*Blast,*" I muttered under my breath. I straightened and cast around the room in desperation, hoping that Matthew hadn't found it. I didn't see it at first because the unlit lamp cast a shadow across its black cover, but there it was, on the table where I could have sworn I hadn't left it the night before. If Matthew had found it he would have said something, and as far as I knew, nobody else from the Stable or the Barn had been in the house that morning. "Mrs-bloody-Danvers," I snarled, snatching the book up. I had no intention of reading it – just a glimpse of the name on the cover was enough to set my skin crawling with revulsion – but I dropped it and the book fell open on the floor. I bent slowly and picked the wretched thing up, my eyes already scanning the page despite myself.

He wrote well – convincingly, I gave him that – but it didn't take much imagination to see where Staahl was coming from. Even from the first few snatched lines I could hear the echoes of his voice inside my head: the insinuation, the choice phrases loaded with meaning, vile, sickening, depraved. I heard the click of the door behind me and snapped the book shut, the sound loud in the quiet of the room.

Maggie didn't even bother to feign surprise at me being there. "Good morning, Dr D'Eresby, I see you have found your book." Not *the* book, but *your* book – as if it had been written for me. She came towards me with the same smooth movements of her grandfather, which in him were elegant and lithe, but in her were, quite frankly, sinister. "I understand that your area of research is in a similar vein to Professor Staahl's. All those monsters; it takes strength of mind not to become confused, no – *disturbed* – by what one reads. I think you would agree?" Her low voice held a mocking edge, which I imagined she used to reduce subordinates to a quivering mass. *Don't get riled, don't let her get to you. Danvers – Danny, Danny, Danvers...*

I smiled politely. "I'm sure that insanity is more your line of work than mine."

She didn't like that; I could see it in the way the lines around her mouth sharpened and her eyes became shrapnel. Yet her voice didn't betray her.

"Poor Professor Staahl. It is so easy for a man to become beguiled by the whispers in his mind, especially when he has certain *vulnerabilities*." She licked at the word, flipping it with her tongue before spitting it at me. "Still, there is always a chance when help is at hand. I do so hope that *you* are robust enough to cope with what life might throw at you, Dr D'Eresby. It would be such a shame if it proved otherwise."

What was she talking about? At least Staahl's ramblings were crystal clear in their madness. With Maggie there were half-truths and might-bes and what-ifs all wrapped up in fog, as was, no doubt, her intention. She made a career of toying with people's minds, and now she practised on mine. I had never known what to say to the bullies at school, and I didn't know what to say to her now. I remained impassive so as not to feed her guile.

"I'm remarkably resilient and thick-skinned, Maggie, but I thank you for your concern." Resilient – yes, to a degree, but thick-skinned? *Oversensitive*, Dad's father used to call me. "*Toughen her up, Hugh, there's no place for a simpering ninny in this world. She'll thank you for it in the long run.*" Sensitive soul, my grandad.

I didn't wait for her reply, I didn't dare, but it reminded me of the need to speak to Henry sometime soon. I removed myself and the book from the room, hoping that it didn't look as if I were in flight, and ran up the stairs two at a time, and into my bedroom. Scouting around for somewhere to conceal the book, in the end I hid it in the bottom of my travel bag and stuffed it back under the bed.

I saw Henry sooner than I anticipated. He and Matthew had their heads together at the computer screen, reminding me how alike they were. They both looked up when I entered the study. "Henry, please may I have a word with you?" I asked, not sure how to approach the tangled question of his daughter except directly. Father and son traded glances, and Matthew flipped the lid of the computer shut. "I'll leave you to it," he said, and closed the door behind him.

Henry drew another chair out from beside the desk and lowered himself into the seat.

"It's Maggie," I blurted out.

"Problem?"

"Yes, I think so," I said more steadily, thinking about how to continue. "You know that she resents me?" He nodded. "Well, she's making it abundantly clear that she doesn't like me or want me here, and it's getting worse and I don't know how to deal with it – deal with *her*." I looked anxiously at him and made a conscious effort not to fiddle.

Henry tapped his fingers together. "Have you spoken to my father about this?"

"Not recently, no. I don't want him put into a situation where he has to choose between his granddaughter and me. He has enough to deal with at the moment with… well, with Ellen, if that makes sense."

"It does," he said, slowly. "Maggie has problems of her own…"

"Yes, I understand that," I said a little too quickly, recognizing dodgy ground and not wanting to be seen as being uncharitable. "Matthew said something about her reaction to the crash."

Henry didn't look upset at my mentioning it. "It's more than that," he said. "She has never really understood why her mother left her, and it has caused some deep scars that we have never been able to heal."

I looked up sharply – too sharply because he saw my sudden interest at the mention of her mother. "And where is her mother? Surely if she knew, there might be some sort of reconciliation for her?"

Although he tried to disguise it, his face became guarded. "No, there is no chance that they can meet again. Monica was not the best mother for a sensitive little girl like Maggie. When she left the family over forty years ago, it was for good. She won't be coming back." He said it with such finality that the speck of unease that had made itself known to me in the cabin when Matthew had spoken of her stirred again.

"What happened to Monica?"

Henry leaned forward in his chair, lending emphasis to his answer. "I don't know and I don't care. Matthew dealt with her. I was in no fit state at the time." He sat back again and took a few seconds in which he looked at the photograph of himself with his mother before resuming. "But you want to know what to do about Maggie? Well, you'll have to win her respect and she's obviously not going to make that easy. She's not a bad person inside, Emma, though it's hard to believe when you're bearing the brunt of her spleen, I know. But there is a decent core to her; she wouldn't be so good at her job otherwise. My advice – for what it's worth – is not let her see that she's getting to you. She hates weakness because she sees the vulnerability in herself and it frightens her. But I could have a word with her, if you want me to?"

If only it were that simple, and he probably realized it despite the support he offered. I shook my head. "Thanks, but I'll try to work this out."

"I'm not much help, am I?"

"I don't think anyone can help. It reminds me of when I had trouble with some girls at school."

"Did you resolve it?"

"Ye-es, sort of," I evaded, reluctant to explain to what I had resorted when pushed to the limits of my tolerance. They never came near me again and I had managed to avoid being expelled. My father had been furious. I picked up the lethal-looking letter-opener and put it down again hastily before Henry gained the wrong idea.

"Don't be worried about talking to Matthew about it, Emma. Maggie might be his granddaughter but he won't allow her to intimidate you."

Allow her? The woman must be nearly fifty; he could hardly spank her, even if he were so inclined. I peered at him doubtfully. He saw my reservation and smiled sympathetically. "Maggie's strong-willed, I know, but she'll not oppose him."

The fire popped and a piece of burning log slipped through the iron bars of the grate and rolled towards the edge of the hearth. Henry rose and bent down to scoop it up with the small shovel. As he did so, the sun from the east window caught his thick, greying hair. I did a double-take and he saw me looking.

"Ah," he said, running a hand through his hair and smiling ruefully. "My roots need a touch-up, do they? Good thing you saw them rather than an outsider."

"I don't understand. Why…?"

He laughed gruffly. "I see Matthew hasn't said anything to you about *my* irregularities. You don't really think this is my natural colour, do you? Beneath this badger-like appearance, I'm a natural blond."

"Oh!"

"And, while I'm at it, I don't need these," he took off his glasses, "and my eyes are blue, not… whatever these contacts make them – bluey-green, I think. And if I shaved all this hair off my face…"

"You would look just like Matthew," I finished, already seeing the difference it made.

He replaced the shovel and returned to his chair. "Yes, too like him for our safety. Dan and the boys have to take precautions as well – Dan more so because of his age. And I expect you can see how alike Harry is. He's managed so far, but he's becoming more and more like Matthew as he gets older. Only Ellie is darker naturally, like her mother. We can get away with some similarities, but not all of us, not so obviously. The Lynes gene seems very dominant." Although heavier-browed than Matthew, and his hair artificially grizzled to make him appear his age, Henry would still be considered good-looking – probably how Matthew would look were he twenty or so years older.

"Do you know why the gene is so dominant?"

"The short answer is *no*, although we have identified the particular alleles that give us our distinctive qualities. What we don't know is why they became dominant and remained so through the three generations. Matthew says his grandmother had the same colouring, from what he can recall. He doesn't remember his mother so well, she died when he was very young, although I expect you already know that?"

I made a noncommittal sound, remembering that Matthew concealed his great age and true identity even from his son, and diplomacy – as well as the family's safety – demanded I pretend to be equally unacquainted with the facts.

"Henry, something both you and Matthew have alluded to, it's been bothering me…"

"What's that?"

"You said *outsiders* earlier. But *I* am an outsider, Henry…"

"No, Emma, forgive me for interrupting, but you're not. My father has made that very clear."

"But I haven't been, er, *vetted*, I think Matthew called it. Or is being here part of the vetting procedure?"

Henry laughed out loud and slapped his knees. "You heard about that, did you? No, you're not to be vetted. If Dad trusts you, I wouldn't dare presume to gainsay him."

"Dare?"

"Oh, not in that way. Matthew has never resorted to threats or violence. In fact I can't remember a time when he even raised his voice – he never needed to and he certainly never lifted a hand to me when I was growing up, although I deserved it at times. I wouldn't have wanted to provoke him though, no sir-*ee*." The shattered window in the cabin and Sam's broken jaw came to mind. I said nothing, and Henry continued. "No, Matthew's decisions usually turn out to be correct, even if this is an unusual situation."

I regarded that as an understatement, acutely aware of Ellen's image sitting in full view on Matthew's desk. "And it doesn't bother you that I'm here, Henry?"

"It took some getting used to, I don't deny it. Matthew told me about you a long time before we met a few days ago. At first I didn't know how to feel, but I've seen the change in him. He's more like I remember him before the accident, less withdrawn." Henry rubbed the bridge of his nose in the way that was becoming very familiar. "My mother will die, Emma. Matthew loves her and he has done the best he can for her, but he cannot turn back time. In some ways your coming along when you did has been a blessing – in disguise, I grant you – but a blessing all the same. It'll allow my mother to die knowing he's not alone, and that will ease her leaving."

I considered the man in front of me whose generosity of spirit far surpassed my own, who regarded me so benignly, and wondered – not for the first time – if I would be so giving in similar circumstances.

"Matthew said that Ellen would like to meet me."

Henry nodded and he chuckled good-humouredly. "So she would. I take it you're not so keen?"

I shrugged apologetically. "In the circumstances it would be a little strange. I wouldn't know what to say to her and I can't see how meeting would help in any way. If anything, I would have thought that it would be disturbing for her."

I could hear myself trying to persuade him of the veracity of my argument, but he smiled gently, making me feel guilty instead. "I think it goes back to what I said earlier, Emma – that Ellen is curious to know who she is leaving her husband to, but also, I suspect – knowing my mother as I do – that she will want to share some information with you. She bears you no resentment, you do realize that I hope?"

I felt myself redden and squirmed in my chair. "I don't know why she doesn't – I know I would – but if you think it will help her, then, yes, of course I'll meet her." I didn't want to, Heaven knows I didn't, but it seemed the right thing to say at the time given her willingness to forgive my usurpation of her husband. Would any circumstance make this right other than her death?

Henry seemed pleased by my response. "I'll let Dad know and we can get something fixed sooner rather than later; time isn't on our side." He smiled sadly and I felt for him. "Still," he said, "are you looking forward to this afternoon?"

"Why – what's happening this afternoon?"

"Barbecue," he said.

9

Barbecue

The air was rigid with cold. Newly fallen snow formed a crust of ice that ripped and splintered the rays of the late-afternoon sun.

I stood in the deep shadow of the house and placed a tentative foot on the frozen surface; it bore my weight. Stepping into the light, I followed the gentle slope down from the house towards the river. A line of tracks revealed where Harry, Joel, and Ellie had traipsed back and forth collecting wood all morning for what Henry had been pleased to call the "barbecue" but looked more like a colossal bonfire. I turned around at the sound of fleet steps, my breath hanging in the air like the smoke of a steam engine.

"You look suitably wrapped up," Matthew approved, casting a quick eye over me.

"So do you," I returned. "But you don't need to be, do you?"

"For the sake of normality I do. It'd give the local wildlife a shock if I didn't."

"To say nothing of me," I sighed. The idea appeared to amuse him and he seemed about to comment, thought better of it, and put out his hand instead.

"Come on, let's join the others."

I trudged over the snow, revelling in the slight give of the crust beneath my feet and the correspondingly satisfying *crusp* of sound that accompanied it, leaving a broken set of imprints behind me. It had been two days since my episode with the coffee, but my senses remained ever so slightly heightened: every sound, every touch, every smell sharper and more vivid than before.

Ellie laboured in the process of dragging a log, three times her length and almost twice as thick, up from the riverbank, but a snapped-off branch kept catching in the snow like a ploughshare.

"Boys…" Matthew indicated with his head.

"Yeah, sure, onto it." Harry trotted over to his sister. "Yo, El – need a hand?" He gave her a beatific smile and she gave him a scouring glance in return, and dropped the log.

"Not from a weakling like *you*." She picked it up again, daring him to come any closer.

He called to his brother. "Hey, bro', our little sister needs a hand." Joel chucked a log on the pile and joined them. "What'd' ya reckon?"

Joel didn't need to be asked twice. "*Ri-ght!*" He bent down and casually scooped a handful of snow, patting it into a ball as he moved to Harry's left. As the boys separated, they crouched and began to close in on their sister, stalking her like mountain lions. Ellie deposited the log with a thump, her eyes narrowing. It appeared grossly unfair, two against one, but Matthew followed the manoeuvres with acute interest. Their parents had crossed the ground to join us, Dan grinning in anticipation. Jeannie, on the other hand, didn't look at all happy.

Joel's low chuckle sounded menacing in the bitter stillness of the air. Ellie backed off, looking right and left until she had clear ground between herself and her brothers. Step by step the boys closed in on her until they were no more than a car's length away. Without warning, Joel hurled the snowball with immense force in her direction. As she ducked, they lunged, their arms already extended to imprison her. As quick as I could draw breath, she leapt like a hind, springing from a standstill onto Harry's forearm and then Joel's shoulder, up and over and away, landing lightly on the snow a dozen feet behind them, laughing at the consternation on their faces.

"*Geesh*, how do you do that!" Joel exploded.

I looked up at Matthew. "Yes, how did she?"

"It's one of the benefits she seems to have inherited." He ducked as a snowball sailed over his head, landing harmlessly beyond him. *Whumph*, another snowball landed close by, then another, hitting me on the arm. Matthew's head whipped around. "Looks like an outbreak of hostilities," he grinned.

"Joel, Ellie, stop that," Jeannie called out.

"Looks like it," I agreed, shovelling up snow in my gloved hands and moulding it the best I could. I dodged another, suspecting they viewed me as a soft target. "This snow's too dry," I complained, avoiding yet a third.

"Try the snow underneath the new stuff," Matthew suggested, launching a snowball that hit Joel squarely in the middle of his chest. I dug down and tried a handful of the older snow, which compacted more easily. *Flump*.

"Ouch," I muttered as a snowball hit my thigh.

"Harry, you mustn't…" Jeannie scolded him.

Thwack. I hit Harry with a satisfying lump of snow, his dark jacket bearing the evidence of the white explosion, and narrowly avoided Joel's missile from my left. Matthew covered me while I rapidly formed another ball, launching as Joel reloaded, hitting him on his leg. Ellie secured a sound win against me, much to my fury, before Matthew scored a hit on the back of her hood that had her spinning around to defend her rear. He caught a snowball as it was about to hit my face and relaunched it successfully. Already gasping, I tried to keep up with the speed of snowball production and attack.

"Incoming!" Joel yelled as Matthew fired off a series of missiles with breathtaking speed, each one meeting its target. "Ye-*es!*" I celebrated.

A brief pause followed as Joel signalled to his siblings, and the three separated and went into an attack formation.

"Stick together," Matthew advised. "Don't let them separate us." By "*us*" I knew he meant they were targeting *me* as they sank lower to the ground, snowballs in hand and a predatory look on their faces, their eyes following my movements. This, I thought, is what it must feel like to be hunted and, despite the familiarity of the setting and the benevolence of the group, a thrill – almost like a whisper of fear – clawed at my throat.

Matthew hunkered down into a defensive position, placing his body between the circling group and me. With a shudder I realized I had seen him do the same before, when the bear readied itself for attack not so very long ago.

Harry tested the balance of a snowball, eyeing up the growing gap on Matthew's flank. Matthew edged to cover it. Ellie worked the opposite flank as Joel moved in on the centre, trying to find a flaw in Matthew's defences. I saw the hooded intent in their eyes, I sensed the urgency behind their stealth… and something inside me snapped.

I turned and bolted for the shelter of the bonfire. "*Emma!*" Matthew called out in frustration as I ran.

"Sorry!" I threw back at him over my shoulder, making for the relative safety of the heap of burning timber.

My ruse worked better than I thought. "Ye-*hah!*" Joel and Harry yodelled, splitting up, each running faster than I had ever seen them move before to circle the bonfire before Matthew could intercept. *Clump*. I spun round. *Thwump*. I ducked sideways as a third ball flew past, then a fourth. A rapid volley hit me from three sides, feeling more like balls of ice than snow. Oh, *heck*, perhaps this hadn't been such a good idea. All three siblings had positioned themselves for the attack when, out of the corner of my eye, I saw Matthew launch himself at Harry, knocking him off his feet. There ensued a brief flurry of limbs; then Harry yelled, "OK, OK – I surrender," and lay panting on the snow, as Matthew leapt up and rounded on the other two youths just as Joel took careful aim and walloped a snowball with full force, knocking the breath from me.

Groaning, I bent double, clasping my stomach with both arms, and collapsed to the ground in agony. A stunned silence fell on the group.

"Joel, you *idiot!*" I heard the sound of running feet. "I told you not to throw so hard. Matthew, *Matthew* – Emma's hurt." Panic jangled Ellie's voice as she bent over me. I moaned, barely opening my eyes. Her anxious face was replaced by Joel's mortified expression.

"Emma! Geesh, I didn't mean to hurt you. I'm so sorry. Matthew, Emma needs you!" He looked around in desperation, but Matthew hung back

"Joel…" I mumbled, my hands clasping at the snow in torment, my legs writhing.

"Joel…" I whispered, my lips barely moving.

He leaned closer still. "Emma, what is it?"

I fixed his harrowed eyes with mine. "*Vengeance – is – mine*," I hissed and whisked one hand up to pull his jacket open while neatly depositing a large handful of compacted snow down his neck with the other. He yelped and jumped back, nearly knocking Ellie over in the process, scrabbling at his coat as the snow melted in icy streams down his chest.

"You… you…" he spluttered as he made a grab for me, but I escaped from beneath his legs across the snow to where Matthew stood watching, his whole body shaking with laughter.

"That's gross, you *cheated!*" Joel accused, leaning forward and pulling his jacket open, shaking what remained of the snow from his clothes.

"Hardly," I called. "I just used a diversionary tactic, that's all. Oh, and by the way…" I held up a gloved finger just to make my point, "… it worked."

Joel scowled at me, but the water must have been less cold now because the scowl didn't reach his eyes. "You took advantage of my good nature," he said mournfully.

Matthew finished sweeping snow from my shoulders. "You should know better than to let your defences down, Joel," he said, suddenly serious. "That's how you get stabbed in the back." I detected the ghost of his past, but within seconds he smiled again, and only he and I knew of the betrayal to which he referred.

"Yeah, right, I'll try to remember that next time."

"Who said there is going to be a *next time*?" I asked, primly, thinking I would undoubtedly be the loser in any subsequent game. Matthew lightly tugged my plait like a bell pull. "Oh, I'm sure it can be arranged."

Joel erupted into a broad beam at the thought, but as Jeannie left Dan's side and came towards us looking decidedly annoyed, with her thin features drawn into a point, the smile fell from his face.

"You nearly gave me a heart attack with your antics, Joel. You shouldn't use your training like that – it's dangerous. You might have really hurt Emma. Matthew, I've made it clear that I don't want him or the others encouraged to use their abnormalities." She made them sound unclean.

Joel rolled his eyes. "Just leave it, Mom, it was only a *game*." He turned his back and stomped off to kick a piece of wood back into the pile where it had fallen free of the bonfire.

Matthew watched him, unsmiling. "Joel needs to practise his chosen craft just like the rest of us, Jeanette – it's what will keep him safe in the future. And he's no more to blame for the *antics*, as you call them, than anyone here. As for your children's *strengths*, it's as much a part of them as breathing is to you, and you know that. Your denial will serve no purpose other than to ostracize Joel. He needs to know that you accept him as he is." This obviously represented an old bone of contention, a festering ulcer that erupted now and again that responded to treatment, but never quite went away.

Jeannie's mouth pulled down in a sour bow. "You know how I feel about it, Matthew."

"I do," he said patiently, "but nothing is going to change because of it."

She gave him an odd little look that I couldn't interpret, before turning away to rejoin Dan, who hovered anxiously with Ellie. Harry had gone after Joel, and the two of them were having a heated discussion as far as I could tell by their body language.

"Whoops," I said, watching her retreating back.

"Indeed – whoops." Matthew concurred. "There are one or two unresolved issues, which I think you might have gathered from that exchange."

I nodded. "Yup – a lack of humour is one of them."

Matthew broke into a smile despite himself. "It certainly is. She'll be all right, but I'm more concerned to keep Joel onside; he's not had an easy time of it. Now, we'd better see how the pig is getting on if you want to eat tonight."

I sniffed the air appreciatively. "I thought Henry was joking about a barbecue!"

Matthew frowned. "I don't know about a *barbecue* – I would have called it *spit-roast pig* – but nomenclature can be very misleading..." I walloped him through his thick jacket because he teased me again, and he *oinked* and made piggy snuffling noises in my ear until I laughed and protested at my torment. Matthew then called the boys over to stoke the fire, and whatever Harry had said to him appeared to have worked because Joel had regained his good humour. As he loped past us to the bonfire, he mouthed "*I'll get even*" at me, and I hid behind Matthew's strong back, thumbed my nose at him and mimed, "*Oh yeah?*"

The fire ate deep into the wood, growling and hissing as each new piece became engulfed by flame. Soon the whole inferno lit the darkening sky, sparks like glowing moths rising on the warmed currents of air. I stood back, feeling my skin beginning to singe.

"That's a great fire, Joel."

He smiled sideways at me. "Thanks – that's big coming from a cheat."

"I'm sorry about that. I didn't think it would get you into trouble with your mum."

He shuffled the snow about with the toe of his Army boot. "Yeah, well, that's not your fault. Mom's not keen on me being a grunt. Thinks I should've stayed on at school, gone to college, you know – like Harry and Ellie – but that's not what interested me. School was boring." He stuck his hands in the pockets of his jacket, looking defensive. "That's not what you want to hear, right? You probably agree with her."

Over on the other side of the fire, Jeannie seemed to be mellowing rapidly with a glass of mulled wine in one hand.

"Would you like some wine, Joel?" I asked, wondering if it might help him in the same way it seemed to be doing for his mother.

"Uh – no thanks, Emma, I don't drink."

"But… you said you liked whisky…"

"Nah, I said that to wind Mom up. I'm dry." He took in the expression on my face, "Yeah, hard to believe, right? I don't drink, I don't smoke, and I'll never do drugs. Not what you expected, huh?"

"OK," I said. "You've undoubtedly got me there. That just about makes us even, don't you think? Truce?"

"I guess so." We shook on it.

"Joel, it isn't my business what you want to do, but if it makes any difference, my father and both my grandfathers were in the Army; in fact, it's a bit of a tradition in my family. I can't see what's wrong with it as a career if that's what you want to do. Dan seems to think you're pretty good at your job, and I know Matthew does too."

He made a face. "Yeah, they've been great. If it hadn't been for Matthew…" He stopped abruptly, pulling me to one side as a pocket of gas exploded, shooting a burning lump of wood in our direction.

"Thanks," I said. "You were saying…?"

"Sure. Matthew didn't push the school bit when everyone else did, so I spent a lot of time with him. He used to listen to a load of crap – sorry, *stuff* – from me when I went through a really heavy time at home. I was messed up pretty much – I even left home for a time when I was fifteen. He persuaded me to come back though."

"He knew where you were?"

"Definitely – he made it a condition when I wanted to leave for a while. He made sure I had a place to stay, money, everything – but I made him promise not to tell anyone or I wouldn't've come back." He shot me a look. "Nobody knows this, right? *Nobody*."

"I understand. I won't say anything, I promise."

"Right, I reckoned you wouldn't; that's why I told you." He ran his hand over his Army crew cut, backwards from the nape of his neck to the top of his head, looking older. "When I'd sorted myself out and knew what I wanted to do, he helped with all the application forms for the Army, that sort of thing. And… oh yeah… he taught me to fight – weird stuff too, not what the Army teaches. It gave me an edge when I joined. I've been promoted already," he said with a degree of pride, "though you've not seen me at my best," he appended, grimacing.

I thought Joel more self-effacing than he would have me believe. "Matthew has a few years on you, I wouldn't worry. He obviously thinks you have what it takes or he wouldn't have bothered to teach you."

Joel shrugged. "Sure, but where'd he learn stuff like that? You haven't seen him use it yet. It's weird, but it works."

I wondered if I had inadvertently seen it, although I wouldn't know whether the techniques he employed so effectively against Staahl and Sam would be considered *weird* or not.

"Mom hates it though. She thinks he encouraged me not to go to college, but she's wrong. I would've left school anyway; he just gave me a direction."

It sounded all so familiar, this conflict of expectation, except my grandfather died when I was still a child and I had no one to turn to except Nanna. Grief for the lost years spent in hurt resentment, and for my grandmother, whom I never expected to see again, welled unexpectedly and I swallowed it before Joel noticed. He stared into the heart of the fire with his own thoughts.

"You know, Joel, my father didn't want me to be an academic, and I found it hard to forgive him that. He kept on pushing until I wanted to throttle him. He wouldn't listen to anything I said and I felt so guilty for not doing what he wanted."

He put his arm around my shoulders like a brother would, a touching gesture I appreciated.

"Yeah, I know what you mean. Do you guys get on now, after all this time?"

"Now that I'm old and grey and ready to retire to my grave, do you mean?" I replied, glad to lighten the mood with good-tempered sarcasm.

"Hey, you're not old at all; you're pretty ho…" He took his arm from around me.

"OK, OK," I said briskly to save his embarrassment. "My father and I sort of get on now, but it's only happened recently – since I've known Matthew, in fact."

Joel grunted a laugh. "Yeah, he has that effect on people."

I hadn't thought about it like that. "I suppose he does, yes. Where has he gone, by the way?"

Joel looked around. "To see if the pig is ready, I guess. I'd better give the old man a hand. Huh, I wouldn't say *that* to his face, of course."

I laughed. "No, you wouldn't dare." But we both knew that he would because they had the sort of relationship built on mutual trust and respect that meant that he could get away with it.

I stamped my feet on the frozen ground to get my circulation flowing again, and looked around for somewhere to sit. The hump-backed log Ellie had been fetching to add to the fire still lay in the snow where she had dropped it, yards away from the low bank above the fast-running river. It would make an admirable seat if I could turn it forty-five degrees. The shattered remains of the branch had left a deep furrow where it had ploughed the snow and stuck fast, and it was all that I could do to lift one end. Yet Ellie had dragged it all the way from the river edge where it must have lain for years half-submerged, worn smooth by grit-laden currents until the surface shone silver-grey in the half-light.

I perched on the ridge of wood but it heaved and rolled, sinking deeper, and I rolled with it, my legs sticking up like a beetle on its back. I struggled to get up, but it was too much effort and I lay in the bed of snow and contemplated the blue-washed sky instead. The first stars were just visible and growing in vibrancy every second, pulsing and pushing day into night. The sounds of the family around the bonfire faded, consumed by the urgent voice of the river, and a light breeze, kicked up by the fast-flowing water, sent tremulous fingers of anticipation through the fine, bare branchlets of the willows. All round my head, a hundred lesser voices joined in volatile chorus as explosive frost penetrated pockets of ice within the snow's surface, minute detonations reverberating against my ears. The raw edges of my senses quivered, feeling the tiny vibrations of approaching footfall.

A darker form came between the stars and me. "Are you quite comfortable down there?"

I smiled dreamily up at him. "I'm listening to the snow."

Amusement chased over Matthew's face as he leaned over me. "Of course you are. Do you do this sort of thing often?"

I had a little think about that. "Only on Thursdays," I said at last.

He shook his head. "Ah, but this is Wednesday."

I kicked my legs like a colt. "I don't like to be predictable."

"Heaven forbid you should ever be that! Would you like a hand out of there?" I stuck both hands out to him in reply and he pulled me to my feet. "What were you trying to do, apart from listening to the snow?"

"I tried to move the log so that I could sit on it, but it was being recalcitrant. I do so hate it when inanimate objects have a mind of their own."

"Very trying, I agree. You could have asked for some help, you know."

His family were building something in the snow with a great deal of whooping and snow fights in between raising what looked like walls. Dan had joined in, avoiding most of the confrontation, but not entirely, as his heavy winter coat was layered with snow.

"They were having too much fun; I didn't want to disturb them."

"Where would you like it?"

I turned around. Matthew had the log balanced under one arm, its contorted length compliant in his control.

"I thought between the fire and the river so I have the best of both worlds."

"Good choice," he said, selecting a level piece of ground and driving the broken spur of the log into the snow so that it didn't wobble but formed a relatively level, stable bench.

The pig had been suspended on a makeshift spit made of spars of green wood. It straddled the edge of the fire, the flames still too fierce to place it directly over the heart of it, but the margins glowed orange and hot, and the pig's skin prickled as the meat cooked. I swivelled my legs over the log to watch the last light of day glimmer on the dark waters and felt heat warm my back. Matthew sat next to me with his legs stretched out in front of him.

"You knew I wasn't hurt earlier, didn't you?" I said to him.

He bent over and gathered a handful of snow in his bare hand and crushed it into a ball, moulding until it became a sphere of ice.

"You weren't in pain – or none that I could detect." He threw the ice ball at the river where the churning water swallowed it. "Why did you run? I would have protected you. I wouldn't have let them get to you, and you would have been safer with me."

I detected a note of disappointment, as if he thought that by running I demonstrated a fundamental lack of trust. I tried to find a way of describing the sudden sense of panic and fear that seeing him, surrounded and at bay, had caused, that it wasn't my own safety that had concerned me, but his own – irrational as that might seem. I lifted my legs and bashed my feet together watching the snow fall in clumps off my boots.

"I know you could have protected me, I just thought that perhaps if I ran they would split up and be easier to defeat; you know, divide and rule, and all that. It did work a bit, you have to admit; you took out Harry, didn't you?"

Firelight threw his face into sharp relief. "But not before Joel and Ellie managed to get in a few hits."

I began to laugh. "Matthew, it was only a bit of fun…" and faltered. His eyes had become black, his irises consumed by his pupils, and I saw no responding humour in them. As soon as I spoke, I understood the significance of it for him. If I had reacted the way I did, if I ran and prevented him from keeping me from harm in a mere contest with his family, what would I do if I were similarly threatened and the weapons were made not of snow, but steel and iron?

"It *was* just a game, Matthew," I whispered.

He stared straight ahead of him and back in time. "It is never *just* a game, and even a game can serve a purpose."

All I could see were the faces of the hunters and the hunted, and words rushed from my mouth before I could stop them. "I couldn't bear... I *couldn't bear* to see you hunted, not even by your family in a stupid game with... with *snowballs*," I cried.

A look of wonder replaced the disappointment. "You did that for *me*?" I nodded. "Emma... sweetheart, I wasn't the target, *you* were, and you made it easier for them to pick you off..."

"But it gave you a chance," I interrupted fiercely.

"And at what cost? Why would I want a chance if you had none? What purpose would that serve?" We were beyond talking about a snowball fight, touching on what haunted us both. Matthew stroked the side of my face with the tips of his bare fingers. "I have none of your physical vulnerability. I can persist when you cannot. What would I do without you, Emma? What would be the point of my existence then? I can't go back to how it was before. I couldn't face life without you, not now, not after this." The familiar tight lines creased the sides of his mouth, and the muscles around my heart compressed in response.

"Matthew, you talk as if we're about to be attacked at any moment."

"I want us to be ready for any eventuality, no matter how remote a possibility it might be. It doesn't hurt to be prepared. Call it a habit of a lifetime." He smiled grimly.

"It does matter if you spend it looking over your shoulder."

"You knew that would be part of a life spent with me. I tried to make that clear."

"You did, but perhaps I didn't realize how it would pervade every facet of our lives. I think I am only just beginning to understand that."

"And…?" he asked.

"And, what?"

"Are you having second thoughts about your decision to stay with me – about *us*?"

I scanned his face, seeing his eyes unwavering but apprehensive, at the straight line of his nose before it dipped down to the curve of his mouth. I saw the way his eyebrows drew together in a pleat in the middle of his ever-young face as he frowned at me, and how the whole came to the neat, blunt point of his chin before sweeping down to the little hollow at the base of his neck that I loved so much. I thought of never seeing that face again, not hearing his voice in the vibration of his chest as I rested my head against him. To never again feel the strength of his arms holding me, or the love radiating from him when he caressed my hair or whispered my name. I shivered as a new wind brushed the back of my neck despite the warmth from the fire.

"I cannot contemplate life without you, Matthew, whatever that life might bring."

"Emma, being with me places you in constant risk of my exposure and whatever that might entail. Your existence does not threaten me as I do you."

I shrugged in a display of nonchalance I did not feel. "So be it. That's my choice, isn't it? I'll stay for as long as you want me."

"Hah!" He laughed sharply, causing me to look at him in surprise. "I'll take you at your word. That's a lifelong commitment you've just made."

"Then I am content," I said earnestly.

He placed both hands around my face, forcing me to look at him although his eyes were bright in mine, as painful as the sun. "When it comes to your safety, promise that you will listen to me, Emma, and do what I ask." He saw my hesitation and his eyes burned steadily hotter. "At some point in the future, there might be no room for your mule-like obstinacy. I need to know that I can trust you to let me protect you."

I held his gaze. "And vice versa, Matthew. I'm not promising anything unless I know that you will do everything in your power to protect *yourself* and keep from harm."

He dropped his hands and my face felt suddenly colder. "Of course."

"Of course, *what*?" I demanded.

"I will do everything in my power to keep myself from harm." That was suspiciously easy to extricate from him. I attempted to read his face but he bent down to gather more snow. "Now it's your turn," he stated flatly upon completion of his task.

"I will endeavour to comply with your wishes, Matthew."

"That's not good enough. I want you to promise me."

I shuffled on the log and stamped my feet on the ground, up and down, in front of me. "I'm getting cold," I muttered.

"And that won't work either. Say it."

"Oh, all right, then. I promise I'll try to…" He skewered me with a look. "I promise I *will* listen to you."

"And do as I ask to keep you safe."

I felt more and more like an intractable teenager. I blew out my cheeks and screwed out a tart "*Yes*".

"Yes, *what*?"

"I *promise*."

He clapped his hands together with a satisfied grin. "Right, good – that wasn't so bad, was it?" I pouted, still feeling that somehow he had extracted more out of me than I had him.

The fire had reduced into a sizable mass of incandescent embers, and the pig now roasted over the middle of it. Every now and then, fat escaped from the skin and a spear of flame leapt from the fire. Twizzling around, I welcomed the warmth on my face.

Joel approached with something in his hand. He offered an insulated glass. "I thought you might like some of Grams' *gløgg*. This one's non-alcoholic and it's hot."

I took it from him. "Thanks." I sipped cautiously at the dark red liquid, the colour of dried blood, and coughed. "Wow, that's... *strong*." I took another sip, feeling it scouring my throat. "I – love – it," I managed, wiping my eyes.

"There are no half-measures with Pat," Matthew observed.

"Right," Joel agreed. "I'd better get back to help out with the ice house."

Matthew and I watched as he joined his siblings and father. From where we sat, it looked like he directed operations.

"I used to do something like that when I was a child." I reflected. "My grandfather would take us down to the Meadows, depending on how much snow we had."

Matthew pulled my hood up, insulating my neck and ears from the deepening cold. "Did you build ice houses?"

The glass warmed my hands through my gloves, and its contents my tummy. "Sort of. Beth and I used to build snow forts. It could take us all day – sometimes two – so Grandpa would bring a primus stove and he would make us tea." I recalled the hissing blue flame and the smell of bottled gas and wet snow and damp gloves. "He couldn't do much building himself because of his war injury, you see. It left him breathless much of the time, and he was very old by then. Anyway, we would build and build – so much better than a sand fort because we didn't have to beat the tide – and then he would mount a standing attack having laid siege by withholding our tea and sandwiches until we were *starving*, and we would have to defend ourselves." I lifted one leg over the log so that I straddled it as if on horseback. "We always had to build castles based on the real thing, and they had to be historically accurate, of course: a classic motte and bailey, Celtic hill fort, star fort, concentric castle, you know the sort of thing. I think over the years Grandpa took us through every type he could think of. We learned so much without him ever teaching us a thing. We were disappointed if it didn't snow." I picked at a piece of rough bark where it had become trapped between the trunk and the stub of a branch. "Anyway, that's what we did."

Matthew was a good listener and I grew a little self-conscious talking about myself. He pushed the end of my scarf beneath my hood, securing it. "No wonder you like history," he observed, his smile indulgent.

"It was more than that, though. Beth enjoyed the building and the defending as much as I did, but I don't think that it ever burrowed under her skin in the same way it did mine." I paused, thinking about our different attitudes to the past. "I know that it sounds contrived, but history makes *sense*. I don't know why people can't see the relevance of it. Whatever happened yesterday is part of today and helps shape tomorrow." I could hear myself becoming emphatic and blushed under Matthew's scrutiny. "What did you do when you were little?"

He looked at me for a moment longer, as if he were there with me in the snowbound fields of my childhood, picturing me as a young girl with a long plait of bright copper against the white. He blinked and came back to me.

"It would depend on the winter, of course, but most years my father would take me sledging or snowballing with Nathaniel or my cousins. If the conditions were right, he'd have the horses hitched to an old wagon carcass, which he had mounted on some sort of runners that looked like long skis, and we used it like a sleigh. But the best times were when the fields flooded and froze and we went skating…"

"You had skates!"

"Indeed we did. My uncle brought some back from the Low Countries before… well, obviously before things became strained between him and my father." Matthew kicked at a hummock of snow in front of him, scattering the fine crystals. "They were good times. We had skating parties on the ice, or huge snowball fights, and we would have a bonfire on the banks of the river, like this. Just like this. And if the time was right, we would have a pig slaughtered to cook on it." He interrupted his own narration. "Have you ever seen pink snowballs?" He observed me obliquely, and it took a second before the penny dropped.

"Ugh, *blood* snowballs? That's revolting!"

He grinned. "It's better than what we did with frogs in spring…"

"Stop! I don't want to know," I protested, covering my ears.

He took my hands away and held them in both of his, rubbing them to keep them warm. "But then we had the fields drained so the crops were more reliable, but we needed *really* cold, prolonged frosts before the fish stews or the moat froze. The water was much deeper than the flooded fields, and you needed that depth of frost and it didn't happen as often." He leaned over and drew a small circle in the snow between where our legs nearly touched and idly dotted the centre of it. "Anyway, those were good times," he said again, "before

Nathaniel had to take on more of his father's workload and things became difficult for all of us." He stabbed the centre of the circle with his finger, then scrunched the snow up in his fist, letting it fall. The fire spat and soared at regular intervals now, and the smell of roasting meat wafted towards us.

"Is that why you do this?" I asked, nodding towards the fire and his family, whose figures were silhouetted or illuminated as they moved around the flames.

"Yes, I enjoyed it when young so it seemed an equally good thing to continue with my family."

"Even if they don't know the origins of the tradition?"

"Indeed, but I'm glad you do now."

We were quite content to sit silently in each other's company listening to the jibes between the siblings, and the occasional rejoinder from their mother to moderate their frequent attempts to wrong-foot one another and slam the victim into the snow. They reminded me of puppies testing their strength and dominance against each other, except that puppies had none of their endurance, speed, or dexterity. Ellie received no quarter for being female, and she apparently expected none. Her particular speciality seemed to be in avoiding being captured, as well as deft footwork that landed her behind one of her brothers, upending him before he realized where she was.

A stray hair had found its way into my mouth, and I removed a glove to locate it better with my fingers.

"Emma, Henry had a word with me earlier."

I found the hair. "Oh?"

"He said that you're willing to meet Ellen." He didn't give me a chance to confirm or deny it. "So I thought that we could drive over there tomorrow." He made it sound like a pleasant day out in the country.

Nerves instantly tightened. I forgot the hair. There remained the possibility that it might snow overnight, or even tomorrow – heavily. I scoured the clear, dark night – stars abundant from horizon to horizon.

"And the weather should be fine," he added, lips twitching.

I huffed. "Can you read my mind, or something?"

He slid along the tree trunk and slipped his arm around my waist, kissing a wave of hair that had escaped from my hood. "No, but I know *you*. It'll be all right, Emma, and it'll give an old woman a great deal of pleasure to meet someone else. She doesn't have many other visitors except for us."

Joel and Ellie had broken off hostilities and were moving around the remains of the bonfire, using sticks to roll silver-wrapped parcels out of the embers.

"That's emotional blackmail, Matthew."

"Yes – as I said, I know you."

I failed to push him off the log, and he tickled my stomach, making me squeal with agonized laughter until I begged him to stop.

Joel's voice cut through my remonstrations. "Behave, you two. Hey, Emma – catch!" Something the size of a tennis ball flew towards me and I automatically reached out to catch it, but Matthew intercepted the object, snatching it as my hand began to close around the foil ball.

"That was meant for me!" I objected, trying to take it from him, but he held it out of reach.

"Yes, it was, but I don't think you would have wanted it."

"Aw, spoil my fun, why don't you?" Joel moaned from where he still stood, outlined by the fire.

I looked at him suspiciously and then at the silver ball radiating heat in Matthew's hand. "That was a dastardly trick to play on me, Joel Lynes. You've broken the truce and you don't even know if I *like* baked potatoes – most underhand. And I bet there isn't even any butter on it."

Joel guffawed. "Yeah, you're right, that was bad of me. I'll have to make sure that the *old man* isn't around next time."

"Excuse me," Matthew said politely, rising from the log as if taking his leave of the dining table.

If they were fast, Matthew was faster. He had closed the space between them before Joel had time to react, taking his legs from under him. But Joel anticipated the move and, as he went down, twisted and managed to get his feet on the ground, going into an immediate defensive crouch.

"Good one, Joel," Harry called encouragingly. They were standing outside the diminishing circle of light and I went to stand with Dan and Harry, who were watching the developing interplay intently. Joel remained low and watchful as Matthew prowled along an invisible line, moving ever closer towards his prey.

Joel lunged for him, shoving his right leg behind Matthew's left, grabbing to throw him, but Matthew pivoted on one foot, stepping over Joel's leg and away from him as Joel brought his right arm around in an arc to try to catch Matthew on the side of his neck.

"Whoa, that was close," Dan murmured.

The opponents circled each other, Matthew's face expressionless, Joel's with a cocky grin. On the other side of the circle, Ellie muttered to herself, repeating the same word over and over. I watched her lips and, with a jolt, realized she chanted "*Matthew, Matthew, Matthew*" like a mantra.

Joel dropped down again and Matthew stopped moving, straightening his back. It looked as if he were inviting Joel to attack although he never took his eyes from him for a moment.

"Come on, old man, you're getting slow," Joel drawled; then, without warning, he stepped up to Matthew, landing a hefty punch to his stomach and another to the side of his head. I clapped a hand over my mouth to stop from calling out.

"He's fine, don't worry," Dan said as if he'd seen it all before.

"Better," Matthew remarked, feeling his jaw and dropping his gaze as he did so. Joel took advantage and struck out again but, quick as a rattlesnake, Matthew feinted first to Joel's right, then to his left, taking him off-guard, whipping Joel's own arm into a stranglehold around the boy's neck. Joel tried to struggle but Matthew had him pinned from behind, and the more he moved, the more he choked against his own arm. "Better – but you're still dead. Don't leave your enemy standing or in a position to strike. Incapacitate if you can, or kill them if you can't, but don't give them a second chance to take you down – they wouldn't do the same for you. Oh, and apologize to your elders and betters," he added with a glint in his eye, letting his great-grandson go.

Joel rubbed his arm, a smirk crossing his face. "Aw, Matthew, that's not nice. Emma's not *that* old…" he managed to say before he realized he had gone a step too far. "I didn't mean it!" he panicked. "Emma, I apologize…"

"Too late," Matthew said grimly, striding towards him and picking him up like a sack of hay. He moved swiftly towards the river with the writhing youth on his back, all the boy's Army training futile against his superior strength.

"Oops, you've pushed him over the edge," Harry called out after them as they disappeared into the darkness. A faint splash echoed from the direction of the river and Matthew walked casually back alone and into the circle of light. "That potato should be cool enough to eat now," he remarked pleasantly to me.

"Boys' games," I rebuked, turning his face into the last light of the embers only to discover not a mark on it. "I take it Joel will be fine?"

"Of course," Matthew said, "but the meat won't be if we leave it for much longer."

He went to help Dan lift the pig off the wooden stake driven through its length; there was something primeval about the whole scene.

A sloshing sound approached from the other side of the bonfire and Joel slouched back, dripping.

Jeannie fussed up to him, a little unsteady after an evening spent drinking mulled wine, but clear-headed enough to scold him. "Look at you – you'll catch your death one of these days. Go and get changed."

He flinched away from her as she brushed gathering ice from his jacket as it began to freeze. "Chill, Mom, I haven't caught as much as a cold in my life. Don't fuss. Hey, Harry, did you see that move? Cool, huh?"

"Yeah, it was great; *your* move wasn't bad either," Harry laughed, dodging a blow from his older brother. They wandered off leaving their mother with a peculiar mix of soured regret on her face as she watched them.

Meeting Ellen

Therefore the Love which us doth bind,
But Fate so enviously debars,
In the Conjunction of the Mind,
And Opposition of the Stars.
ANDREW MARVELL (1621–78)

I'd had better nights. I slept fitfully until about two in the morning then woke, finding Matthew gone from my side. I had eaten too much pork too late into the night, and I lay wakeful, feeling the weight of indigestion in my stomach and nervous anticipation heavy on my mind. I considered going downstairs to join Matthew in his study, but while he didn't need to sleep, I did and I would need all my wits about me for my meeting with Ellen tomorrow – bother, no – *today*. I tossed fretfully for another hour or so until the relentless onset of time drove me back to sleep.

The day dawned as exquisite and bright as the night before had promised, illuminating the gilded frame of the triptych on the bedside table. I took a moment to ask for wisdom and patience during the forthcoming day, and gazed at it for a while, trying to absorb some of the tranquillity it exuded before gathering myself and slipping out of bed. I was up and dressed when Matthew came to find me in the kitchen.

"Sleep well?" he asked, more out of hope than expectation.

"Fine, thanks," I said, although he had already seen the dark shadows beneath my eyes. "I'm ready if you are."

The door to the kitchen opened silently as Maggie came in.

"Good morning, Maggie, we missed you last night," Matthew greeted her without resentment.

"I'm afraid that I had urgent work to attend to." Heavy-lidded eyes flickered in my direction and then away, as emotionless as her expression.

"Oh? Something interesting?" Matthew asked.

She smiled stiffly. "That remains to be seen. It has the potential to be most riveting." Again her eyes slipped towards me, a look Matthew caught, his brow creasing imperceptibly. "You're off to see Grandma, aren't you? Do please give her my love."

I heard Matthew's teeth snap together in temper. He stepped forward, but I pulled at his arm. "Matthew, we need to go. Come on," I said.

He didn't refer to Maggie in the car, but he was clearly thinking about her as he hit the accelerator on the open road. I gripped the sides of my seat and he slowed enough for me to start breathing normally again.

"Sorry," he apologized.

"That's OK," I said. "Maggie has a way of finding a tender spot and pushing at it until you squeal, doesn't she?"

He nodded appreciatively. "That just about sums her up, yes – neatly put. But she hasn't been this viperish since her teenage years and, even then, she directed it more at the world than her family, although she gave Pat a hard time to begin with."

"It's aimed at me, not anyone else, Matthew. She'll probably be as sweet as pie when I've gone." I stared through the window at the glorious scenery, not relishing it as much as I would have done in other circumstances.

He thrummed his fingers against the steering wheel. "You're not going anywhere. She has nothing to fight against, especially not you. I sometimes wonder if she will ever realize that and stop making her life a misery."

And mine, I thought, *and everyone else's*. I considered it time to talk about something else – anything else.

"Last night Joel said something about never having had a cold; did he mean that literally?"

We caught up with a silver car experiencing difficulty negotiating the sharp bends safely, skidding a little on the icy road.

"Snow tyres too worn," Matthew muttered, unusually impatient. He found a straight stretch and overtook without hesitation. When I opened my eyes, the silver car had disappeared out of sight behind the last bend.

"None of them have ever been ill – nor Dan or Henry. Nor Maggie," he added. "They've never had any childhood infections, myopia, asthma – anything like that. It was one of the things that made Monica suspicious. She kept taking Maggie and her older sister, Ellen, to chickenpox slumber parties, but they were the only two who never caught anything."

He concentrated on overtaking a lorry carrying timber before the road curved between canyons of trees and rock, plunging us into semi-darkness.

"Jeannie doesn't like the fact that her children are different, does she?"

We sped around the curve and out into the blinding sun

of the open sky. I squinted in the light, noting that Matthew didn't.

"She finds that aspect difficult to cope with, yes. She's always appreciated their intellectual ability of course, although she's blind to Joel's – too blinkered to see his potential." A note of frustration crept into his voice. He did not appear his calm, urbane self this morning, and I wondered if he looked forward to the forthcoming meeting quite as much as he would have me believe.

Valmont was nothing like any of the nursing homes I had visited in the sad last days of my great-aunts, where faded furnishings matched the dulling eyes of those who had once been so vibrantly alive. It stood in its own expansive grounds on a knoll, with far-reaching views over wooded hills and valleys to the mountains in the distance. The front of the building overlooked terraced lawns, now white under a heavy swathe of snow.

Matthew helped me out of the car. "Before we go in, don't be surprised if anyone refers to me as Ellen's grandson."

I reached up on tiptoes and kissed his cheek, quickly wiping away the lipstick I left there with my thumb. "I would be more surprised if they referred to you as her *husband*," I pointed out. He acknowledged the logic behind my thought. "So, what do I call her? Mrs Lynes, Ellen, *ma'am*...?"

He looked at me sharply, then saw that I teased. I felt in need of some distraction to keep my larynx from tightening so much that I was afraid that I wouldn't be able to call her anything at all.

"Don't you dare call her 'ma'am'. '*Ellen*' will be just fine."

The inside of the building looked as attractive as the exterior, but it managed to be homely at the same time. The cool whites of the walls and rich reds of the carpets in the hall – where an extravagant arrangement of fresh flowers sat on an elegant table – gave the interior more the appearance of an expensive hotel than a nursing home.

A short, middle-aged man in his early fifties, with thinning once-dark hair and olive-toned skin, approached us with an extended hand. "Dr Lynes, it's good to see you again. I'm sorry to have missed you the other day."

Matthew shook his hand warmly. "Charles – hello. Emma, this is Dr Charles DaCruz. He has been Ellen's physician for the last six years or so. Charles – this is Dr Emma D'Eresby." He didn't expand upon my relationship with him, but from the way the doctor looked at me, he had already made an assumption that fitted neatly with our charade.

"Dr D'Eresby, well, Mrs Lynes *has* been looking forward to meeting her grandson's friend."

My mind boggled at what Ellen must have been saying, and forced a look of pleasant interest. "Has she? That's... good." My voice came out as thin and strained as my smile, and Dr DaCruz looked momentarily baffled, fingering the side of his eyebrow. "Well, yes," he said hesitantly, "she's talked of nothing else for the last few weeks."

I felt myself pale and Matthew took my hand. "We'd better get along, Charles," he said, already moving down the hall.

"I'll need to have a word with you later before you go, if I may, Dr Lynes," he called out after us. Matthew waved his hand in response before we turned a corner and were alone in the plush-carpeted corridor.

"How do you remember what to say?" I rushed when we were out of earshot, my back against the wall to steady me. Matthew planted a kiss squarely in the middle of my forehead as if trying to instil courage.

"You get used to it – *you'll* get used to it. Lying isn't so difficult when you have a good enough reason to, and most of the time you can avoid doing even that." He tipped my chin up and smiled into my eyes. "Ready?"

I groaned. "As I'll ever be."

I waited outside the double-width door to Ellen's room, while Matthew went in first to see her. I considered this worse than waiting to see the dentist, more gut-grindingly awful than the minutes before my doctoral viva interview, and almost as bad as telling Guy that I never wanted to see him again, and seeing the look of desperation cross his face as the initial shock wore off.

I paced up and down the lobby, the dense carpets absorbing the sound of my feet, listening for the familiar sounds of nursing homes: an aluminium tea trolley on lino floors, or a TV bellowing out sports results nobody listened to. The stillness was almost sepulchral, except that I found peace in it, a quietness that comes with the acceptance of death before it becomes reality.

I don't know what I expected to find in the room beyond the door. Ever since I had first heard of Ellen's existence, I had tried to picture her. Before I knew that she still lived, and when I'd believed Matthew to be a widower, I had tried to visualize the woman whom he had loved and with whose memory I believed I could never compete. Even the photographs of her as a young woman somehow did not relate to the frail old lady sitting just feet away from me now.

What did I feel – revulsion? Resentment? This was Matthew's *wife*, a woman the same age as my grandmother, who – like Nanna – hung between death and life. God forgive me, but is this what I would become should I live as long? A brittle carapace waiting to die, binding her husband to her with bonds of law and loyalty, preventing our union with fingers embedded in his life as she was slowly torn from him by time.

Curiosity? Jealousy? For living this long, for being alive at all when the crash should have killed her? How could I resent a woman whose only transgression against me was to love and be loved by him first, and whose bitter tragedy saw her spend the rest of her life in the coffin of her body? She, who was the innocent, vulnerable victim of my jealous resentment – undeserving and unknowing – although I struggled against my darker thoughts and, for the most part, won.

Leaning my forehead against the smooth surface of the wall, I squeezed my eyes shut. Could someone *please* explain to me why I ever agreed to come?

Because I owed it to her.

Compassion, then, and pity? Yes, because she wanted to see me, and I should be secure enough in Matthew's love that I could shake off the chains of envy and fear and wish this woman well.

By the time Matthew came to fetch me, I had sat, with a degree of composure, on one of the armchairs provided for relatives and visitors pretending to read a glossy magazine devoted to the apposite subject of health insurance.

It wasn't one room, but a series, like a comfortable suite rather than full-time nursing care. Encapsulated in a custom-built wheeled chair, a tiny, frail woman of great age sat in the bay window full of light. A heavily built man with the shoulders of a boxer looked up from his newspaper as we came in, folding it and standing in readiness to welcome me. My courage began to fail.

"Come in, come in – don't stand where I can't see you." I heard nothing fragile in the old lady's voice, sinewy and strong with traces of her Texan roots still evident.

"Now, Ellen, that's no way to greet your visitor, is it, Mr Matthew?" The man spoke slowly and deliberately, rolling his words out on deep, bass notes like an old song from the South. He ambled over to the chair and started to turn Ellen to face us as Matthew applied gentle, but insistent, pressure on my lower back, propelling my unwilling legs forward.

"That's better – I can look at you now," she said, her sharp eyes appraising my fixed face and wide, edgy eyes.

Matthew kept his hand on the small of my back, out of sight. "Ellen, this is Emma D'Eresby."

"Yes, I know who she is." Ellen peered at me, not making any attempt to disguise her scrutiny. I felt myself blanch further. "You look like a jittery colt with the wind up its tail. I won't bite, even if I could with these damn wires everywhere. I promised Matthew I'd behave and Eli here won't let me have any fun, anyhow."

The large man shook a finger at her. "We can't have you enjoying yourself, now, Ellen," he chided her with a twinkle, making him far more amiable than his bulky body suggested. "It's nice to meet you, ma'am," he said genially to me. I smiled in response. He busied himself around the back of her chair, adjusting dials and checking wires.

Matthew cleared his throat. "Emma's been looking forward to meeting you, Ellen."

"Don't lie, Matthew. Who would want to meet a crabby old woman like your grandmother?" Her tone might be tart but her eyes sparkled. "Come and sit by me, young lady, so we can get better acquainted. I want to know how you met my grandson and what you two have been up to. I hear you've not ate supper before sayin' grace, if you get my meaning."

"There's no call to be speakin' like that!" Eli scolded. Ellen pitched a glance at Matthew, who struggled to keep a straight face.

"Stop fussing around me, Eli, and go read your newspaper someplace else."

Eli heaved a sigh and picked up his paper from the table. "You play nice, now, Ellen, or you'll have some explainin' to do when I get back."

"Yes, yes, I hear you. You go too, Matthew – this is no fit talk for your ears." She took me by surprise by winking at me, and she lost a little of her formidable persona.

"I'll go and find Charles then, as I'm not wanted." Matthew grinned, his stride taking him to the door.

"No, we sure don't need any men about, do we?" Ellen said to me.

"I heard that," Matthew said over his shoulder.

I spoke without thinking. "I think you were meant to." The door shut, and Ellen and I were alone.

"I expect you're wanting to know why I asked to meet you?" She had lost none of her shrewdness, but her tone had softened considerably. She retained enough mobility in her neck to be able to turn her head forty-five degrees either way and she watched for my reaction.

"I think I can guess," I said, a little stiffly.

Ellen cackled a laugh. "I'm sure you can, honey. This isn't the most normal of situations, is it? But then Matthew's not a *normal* sort of man, is he, as I'm sure you know."

I didn't have anything to say to that. I studied her surreptitiously. Her fine, silvery-white hair had been carefully dressed to look full, her clothes specifically chosen to complement her colouring, which, despite her age and infirmity, still had a glow of sun about it. The pale lemon wool twinset wasn't worn with pearls, but with an unusual gold necklace, exquisitely fashioned like a snake with the head swallowing the tail. Two large rubies glowed as eyes. Ellen saw me looking at it.

"Matthew gave it to me as an anniversary present when this sort of thing was all the rage; but it will seem old-fashioned to you now, I expect."

I shook my head, feeling as if I were being drawn into a conversation that had nothing to do with jewellery. "I like old things," I contested, before I recognized what I had said.

Ellen laughed. "Well, that's a mighty good thing too since you've *snared* my husband." I tensed but Ellen continued to chuckle. "Aw, don't mind an old woman. To tell you the truth, I've been waiting for this for nearly fifty years. I always knew Matthew would meet someone else; it was only a matter of time." She paused as she looked at me.

"I'm sorry," I said.

"Don't be. I can't pretend that I've found it easy waiting all these years, and it would've been easier still if I'd been dead when he met you, but now it's happened, I'm kinda glad that I'm still alive to see it – to meet you. I can see what caught his eye. You're a thoroughbred if ever I saw one, and Matthew has an eye for fine things." I shook my head, embarrassed. "You'll have to forgive me; I'm too old to waste time beating about the brush. I say what I think because I'll be dead before I can say it otherwise. But there's more to you than looks, I guess, otherwise he could've had any of the women who'd have gladly flung themselves at him. Do the nurses still chase him?"

I needed to gauge the source of her query before I answered, because one false move at this juncture might throw the whole meeting off-course. But since I didn't know the direction of her question, it seemed any response would be like walking along an unknown cliff edge. In the dark. I opted for direct honesty, rather than subtle diplomacy. "Yes, nurses, doctors, and the students – in fact anyone who has eyes and hormones in the right place."

Ellen grunted a laugh. "Yes, indeedy, you can't take him anywhere, never could. I bet you've seen them too, haven't you, honey? All those girls who are taken by his good looks and gentlemanly ways. But then they don't know what we know, do they? And I wonder – I wonder if they would be so enchanted if they did?" She eyed me speculatively. "But you and I, *we* know, we accept him – despite his bein' so different and all." She coughed a little and I could hear the hollow fragility of her lungs. "You know, honey, when I met Matthew I didn't know anything about him. My brother, Jack – he was his friend from the athletics team – he brought Matthew home with him one holiday. Matthew was so handsome and so quaint my parents just loved him to bits, and although he was studying to be a doctor, he knew a thing or two about farming, and he knew horses better than anyone, so that wasn't so bad. My parents had a ranch – I'm from Texas, if you hadn't already guessed – a big place, and they hoped he and Jack would run it one day when they passed over. But that wasn't to be." Ellen's voice stilled and her face softened as she summoned the sun-warmed memories of her youth. I sat quietly next to her, not yet understanding my role but absorbing each detail of Matthew's past as she revealed it to me.

"Everything was just dandy until the war. Well, I say dandy – Henry had come along by then and he grew so well – *like a field of dreams*, my papa would say – but I noticed Matthew was somehow not the same as other men, always working through mealtimes. He didn't need much sleep and looked as good as he did when we married and I didn't mind *that*.

But when he came back from the war, he hadn't changed, not one little bit, and that was real confusin', because all the other wives, their husbands came back and they were wounded in their heads or their bodies – sometimes both – and they would talk about how difficult it was for them. But Matthew, he carried on as if nothing had happened, except for Jack – now that took him *bad*."

"In what way?" I asked, curiosity getting the better of me.

"Jack was killed in Italy in 1944. It hit us all hard, my mama and papa especially. But Matthew, he found it *real* difficult to get over."

"Why – did he ever say?"

"Not really, but he couldn't save him when Jack was brought into the field hospital and he couldn't forgive himself that, you know? I think that's why he keeps me alive when I should have died in the accident. I should have died times over but he has always brought me back. Sometimes I think that he does it because he can't abide losing anybody else." She smiled sadly. Somewhere nearby, a clock struck eleven with a melodic *ting*. "I saw what you meant to Matthew when that man attacked you. And then you left, and he was nearly beside himself because he thought he had lost you." I frowned involuntarily, wondering how much Ellen knew about me. She must have guessed my thoughts because she continued. "Matthew told me he had met you. He's not good at keeping secrets – they eat him up inside and I can always tell – so he has always been honest with me, though I expect he still keeps things from me – dark things – from his past." She eyed me quizzically and I kept my face blank.

"*When* did you know about me?" I asked quietly.

"Right off, before he even knew it himself. And when I asked him who you were, he seemed surprised at first, as if it hadn't occurred to him. But then he knew and I could see it in every look, every word – he just went right on and lit up whenever he spoke of you. He tried not to of course, but it just shone out of him. I was dead envious. I don't remember him ever doin' that for me and I wanted to know what it was you had that I didn't – when I was your age and younger, that is. At first I thought that he might leave me, abandon me, even though I have said to him time and again over the years, '*Matthew, if you find someone else, I'll give you a divorce and you can be free of me.*'"

I looked at her squarely. "He would never do that to you."

"I know, I know, but what can I give him now that he has you?" Her eyes travelled over my face and my hair, noting my clothes and the youthful suppleness of my body when I crossed my ankles under my chair. Her glance then fell on my earrings, and I reached for them self-consciously. She looked away.

I broke the awkward moment. "I don't think Matthew sees it that way. You are his wife and… I am not."

"That is true." I thought I perceived a note of triumph. She sighed and closed her eyes and, for a moment, it seemed she slept.

I looked around the room. Despite the medical equipment to one side, it appeared more like an elegant drawing room, expensively furnished and beautifully maintained.

I became aware that Ellen had opened her eyes and now analysed me openly.

"Matthew says that you study history."

"Yes."

"And you work at the college. You must be clever to get a job there. Matthew is very intelligent, you know."

I wondered where this might lead. "Yes, I know."

"I didn't go to college; it wasn't expected back then. My parents thought that I would get married and make a home and I did…" She paused. "I wouldn't have chosen a life like the one I had with Matthew. If I had known about him before we married, perhaps I wouldn't have. I never wanted anything much out of my life but a good husband, a family – and I had that – but I found it hard sometimes, the way we had to live. And when Matthew didn't get any older-looking and we had to move on and lie about who we were – who *I* was, and Henry too – that near broke my heart. But I had to choose and I did. I stuck it out and I'm glad that I did now, despite all this…" She moved her head from side to side, her body staying lifeless and still. "Tell me about your folks, honey, and where you come from."

I gave her an outline of my family, and all the time she watched and listened, summing me up from the short life I'd had.

"My papa would say Matthew's family tree was short of a few branches. Matthew didn't talk much about his parents; he said they died sometime before we met," Ellen stated, obviously fishing to see if I knew more.

"I believe so, yes," I hedged.

"You sound like him a little. My mama always used to say how he was an English gentleman in disguise, and he would laugh and say that he had better stop reading Austen. I always remember that because it reminded me of Texas – you know, Austin, Texas?"

"Yes, I've heard of it."

"I read one of her books but it didn't interest me that much, and I had Henry to cook for – he was always hungry, he and his friends – and I would rather be reading recipes than reading books. Do you like to cook, honey? I loved to cook; that's what I miss most."

Food again, always food.

"I'm afraid I'm a lousy cook."

A little look of satisfaction crossed the old woman's face, just a fleeting glance, before it vanished. "No matter, honey, Matthew was never interested in food anyway, more's the pity." She appeared a little weary and she coughed gently.

"Can I get him for you?" I asked, trying to imagine what I would do for Nanna in similar circumstances.

Ellen smiled at me for the first time. "Now there's a kindness. No, honey, Eli will be here in a minute to fix these damn lines and you'll be wanting something to eat yourself."

I had so many questions, but time was stolen from me by her frailty and great age.

"Ellen, I know that this might sound impertinent, but I'm concerned about Maggie. I'm worried that because of me, she could do something that will upset Matthew – or even worse. I think she mi…" I stopped abruptly as the door opened and Eli came in looking efficient.

"Don't you ever knock?" the old woman said in a tone that would have had me quail.

Eli brushed her remark aside with a cheery grin. "And what might you be doing that I should need to knock? Now, Miss Emma, Mr Matthew asks if you would like to join him for lunch. I'll take you to him, if you would like?"

I stood up, recognizing the first signs of hunger, but reluctant to leave with so many unanswered questions. I turned to Ellen, ready to speak, but she spoke first.

"Go along now and get something to eat, but I'll expect you back later – I haven't finished with you yet." We exchanged the briefest of looks and I followed Eli.

"Don't you go doin' anything I wouldn't when I'm gone, now," he said, as he reached the door.

The delicate invalid snorted defiantly. "And what might that be, I ask you? Chance would be a good thing."

Matthew waited for me in a small dining room; we were the only ones there at present. He stood up as we approached, his face more pensive than he probably intended me to see.

"Thank you, Eli." Then to me. "How did that go?"

Eli answered before I could. "I half thought I'd find a pile of bones and the old lady still chewin' when I went in, but they were gettin' on just fine. I think your grandmother really likes Miss Emma."

Matthew relaxed a little. "Good."

"But I think that there's still a way to go," I said. "Ellen wondered if I could go back after lunch. There are things we would like to discuss." His forehead rumpled slightly, but he nodded.

Eli chirped, "Don't worry, Mr Matthew, I'll make sure Miss Ellen's good and fed so she'll not be a bother." Matthew smiled tightly in response and I could tell he wanted to ask me what happened, but Eli remained within earshot.

"I'm starving," I said, sitting down at the table nearest to me.

Eli took the hint and rambled back the way we had come, his broad shoulders almost filling the corridor as he went.

Matthew sat down with me. "So?"

"It's fine – we're fine – but as I said, we haven't quite finished and I promised I would go back after lunch."

He sat back in his chair, still frowning. "Yes, of course." He hesitated. "So there's nothing you want to ask me?"

I thought about it. "Not yet, no, but I'm sure there will be. Did you see Dr DaCruz?"

"No, he wasn't available. All right, be mysterious if you wish. I'll get it out of you later."

I smiled sweetly. "Is that a promise?"

"You know me and my promises…"

I laughed and picked up the menu.

After lunch – my lunch, that is – I begged Matthew for some time outside. For all the elegance of the place I couldn't take the heat, and I longed to feel the raw cut of the cold air.

The snow lay too deep in the gardens, and we ended up walking around the exterior of the big house where the recent snow had been cleared to leave a gritty path. I asked him how many residents there were in total.

"Six at any one time, including Ellen. They come and go, of course." He didn't need to elaborate, and he directed a look over the side of the house we were passing. I recognized the bay window of Ellen's room and I wondered if she could see us walking together.

"Ellen told me that she didn't know about you when you married; she found it quite difficult at first." Matthew kicked a lump of ice out of my way without commenting. I went on. "She thinks we sound similar. Her mother thought you were an English gentleman in disguise."

"I remember. I had to work on my American accent."

We neared the corner towards the back of the house where the bins and utility area cluttered around the fire escape. A young woman, startled by our sudden appearance, hurriedly stubbed out her cigarette and went back inside, leaving a fug of tobacco smoke behind her.

"Ellen also said something about her brother – Jack."

Matthew halted, bringing me to a stop with him. "What about him?"

"That's what I was going to ask you. What about him?"

"He died. I tried to save him, but I couldn't. That's it."

By the way he glowered at the large metal bin near the back door, there was more to tell. I waited. "I don't like losing the people I love, Emma, you know that. We were like brothers, the nearest I had to a close friend since… well, almost since Nathaniel. I was with him when he died, but if I had been there sooner I might have saved him." He scowled at the bin and kicked it.

"What happened?"

A member of staff in an apron came out to investigate the noise. Matthew grabbed my arm and walked us briskly on, leaving the man to still the reverberating bin.

"I was operating on another soldier when they brought Jack in. I couldn't leave the boy on the operating table – it was the height of the Italian campaign and casualties were heavy – there weren't enough of us and we were pretty stretched. I had to make a choice. When I reached Jack, he'd already lost too much blood; there was nothing I could do."

I skidded on a patch of ice and Matthew steadied me.

"You weren't the only doctor there, were you? You weren't the only person responsible."

"You don't understand, Emma. I was the only one who had a chance of saving him. I was his friend and I didn't save him – I didn't even try."

"What do you mean, you didn't *try*?"

He shook his head angrily. "Nothing. I didn't mean anything by it. I couldn't save him, that's all."

I wrenched my hand out of his. "You're right, Matthew, I don't understand. You're the only one holding you responsible; isn't it time you stopped beating yourself up over it?" I hated to see him get upset over something that had been beyond his control, and I probably sounded less sympathetic than I meant to.

"Maybe." He hunched his shoulders and crammed his hands in his pockets without looking at me.

We had circumnavigated the building and reached the car park.

"Look, Matthew, Ellen has spent her life without getting the full picture from you, and I won't do the same. When it comes to things that affect you so fundamentally, I need to know *everything* that's happened. It's not fair to expect me to accept the holes in your life – I need to know. No more secrets, no more lies, remember?" He continued working at a spot of loosened ice with the toe of his shoe without looking at me. "*Matthew…!*"

"Yes, all right, Emma, all right, I heard you," he snapped. I all but stamped the frozen ground in frustration. "I heard you," he said more reasonably, holding out his hand to me in reconciliation. When I didn't take it, he didn't let his hand drop. "You're right, I know you are, it's just…" I put both my hands stubbornly behind my back. He lowered his arm. "You are right, there is no room for secrets between us, but I have spent a lifetime hiding who I am, what I am – even from those I love most – and it has become a habit. I won't – *can't* – change overnight, Emma. I need your help."

He must have known I couldn't resist such an appeal and saw that he had persuaded me, because he reached around my back and unhooked my hands without opposition, and brought them both to his lips, holding them there while I melted inside for him.

"Jack," I reminded, not so beguiled that I forgot my question.

He kissed my hands once more, still holding them tightly in his own. Despite the cold, the midday sun had some warmth to it. He raised his face, his eyes open, absorbing the full force without blinking. After what seemed like a long minute, he looked at me again.

"Over a number of years, I toyed with the idea that I might use what benefits I manifested to help others. Initially, I attempted using my blood, hoping it might convey some of the advantages of my longevity." He grimaced. "It didn't. More recently, and as my own knowledge has developed in light of scientific advances, I tried other avenues, including using my own stem cells, and gene therapy. But when it came to Jack back then, I had few options. I couldn't bring myself to intervene – I froze."

"You mean, you've tried things before – on people?"

"On animals, mostly, but on humans also, yes." He tensed, sensing disquiet in me as it flowed through my hands and into his.

I breathed evenly, keeping my tone non-judgmental. "And did you have any success with your… experiments?" A solitary cloud drifted across the sun, and Matthew's face fell into shadow.

"No."

The wind on my back blew cold; I shivered. I heard the crunch of feet on the gravel behind me and turned. Dr DaCruz's skin appeared sallow in the bright sunshine.

"Dr Lynes, if it's convenient, can I have that word with you now, please?"

"I'm going in to see Ellen," I told Matthew. He nodded, and I left the two men standing in the ice-bright sun.

Ellen looked perkier when I rejoined her. She had more colour in her cheeks and her eyes were clear and pin-sharp again. Eli made busy in the corner of the room with some monitors. He looked over as I came in and beamed at me.

"I trust you and my grandson had a good lunch?" Ellen asked with a glitter in her eye.

"Thank you, I did," I said, keeping a straight face. "I trust you did too?"

She gave a short rapport of a laugh. "Whatever they feed me through these tubes, it keeps me alive, if not quite kicking. Eli, go get your lunch; Emma will look after me."

Eli lumbered over to us. "If you need anything, Miss Emma, you just push this button and I'll come quicker than maybe."

"Perhaps I'll just up and die and solve all our problems before you get back, Eli Coots," she said, looking sideways at me. I narrowed my eyes at her.

He waggled a finger. "Now don't you go doin' any such thing. We still got that bet on and I aim to win it."

Ellen addressed me. "The old fool thinks I'm going to live till next Christmas just so he can fill his pockets with his winnings, but he's got another thing coming if he thinks I'm going to let him win. I *never* lose a bet."

Eli's normally jovial face became serious. "I won't have you dying on my watch, not if Mr Matthew and I has anything to do with it."

Ellen closed her eyes and the subject. "All right, all right, Eli, you go along now. I'll still be alive when you get back." As the door closed behind him, Ellen's eyes flicked open. "Now what's this you were saying about my granddaughter?"

I outlined my fears about Maggie's instability and the animosity she demonstrated against me, taking care to emphasize my concern for Matthew's well-being, rather than my own.

"I blame her mother," she said, finally. "I didn't like her when Henry brought her home like some stray wild thing.

Monica was good to look at all right, and clever – too clever – but untamed, and she only thought of herself. Headstrong too – she never listened to anything anyone had to say. Neither Matthew nor I liked her much, but Henry was dead set on her, and young – not yet twenty – and she scheming. She smelled money and she wasn't going to let it go even if it destroyed everything and everybody she was supposed to love." The sun had migrated to the other side of the building and no longer shone through the bay window. Already lower in the sky, it cast long shadows on the lawn of snow.

"But I blame myself too. If I hadn't been so damn angry with her for taking the girls to those doctors, if I had just shut the hell up and let her drive, perhaps we wouldn't have crashed." The old woman's chin quivered and I put my hand on hers where it rested on the arm of the wheelchair. She looked down at it, slightly confused, and I remembered that she couldn't feel it. "Thank you for the thought, honey. Sometimes I recall that day better than yesterday, and I wish I did something different, and then, perhaps... No matter; if wishes were horses, beggars would ride. It was Maggie who started crying, you see, and Monica shouted at her. Little Ellen told her mama that she was so cruel, and Monica turned in her seat and hit her. And then we skidded and crashed. My little Ellen..." she whispered, her eyes filling with tears.

"Please, don't talk about it if it upsets you," I pleaded, feeling her sorrow.

She looked at me sadly. "You need to know, honey. You're not just taking on my husband, you're taking my family as well – the good and the bad."

In saying so I also recognized, with a lurch, that she had accepted me as her successor and bequeathed me her husband and family.

"Maggie was always a headstrong little girl, just like her mama. When she loves she loves a lot, but when she hates, there is no force on this blessed earth that will stop her, except herself. She hates her mother with a vengeance, you can be sure of that, but she also loves her granddaddy, and I don't think you need worry yourself on that score too much. But *you* now, if she has taken a dislike to you, only she can change that and it's best to keep out of her way until she does. She has a wicked temper on her. I was more of a mama to her, you see, and she won't like you takin' my place even if Matthew wishes it. There now, it looks like you've been rode hard and put away wet. You're not to worry, honey, Maggie's not so like her mama in all ways. She has a heart and she loves her family even if she doesn't show it. She won't do anything to hurt them."

I noted wryly that Ellen didn't say, "*you*", just "*them*".

"Do you know what happened to Monica?"

"I neither know nor care. She could be rotting in hell for all I know and that'd be the best place for her. I asked Matthew once, but he didn't want to talk about it and he said that she'd "*gone away*", whatever that might mean. We never did hear from her again, so she's probably dead." She said the final word with relish and I gained the impression that she would have liked to have pulled the plug on her daughter-in-law's life, given half a chance.

"Emma, honey, I can see you're not like that brazen buffalo chip and you have more about you than Jeannie ever did. I can see why Matthew likes you, and were I sixty years younger and had the use of this body, I would have fought you to the death to keep you away from him. But it seems that he has another life ahead of him and I don't want him to spend it alone, and you don't seem to mind him being the way he is, and he loves you, so…" She paused to catch her breath.

"So you look after him, won't you? You need never fear him wandering, and he'll never hit you. He's good in *all* the ways a husband should be, if you get my drift, 'though I was never as inclined in that way as perhaps he would have liked me to be, though he never complained." She stopped, and suddenly looked anxious. "Has he ever said anything to you?"

I shook my head vehemently at the thought of Matthew and me discussing their sex life, considering we didn't have one of our own.

Ellen seemed relieved. "Well, perhaps that side of things interests you more than it did me?" I heard the question attached to that statement, but declined to satiate her curiosity, that being a step too far in the honesty stakes. "Well, now, that's none of my business any more, is it?" She chuckled throatily, a bubbling wheeze deep in her chest. "I asked about your family earlier and that was no idle chat. Matthew has been a good husband to me and a damn good father to our son, but living with him means sacrifices and sometimes they can be hard to make. Emma, my parents meant everything to me and I had to give them up if I wanted to stay with Henry and Matthew. There will come a time when you, too, might have to make that choice when you can't hide Matthew's differences any more."

"Did you never see your parents again once you'd left?" I asked.

"Sure I did, honey, when I buried them. You have to think long and hard over whether that is a sacrifice you are willing to make. I don't resent it now. Matthew had his reasons for not telling me, but you have to remember that when I married him, I didn't know what you do. I had to choose when I already had Henry to consider. You owe him nothing and you can walk away if you so wish."

"I owe him *everything*, and I have already made my choice; I won't go back on it now."

She nodded her head slowly, like one of those dogs you see behind the rear seats of cars. "That's good; you have strength. I thought as much. Now, I have something to ask of *you*." She took a series of shallow breaths and I waited. "I am dying, Emma. Yes, I know that I have been cheating death for so long and the good Lord knows I have begged and *begged* Matthew to let me go so many times over these years. And if he had, we wouldn't be talking like this right now, and he would be a free man. Anyhow, it won't be so very long now and you can have him to yourself…" I started to protest, but Ellen just smiled and rocked her head. "I don't doubt the goodness of your heart, honey, but you and I both know that while I'm alive Matthew is torn between us and I don't want that for any of us. My time is near and I have made Charles *promise* me that he won't tell Matthew because I don't want to be saved any more. I want to die and be at peace, if any is coming my way. I am content with what I have been given, and knowing now that Matthew has someone he can share his life with – someone who understands him – makes it the easier to leave."

I might have been forgiven for rejoicing, but I no longer considered Ellen as a collection of disembodied labels: wife, mother, quadriplegic – barrier to my own fulfilment and happiness – but a vibrant personality who, for all the slow erosion of her life, remained little changed from when Matthew married her.

"What is it that you want me to do?"

"I want…" Ellen began, slowly at first, "… I want you to stop Matthew from resuscitating me."

"How can I do that?" I asked, horrified.

"Do whatever you have to, but keep him away until it's too late, until I'm dead and you are sure of it. Lie to him, sabotage his car – anything but *anything* to stop him from reaching me in time."

"I can't do that, it's against everything he believes. He would never forgive himself."

"Honey, I've got to die *sometime*." For all her infirmity I perceived granite in her blood. "He's got to let me go and you're the only person who understands what this means to me; I know it, I can see it in your eyes. I can't ask anyone else to do this, my family is too closely tied up in it and they won't act against Matthew's will. And Eli – God bless him – he would cross the Red Sea if he could to save me. We've been friends far too long to ask this of him. But you understand, Emma. You see things differently to most folks, don't you?"

I found I had been concentrating on the second hand of my watch. Now I looked up. "Yes," I murmured.

"Then you will do this one thing for me?" she asked, but too eagerly. She didn't say it, but she must have realized that she might as well have asked me to switch off her life-support machine there and then. It wasn't as simple as she made it sound. Not only did I have Matthew to consider – and Heaven only knows what would happen if he discovered I had been complicit in her death, because that is how he would see it – but I would also have to square it with my own conscience. She had correctly deduced that I would not wish her to be tied to a life of suffering, that I viewed death as the next step in life, not an end to life itself. Yet I remembered how devastated I felt when Matthew told me that Nanna neared death, and how only time and reflection had allowed me to see it from her point of view. Could he not tell how close Ellen was to the end of her days, and would it not help him if he did? The delicate chime of the nearby clock beat out the hour, reminding me of the lateness of it. Ellen hadn't told Matthew because she feared he would try to save her, as he had always done before. She asked me knowing that, aside from everything, I had a vested interest in her death.

Which was why I couldn't do it.

"Well, honey?" Uncertainty quavered in the old woman's voice for the first time.

"No – I'm sorry, Ellen, I can't."

Her face fell. A look of panic, followed in quick succession by disbelief, disappointment, anger, then panic again. She had been relying on me. It explained why she wanted to meet me in the first place. She planned to ask all along.

"Ellen, I *can't* do as you ask because of what it might do to Matthew, and I *won't* do it because it is tantamount to euthanasia. But I can do this: I will relay your wishes as you have described them to me. If the opportunity arises, I will tell Matthew that this is what you want. I won't try to hide anything from him though; I won't do anything that might give him cause for regret."

The slight tremble that had set up in her lower lip had ceased as I spoke and now she viewed me sharply. "You might find yourself in a similar situation one day, Emma, when *your* successor sits in front of you and you are in no position to rule yourself. Then what would you do if you were faced with this living *death*? What would you do in my stead?"

I didn't rush to answer and only did so after a degree of thought. "I would probably do what you have done, Ellen, and hope that the girl makes a different decision and that she can live with the consequences of it because I wouldn't have to."

Only the soft rasp of her breath breached the silence that followed. Finally, she spoke. "Well, well, there's more gut and gumption to you than I would have thought. Fancy denying an old woman her last wish." And to my surprise, Ellen laughed softly, phlegm rattling in her throat. "I will bide my time till death defeats us both, and I go my way and Matthew goes his."

"I'm sorry, Ellen," I said, and meant it. Her eyes shut. Her deeply folded face had paled and become drawn with all the effort she had poured into the conversation, and I felt an overwhelming urge to comfort her.

"I know you are, honey, but I had to try; you were my last hope." Her eyes fluttered open again. "There now, call my husband for me, will you? I'm feeling a little tired."

I rose to do as she asked but, as I did so, she suddenly said, in a voice stronger than she had used all afternoon, "This is the last time we shall meet, Emma. The next will be at my grave. Look after him; he's worth the sacrifices you will surely have to make." Her voice faltered and her eyes closed again and for a moment I thought that she had stopped breathing. Then I saw the steady rhythm of her chest as she inhaled, small but distinct, and I breathed again also.

"Goodbye, Ellen," I said softly, and went to find Matthew.

11

A Matter of Time

We were both quiet on the way home as the sun set. Amber clouds lit the horizon with the promise of more snow. When I chanced to catch his eye, Matthew did not return the look, his expression indecipherable.

That night he slipped from my bed when he thought I slept, and went downstairs. Through the thickness of the walls I heard a faint *click* as the door of his study closed behind him.

I was still alone when I woke and, although he had said nothing untoward the evening before, a deep unease settled over me when he didn't appear after breakfast. I knocked on his study door but received no answer, and poked my head around the frame to check. The first flakes of snow beat soundlessly against the window and the room felt cold. I went instead to the joining door between the Barn and the main house, hoping Henry would know where Matthew had gone.

Pat looked up from a delicate piece of patchwork she was assembling on the family table, her eyes refocusing over the tops of her glasses.

"Henry and Matthew are at the lab this morning. Didn't Matthew tell you he was going?"

"I was asleep – he probably didn't want to wake me. It doesn't matter, Pat. Thanks."

Feeling forlorn, I declined her offer of a cup of tea, and went back to my bedroom, but it, too, felt chill and I sat on the edge of my bed swinging my feet, malcontent. I should have been elated: Ellen was dying, but I found no joy in her imminent death, no more than I did in Nanna's.

My heel caught against something and I swung off and bent down to peer underneath the high bed frame. My travel bag resided where I had left it and, unzipping it, I pulled from its depths the matt black book concealed there. I held it in my hand, deciding what to do with it and thinking murderous thoughts about the giver. It wasn't a hard choice and at least it offered an antidote to boredom. Tucking the book under my arm, I sought the solace of Matthew's study.

The fire bit eagerly into the wood as it caught the dry timber, bleeding warmth into the room. Outside, snow fell more heavily, beating frantic time to the Prokofiev I had selected as if orchestrated for it. I crammed my legs in the chair by the fire and opened the cat-black book wishing I had more self-discipline to resist its dubious appeal.

Staahl's distorted view of the world became clear from the way he wrote. He had unstitched texts from the last six centuries, many of which were familiar to me, and imposed upon them a warped logic that echoed the demons of his mind. I recognized the vein of corrupted thoughts he whispered to me that night in the atrium as he stole my blood. I shuddered, threw the book on the floor in disgust and in rejection of everything he stood for, and chewed disconsolately on my cross.

A sudden draught lifted the soft hair at the nape of my neck and my skin prickled.

"I thought I might find you in his study." Maggie stood in the open doorway, her severe mode of dress in stark contrast with the shocking pallor of her skin. She came into the room when I didn't respond, quietly shutting the door behind her. She leaned against the frame. "My grandfather isn't here."

"I know," I said, surly at her for pointing it out and wondering how she could make such a simple statement sound so sinister. Her long-fingered hand slowly stroked the wood of the panelling.

"You like being in here, don't you? It's where you are closest to him, surrounded by his things. Do you feel more in control of him when you're here? Or do you gain gratification from being near to the objects he has touched?"

Both rattled and irritated by her intrusive insinuations, I had no desire to be drawn into a conversation. "I'm not in the mood to be psychoanalysed by you, Maggie. I'm not one of your patients."

She walked over to the mantelpiece and stared appreciatively at a statue of a stallion made of polished bronze, so lifelike I could almost see its flanks flinch under her fingers as she ran her hand along its back. "You have a strained relationship with your father, don't you? I wonder whether it has made forming relationships with men more difficult. Or do you find older men more attractive? Perhaps you find their greater experience reassuring – seek security in their dominance. Do you like being dominated, Dr D'Eresby?"

"I've had enough of this," I snarled, standing abruptly to leave the room. I had almost reached the door when she called after me.

"Have you noticed that my grandfather doesn't keep any clocks in the house? Not one. *Tick-tock, tick-tock,* no *clock.* Would you like to know *why?*" I stopped and she saw my quickening interest. "Yes, of course you would. He doesn't keep clocks because he doesn't want to mark the passing of time. The only timepiece he has is the watch his wife gave him on their wedding day. You must have seen it; he always wears it to remind him of her. He cannot bear to be parted from her, even now, even after so much *time*." She cocked her head on one side. "What an interesting choice of music: discordant, so ill at ease with itself. How apt for someone who has never really belonged."

Blast the woman – whom did she mean? Matthew, me – or did she refer to someone else? She listened seconds longer then picked up one of a matching pair of simple jade-green vases of great antiquity that sat at either end of the mantelshelf. It crossed my mind that she would drop it and blame the breakage on me, but she put it back carefully where it belonged.

"My grandfather has such exquisite taste in the objects with which he surrounds himself. Do *you* like them? Do you touch them, caress them, when you are alone? You can tell me, I won't be shocked. There is nothing I haven't heard over the years and I *promise* I won't say a word." She held an elongated finger to her lips, her voice silky like a scarf being drawn too tight around a throat.

I remembered what Ellen had said about her embedded hatred and saw the truth of it. "Is there a point to any of this, Maggie?"

Her movements measured, almost stately, she bent swiftly to the floor and retrieved the book I had flung there. "You seem to have dropped your book. What a shame. I hoped you might find it stimulating – such an interesting subject by a *fascinating* man." Her hand rested ghost-like against the cover and she tapped her fingers, once. "Of course, he told me all about you."

I felt my eyes widen involuntarily. She knew him – she *knew* Staahl. My guts cramped, leaving me leaden inside.

Maggie's face cracked into a hard smile. "Ah, I see that you understand now," she said softly. "It took you a little longer than I expected. A little slow on the uptake, aren't you? Professor Staahl and I have had many conversations over the last few months since he became my patient. I was really quite pleased when his case was assigned to me. It gave me the opportunity to get to know you better through him, to have some insight into why you are pursuing my grandfather." An edge had crept into her voice, slicing through the numb fug her words had woven. "Professor Staahl has been surprisingly enlightening, with the sort of clarity the delusional often have. He has a quite… unique mind, but then you already know that, don't you?"

My throat contracted into a tight band and, through teeth clenched in an attempt to keep calm, I forced out words that I had hoped I would never have to say again.

"What do you want?"

Carefully placing the book on the chair as if it were an object of great value, she wandered past me towards Matthew's desk at the far end of the room. She trailed her fingers over the surface of the cittern as she passed, the strings resonating eerily long after she reached his desk, touching lightly first one photograph frame, then another, until her hand rested on the picture of Ellen and Henry. She picked it up, smiling fondly. "Ellen is like a mother to me," she said, as if I cared at that moment. "She is like my mother should have been."

"What do you *want*, Maggie?" I asked again, frustration and unease vying for domination.

She continued as if she hadn't heard me. "When the crash took my sister, it took my mothers as well – both of them – my good mother and my bad mother. Monica left me. She didn't want to be with me because I was bad and I caused the crash. I killed my sister and she couldn't stand being near me any more." She expressed no sadness, more an acceptance of her culpability.

"You didn't cause the accident. She didn't leave because of you. You were only a little girl and not responsible for *any* of it."

Without warning, her arch control dissolved into a rictus of spite. "What do *you* know? You worm your way into our lives where you don't belong. You insinuate yourself between my grandfather and his wife. You are *nothing* to him, don't you understand? He will always love my grandmother, he will always save her. No one wants *you* here." Touching the photograph of Ellen, as if she could conjure her from the surface of the print, she became completely calm again. "When you are gone, he will love her again and everything will be as it was."

I faced her squarely with more bravado than I felt. "I'm not going anywhere, Maggie. I'm sorry if you find that difficult to accept, but I didn't know that Ellen was still alive when I met Matthew, and I have no intention of coming between them now. He loves Ellen and he won't abandon her, but nor will I leave Matthew. I will wait for him, whether you accept that or not."

She replaced the photograph on the desk. "What do you want from him? His money? I don't expect you earn much and he is *very* wealthy. What did you plan? To hook him before somebody else does, or… is it something else?"

"I don't know what you're talking about."

She picked up the letter-opener and her eyes followed her thumb as she ran it down the silver edge. "*Monsters,*" she hissed. "*Outcasts. Torture.* Kort told me all about your research; it's what he found so inviting about you. It is why he feels such an affinity with you – like minds, like *tastes*. Is that why you are here, so that you can indulge your obsession through my grandfather's deviation from the norm?"

I looked at her in horror. "What have you said to Staahl, Maggie? What have you told him about Matthew?"

A sneer distorted her mouth and she drew herself upright until she stood haughty and aloof above me. "Told him? About my grandfather? What sort of *fool* do you take me for? I might be surrounded by the insane, but don't imagine for one moment that I am deceived by their madness any more than I am taken in by *you*. Staahl saw through your façade – he knew what you wanted, the games you were playing that night. He went too far of course, but that is to be expected of a man of his predilections. I understand *why* you need my grandfather – you need him to justify your actions that night, that much is clear. What I don't understand is how you've deluded him into believing you care about him…"

My temper flared with the obscenity of her misrepresentation, my voice rising with fury. "Is that what Staahl told you? And you believed him? Or is it because that's what you *want* to believe because you can't possibly acknowledge that Matthew loves me for any other reason than he does?" A sudden gust of wind catapulted snow against the windows, rattling ice like impatient claws on the glass.

"*No!*" Her voice rose shrill, contempt twisting words as they came slewing from her mouth, following the bitter corkscrew of her mind. "He only loves Ellen. There will never be anyone else, only her."

"For goodness' sake, Maggie, Ellen's an old woman and she will die one day – she has to. She can't live forever."

She raised the letter-opener like a dagger and I hastily backed away. "No!" she screeched. "No – he'll save her, he always saves her. There's no room for *you* here. You're an aberration, a scheming *whore*. He will see you for wh…" The door slammed open, cutting her short.

"What's going on?" Matthew's voice, sharp with authority, broke through her incoherent ramblings. Snow fell from his jacket as he rapidly placed himself between us.

Maggie pointed the letter-opener at me, shaking uncontrollably. "*She's* stealing Ellen's place. She's not what she seems – he says so. He's told me, he knows her. He knows what she wants."

Matthew lowered his voice, dampening her hysteria. "Nobody has taken Ellen's place, Maggie. Everything is fine – Ellen's fine."

Standing behind Matthew in the doorway, Henry's unease stretched across his face. He moved unobtrusively until he was by Maggie's side and, putting his hand on her arm, reached for the knife.

She wrenched roughly away and took a pace forward, glaring at me around Matthew. "Why did you let her come? Why didn't you stop her? Tell her to go away and then Ellen can come back."

Matthew spoke to me without taking his eyes from her. "How long has she been like this?"

"About twenty minutes. She's ill, Matthew, she needs help."

Maggie's lips pulled into a sneer. "She's *ill*; she needs *help*," she mimicked, like the spiteful mocking of a teenage girl.

Henry took her by the elbow. "Come with me, love, you need to rest."

She threw his hand off with more force than he obviously expected, jabbing the letter-opener in my direction. "*Get rid of her!*"

"Margaret!" She halted and looked for the first time at her grandfather directly.

"Margaret, Ellen is dying; she will not come back."

I caught my breath – so he knew. Ellen must have decided to tell him after all, and that explained why he had been so quiet on the way back from Valmont.

Maggie's face crumpled and a low moan escaped from between her lips, becoming a denial. "No-o, no, no, *no*." She fell against Matthew and became a little girl again. "You can save her – say you will save her."

He removed the knife from her now limp hand, and held her upright as she threatened to collapse. "I can't help her any more, Maggie. Ellen has come to the end of her life; you have to let her go." I couldn't see Matthew's face, but I could hear the resignation in his voice.

Henry took her weight from him, fraught, deeply drawn lines around his eyes betraying the shock he felt as his daughter plummeted towards despair.

"I'll take you to see Ellen when you've had a rest, when the snow's stopped. She'd like to see you." He steered her in a line towards the door, and she appeared shrunken now that the anger had gone, a pitiful shade of what she had been.

Matthew dragged a hand across his face and put the letter-opener back on the desk where it belonged.

"What will happen to her?" I asked.

"She didn't hurt you?"

"No, I'm fine. What will happen to her, Matthew?"

"Henry will sedate her, then we'll see how she is once she's had a rest. She's been overworking recently." He didn't say what I knew he must be thinking: that my presence in the house had pushed her beyond the boundary of wisdom into the emotional wilderness where she now wandered.

"I'm sorry."

"It isn't your fault, Emma. She's been unstable for a long time but she has always refused help. Perhaps this is the best thing that could have happened, if it enables her to get what she needs." He spoke softly. "Are you sure you're all right?"

"I'm fine," I said again, a little shakily this time, "and I meant I'm sorry that this has happened to you and to Henry – to all the family – it's traumatic. You know about Ellen?"

"Yes, Charles DaCruz told me. How did you find out?"

"Ellen told me yesterday, but she didn't want you to know and Dr DaCruz was *not* supposed to have told you either."

He shook his head, drops of water from the melted snow in his hair catching the light. "He didn't in so many words. He wanted me to know that she has myocardiopathy. It's a disorder of the heart muscle and it's untreatable – he didn't need to tell me she's dying. Why did she tell you and not me?"

"Ellen thinks that you will try to save her again and she doesn't want that – she wants to die."

"Oh." He remained quiet for a second. "There's nothing I can do to help her; I have to let her go as well. I'm not sure how easy it's going to be, not after all this time." He looked so sad at this thing that lay beyond his control, after so many years of cheating death.

I laid my hand on his forearm, feeling the tension working the muscles under his clothes. "I don't think it can be. Even when death's expected it still comes as a shock; we just have to get through it somehow."

"We?"

"I know I've only met her once and I'm not trying to say that her death will mean very much to me in emotional terms, but it will to you and to your family, and I wasn't going to let you go through that alone. Unless you'd rather?" I was careful to let it sound as if I wanted him to have a choice but, in reality, I didn't know what I would say if he said he'd rather grieve alone.

He put his hand over mine. "Would it be selfish to want you with me?"

I leaned my face against his chest, and mildly chided him, "Where else would I want to be, silly?" And I felt him relax a little.

Resting his chin on the top of my head, he put his arms around me and rocked us. Suddenly, his body stiffened and he released me. "What the *hell's* this?" He snatched the black book from where it lay on the chair and held it up, his eyes igniting. "Did you get this?" I shook my head. "Did Maggie give it to you?" He didn't wait for an answer – he didn't need to, he saw it in my face. "What did she think she would achieve with this *filth*?" He hurled the book into the fire and the flames leapt greedily, the pages curling in the fierce heat. "Damn it to hell, if I had known…"

"Don't, Matthew, she's ill, and she's been talking to Staahl; he's one of her patients. Goodness knows what he's been filling her mind with."

"*Staahl*?" He swore again, stabbing a finger in the direction of the burning book. "I didn't *ever* want you to have to see anything like that, to be reminded of him, of what he did to you. And for my own granddaughter to flaunt it…" He ground his teeth and I cringed at the grating sound they made.

"You knew about the book?" I asked, disbelieving.

He hunched his shoulders. "That one? No, but ones like it – yes. I wanted to know the mind of a man who could have done such… things to you. His thoughts are perverted, distorted – they make my blood boil. I sometimes wish I had killed him…"

"No, you *don't*," I said firmly, my hands on his forearms. "That would have achieved nothing except trouble, and we wouldn't be here together now if you had. Did you know Staahl was Maggie's patient?"

He responded to my touch and began to calm, his tight shoulders easing. "It makes sense, I suppose. She's head of the psychiatric assessment unit at the hospital. She would normally have told me, so I assumed somebody else had taken on his case. She's never kept something like this from me before. What did she say to you?"

"Not much that made sense, but she repeated the same nonsense the detectives insinuated about me going to the atrium to meet Staahl, and that it was some kinky game that got out of hand."

"She should know better than to be taken in by a delusional obsessive."

The book was taking its time to burn. I willed the flames to hurry and do their job so that I didn't have to be reminded by its charcoalled carcass any more.

"Matthew, do you think she'll have said anything to Staahl about you?"

"I don't know. I'll see what I can find out when she's had a couple of days rest. Don't worry about it." But, by the concern etched into his face, I knew that – whatever he wanted me to believe – he did.

12

Some Semblance of Peace

A strange sort of peace fell on us over the next few days, as if learning of Ellen's imminent death sealed a bond between all the family. For me, there could be no pleasure in the knowledge that her death would release Matthew. Yet, now that the waiting was almost over, the full stop to the sentence of her life would bring with it a sense of fulfilment, a life brought full circle and to its natural conclusion. I knew Matthew yearned for such freedom for himself and that I would deny him his wish if I could, for dread of losing him.

Maggie emerged from her room bewildered and frightened, but sentient enough to understand the implications of what she had said and done. Between them, Henry and Matthew organized discreet assessment and treatment for her in a nearby private residential unit. There, she would be able to rest, and come to terms with her grandmother's impending death.

Matthew and I spent more time together, often in the study, where I could work with maintained concentration on the research paper I had started the previous term. In between times, we went out on the snowmobile across the brilliant snowfields and further, into the foothills of the mountains beyond the river. And finally, he persuaded me to drive his car.

I ran my eyes along the sleek bodywork, wondering how long it would survive my attempts to drive it. "Do I *have* to?" I groaned, as he held out his keys to me across the roof. He had not been in the least impressed by my reluctance to drive in a foreign country.

"No, not at all, especially if you don't want any independence and wish to be forever ferried around by everyone else like a tick on an elephant's back."

The image was gross so I blew a raspberry at him. "Cheers, thanks for that – boost my confidence, why don't you?" He grinned and threw me the keys over the top of the car.

The worst part was getting used to the acceleration of the powerful engine. It had a will of its own like a dominant dog, one touch of the accelerator sending it straining forward, dragging me terrified behind it. But it was fast, and I liked *fast*. Matthew maintained complete composure while I was behind the wheel; gradually his confidence in my ability to stay on the road calmed me, and I grew used to the feel of the car and began to enjoy driving it, feeling it respond to my commands.

We arrived back at the house in one piece.

"That wasn't so bad, was it?" Matthew said as I switched off the ignition.

"You can take that smug tone out of your voice, Matthew Lynes. You never know, I might have longed to be a tick in someone's flesh."

He swivelled in his seat, fastening me with a rascally look. "Is *that* the itch I'm always wanting to scratch? I did wonder."

After that I didn't protest if he suggested I drive, and he made no further reference to parasitic insects.

Matthew read next to me as we lay in his bed. I had just finished rereading *Crime and Punishment*, and was reflecting on Raskolnikov's acceptance of his fate as just retribution for his crimes. I closed the book and laid it on my stomach while I considered it, staring across the room at nothing in particular.

Matthew turned a page. "Have you remembered that we are expected at the New Year's Eve party at college tomorrow?"

"I hoped you'd forgotten about that. I can't say that the thought of it fills me with great joy. I suppose it's compulsory attendance?"

"It is, but it's not particularly formal so you don't have to sit and eat and behave yourself." He hesitated and glanced at me. "Are you worried about the attack in October?"

"A bit," I admitted. "I keep thinking about it the closer it gets to the beginning of term. Silly, really."

He closed his own book and put it down next to him. "Not in the least. When have you had the opportunity to come to terms with it?"

I thrummed my fingers, thinking of the weeks spent without him in Stamford, isolating myself in the bedroom of my childhood. I had avoided thinking about Staahl then; I had had better things to do. I shrugged dismissively. "I had plenty of time at home."

"Did you talk to anyone about it? What about your mother or your sister? Or the doctor you saw, the one you said who knew me?"

"No, I didn't want to talk about it, and it wasn't what was on my mind at the time, anyway… I just want to forget it."

"Hmm, I'm not convinced it'll be that easy. Still, for the purposes of tomorrow, there's nothing to worry about as I'm not letting you out of my sight."

"Does that mean we're going as a… couple?"

He rubbed his eyebrow. "Well, we are, aren't we?"

"It still feels weird. I mean, I find it odd because of Ellen. It feels like we're two-timing her, even though…" I stopped, not sure whether she had wanted him to know the tenet of our conversation.

"Even though…?" he prompted.

"She said that she wants you to be happy and that… well, to all intents and purposes, she is *bequeathing* you to me." I could feel a surge of heat to my face and I studied the end of the quilt where it rose in a mound over my feet. He startled me by laughing, shaking his head from side to side. He saw my bemused look and controlled himself in stages.

"Sorry," he apologized, "but that is so like my wife. Even from a distance she has always been able to exert a certain influence on the family." He laughed again. "And how did you react to her kind bequest, given she has absolutely no say in what you choose to do?"

"Um, well, I understood what it must be like for her to relinquish her husband to another woman, so, actually, I didn't mind her control as much as I might have done in different circumstances."

He sobered rapidly. "That's put me thoroughly in my place. That'll teach me to leave the two of you alone together. However," he added, 'I think that it answers your question."

I wrinkled my forehead. "Which was…? I've forgotten."

"We can count ourselves a couple and anyway, from a public point of view, I'm not married, so it won't appear untoward. Is that acceptable to you?"

"Definitely… sort of." I caught myself unawares by a yawn.

Matthew took my book from me and kissed my hair. "Well, *definitely… sort of* will have to do for now; it's time you had some sleep."

"I'm not tired." I yawned again. "Anyway, there's something I've been meaning to ask you for-*ever*." I rubbed my eyes.

"Can't it wait until tomorrow?"

I snuggled into his side and he pulled the covers over my shoulders, tucking the draughts out from around my back. "No."

He smiled softly, keeping his arm around me, strong and comforting. "Go on then, if you think you can keep awake long enough."

"Why *did* you become a doctor?"

"That's simple enough – I didn't want to initially. I went to Cambridge to read divinity, intending, I suppose, to ameliorate some of my uncle's influence, and it did, to an extent. But it posed more questions than it answered and, being a bit of a restless youth, I joined one of the bands that became the Eastern Association to train in arms…"

"Why?"

Matthew started to rub my back and I fought sleep to hear his reply. "Well, my father had no need of me at home to help run the estate, and with the degree of unrest in the region, it seemed like a good idea at the time." He started to draw a large circle on my back, spiralling smaller and smaller to a midpoint between my shoulder blades as he spoke. "Then I realized that I did no more than bide my time and that I needed to find something else that would bridge the gap I felt. I went back to Cambridge to take up the study of medicine and while there, met a man – a few years younger than me – who wasn't like anyone else I'd met from the College of Surgeons. He was quite radical in some of his ideas – a Parliamentarian – but more than that, he believed that medicine should be available for the common weal, not the prerogative of the chosen few in the college. And I agreed with him. Too much custom and prejudice surrounded the study of medicine and it proved a disincentive to research and new ideas. Most of all, it kept it cloistered from those who needed it most."

"And that mattered to you?"

"Yes!" he shot out, making me jump. "Yes, it did," he said more quietly. "I had found my calling, if you will, and a good friend in Culpeper, and so…"

"No," I said, stopping him mid-sentence and raising myself on one elbow. "You cannot keep doing that – mentioning a famous name and then carrying on as if nothing out of the ordinary has happened. You were friends with *Culpeper*?"

He looked sheepish, as well he might. "Yes, Nicholas and I were good friends. Can I continue?" I lay back down again, my head reeling from his latest revelation of a friendship with one of history's most celebrated herbalists.

"I completed my initial studies in medicine, but the war broke out and I rejoined the Parliamentary force. But my father's health began to fail and I went back home, and then… then we had that trouble with William."

I turned my head to look at him again. "That's one way of putting it, Matthew."

He smiled grimly. "Quite. Anyway, that put paid to my studies for a while, and then… Emma, will you *promise* that you won't overreact?"

Instantly on my guard, remembering his revelation at the cabin that his wife still lived which nearly put paid to any future together, I sat up. "Why, what else haven't you told me?"

"Before the incident with my uncle, I had been betrothed." He waited for me to detonate.

I pictured Mrs Seaton's animated mouse-like face telling my father and me the few known facts of Matthew's life in

Rutland as we sat in the dilapidated grandeur of her once-fine house. "Yes, I know – to a Harrington heiress." Even without looking I would have sensed his palpable relief.

He parted a strand of hair that had fallen over my eyes. "You know? You never said. We couldn't marry, not after what had happened to me and anyway, the rumours put paid to the match. I can't blame her father for breaking the engagement and I wasn't in any fit state to be a husband to her, but still…" I thought I could hear regret and I had to fight the wave of jealousy for this long-dead girl.

"Did you love her?"

A smile lifted his mouth. "Love her? She was pretty, young, rich, eminently marriageable – all told an excellent union for my family. What was there not to love?"

Frustration born of envy burst from me. "How should I know?" I fumed, exasperated. "I wasn't there."

"No," he said, musing as he stroked my bare foot closest to him. "You weren't. Now *that* would have been an interesting scenario."

I faced him, crammed together on the bed as we were, all tiredness evaporated. "Get to the point: did you or didn't you love her?"

"Does it matter now? After all these years and after everything you and I have been through in these last few months, does what happened between me and this girl have any bearing on our relationship now?"

I pulled the bed covers over my shoulders, leaving only my foot protruding. "I know it's stupid of me, but yes, it does matter because it's still part of you, however long ago it was."

He tilted his head on one side in the appealing way he had, regarding me with irises darkened by the dim light of the room. "I admit to having been fond of her, Emma, but I hadn't yet come to love her; I didn't know her well enough for that." His quiet reassurance rendered my thoughts irrational. "But she did partially influence me in my determination to follow medicine as a vocation."

"How so?"

He watched his own hand travel from my foot to my ankle, then just above, pushing the leg of my pyjamas up my calf, running his hand back down the front of my leg and repeating the action.

"I left home after all the trouble in the village, but before it reached a point where the authorities became involved. The rumours about me were considered to be idle gossip although it was gathering momentum, and it was only a matter of time before it grew out of hand. It caused my father distress and made it difficult for members of our household to come and go in the community without some comment or other being made about my oddity." His hand ceased its travels up and down my leg. "And then when some of the women started wearing mistletoe sprigs around their necks when they came to the house or even in church – can you believe it, in *church* – when I was there…" His eyebrows drew together.

"Matthew…" I leaned forward and tried to prise his fingers from where they dug into my ankle. He released me, mortified, staring at the red marks appearing on my pale skin. I put my hand over it, breaking through his field of vision. "No, it's fine. Tell me, what was it about the mistletoe? I don't understand the significance."

He took my hand away from my ankle, and gently covered the area with his own.

"Mistletoe: *it remedies witchcraft* – if you read Culpeper's thoughts on it in his *Herbal*. It reflects folklore. So you see, I had to leave before it went any further. You know what happened to people accused of witchcraft and sorcery – I don't need to spell it out." He winced as I smiled. "The pun was unintentional."

"Yes, but quite funny. What did that have to do with the Harringtons?"

"I left but I kept an eye on what was happening at home…"

"How?"

"Through Nathaniel – oh, you won't have found anything written in the journal. I swore him to an oath of secrecy, which he kept, and once my father died and Nathaniel had gone to the New World, I lost all my connections to home and I left for ever."

I wriggled impatiently. "The Harringtons?"

"Patience, my love, I'm getting to that. Lucie Harrington married my cousin – my aunt Elizabeth's eldest boy. Through Nathaniel I heard when she had children – two girls – and the ups and downs of the family. I know it sounds as if I used Nathaniel to spy, but it wasn't like that, it was more…"

"That you needed to keep in touch with reality. I understand," I finished.

"Yes, I thought you might. Well, anyway, there was a minor outbreak of pestilence and Lucie caught it. It took her two weeks to die a horrible, lonely death. She had isolated herself to protect her husband and children. I could do nothing for her, nor… nor for all the others I met who caught the plague, or who had ague, or were bitten by a snake or a mad dog. For them all, for the good that I *could* do, I became a doctor. For some salve for my own soul, I became a doctor. I knew I could kill effectively enough – it's so easy to take a life – but to heal, to give life where none could reasonably be expected, that's different, that's verging on miraculous."

"And do you include yourself in those who require healing?"

Matthew frowned fractionally. "You know I do, because I want to understand the process that caused *this*." He used his hands to indicate his body.

"So that you can find a *cure*…" I grouched.

"Emma, don't start," he warned.

"And then you will change, and then…"

"Emma, *leave* it." He leaned towards me.

"And then you won't be *you*, and you…"

He didn't let me finish, putting his hand over my mouth against my protestations and his other arm around my waist so that I couldn't writhe away. He rested his forehead against mine as I squeaked and wormed to get free, cross with him for restraining me, but more so for wanting to change who he was, and absolutely petrified for what that might mean.

"Emma… sweetheart…" He lowered his voice and I found I couldn't resist his balm, and gradually ceased struggling. "Why are you so frightened? Where is all this fear coming from?" He took his hand from my mouth and placed it against the side of my face instead, looking at me in a way that made me want to melt into him, to absorb him, so that he would never be free of me, forever bound molecule by molecule for the rest of time. How could I begin to put into words what he meant to me when the very thought of it engulfed me in feelings so intense that they threatened to break through my reserve at any moment? I felt tears, heated by the intensity of emotion, sting the corners of my eyes.

I took a ragged, deep breath. "I can't… *bear*… the thought of this world without you." Pulling away from him, I climbed off the bed to stalk to the other end of the room by the windows, willing myself to control the tightness in my throat that would give me away if I spoke.

"We've talked about this," he said, reasonably.

I nodded so that I didn't have to say anything, wrapping my arms about me more as a defensive measure against what I might do, or say, than against the chill air away from the fire. "I know," I managed after a moment. I turned my back on him and opened the shutters for something to do. The black blank glass reflected my pale image and behind me, across the room, the bed I had just left.

"I know I'm being selfish and I realize it's irrational. And I know that I'm not the one whose wife is dying…" I bit my lip, flapping my hands to regain control. "But in the same way that you find it hard to let Ellen go, I can't imagine time without you… agh, *drat* it, I can't explain what I *mean*," I erupted, punching the air in my frustration. I composed myself, my fists scrunched so hard that my nails bit into my hand bringing welcome pain, and spoke slowly and deliberately. "I know that we can never be together other than for the short time we have been given, and that's killing me. But, even if – *when* – I die, I know there is some small part of this planet where you still walk and live and breathe, I shall have some comfort even if… even when I am in the presence of God and it shouldn't matter any more."

"Emma…"

I spun around to look at him. "And I know… I *know* that this is entirely selfish on my part because… because if the roles were reversed and it was I who had to live without you…" I couldn't continue; I took one look at his distraught face and I buried my own in my hands; the thought of eternity without him too much – too soon – too *real*.

He was in front of me before the first tear had fallen, catching it as it fell. "Emma, my love, you cannot live your life so full of fear; it will destroy what happiness you have, what *we* have."

"*You* do, you and your family live in *constant* fear of… of discovery," I accused, wiping angrily at another humiliating drop, shrugging his hands off my shoulders in case his attempt to comfort me totally undermined my efforts to keep some scrap of dignity. He bent his head to level his eyes with mine.

"Yes, I know, but we don't let it dominate us. We are aware of it and we take sensible precautions, but we don't let it make us miserable, we don't let it tear us apart at the seams. How can I live with you, knowing that I make you so unhappy?"

I glared at him. "You don't – don't say that."

"Then be happy for what we have now, not unhappy for what might be. We don't know what the future holds, any more now than when I fought my uncle, or when you faced Staahl, or when we met each other. Emma, you are the very heart of me; if you are happy, then so am I." I sensed his distress, which I had put there, and my heart crushed under the weight of it. I flung my arms around his neck and pressed my face into the side of his until I felt my skin begin to bruise under the pressure.

"Matthew, I would do anything rather than hurt you."

He pulled away from me unexpectedly, his hands grasping both my arms. He laughed a short, almost harsh laugh. "Anything?"

I nodded. He gave me a strange glance that I couldn't decipher, before his face cleared and he smiled, a longing, wistful smile. "Then be happy, that's all I ask, and I will do everything in my power to make it so." He put his arms around me. "I think," he said, "that all this talk of death is too melancholy for what we have together, and certainly for this time of night. If I'm not to be accused of battery tomorrow, you need your sleep to remove those dark rings under your eyes otherwise, Heaven forbid, I might have Sam on my case. Which reminds me, I want to have a look at your ankle."

I shook my head and sniffed. "There's nothing to look at."

"I think that I'll be the judge of that," he said, scooping me up. He sat next to me on the bed and pulled up my pyjama leg, making a face as he saw the marks his fingers had left. "I shouldn't be trusted to look after you. I'll get you an ice pack," he muttered, disappearing out of the room, his rapid footsteps light on the wooden treads of the stairs as he made for the kitchen.

I lay back against the pillows and heaved a long, shattering sigh. It wasn't my ankle that needed a salve, but my heart.

New Year Resolution

"Culpeper," I said out loud.

Matthew waited until the driver in front of us had turned off the main road, before accelerating again. "What about him?"

I had spent the morning in between packing and tidying my room mulling over what we had discussed the evening before. I had slept late and consequently felt considerably better after a long rest. In the bright light of a golden sun, my performance the previous night seemed ridiculous, infantile, but I had enough self-awareness to understand that, although the tears had stemmed from tiredness, the depth of my reaction tapped a deeper, unexplored well of emotion that was all too real.

"Did he know about you?"

"He knew as much as I did, yes." He focused on the road ahead.

"Did he try to help you find out the cause of your changes?"

"Well, it wasn't that clear-cut. At the time, I was only aware that I grew stronger and healed faster. I didn't know how long I would live. It didn't occur to me that I wouldn't die within a normal lifetime." He spun the wheel to avoid a large lump of ice that had fallen onto the road from the slope above, neither slowing nor showing any sign that he gave it any more consideration than the movement required to turn the wheel. He wasn't a reckless driver – far from it; just that his reactions were fast – so fast that he sometimes manoeuvred the vehicle before I even realized he needed to do so. "Nicholas was as fascinated by my body's healing ability as I was appalled by it. Without his support and his lack of prejudice, I think I would have gone mad."

"I'm glad you had someone you could confide in."

"Yes, he was a good friend, but he had his own tragedies to deal with and I couldn't burden him with mine, so I left."

I inwardly flinched as he referred to his situation as a tragedy; without it, we wouldn't be together and he would have died from the natural processes of time.

Obviously reading my thoughts, he reached for my hand and we were quiet again, the road busier than before as people made their way to parties or their families for New Year, much as we did.

I missed Matthew's family already. Despite Maggie, they imparted a warmth that was both wholesome and welcoming, and more normal than my own had felt to me at times. They fell in and out of discussions and arguments and laughter as easily as water runs from a tap, but always with a sense of solidarity, a unifying force that kept them together. Perhaps that is what made being with them easy and leaving so difficult. They were a family – Matthew and Ellen's family – and although Ellen didn't live with them, her influence was still strong in Matthew's insistence that she be included as far as possible in the decisions that affected them all. And rightly so.

"Matthew, would you mind terribly if we didn't go as a couple tonight?"

His fingers tightened on mine. "Why?"

"Mainly because I don't feel right about it while Ellen's still alive – it's disrespectful, somehow…"

His expression didn't change. "Oh."

"And… there's another thing. I don't want what we have – us – to be the source of other people's entertainment around campus. You know how corrosive gossip is. Can we continue as we have for a little longer, without going public?"

I could hear a thread of uncertainty in his voice, something I wasn't used to.

"Isn't it a bit late for that? Matias and Elena know – and then there's Sam."

"But you did say that Sam won't say anything after that silly nonsense before Christmas, and his jaw should have healed by now, and I know Matias won't, and I can threaten Elena with certain death if she says a word to anyone."

Matthew's mouth softened into a smile. "You're not having second thoughts, then?"

"No! I'm not, not at all. I just want to protect what we have. There's going to be enough to deal with without tittle-tattle as well." I looked anxiously at him. "You don't mind really, do you?"

He shrugged ruefully. "As long as there's no embargo on our being together in private, I think I'll survive." He let go of my hand and placed his back on the steering wheel, indicating to turn down the long, tree-lined drive to the college. "Anyway, you're right about Ellen; sometimes the closer we are to everything… changing… the more impatient I get. God forgive me, you know that I don't wish for her death…"

"I know, and so does God for that matter, and if it's a question of forgiveness, I'm more concerned that you can forgive yourself because nobody else here – and that includes Ellen, by the way – is holding you to account."

He turned the car into the car park, now almost full with staff cars as the new term beckoned. "So we're good friends, then. This is going to be interesting. Think you're going to be able to keep it up for long? You're not as practised in deceit as I am."

I shuffled unhappily at the word. "I'd better get used to it, hadn't I, if I have to make it a habit of a lifetime?"

"Starting from now," he muttered.

I followed the direction of his gaze. The director of psychology, Professor Gerhard, was climbing out of her car directly opposite us. There was no way we could avoid being seen.

"O-K," I breathed, "in for a penny… I'll see you later." I grabbed my bag, opened the car door and stepped into the cold air before Matthew could stop me.

"Hi – Siggie! How are you?" I called out to her, rapidly distancing myself from the car as she looked up.

She smiled and waved as she recognized me. "*H*-ello there, Emma, and how are *you*?" Her benign face lit with a smile. "You look very well, I must say – much better than you were, I think?"

I took her by surprise by embracing her and taking the bag from the back seat of her car. She started to turn around to see where I had come from, but I tucked my arm through hers and began to walk us towards the steps.

"I am so much better, thank you. Britain can be quite dreary in December, but then home is the best place to be when you're recovering, don't you agree?"

She looked a little overwhelmed by my sudden animation but didn't resist as we walked up the steps together. "Yes,

yes, home is quite the best. Is that where you've been for Christmas?"

I took a swift look behind me as Siggie became momentarily distracted by someone calling her name from one of the windows above. It looked as if Matthew was still in the car, bent over the steering wheel, laughing.

"I've been with family." Not *my* family, perhaps, but who's quibbling over a little semantic disparity? "What about you, Siggie?"

We reached the quad, where snow had been cleared in swathes, dark lines of paths criss-crossing like doodles on a page.

"I went back to Germany. We didn't have this much snow in Cologne and I missed it. Saul stayed in Denmark over the holiday and he said they didn't have a flake of snow all season. Now, are you coming to the party tonight? Yes, of course you are, how stupid of me. I will see you then and you must tell me all about what you have been up to, yes? You must tell me all about it. Let me take my bag, thank you." Briskly taking her bag from me, she patted my arm, and I wondered what she meant by "it", since I doubted whether she was interested in what I had been given for Christmas.

I stood in the middle of the quad in the sunshine and considered going back to the car. I had left so quickly that I'd forgotten to take my luggage. I decided I could do without it until later and continued to my apartment.

I didn't need to wait. Matthew had beaten me to it and left my bags neatly on my bed with one of my lilac Post-it notes resting beside them. On it, in exquisite lettering despite his haste, he had written: *"Very impressive for a beginner. I'll meet you there."* Nothing more, just a promise and an echo of him still hanging in the air. It was the first time in weeks we had been parted for more than a few hours. I felt a screw of loneliness. Loathed to wallow, desperate times called for desperate measures. I took my bar of chocolate and trotted along to find someone with whom to share it.

"Emma, you are back!" Elena cried when she saw me, her Russian accent stronger since being away from English-speaking friends.

"Elena, so are you!" I reciprocated, grinning and giving her a heartfelt hug. She looked bright and perky after her holiday. "I come bearing gifts." I waved the chocolate, hiding the present I hadn't been able to give her before Christmas behind my back.

"Oooh, that looks expensive, Em; is it as good as it looks?"

"Better. Do you have time now to tell me about your holiday, or do you want me to come back later?"

She grabbed my arm. "Don't you dare. I have the tea, the water is hot, you have the chocolate – *now* is *perfect*."

She bounced into the kitchen to re-boil the kettle and came back, her face rosy. Her eyes sparkled.

"You're looking very well, Elena; what have you been up to?" The kettle clicked off and she jumped up again. I followed her. "Go on, you're dying to tell me."

"Tell you? Why should I have anything to tell you?" She turned the kettle around on its plate in a slow, obvious movement. I passed her two mugs and she made a show of pouring the hot water into each of them.

I was missing something here. "Well?"

She handed me a mug and, as she did so, the light from the ceiling refracted through something on her hand that shot blue spears of light.

"Oh!" I exclaimed, nearly dropping my tea. "You're engaged!"

"*Da*, yes, yes! You are so *slow*, Em." Her face flushed with excitement. "Do you like it? We bought it in St Petersburg. Matias proposed to me outside the Winter Palace. He knelt in the snow in front of everyone and they all stopped to see and they clapped and cheered. It was *sooo* romantic. Then it began to snow and he got a tourist to take a photograph of us. Do you want to see it?" Her words rushed out in a steady stream without pause for me to admire her ring, which danced around in front of my eyes as she waved her hands excitedly.

I felt blindingly happy for her. "That's fabulous. Oh, I'm so *happy* for you both. Elena, this is the best news I've heard in a long while. I know I'm not supposed to congratulate the woman, but congratulations – that's amazing, well done!" I gave her another hug. "It's lovely," I breathed, admiring the central blue stone with lilac shot through it like watered silk, supported by rows of tiny, brilliant-cut diamonds on either side as it hung in suspension between them. It sat perfectly on her slender finger, so new to her that, even as she tasted the first square of chocolate as we settled down with our tea, her eyes were drawn to the unfamiliar fire on her hand.

She came out of her trance. "I get the photo for you to see." In an unframed glossy photograph, the two of them stood in falling snow, the Winter Palace partially obscured in the eddies of frozen white.

"There, isn't it romantic?" she said, her eyes misting slightly.

"You look so happy," I said quietly, and realized that part of me envied her uncomplicated life.

"We are so *very* happy. And what about you and Matthew, are *you* happy? Do you have any news?" She came and sat down beside me on the sofa and we looked at the picture together. I had not seen her since before Christmas, when

I prepared to leave for the cabin in the hope that I would return similarly engaged.

"Yes, we are happy. We belong together – does that make sense?"

Elena nodded emphatically, her short hair bobbing up and down. "Of course, but you do not look – how do you say it?" I didn't feel like helping her with her vocabulary today, in case I guessed what she was trying to say correctly.

She leapt up from the sofa and came back a moment later with a Russian/English dictionary, already leafing through it. "You do not look *ec-sta-tic*. You should be esc-static, Emma, yes?"

Matias and Elena looked out from the photograph at me, a couple in the eyes of the world about them, and loving it.

"Elena, if I tell you something, will you promise me that you will not tell anyone else?" She peered at me doubtfully. "You can tell Matias, he needs to know as well," I verified and she nodded gratefully. "Matthew and I *are* together, but we don't want anyone else to know. It's too soon in our relationship and…"

Elena's eyes filled with sympathy. "It is too soon since his wife died, *da*? It must hurt him deeply still." Her hand fluttered over her breast in simulation of a wounded heart. This was easy, too easy, to deceive my friend and I said nothing, hating my dishonesty.

Elena took my silence as confirmation. "But you love each other, so all will be well and his heart will mend because you will be there to help him." She smiled in the certainty of her knowledge and I felt thankful because – despite the irony of it all – she was right.

I stood up and stretched, arching my back to ease the muscles. "I suppose we'd better get ready for the knees-up tonight."

She wrinkled her brow, her dark, arched eyebrows knotted in confusion. I laughed. "*Knees-up*. It's a colloquial term used to describe having fun, a bit of a do, bash, party, rave – that sort of thing."

"Ah," she said, "I have missed your English words, they make me *crack up*. Yes, we must get ready for the knee-up, good."

"Give me an hour to sort myself out. Oh, and by the way, this came too late for me to give to you before you left. Happy Christmas." I left her enthusing over the fringed silk evening wrap, the colours of which reflected the multicoloured euphoria in which she spun.

Back in my apartment, the bathroom mirror slowly cleared of condensation and I wiped the residual drops from its surface. The face that looked back at me was not ecstatic, it was true, but nor was it unhappy, despite my fears from the night before. I saw hope in my eyes, and the light of love, something that I hadn't seen for a very long time. I would have to keep it hidden for a while longer, caged like an animal waiting for freedom, longing for release.

14

Party Beast

It seemed like an age ago that I had stood in the exact same spot and watched the light fall in squares across the quad. Now snow lay either side of the path we followed to the door of the reception room, and this was no longer a new experience in a foreign land, and Matthew would be there, waiting for me. I hung back, nonetheless, nerves fluttering in anticipation.

"You OK, Emma?" Matias asked kindly, no doubt remembering what had happened last time I attended a college function. I rejected the image as soon as it emerged from those parts of my memory where I dared not look. Instead I searched the windows for a familiar form, but too many people crowded the room to see clearly. "He'll be there," Matias reassured. "He said he would."

A disorientating blast of sound hit us as we entered the room. Shrill voices of the women rose above the deep tenor of the men. Heady scents of perfume and alcohol mixed with the odour of dry-cleaned clothing and the occasional taint of sweat – smells now unique and identifiable, whereas, before the incident with the coffee, I would hardly have noticed. I recognized a few faces and smiled in response to their greetings, but didn't stop until we reached open space, where the assault on my senses proved less savage.

I sensed him before I saw him. Matthew was with a small group from his department at the end of the room where he had been when we first met, and he watched me intently. As soon as I saw him, he looked away casually, but the connection between us remained unbroken, like the thread of a spider – silk-thin, but stronger than steel. My pulse flustered briefly and settled to a steady beat in time with the music bouncing off the walls.

Matias waved to him, kissed Elena briefly, and went to join the huddle, deep in conversation before she had time to protest his absence.

We had managed to skip past the Dean and the bursar, who were hovering near the table by the door, doing what seemed to be a surreptitious roll-call of staff as they entered the room. The Dean saw us and his hooded eyes brightened, and I noted with an element of despair that beneath her silk shawl, Elena wore a wrap-over dress in a deep red jersey fabric that left little to the imagination.

"Ladies," Shotter oozed, "and a very pleasant New Year to you both." Since his gaze didn't leave Elena's bosom, almost level with his eyes, I couldn't be sure whom he addressed. Neither could she, and her skin flushed under his stare. Beads of perspiration broke out along the envelopes of skin that seemed to have increased since I last saw him, and the Dean patted a large, yellow silk handkerchief along them.

"My, my, but it is warm in here," he puffed. He wrenched his gaze from Elena and focused on me. "My dear Professor D'Eresby, you are looking very well, I must say – quite blooming. I do hope you are fully recovered from your... eh... ordeal." He didn't wait for an answer but turned away, scanning the room. "I rather expected to see Dr Lynes with you this evening." He brought his ice-pick eyes back to investigate my face.

"Dr Lynes?" I said casually. "Why?"

Elena twitched next to me.

Shotter dabbed at his bald, spotted head with his hankie, resembling a bloated toad. "My mistake, I thought that perhaps you are in a better position to know where he might be." He smiled, but a patient in a catatonic state could have made a more convincing job of it, and his cold interest prickled my skin.

"I'm so sorry not to be able to help," I lied, "but have you heard Professor Smalova's news?" Elena smiled gleefully in anticipation. "She and Professor Lidström are engaged. Is that not a wonderful way to start the New Year?"

Elena beamed happily, showing him her ring. The Dean hid his disappointment well, congratulated her and, with a furtive farewell to her ample form, bid us all a happy New Year again, and departed for more rewarding pastures.

"Is this dress too much?" she whispered when he left, sticking her chest out even further and looking down at her curves. Dear Elena, she seemed to be in a state of perpetual confusion over her frontage.

"It's fine. You're making the most of what you have rather effectively, but you are perfectly decent, it's Shotter who isn't. Good thing Matias wasn't here – he'd have popped a rivet. Did you mind me telling the Dean about your engagement?"

She held her hand above her head and twinkled her ring in the clear fairy lights along the wall. "No, I don't mind who knows; I want *everyone* to know." She pirouetted, nearly bumping into an elderly, diminutive professor behind her.

"*Everyone* will, at the rate you're going," I laughed, picking up a glass of wine and handing it to her.

One of our rather earnest colleagues from the history faculty came up to us then and wanted to talk about the forthcoming international conference in June, which the college would host this year. I hadn't given it much thought, but in terms of preparation, it was only a brief moment away. I had that strange sinking feeling, the sort you get when it's time for bed and you suddenly realize that you have a six thousand word essay to be given in the next morning.

"And I expect you will be pre… presenting a paper?" he stammered. I hadn't seen much of the portly professor since I had first met him at my reception back in September. Colin Eckhart was well known in our circles for his thorough preparation and meticulous research, his pedantic delivery, and even poorer social skills. Elena and I exchanged glances in the safe knowledge he wouldn't be looking at either of us.

"I haven't been asked," I replied, hopeful that I wouldn't be.

He shuffled an inch closer than comfortable, his cumbersome movement hampered by his brown velvet jacket, the buttons and cuffs worn bare from repeated use since he'd bought it in the eighties. He looked just over my shoulder at a blank spot on the wall.

"You will be," he stated, darting me a quick look. "They need someone who specializes in your field and there isn't anyone else."

"Thanks," I said sardonically.

"Not at all," he said, totally missing the point. "I think the Dean wants to showcase you. We've never had someone from C… Cambridge before."

"So it's nothing to do with my academic brilliance or scintillating wit, then?"

He pushed his big-framed spectacles back up his nose. "No, no, not at all."

Behind him Elena pulled faces at me, trying to make me laugh.

"What about Elena?" I said. "She would simply *love* to present a paper." Elena's face fell.

He leaned forward, forcing me to step back. "Oh no, Professor D'Eresby, Professor Smalova has nothing to offer – n… nothing at all." He spied another colleague and, without further ado, launched in his direction.

Elena grabbed my arm and pulled me out of earshot.

"You should have seen your face – you were so *funny*," I gurgled.

Elena hopped up and down like a rabbit on a pogo stick. "That man is so rude. Nasty, *rude* man," she fumed.

I put out a cautionary hand. "Stop, Elena, you're drawing attention to yourself." I indicated her bouncing cleavage and she stopped abruptly, smoothing herself back into place.

"Rude man," she muttered again.

"He doesn't mean to be, he just meant that your field's the wrong period for the conference. Post-Revolutionary Russia is hardly European Medieval and Early Modern history, is it? I don't think he realized that what he said sounded a bit… off. What he said to me was just as bad, wasn't it?"

"I suppose so," she huffed. "Somebody should tell him he sounds rude."

Eckhart had targeted someone else, and the young man was backed against the wall with a look of perplexed agitation, which Eckhart failed to notice as he ploughed on regardless.

"I don't think he knows the effect he has on other people," I said, regarding him with interest.

"You think?" Elena rolled her eyes as the young academic bolted the first chance he had.

"It must make life pretty tough for him, being out of step with the world all the time," I continued, half to myself.

"Who are you two watching?" Matias rejoined us, glass in hand, and followed our line of sight. "Elena, am I not enough for you, that you are already looking for another man?" he said, clasping dramatically at his chest before chucking Elena under her chin so she smiled coyly at him. "And as for you," he said, giving me a stern look, "wait until Matthew hears about this." He broke into a wide grin as he caught the eye of someone behind me.

"What am I supposed to be hearing about?" The merest touch on the small of my back had me pushing against Matthew's hand to feel the pressure more intensely, but he removed it and stepped around to face us as if he hadn't seen me for months.

"Elena, Matias has just told me; I'm so pleased for you both." Alive with genuine delight, he bent forward to kiss Elena warmly on both cheeks, sending her flushing scarlet. When he looked at me, however, his cool smile was merely polite and at odds with the wave of pleasure I felt emanate from him. "Emma, hello." He bent forward to kiss my cheek, his mouth close to my ear. "We're being watched," he murmured, before drawing away again. "It's good to see you looking so well. I'll catch up with you later, perhaps."

"That would be… good," I said lamely. *"You'd better!"* I threatened as he moved away, and I swear he heard me, although I had said nothing.

"Matthew is looking very… fit," Elena squeaked, recovering.

Matias lifted an eyebrow at me. "He is, isn't he? I think life must be suiting him at the moment. Can't think why that might be, hey, Emma?"

"I couldn't possibly say," I replied, watching Matthew out of the corner of my eye as he stopped to talk to Sung.

Matias coughed. "You're drooling." I nudged him in the

ribs, forgetting he would feel it more than Matthew. "Ow," he said, rubbing them. "Elena, Emma's hurt me."

"You probably deserve it," she said, without looking at him. She grabbed my arm. "Look, there's Sam. Hey, Sam!" She called out.

"Elena, no – *wait!*" I hissed, but too late. He turned at the sound of his name, wavered, as thrilled to see me as I him, but Elena dragged me, unwilling, in his direction.

"Sam!" she exclaimed, stretching up and kissing him. He flinched and drew away. "Ooo, you look awful – what has happened to your face?"

I examined a seasonal display of dried foliage on one of the side tables, and waited for his response.

He grunted. "Skiing accident off-piste before Christmas. Ran into a tree, broke my jaw."

I couldn't help the tiny smile as I thought of Matthew's hand being described as a tree. Still, it was a lot better than the truth. Trust Sam to have a macho reason for having a smashed face. I took a quick peek. He didn't seem too bad, all things considered, but his eyes were heavy and dull and it didn't appear that he'd had a holiday at all.

Elena murmured sympathetically, then wiggled her ring finger in front of him. "Matias and I are engaged to be married; what do you think of *that*?"

Sam looked despondently at her and then at Matias. "Yeah, sure, that's great."

Elena's smile faded.

Matias cleared his throat. "Anything interesting lined up for the semester, Sam?"

Sam shrugged. "Not thought about it much. You?" He cast a swift look in my direction and then over at Matthew, who now had his back to us.

Elena frowned at him. "You are very miserable, Sam – you have not even said hello to Emma. It's good she is back, no?"

He threw back the remains of whatever he was drinking and wiped his hand across his mouth. "Yeah, just *peachy*."

She tried again. "And look what Emma gave me for Christmas, isn't it beautiful?" She twirled in the silk wrap, the rich tones complementing her skin perfectly.

Sam's lip lifted in derision. "*Nice.*" With one efficient slice of a word, he cut her smile. Her face fell. Matias said something unintelligible in Finnish, and put a protective arm around her.

"Selfish pig," I snarled at Sam. "It's not you, Elena, he's having a go at me. If he has any sense of decency he'll apologize, but don't hold your breath."

Elena gaped at me, then at Sam, but I didn't wait to hear his response.

The room stifled, hot and heady, the too-loud music vibrating my senses like a taut wire. I felt fed up and desperately thirsty. I ran my eyes around the crowd and Madge caught my eye; she beckoned to me. I pretended not to have seen her but she motioned again and I inwardly sighed as I went over.

She peered at me, her sallow skin stretching in taught nicotine lines into a leer.

"Ah, the Iron Maiden. You're back from the dead, I see. All alone? Not married yet?"

"And good evening to you, Madge," I sidestepped, ignoring her reference to me as an instrument of torture. "I trust you had a pleasant holiday?"

She waved a hand dismissively.

"All right, all right, I get the message. Where's Sam, anyway? I've not seen much of him recently and he could always be relied on for entertainment."

"Neither have I," I replied truthfully. "He was over there with Elena and Matias." I made to move on, but her claw-like hand grasped the sleeve of my evening jacket.

"Don't go, my dear." Her leathery face sharpened as she poked her head around me. "Well, well, I see the elusive doctor has graced us with his presence once again. What brings him here, I wonder?"

I swung around, but I should have known better than to think she had made some random social comment. I saw Matthew and became rigid. He was talking to one of the most striking women I had ever seen, her darker-than-chestnut hair rolling in glossy waves down her back. From the way her wide, dark eyes devoured him, she thought she had met her equal in looks. He said something and she laughed, perfect lips parting as she took in his face.

Madge skewered me with her black irises, looking more like a shrew than ever. "Now, do you think that the Ice Man has found a little fancy at last? Someone to warm his heart and his bed? Or do you think he's gay?"

I knew exactly what she was up to but, despite my best efforts, my irritation must have shown, because her mouth twitched in expectation.

"I hope Dr Lynes doesn't know you call him that, Madge – it's offensive."

"Gay? Do you think so? Perhaps you could find out when you next speak to him; you are friends, after all. Oh, you mean *Ice Man*, don't you? Do you know why I call him that?"

I ground my teeth because as much as I didn't want to give her the satisfaction of asking, I *did* want to know. She saved me the bother.

"Because in all the years he's been here, countless women have broken themselves trying to get his attention, or into his bed, and he's never even noticed – until now." She missed my sudden intake of breath. "He's like an iceberg: so much more going on beneath the surface than on top." Madge stroked my arm. "That's Staahl's replacement he's talking to. Isn't she the most exquisite creature you have ever seen? He's obviously taken with her, but then, who wouldn't be?"

She scanned my face for a reaction, but I had been watching the pair of them laughing and talking, drawing the attention of those around them as they lit up the room with their combined beauty, and I waited for the familiar trickle of jealousy, waited for it to turn into scalding envy followed by cold fear at the thought of losing him. And I felt nothing – not a speck, because he felt nothing for her. It was all an act on his part, like the affectation assumed by the face of an accomplished player. I concentrated on him, willing myself to divine something other than the wall of indifference he hid from her, but I perceived nothing.

It was all Madge could do to stop herself salivating. "Well? Beautiful, isn't she?"

I turned my back on them. "Isn't she just. You say she's Staahl's replacement?"

Madge seemed confused by my lack of interest in Matthew's love life, so she changed tack. "What happened to you – it was terrible." There was a question there somewhere.

I pulled my sleeve to free it of her hand, but she clung on. "Yes, it was."

"Why did Staahl do it?"

I yanked my arm more roughly than I meant to and she drew her hand back in surprise. "I don't know; he's mad or bad. Does there have to be a reason?"

Her voice rasped out through smoker's phlegm. "Gerhard, you're a head doctor, help us out here."

The professor twisted at the mention of her name. I hadn't recognized her from the back. She smiled when she saw me, a genuine good-to-see-you-again smile.

Madge grunted. "I was just saying to Emma, what is it that makes a man like Staahl do what he did to her?"

Siggie's face straightened. "This is not the best topic of conversation, Madge. It doesn't take a degree in psychiatry to see the man's insane. Ignore her, Emma."

"I was trying to," I said.

Madge shrugged. "That's not what I've heard."

"Heard what?" Siggie said sharply, frowning at the smaller woman.

"Staahl's not insane," Madge purred.

My head pounded as the room narrowed to the point just in front of me, and my voice came out pinched and thin.

"What do you mean? Of course he is; why else would he attack me?"

She licked her lips. "You tell me. So, you haven't heard the rumours then?"

"Obviously not," I said coldly.

"It's all probably lies," she shook her head in a show of regret, "but they are saying that perhaps he went to the atrium because he was *invited*." She rocked back on her heels and waited while I froze, blood thickening in iced veins, my feet stuck fast to the polished floor. It wasn't that I hadn't heard this before – the detectives had suggested as much, and Maggie had made it quite clear that she believed it possible – but I hadn't realized that the accusation had become common knowledge on campus, and from there it was only a short step away before rumour became fact.

Gerhard's expression reflected her disgust as she rounded on Madge. "What do you think you are doing to the poor girl? Hasn't she been through enough without you stirring up trouble?" She turned her back on the woman and looked with a degree of concern at me. I gazed back, numb. "Emma, now listen to me: Staahl is mad. What he did was a reflection of his insanity and has no bearing on you or your own behaviour. Ignore the gossip – there's always gossip, but it is nothing, do you understand?"

I found my voice although my lips moved of their own accord. "Yes, it's all right, Siggie, thank you. I'm sort of used to rumours in my job. I know when to take no notice." I forced a smile. "I'm getting a drink. Would you like one?"

Surprised by my apparent composure, Siggie shook her head, and I didn't wait to see whether Madge wanted anything, as she didn't exist at that moment as far as I was concerned.

I found a table tucked away at the back of the room where the light was dim and I could escape the frenzied attack of the music. I grabbed a glass of fruit punch, willing my hands to stay still as I slopped the liquid clumsily. I drained it, and refilled it from a full jug, drinking thirstily and feeling the afterburn of spices in my throat.

The full implication of what the woman had said dawned on me through the matted jungle of misshapen thoughts. If it was thought that I had invited Staahl to meet me that night in the atrium – as Maggie had said and as Madge implied others believed – then an argument could be framed in which *he* became the victim and I the lure. If, in the minds of the public, I led him on, then no matter what the outcome of that meeting, I would be deemed partially to blame for what had happened to me. And worse – much, much worse – if Staahl were considered fit to stand trial, I would be forced to face him in court, and if I had to, so would Matthew, and who knows what poison would seep out of deep wounds then. I leaned both hands on the table in front of me, taking first one breath then another until the welling sickness abated.

"Hi-ya!" Elena hailed me. "You've been gone a long time."

I took another gulp of the punch – sweet and cool – and drank deeply, finishing the glass. I poured another. "Yup."

"Sorry about earlier. I didn't know you and Sam are still not talking. He was being very grumpy but he *did* apologize. He said he did not have a good holiday and he was very sorry he said those things."

"Uh huh."

She cocked her head on one side. "Are you OK?"

I caught a glimpse of Staahl's replacement through the gyrating bodies of some dancers. She eyed Matthew from a distance and even from where I stood, the way she looked at him with an exploratory, hungry expression made me seethe.

"I wish everyone would stop *asking* me that," I muttered brusquely, and Elena's face dropped. "Sorry, of course I'm OK, thanks for asking. I'm just grouchy; it must be PMT. Can I get you a drink? Where's Matias?"

"Over there with Matthew. Do you want to join them?"

To my disgust, the woman steadily made her way towards them through a throng of admiring glances, her hips swaying provocatively in the clinging, silky fabric. I was in no mood for playing nice. "I think we'd better," I growled.

Mere feet away from him when I blocked her path, she came to a halt in front of me, eye to eye. She looked me up and down. "*Excuse* me," she said, initial surprise replaced by a superior pout at her progress being impeded.

"Emma…!" Elena whispered.

I took another sip of my drink, regarding the woman with a pleasant smile I didn't feel. "Yes? Can I help you?"

She tried to step around me but I countered her move. "I want to get past."

I made no attempt to budge. "Do you?"

Elena tapped me on the shoulder. "Emma – come on."

I eyed my near-empty glass with disappointment, but a refill would have to wait.

The woman all but stamped her elegant foot. "I want to get past; you're in my way." Her voice had an unpleasant sneer woven through it and she had tight little pucker marks around her mouth like a cat's backside. She wasn't used to being thwarted.

She tried to get around me again, looking over my shoulder to see if she could catch Matthew's eye, but couldn't get far with the crush of people either side of us.

I felt disinclined to move. "Am I? I'm so sorry."

Elena tugged at my arm. "Emma, what are you *doing*?"

"I'm standing here having a drink. Have you had one of these?" I held up the glass for her to see. "It's really very good."

"Get out of my *way!*" The Staahl-woman snapped, her mouth twisting into an ugly snarl. Just as I thought, her beauty was merely physical. Beneath the surface she was a pit of scorpions.

"Be my guest," I invited, standing suddenly to one side. She strode past, scorn replacing annoyance as she flicked her hair over her shoulder.

I waited until she neared arm's reach of Matthew, her face once again a picture of serenity. "Your knickers are showing," I said, just loud enough for her to hear. She whipped her hand to her pert and perfectly formed behind, craning automatically to see.

I walked past her, Elena's eyes agog. "What were you doing?" she piped. "That was so *bad* of you. What would Matthew say if he knew?"

"Knew what?" he asked, skewing on one foot to greet us.

"Emma's been playing games with that new woman over there." Elena pointed to the retreating figure of Mrs Staahl as she scurried self-consciously towards the door.

He gave her a cursory look. "Why?" he asked me.

"Hello," I said, eyes wide with innocence.

"Ah, I see," he said, taking my glass from me and sniffing it. "And what has the poor woman ever done to you?"

"It wasn't what she was planning to do to *me* that bothered me," I replied sniffily, trying to retrieve my glass.

"Emma, did you *want* alcohol tonight?" he asked, holding it just out of reach.

I wavered. "It's fruit punch."

"With a hefty slug of brandy. Do you want to finish this or would you like me to get you something else?"

I wrinkled my nose. "Oops," I giggled.

"I'll get her a coffee," Elena offered.

"*No!*" we both said, simultaneously. "Thank you, but no. It'll wear off soon enough," Matthew added. Matias indicated in Sam's direction with his glass.

"Talking of which, Sam's looking the worse for wear. Looks like he encountered a slight problem recently. I nearly added to it myself this evening; he was being bloody obnoxious. I wonder what sort of problem that might have been?"

Matthew rubbed a finger down the length of his nose. "Oh?"

"He looks awful." Elena craned over her shoulder to where Sam barely listened to an enthusiastically gesticulating young woman.

"He said it was a tree," Matias continued. "A skiing accident."

Matthew looked blank. "Really?"

I giggled again.

"But I couldn't see any impressions of bark, looked more like he'd run into a *fist* to me."

"But it wasn't his…" I began, my head too fuddled to see the warning flash from Matthew, "… fist." I finished. Matthew groaned. "But it wasn't," I insisted, shaking my head, making it more woozy than it already felt.

Elena looked from me to Matthew. "What do you mean, it wasn't a tree? What was it? How do you know? Did he tell you?"

Matias rested his arm around her shoulder, fixing Matthew with a caustic grin. "I think you'll find Sam got into a fight over some girl, isn't that right, Matthew? Had to go to the med centre, did he? He always was a bit of a fool where women were concerned, doesn't know where to draw the line." He cast a knowing look in my direction and I felt again the sting of Sam's open hand across my face and the taste of blood in my mouth. I put my hand to my cheek and looked away, conscious I mustn't say anything more.

Matthew responded evenly. "I think that just about covers it, but of course, Sam doesn't want it to be made common knowledge – too embarrassing, or perhaps he's protecting the girl's honour."

I met his eyes briefly, keeping quiet.

Elena's brow wrinkled. "Who is this girl? Sam has not said anything to me. I thought that it was only Emma he liked."

Matias squeezed her shoulder affectionately. "You don't have to know every little thing that goes on in people's lives, kitten, even if you would like to. And remember, Sam wants to keep this quiet, so…"

"OK, OK, I say nothing, but Emma," her eyes probed as she turned her attention directly to me, "do you know who this girl is?"

I returned her look with a baleful stare, the initial flush of warmth and bravado from the alcohol subsiding, leaving a hollow, sloshing sensation in my stomach.

"Actually, I feel quite… unwell," I stated.

Elena flapped a reproving hand at me. "You should not have alcohol, you know it makes you sick."

"I think I'd better go now," I agreed.

Matias took a theatrical step away from me. "Over to you, Matthew. This is your department, I think. Elena, come on, I could do with another drink and there's food over there that needs eating."

"I'll go with Emma…" Elena started to say, but Matias was already guiding her in the opposite direction.

"Let Matthew take care of her," he said, a broad beam on his face as he looked back at us over his shoulder. "He's the doctor."

"Neatly done, well extricated." Matthew joined me minutes later in the quad, taking off his jacket and putting it around my shoulders.

My tummy rocked queasily. "It wasn't entirely a lie."

He put his arm around me and we started to walk back across the moonlit snow towards my apartment. "I know, but it'll pass, especially if you are able to eat something." We walked on for a few paces. "Emma, I'll go and see Ellen tomorrow, if that's all right."

Earlier feet had compacted the snow and it lay in wedges of ice that imploded as we walked over it. I felt better for being outside in the cold.

"Yes, of course, you must. Will you tell her you know she's dying?"

"I don't know; I might." Our footsteps echoed in the empty air and I came to a halt. He stopped with me.

"What is it?"

My breath steamed, creating a ghostly vapour around my mouth before vanishing.

"I realize it's none of my business, but I really think you should tell her that you know and that you won't intervene – it would be kinder. She's frightened of being brought back again; she's had enough."

"Is that what she told you?"

"Yes."

The moon lit Matthew's face as he raised his head to look at it, barely mortal in its eternal light. He breathed out in a sigh and looked down at me, his face falling into shadow. "In all the years I've known her, I've never heard her once say she's afraid. I'll tell her."

We walked on, conscious of the night's silence and our part in rupturing it. In less than a quarter of an hour, the college would resound to the breaking of the New Year, but until then, the stillness remained ours. Matthew held the door to the empty hall for me. "Do you want to talk about it?"

I ducked under his arm and waited until he joined me. "Talk about what?"

"What Madge referred to."

"Oh, that. Did Siggie tell you?" We climbed the stairs to the first floor, Matthew slowing down to my pace. "I hadn't given it much thought."

"You were worried, Emma. Even from where I stood I felt it." We finally reached my door. "Well, do you?"

I took my key out and slid it into the lock. He put his hand over mine, his face gently questioning.

"No. I don't." He held my eyes for seconds longer, then nodded once. "Are you staying tonight?" I asked him, as I switched on the light and turned to face him. He hesitated by the door, looking lost for a moment.

"If you want me to."

I held out my hand to him. "Do I *ever* not?"

Stepping over the threshold, he smiled suddenly. "Do *you* need to ask?"

CHAPTER

15

Interlude

It wasn't that the cold was any less intense by mid-February, but the days were definitely longer. By the time classes ended and the stream of students flowed in a noisy gaggle from the lecture halls, they walked to their rooms in the last light of the day.

In between snowstorms, I dodged snowballs and kept a weather eye out for the occasional student whose idea of fun was to career into a tutor, knocking them into the snow piled on either side of the path, and blame it on the treachery of the ice.

Professor Eckhart fell victim to the prank on several occasions, his confused expression the cause of much hilarity from the watching youths as he tested the slipperiness of the path with a pronounced degree of caution. I didn't find it very funny: he represented easy prey to a world that didn't understand him and made no attempt to do so.

Crossing the quad on my way to my tutor room, I witnessed a sudden dash and a flurry of limbs as the professor propelled through the air, landing with a dull *thud* in a pile of snow near to me. A boy was already up and grinning just a few feet from us, making a victory sign to a huddle of students nearby.

I frowned at them as I went over to the beleaguered man. With the long strap of his case wound awkwardly around him, he struggled to disentangle himself from a deep drift. I took the case and he rolled untidily to his feet, pushing his dated glasses back up his nose where they had fallen askew.

"I think that this young man kn… knocked me over on purpose." He blinked rapidly in the direction of the student, whose straggly beard looked too old for his face. I had seen him before, when his face was clean and fresh and he wasn't trying so hard to impress his peers. He didn't even have the decency to hide his amusement, laughing openly at the owl-like academic.

"I'm sure it was just an accident, professor," I said, aiming a cutting look at the lad. "He wouldn't want to risk looking like a prat in front of his friends. Besides, his faculty head might get to hear about it."

The student stopped laughing, but gave me an appraising look as if he wanted to say something. I stared in challenge and he changed his mind, slouching off in the direction of the group, and the students' canteen.

Eckhart appeared to have forgotten the incident already as he continued to brush loose snow off his coat over my feet. "A… actually, I was just on my way to see you," he puffed. "I have so… some excellent news." I smiled politely and he stepped up conspiratorially. "The Dean has asked me to tell you that he would like you to present the keynote lecture for the conference. What do you say to that, hey?"

I reflected that what I *wanted* to say and what I *should* say were worlds apart, and one of them couldn't be repeated. "Wonderful," I said without conviction.

"I said you would be pleased," the professor enthused. I considered whether I could get away with reworking my inaugural lecture. "Of course, everyone was very impressed with your inaugural lecture so we are looking forward to your latest research – something new."

Blow. My latest research was nowhere near a stage where it could be presented. I had been concentrating so much on my students' work that my own had been put on hold. Besides, despite it being the reason I came to the States in the first place, abandoning my research on the journal to protect Matthew made that line of enquiry taboo. Eckhart smiled and nodded and blinked at the great honour bestowed on me, so I had to smile back and look a little pleased, if only for his sake.

"I'll do my best," I said.

"Marvellous, marvellous," he beamed. "I'll te… tell the Dean," and he turned and shambled in the direction of the cloister and the Dean's study without saying goodbye. Watching his retreating back, I counted the months in which I had to prepare for the conference and concluded that, without distraction, I might be able to scrape something together with some help.

Distractions. Since New Year there had been plenty of those.

Matthew and I had spent as much time as we could together over the past weeks between work, his family, and Ellen. She was deteriorating but still fighting, and I went to see her in late January with the snow still deep on the ground. Frailer than when we last met, she had lost the haunted look of desperation and she thanked me, when we were alone, for the peace of mind Matthew had given her. Just once, when she forgot that Eli was still in the room, did she refer to Matthew as her husband, and Eli looked up, his face sad. He joked more gently with her now, and his movements had become quieter as he watched her slide towards death. When I mentioned it to him on the way home, Matthew said that some days were better than others as Ellen's heart muscles struggled to supply all the oxygen needed to her brain. If he knew the hour of her death, he kept it to himself and I did not ask.

We were in limbo, neither one thing nor the other, betwixt and between. It felt a familiar state of being, but not a welcome one.

At college, we still kept the depth of our relationship to ourselves. Rumours briefly circulated that Matthew had been dating the beautiful new professor of English. It must have been a fragment of deceit of Madge's doing, fanned by a lack of denial on Matthew's part, and by wishful thinking on the woman's, but the gossip died a natural death, starved of the fuel of evidence.

I saw very little of Sam. Elena said he had been going out with the girl we saw talking to him at the New Year party and I hoped fervently that it might be true for his sake as much as ours. I had never been very good at dealing with conflict, especially the festering kind, and Sam showed no willingness to heal or be healed, and this girl – if true – was the first indication that he had moved a step away from me. I didn't want him on my conscience, not after Guy.

I trudged towards my room, head bent but alert for frozen flying objects. I had grown very fond of my little group, whose verve and tenacity for their subject I admired. All, that is, except Leo. He was lazy – he was lazy and *late*. His indolence nauseated me. He relied on his good looks and what he thought of as charm to wheedle his way through college while the others worked, got it wrong at times, listened to advice, put it right, and carried on.

I didn't wait for him today. Today he wouldn't be late. Today he wouldn't use a feeble excuse in which he didn't bother to believe. Today he wouldn't tell me why he hadn't produced the minimum amount of work he needed to keep his degree alive and viable.

I had seen them all individually of course, working longer than timetabled to get to the heart of their chosen subjects, chewing the data over, making it work for them, pulling them back when their theories led the evidence rather than being framed by it. I loved it and it made the hours between seeing Matthew easier and relevant and worthwhile. But I had given up on Leo.

Leo had gone a step too far after I told him that I was failing his latest piece of work, which all too closely resembled that of a well-known academic recently published on the internet. He had slipped his hand up my knee with a lascivious sneer that showed he had succeeded with the same tactic in the past. I had been so outraged that I'd grabbed the closest object on my desk and slammed it into the back of his hand. Matthew told me afterwards that the pen had missed vital nerves and tendons and that the tissue damage was minimal, but I still lay awake worrying that the boy's father would make a formal complaint to the college.

Matthew appeared more pragmatic about the whole thing. "He had no right to touch you, and you had every right to defend yourself."

"I thought there was something in law about justifiable force. I'm not sure if what I did equates to that."

"What you did was to take reasonable measures to prevent him going any further. You didn't know what he was going to do next. Perhaps he'll think twice before he tries that trick on anyone else in future."

It offered some small comfort, but I hadn't mentioned that it bothered me that Leo thought he had a fair chance of getting away with it. Or that I was fair game. Or that my reputation preceded me.

On a brighter note, Holly told me that she'd broken up with Leo shortly afterwards. I would have felt a twinge of guilt except she didn't seem too upset by it and I reflected that he had brought out the worst in her. By the time I saw my reduced group again, she and Josh had started dating and they both looked happy.

I thrummed my fingers on my desk to the theme from *Gladiator*, blocking out the random noise from the corridor outside my room and so deep in thought that I didn't hear my students come in until Josh's face appeared upside down in front of mine. He had gelled his hair into spikes as usual, but this time he had dyed it a vivid shade of apple green. "Hey, what's up, Doc?" He grinned cheesily and flung himself into a chair, pulling Holly into the one next to him.

I tugged my ear phones out and switched off the music. "Very fetching, Josh. What's your real colour, by the way?"

His grin broadened. "I'm a natural blond, why yes I *am*," he drawled in imitation of a Southern Belle. "And what's yours, might I ask?"

I laughed. "Cheeky monkey, I haven't graded your paper yet."

Holly fidgeted nervously. "He didn't mean to be rude, Dr D'Eresby – did you, Josh?"

"I know that, Holly, don't worry, we were just…"

"Joshing?" Hannah suggested with a rare show of humour. Josh cracked up.

I smiled. "I was going to say, 'joking', but yours is much better, thank you, Hannah. Right everyone, let's…"

A quick knock at the door interrupted me, and Elena poked her head around the edge of it, her face flushed. "I've just heard the news from David: keynote lecture – you must be thrilled," she rolled her eyes dramatically.

"*Thrilled*," I grimaced.

"What is *keynote lecture*, please?" asked Aydin in his thick accent.

Elena bobbed into the room. "It means that Emma will give the introductory lecture at the conference. It is the one that sets the… what is the word?"

"Theme?" I proposed.

"*Da*, that will do. Sets the *theme* for the whole conference so it is *very* important that she gets it right."

"Huh, no pressure then, hey, Doc?" Josh had slumped low in his chair, his legs stretched out halfway across the floor. He reminded me of Joel in the way he appeared so laid back, but underneath was as astute as the rest put together.

"Ah, well, now that's where you come in, boys and girls." They all sat up. Elena hovered but I waved her away. "Skedaddle, sprite, we have work to do here. I'll tell you later," I added, in case she thought she was being summarily dismissed. She waved her fingers around the door frame in acknowledgment as she left.

I stood up and walked over to the big window, where the radiator pushed out heat.

"You know how much you reprobates and ingrates love and adore me…" A united groan issued from Josh and Hannah. "Well, now you have the chance to prove it. And it might prove to be good experience as well."

"*Righ*-t," Josh burred, "I get it, this is something we're not gonna like. Cool move, dude." I cringed and he smirked.

Aydin scratched his head through his thinning dark hair. "I don't understand – in English, please."

"Sorry, Aydin," I apologized. "It's like this. I have to give an important lecture in the summer at the conference. You all know about the conference, right?" They nodded. "Good, well, since the theme is faith and heresy in Reformation Europe and I'm the only one here who specializes in that period and this particular topic, I have to lead with the opening presentation. But I've been working *sooo* hard on all your behalf…"

"Yeah, yeah," Josh intoned.

"… that I have very little time to pull this together, which is where you lot come in."

"*You* want *our* help?" Hannah asked.

I dropped the act. "I *need* your help, Hannah – all of you, if you'll give it."

"But what about our own studies?" Holly queried, wide-eyed as she mentally calculated the months she had left in which to complete her thesis.

I came and sat back down in front of them. "Look, I wouldn't ask for your help if it was going to detract from your studies, but I think this will work to your advantage if we can get through the prep it's going to take in the meantime."

"So, what do you propose?" Hannah said slowly, evidently curious but noncommittal.

I took a deep breath. "Right, here goes. Each of you is well on your way to completing research into your chosen area. Each area was well considered beforehand and your work is original and interesting. The keynote lecture can be pretty long. What I propose is that it is used between you to present your own studies to an international audience made up of some of the best minds in our field." I waited as it sank in.

Aydin peered at me curiously. "You would do that for *us*?"

"Yes."

Hannah plonked her bag on the floor next to her. "But what about your own work? You can't give us the keynote spot – we're nobodies. Who'd want to listen to us?"

"Well, *I* would for one. Look, you'd be helping me out here. I can't get my own research completed in time, and anyway, *you* are my work. Just think, I can get the credit four times over off your backs." There was a doubtful silence. "It'll take the pressure off me," I supplemented, trying another tack.

Josh finally shrugged acceptance. "That's really cool, thanks, but you'll have to go on first – introduce us and everything, right?" he said, looking at the others.

"Right," Aydin and Hannah murmured in agreement.

I stood up and rubbed my hands together. "Good, well, that's agreed. Let's get started."

"There's one thing, Doc." Josh looked up at me. "I don't think the Dean'll like us taking your place, you being English and from Cambridge and all."

"What, and miss the opportunity of showcasing four of his best students? He'll love the idea." Uncertain, Josh ran his hands through his green hair. "And don't change your hair, Josh – don't change it for anyone."

I turned away and pretended to get a book from my shelf: *A Mind Worth Knowing: A Medieval Dictionary of Deceit*, by Johnson. My sister had given it to me as a joke years ago; how apt it seemed now. I didn't know how Shotter would react to my change of his plans, but I could guess. Behind me, my four students gabbled excitedly in close conclave. I would have felt the same at their age – have given anything to have an opportunity like this. If truth be told, six months ago I might have seen it as a highlight of my career: the key speaker at an international conference where I would present my lifetime's work to date, where I could present the *journal*.

A rapid set of heavy knocks on the door broke through my reflection and cut the purl of voices dead. I reached for the handle, but it pushed open, forcing me back.

"Professor D'Eresby? Professor Emma D'Eresby?" The man in the dark uniform with matching eyebrows and a gold shield said as he stepped into the room.

"Yes?"

"We're from the Sheriff's Department. Come with us, please."

16

Between the Horns

My first thought was that the journal's absence had been discovered. My second, following on so rapidly from the first that it almost knocked me senseless, was that somehow, and despite all the precautions taken, Matthew's true identity had been exposed.

"Ma'am?"

I dithered, uncertain. Could I refuse to go with them?

The second man, taller and thick set, looked at his watch. I became aware of my students: Aydin, round-eyed and fearful, and Josh, his stance belligerent. I cleared my throat and forced blithe confidence.

"Of course. Lay on, Macduff."

The two men flanked me like the criminal I felt, my heart thumping noisily as we walked down the corridor towards the staircase. Somehow, I had to get a message to Matthew. He would be at work now, but whether in the lab or the medical centre, I didn't know. Why couldn't I have thought fast enough to give some cryptic message to Elena that would have given him time to escape, unless... unless they already had him in custody – alone, caged? Isn't that how it worked? I was being rounded up as evidence. My mind fumbled for answers. I had to warn him.

The men seemed at ease with the role they played. This is what the Gestapo used to do – lull you into a false sense of security, and then, when you thought you were free, haul you back into the interrogation cell and start all over again. However, this was the United States in the twenty-first century and things worked differently here. Normal citizens couldn't just disappear – they had rights, privileges, protection against the excesses of authority. But then I wasn't a citizen and Matthew wasn't normal.

The men stopped in the communal seating area. Checking we were alone, the stocky man lowered his voice. "We thought you wouldn't want your students to witness this, ma'am." He reached inside his long overcoat and, for a fraction of a second, I thought he went for a gun, but instead he withdrew an envelope. "It's not the sort of thing you'd want them to overhear." And he held it out to me.

"What is it?"

"Ma'am, I'd be obliged if you'd take it."

I don't know what I thought I would see. I'm not sure whether, in my startled state, I could think rationally at all. The document bore all the hallmarks of officialdom. I scanned it for Matthew's name, but found none other than my own. I read it again, this time more slowly. Then I laughed, a short, stabbing laugh as relief washed through me, and became aware of the men looking at me oddly. I swallowed, feeling a mixture of release and idiocy as my pulse stuttered back to a more normal pace.

"It's all right," I whispered. "It's for me."

"Yes, ma'am. You are duly served with a complaint and a summons."

"Summons?" I asked, blankly.

"Yes, ma'am." He pointed to the word printed bold and

black on the form. "This is a court summons. You have twenty days to respond to the complaint against you." He prodded the paper again, but he didn't need to, because next to the word "plaintiff" lay others more sinister and laden with malice: *Kort Staahl.*

My initial elation that Matthew was not the focus of investigation had been replaced with horror as I realized that I was. The slow, sapping dread of the unknown deepened as I was shown through the doors of the redbrick courthouse days later. The oak-haired attorney appointed for my defence – a woman in her late thirties – summed me up with quick, dark eyes.

"My name's Louise-Antoinette Duffy," she said, holding out a slender hand in greeting, and surprising me with the strength of the grasp. "I know, I know, it's a mouthful; my mammy's family is French and my daddy's granddaddy was Irish. People just call me Duffy and I like that. Call me Duffy." She waved towards a chair. In her other hand she held a copy of the letter by which I had been served notice of my prosecution. "Take a seat. I expect you know why you're here?"

Apprehension was rapidly replaced by indignation. "How can Staahl prosecute me? I haven't done anything."

Perching on the edge of her desk, Duffy drew her pencilled eyebrows together in a show of sympathy. She finished the dregs of a takeaway coffee and crushed the cardboard cup in her hand. "Can I fetch you a coffee?"

"No, thanks, I don't drink it."

"Professor Staahl is pressing charges against you on the grounds of defamation *per se*. Do you know what that is?" I shook my head. "Simply put, it means that Staahl is saying that you maliciously reported that he attacked you and that this has resulted in him losing his job and damage to his reputation. He also says that you have caused him mental injury."

My mouth dropped open. "But he attacked *me!*"

"That's not what he's saying."

"I haven't said anything malicious, only the truth. And I haven't told the press, or anything, only the police and my family – and my friends. How can I be responsible for him losing his job, for goodness' sake?"

"Hun, that's just the thing; it's been reported in the press and it is known in the town. The college has terminated his position both because of the alleged attack…" I scowled. "… I know, but it remains *alleged* until proven – and because he's been unfit to work. You will have to prove that your allegations are true, but he doesn't have to *prove* that his career has been damaged by your accusations; it is taken for granted that by making the accusation in the first place, you have done enough to ruin his reputation. That's the *per se* bit, by the way."

My heart bulged uncomfortably as I tried to get my head around it.

"And that's not all. In Maine we have a provision in law called the Restatement of Torts, and it states that, and I quote, *'One who gives publicity to a matter concerning the private life of another is subject to liability to the other for invasion of his privacy, if the matter publicized is of a kind that would be highly offensive to a reasonable person, and is not of legitimate concern to the public.'* End quote."

Swallowing the snake of fear sliding up my throat, I protested, "He's insane. How can he be allowed to bring a case against me at all?"

"It's not as simple as that. The case against Professor Staahl hadn't been closed, just put on hold until such time as he's found fit to stand trial or he's seen to be criminally insane and committed to a psychiatric institution." She threw the mangled cup into the wastepaper bin. "You'll be seeing him in court, don't you worry. Till then, he has rights like any other citizen, and he's exercising them against *you*."

I didn't want to see him in court, not now, not ever, but this turn of events added insult to injury. "But hasn't he been in a psychiatric unit since he attacked me?"

She swung one leg as she regarded me earnestly, the edge of her light grey jacket lifting and falling with the motion. "How much do you know about our judicial system, Professor D'Eresby…?" She pronounced it *Deers-bye*. "Can I call you Emma? I just can't quite get the hang of your name." She had a lovely, slow drawl from somewhere in the South that reminded me of films with verandas and mangroves and freshly squeezed lemon juice.

"Emma's fine. Nothing – I don't know anything about American law."

"It's not so very different from your own." I didn't like to admit my ignorance in that sphere either. She placed her hands together at the fingertips. "It's like this. After Staahl's arrest he was sent to a secure psychiatric unit for a period of thirty days for observation."

"Who sent him there?"

"It's the responsibility of the Commissioner of Health and Human Services – hell, I just *love* the titles they give themselves – and the commissioner asks for reports on the defendant from a clinical psychiatrist."

That must have been Maggie's role. Talk about the mad leading the insane. What would her report be worth in court in light of what she had said to me?

"But it's already been much longer than thirty days."

"Yes, it has. In this case, there was some doubt over Staahl's ability to answer for his crime, so he was recommitted for a further period of sixty days and another report commissioned, this time from the State Forensic Service."

"Does that mean that the psychiatrist's report is invalid?" I asked hopefully.

"Hell, no, it's taken into account and they're asked to do more observations. It's a case of double-checking to make sure they've made the correct diagnosis. Anyway, a hearing was held just the other day and Kort Staahl has been found *competent to stand trial*, as we say. That means he faces a charge of Elevated Aggravated Assault, a Class A crime, to be tried in a Superior Court like this one and, hopefully, you get to nail the son-of-a-bitch. But in the meantime, he's managed to get his charge against you in first. Must've been a light schedule, or else the judge believes she can make a quick job of it and squeeze it in. Either way, you're up first." She quirked her head to one side. "Odd, though…"

"Odd? In what way?"

"This is a pretty unusual case as it is, but I wouldn't normally expect an attorney to be so keen to put all the facts of the attack upfront of the jury like this. I'd have thought he'd have held off till after the criminal trial so as not to prejudice his client. Still, Staahl's pressing for this lawsuit, so here we are."

"Do I *have* to attend?"

Duffy flicked her hair over one shoulder and slid off the desk. "Unless you want to be in contempt of court, you do. Of course, you could still refuse, but you'd be likely to face a jail sentence for your trouble, and you wouldn't want to be doing that, now, would you, hun?"

I certainly did not. "No, I suppose not, but he tried to *kill* me, and if it hadn't been for Dr Lynes…" I had to remember to distance myself from him. "I *would* be dead. Staahl's not trying to claim he's innocent, surely?"

Duffy undid the single button of her jacket, letting it swing open, revealing a silky purple shirt tucked into the top of her suit trousers. "Sure what he did was a criminal offence and, even if you consented to it, he'll stand trial for it. But if your claim that it was an unprovoked assault is shown to be untrue, what you did makes it malicious, and that's defamation. The fact is, honey, Staahl *has* lost his job and suffered damage to his reputation. As for the state of his mind, he's saying that he's experienced mental anguish as a result of your allegations…"

"But… but," I stammered, "he *must* have been unhinged in the first place to do what he did to me."

"Well, if he was there's no record of it. Now, we can try entering a plea to mitigate the sentence. If you're willing to admit fault, he might just drop the charges altogether and you're home and dry…"

"No way! I haven't done anything wrong!"

She took a moment in which I felt myself unstitch beneath the severity of her gaze, then she shook her head. "That's the darnd'est thing about this. It's normal – hell, *expected* – that negotiations take place between us and them before trial, to come to some sort of arrangement that means trial can be avoided altogether, but they've refused. He wants a jury trial. What's more, he's not only going for damages, but an injunction against you. Hell, you must've tweaked his whiskers. Even if he wins, the award is likely to be negligible, and the trial'll be all over the media, and what'll that do to his reputation, I want to know?"

"To say nothing of mine," I muttered. *And Matthew's safety*, I thought.

Duffy ran a nail under her chin and scratched thoughtfully. "They must have good reason to risk it; it's all or nothing now. He's claiming you led him on." She dropped it in, scrutinizing my face again for my response. I blanched but didn't say anything.

"You're not surprised by that?" she asked, still watching.

"I've heard the rumour before. It surprised me then, but I've sort of become used to it now."

"You'll have to do better than that if you're going to convince the judge – she'll be watching your reactions. Once an idea's been planted it's damned hard to shift it. Remember, *you're* the victim, you didn't lead him nowhere. Now, I want you to take me back through each minute of that evening."

That was hard, gruelling. Duffy took her time, interleaving detailed questions about the attack with anecdotes from her childhood in a village near New Orleans I'd never heard of. She tried to make it easier, but her questions were direct, incisive, making my stumbling answers look contrived and evasive. At the end of it I felt pummelled and stretched like pizza dough, and my hand, holding a plastic cup of water, shook.

"I know this isn't easy, but the prosecuting team'll be a lot harder on you than I am, so you've got to get your story straight. And, about the way you dress, make it plain and dark – professional-looking. If you wear jewellery, keep it simple. The cross is just fine, but your earrings…" my hand flashed defensively to touch the earrings Matthew had given me, "… they look darned expensive and the jury'll spend their time looking at your earrings and not listening to you. Got anything plainer?" I nodded. "Now, tell me," she picked up a magazine from a pile by her desk and flicked through it without looking, "about your relationship with Dr Lynes."

I had been expecting something like it ever since I entered her small, cramped office overlooking the parking lot at the back. She worded it as if it was understood that we had a relationship, but she could have had no certain knowledge of it.

I ran my cross up and down its chain. "We're friends."

"And that's all?"

"Is there supposed to be more?" I countered, dropping my cross. It fell cold against the skin of my neck.

"I'm the one doing the asking."

I fixed her with as steady a look as I could muster. "Yes, we're friends."

"Dr Lynes came across you and Staahl by accident? Chance? Fate? What?"

"I don't know."

"The prosecution will claim he was following you."

"Dr Lynes? Why?"

"They'll say he was jealous."

"Of what, for goodness' sake?"

"Your relationship with Staahl."

"Relationship? There was no relationship. He was *stalking* me."

"Can you prove that? Did you go to the police?"

"No – no I didn't, but… but Elena…"

"Professor Smalova?"

"Yes – she was there in the diner when Staahl followed me there. She can tell you – he took my keys."

"You saw him?"

"No."

"Did he threaten you, shout at you, abuse you?"

"No, nothing like that."

"Then what *did* he do that made you think he was in any way a danger to you?"

I hunted desperately for words that described how I'd felt that evening, faced by the man who seemed so sinister, so *unwholesome*. "He talked."

"About what?"

"About… oh, I don't know… about how I liked monsters, things like that. It was the *way* he said it; it made my skin crawl," I faltered, seeing where this was going. "He *was* following me," I finished feebly.

"So you said." She walked around the side of her desk, and tossed the magazine onto the pile and picked up another. She opened the front page and glanced down the list of contents. "You told him to leave you alone, when you were at the diner?"

I had been distracted by her movements. "Yes, no – I can't remember. He wouldn't leave me alone. He held onto my bag, he touched me." I felt physically sick as I recalled his touch on my hand.

"But he did leave?"

"Yes, but only when Harry…"

"Dr Lynes' nephew – is that right?"

"Nephew… yes. Harry saw me there and came over and Staahl left."

She rolled the magazine into a tube like a telescope and tapped her hand with it.

"What, he just *left*?"

"Yes, well – no. Harry knocked a drink over him."

"On purpose?"

"No… I don't know. I don't think so."

"Where was Professor Smalova during this *conversation* you had with Staahl?"

"She was in the bathroom, then she went to pay."

"So she didn't see you with Staahl, hear what was said, anything?"

"She saw him leave." I wiped the back of my hand across my forehead and it came away damp. "This is hopeless, isn't it? I can't prove he stalked me; you only have my word for it."

She gave a small smile, the first I'd seen for a while. "No, we have more than that, we have physical evidence…" she nodded at my arms, "… and we have the testimony of a highly regarded surgeon – that's got to count for something. By the way, did you know that Dr Lynes' sister is the clinical psychiatrist in charge of assessing Staahl?"

If I looked startled it was because she referred to Maggie as Matthew's *sister* and it took me a moment to make the connection through my addled brain.

"So you didn't. Quite a coincidence, don't you think?"

I felt almost past thinking anything. I found it bad enough having to regurgitate the events leading up to the attack, but I also danced on coals with any and every piece of information I gave her to prevent any slip, any look, any *word* that might lead someone with an inquisitive frame of mind down a different, more dangerous path, that would make Staahl look positively normal.

"One last thing," she said, "and I don't want you to be unduly worried by this or anything, but have you any idea how Staahl has been able to buy the services of one of New York's better legal firms?" I shook my head. "Because – between you and me – you academics don't get paid enough, and Professor Staahl hasn't any other income that we know of, so where has he come by the means to afford the likes of them, that's what I'd like to know. Sure as *hell* I would."

"Are you saying we haven't a chance?"

"No, not exactly, but it won't make this as easy as getting a tan on a summer's day, that's for sure."

The consequences of failure were too horrific to

contemplate. "And if he succeeds in persuading the judge I'm guilty as charged, what then?"

"You can probably say goodbye to your job prospects in these United States of America for a start – you might even be deported – and it'll make it one step easier for him to go back to work with a clean sheet." She slapped the rolled-up magazine against her leg. "Isn't worth thinking about, is it? So we'd better get this right and get the charge against you dismissed and the judgment he deserves. Ready to go to trial?"

Matthew waited for me in my apartment, pacing up and down in front of the window, his face drawn. I ran to him and he drew me into the protective circle of his arms. He held me until I stopped shaking.

"They've been asking questions," I said, when at last I found my voice.

"It's all right," he murmured into my hair.

"But I thought they were going to ask about you…"

He tightened his hold on me. "Shhh, it's all right – this has nothing to do with me."

But it wasn't all right and I had to make him understand how close to the edge I had come.

"I didn't know what to say when she kept asking me about you – about us – and I was sure I was going to say something I shouldn't because I forget you're not normal. And, Matthew, she's on *my* side; what'll I do if they ask me in court?"

"It's over for now, don't worry."

I could feel him trying to draw the anxiety out of me down the long, fine strand that bound us, but I wasn't ready to let it go, not until I'd told him.

"But it's only over for today. Then there'll be the trial and they'll try to unpick your evidence. Staahl's brought in a hotshot team from New York or something. My attorney is nervous about it."

He leaned back a little so that he could see my face. "Did she say so?"

"No, but it was pretty obvious."

His face broke into a frown. "I wish you'd let me get in someone else to represent you… all right, sorry, I promised I wouldn't mention it again. But why should you be any more likely to say or do something that could possibly harm me, any more than Pat or Joel or Henry might?"

"Because you *are* normal to me. If I saw you as being so very different – if you had two heads or were green – I would remember it. But I've always lived buried in the past, and living and breathing centuries of history is as natural to me as… as stepping from shadows into light. It's easy to forget that you're different," I fretted, "and they'll want to question you, too – as a witness."

"Of course."

"And?"

"And – nothing. They'll ask me some questions. I'll answer them. Everything's fine."

"Would you tell me if it wasn't?"

He paused as if deciding whether he would or not, then smiled. "Yes, I would."

"I think I might have gone to pieces today if I'd known you were being questioned too," I said a little mournfully.

He kissed my hair and smoothed it out of my eyes. "I don't think you would – you're stronger than you think."

I didn't feel very strong at that moment. I had a dim memory, almost lost to time, of when I was very little and something had frightened me, and my father held me and sang to me until I wasn't frightened any more. I had forgotten that until now.

"Have you eaten?" he asked, ever practical.

Lunch seemed a very long time ago and my tummy was thinking about feeling hungry, but hadn't quite made up its mind. "No."

He went into the kitchen. It was his way of distracting me and concentrating my mind on the here and now, and not the dread phantoms on which I would dwell given half a chance. I had only the benefit of a few months to come to terms with what he had acclimatized to over many lifetimes, and while I considered that I had made a pretty good start to what might become an existence of obfuscation and dissembling, I had yet to face a hostile prosecution team intent on gunning me down.

Matthew handed me some bags of vegetables and then selected a packet of pale meat, possibly chicken, from the fridge. I peered into one of the bags containing broccoli; he wanted me to eat a more balanced diet. I felt my forehead wrinkle as I tried to remember what to do next.

"You have to take it out of the bag first," he reminded me with a sideways grin, placing the meat in the frying pan.

I watched the meat hiss and spit, reminding me of Archbishop Cranmer at the stake, writhing as the flames ate the wood beneath his feet. I wasn't ready to drop the subject of the trial.

"We're not supposed to talk about the trial."

"I know." He scrubbed his hands like a surgeon and stirred the already browning meat.

"Matthew…"

He looked up. "What, sweetheart?"

"I'm going to have to take an oath in court, aren't I?"

He found a chopping board and rapidly dissected some carrots. "Yes," he said quietly.

"What if I'm put in a position where I can't tell the truth because of what it might expose?"

"About me, do you mean?"

"Uh huh."

He put the knife down and turned to me gravely. "I can't answer that for you. I'm not going to ask you to lie for me, Emma. You must do what your conscience dictates."

My *conscience*? My conscience didn't know which way up it was at the moment. Once I had sworn an oath, I would *have* to tell the truth, whatever the consequences, and I couldn't rely on awkward questions not being asked – Sod's Law dictated they would.

I poured boiling water over the broccoli. His answer hadn't helped. There were times when I would welcome someone dictating to me, taking away the responsibility of having to make a decision, and this proved to be one of them.

"Matthew, what will you do if you are under oath and you're asked a compromising question?"

He pointed to a pile of carrot sticks on the board. "Would you like these raw or cooked?"

I gave him a pained look and pinched a carrot from the board. "Raw, please, and that's not in the least bit helpful. I'm not asking you to make a decision for me, I just want to know what you'd do in a similar situation."

"I don't know if I can answer you. If it's a question of integrity, I will always try to tell the truth; but if it's a case of swearing before God and having to choose between the truth and protecting my family, I can't say for sure. I would have to judge at the time."

"So you're not so concerned about lying in a court of law?"

"My life is one big fabrication, so no, that's not my main concern, but my soul… well, that's another matter."

I gnawed down the length of the carrot stick, pondering.

"Emma, does it bother you that I would be prepared to lie to the State?"

I waved the carrot in the air dismissively. "The State? No, not really. The State does it all the time and calls it expediency. What does the State care as long as you pay your taxes and refrain from killing thy neighbour – unless it tells you to do so. Anyway, I'm not sure who's side the State would be on if they knew who you were. You'd be wired up to a computer in a windowless room and damn your rights as a citizen in the time it took to sign your life away, and all in the name of State security, or science, or… whatever."

The boiling saucepan rattled urgently. He adjusted the lid and the escaping steam scalded his hand. He examined the already healed skin then folded his arms and leaned back against the counter, regarding me thoughtfully. "You're too young to be so cynical."

"And you're old enough to know better. I'm a historian, what do you expect? History is littered with examples of expedient behaviour, whether by the monarch, the church, even presidents. If it's given a name and a law, the State can get away with… murder." Matthew didn't say anything, so I continued. "All right, then, what would have happened to you if you hadn't left Rutland when you did? What would have been the natural progression of events given the time in which you were living?"

He turned and switched off the stove. "You know what would have happened," he said quietly.

Yes, I knew, but I wanted him to say it out loud. "I can guess, but you were *there*. What would they have done to you?"

He put the saucepan down, my food momentarily forgotten

as he stared at the floor, remembering. "I would have been arrested and arraigned before the magistrate…"

"On what grounds – by what *law*?"

He glanced up at me, his face strained. "By the 'Act Against Conjuration, Witchcraft, and Dealing with Evil and Wicked Spirits'. I studied it at Cambridge; it was fairly new then, one of James I's contributions to humanity." He grimaced. "Matthew Hopkins used it to enforce his peculiar form of persecution, if I remember correctly."

I nodded. "You do. He didn't style himself the Witch-Finder General without reason. At least you wouldn't have been burned at the stake under the 1604 Witchcraft Act, only *hanged*."

He kicked a stray bit of carrot away from one of the cupboards. "They would have had to convict me first."

"Oh, come on, Matthew, they'd changed the law. Under the rules of escheat all your lands and goods would have been forfeit to the crown. There were financial incentives for a conviction; you wouldn't have stood a chance. Your retainers, your household staff, your *friends* – all would have come under scrutiny, and who knows what any one of them might have felt compelled to do to protect his or her interests. Laws change to suit the times. Then it was witchcraft, now it's… terrorism."

"I'm hardly a terror suspect."

"That's not the point, is it? With your particular anomalies you'd keep the Army research guys, or whatever you call them over here, in work for decades. Think what they could do if they harnessed your life-enhancing potential, Matthew. You're a gift to the military: you don't need to eat or sleep, you're unusually strong and fast, and you're nigh on indestructible. They wouldn't be interested in your *rights* then, and don't tell me you haven't thought about all this before, because I won't believe you."

The way he looked at me made me suspect that this had been a matter for conjecture for a considerable length of time.

"Yes, well, that may be so, but they didn't get me then and I have no intention of falling outside of any law or statute now, God willing."

"Amen to that," I said with feeling.

"Your food's getting cold," he said, picking up the plate warming by the side of the stove, and closing the subject.

"Hang the food, I don't *care* about the food, it's your neck I'm worried about."

"Believe it or not, I've managed to avoid detection for the last few centuries and that's not about to change." A note of irritation had crept into his voice, but this wasn't an issue that could be dodged.

"But things have changed, Matthew; they *are* changing. Surveillance is so much better than it was…"

He put a finger over my lips, willing me to trust him.

"We'll see. Now, eat." He smiled, but whatever he might have me believe, I hadn't been far from the truth.

17

The Trial

"Winter's nearly over," Elena remarked, pulling on her coat and buttoning it up.

I glanced out of the window, distracted despite the seething army of ants crawling around inside me. Snow lay as thickly as ever on the branches of the old cedar tree. As I watched, a wedge slid off one of the boughs and I imagined the soft *slumph* as it fell into the yielding cushion of snow beneath.

"Is it?"

"It is, just you wait and see. Spring will be here soon."

I liked winter in Maine. I liked the way everything became clothed in purifying white as predictably as it rained every winter in England. I liked the way the snow muffled the raucous voices of the students, and yet occasional birdsong echoed clear and strong. But at the mention of it, I felt a surge of longing for spring in Cambridge and for the caustic daffodils brushed by lime-green willows along the banks of the River Cam. I longed to walk in the cloistered gardens of the old stone colleges, sheltered from the bitter easterlies and scented by the warming sun. And I missed the Meadows at home, and the greening grass, and the kingfishers chasing low over the water. My throat began to tighten and I busied myself pulling on black leather gloves, feeling more as if I were going to a funeral than a trial.

Matias pushed the door open with his foot, bringing with him the smell of snowbound air.

"They're on their way, Em."

I started to do up the buttons of my new coat, the tailored black brushed cashmere gleaming like animal fur. Matthew had bought it for me to wear to the trial over my most restrained suit. My gloved fingers fumbled clumsily. Matias pushed my hands away and started to do the buttons up for me, ignoring my feeble objections.

"You don't have to come with me, you two. It's very kind of you, but it's really not necessary."

Elena wagged her finger as if she were scolding a child. "Then you should have told your parents what was happening. If they are not to be here, then we will. You should not have to do this alone."

"I didn't want them to know because there's nothing they can do. Anyway, my grandmother's ill and they can't leave her now. And Matthew will be there, so I'll be fine."

Elena tutted. "Matias, tell her she is wrong. Her parents would want to know, *da*? And you said that you must pretend that you do not know Matthew so well, so he doesn't count." She shrugged, ending the argument in the uplifted movement of her shoulders.

Matias grinned in his brotherly, bear-like way that always made me feel better.

"Besides, we wouldn't miss this for the world. A couple of days off work, free entertainment, and all at your generous expense – great." He rubbed his hands together in anticipation, and I managed something of a smile.

Elena might have been about to reprimand him, but the small man with the bushy black eyebrows – Hart, I discovered his name was – who had been appointed to accompany me to and from the court stood at the door expectantly, and she closed her mouth, glancing anxiously at me instead.

"Time to go, I think," I said, sounding more upbeat than I felt.

We arrived at the courthouse early and I waited in Duffy's office as instructed. Minutes passed and I had looked at my watch for the third time when she burst into the room, grabbed a file from a drawer, rifled through it, selected a few pages, and stuffed the file back where it had come from.

"Hun, we have a change of schedule, so don't hurry yourself. That lawyer from New York has made a request and I have some issues we need to discuss with the judge and that'll take a while."

"Is anything wrong?"

"Wrong? No, I wouldn't say it's wrong, as such, but he's requesting a change of precedence and wants his witness to go after ours. It's not that it's controversial, but it's not usual. Hell, even Staahl's local counsel thinks it odd. It's up to the judge, of course, but we'll have a little chat about it first, don't you worry; we'll make it right."

Her entreaty sounded hollow. This was the first time I had seen Duffy flustered, and it sent strobes of alarm through me.

It didn't get any better.

The courthouse was packed. The judge was late and I sat facing the empty chair while the room filled up behind me. Individual voices merged becoming a sea of sounds, rising and falling along with the waves of nausea that had developed over the morning. I promised, no – threatened – myself that, whatever happened, I would remain calm and in control. *I* was the victim. I was the *victim*, and nothing that came out over the course of this trial could change that.

The windows of the second-floor chamber were set high up in the wall so I couldn't see out, but sunlight streamed through, striking the wall opposite, particles of dust caught in the striated beams. It reminded me that even in this place I could find light and hope.

The jury had been selected beforehand and the jurors now sat at right angles in two rows on pew-like benches, like a choir in church.

Duffy leaned close to me. "Don't play with your cross, it makes you look nervous."

I took my hand abruptly from the chain, and clenched my clammy hands in my lap instead. I heard a suppressed laugh from someone on the prosecution team, but I didn't look, I didn't dare turn my head in case I saw Staahl – just in case he saw me.

"Don't take any notice of them, they get up to tricks. You'll be fine, hun. Just remember, stick to the facts – yes, no – nice and clear, don't rush your answers but don't be hesitant either. You'll do OK."

I barely heard her through the humming in my head. I searched for Matthew, feeling through the mass of bodies behind me, reaching out tendrils of awareness until I could find his familiar, comforting presence. But he was not there and I remembered that until I finished giving evidence, he would not be allowed in the courtroom.

A sudden hush fell and Duffy tugged at my sleeve. I rose with her as the judge, round as a bumblebee, approached the bench, shifted her robe so that it fell over the back of her chair, and sat down. The room sighed as the assembled mass sat as one.

The clerk of court read the declaration and announced Judge Everline Dusk to be presiding. There was a general shuffling and coughing as the crowded room settled to watch.

The lawyer from New York, acting as counsel for the prosecution, stood. Slowly, and with all the authority that his belief in his superiority afforded him, he took the floor. He was a big man with a big voice that reached out over our heads and drew us to him and, from the second he opened his mouth, he had his audience hooked. More than patrician, he was a statesman, and worked the room with all the aplomb of an actor in control of his stage.

"Your Honour," he soothed with his bass voice. "Ladies and gentlemen, my colleague, counsel for the defense, will tell you a tale that would, were it true, be monstrous indeed."

I didn't like him.

"My client, a man of standing within an elite academic university – with an international reputation in his field of research and unimpeachable personal record – is, instead, the casualty of this young woman's obsessive disposition." He turned his body in my direction and I felt a swathe of eyes fall upon me. I straightened my shoulders and stared ahead at nothing, avoiding them.

"What is more, I will show you that, as a result of her subsequent actions, my client has suffered irredeemable damage to his career, resulting in catastrophic emotional trauma." He paused as if struck by the tragedy of it all, before continuing. "I will demonstrate that, far from being a victim of a premeditated attack, this woman was the willing… *willing* participant of a fantasy that she *consented* to in a *mutual*, *prearranged* meeting."

I *really* didn't like him. *Willing, mutual, consent, prearranged* – I heard every word and understood every element of the implied meaning – and so did the onlookers. I could sense the swell of morbid curiosity that arose from them – not disbelief, not sympathy.

From a few yards to my left, a low hiss of breath escaping from between clenched teeth had my blood running thin and cold. I didn't hear the rest of the opening address – I felt alone in the courtroom with Staahl, and it was all I could do to stop from getting to my feet and heading for the door like a bolt from a crossbow.

I started when Duffy tapped my hand and said, "I'm on," and stood to make her initial address.

I phased out, concentrating on my breathing, letting her undulating drawl roll over me, resisting the temptation to look at the judge to see if she believed her. I heard snatches of her argument – everything that she had told me she would say – and then she sat down beside me again, shuffling papers in front of her.

She put a steadying hand on my arm. "OK, hun, you're up." I froze, aware only of Staahl looking at me. "Emma!" the woman said firmly.

I came to, feeling the eyes of the entire courtroom watching as I squeezed out from between my chair and the table and walked, with footsteps echoing in the hushed chamber, to the raised dais by the judge's bench and the chair that sat upon it.

The jury stared at me, in eager condemnation it seemed, as I prepared to take the oath. "Do you affirm…" the clerk intoned, sounding bored.

Forgive me, Lord… I offered a silent prayer.

"… that the testimony you are about to give…"

… if I take the truth in vain…

"… is the truth, the whole truth and nothing but the truth…"

... and sin against you...

"... and this I do under penalty of perjury," the clerk finished.

I hesitated, then in a strong, loud voice that couldn't have been mine replied, "So help me God, I do."

A murmur ran through the room and Duffy winked at me. "Sit down!" she mouthed. I sat a little too rapidly and a titter rippled among a few of the watchers. Heat needled my skin.

Duffy rose and straightened her jacket, stepping forward into the empty space in front of the bench with a practised air. She stood squarely, making the most of her medium height, looking solid, dependable, and utterly trustworthy.

"Professor D'Eresby, you heard me describe the vicious attack made upon you on the night of October 31st of last year..."

"Objection, Your Honour." The counsel for the prosecution was on his feet faster than I would have thought possible for his size. "That is prejudicial; the nature of the event is yet to be decided."

The judge waved a hand at him. "Yes, yes. Counsel for the defense will refrain from making remarks that might lead the witness."

Duffy didn't look in the least bit reprimanded. "Thank you, Your Honour, if I might now continue..."

The judge looked over the edge of her glasses. "I wish you would."

A sniggered murmur issued from Staahl's team, and the judge turned on them. "And time would be best served if you keep your comments pertinent." They fell silent.

Duffy resumed. "It is my job to convince the court that you repeated statements of fact which you believed to be true and, in so doing, are not guilty of *defamation per se*, which implies *intent* to cause harm to an individual's reputation. Professor D'Eresby…" She paused. "Do you know, I just *love* that name. You're from England, are you not?"

Staahl's counsel started to rise but the judge waved him back. He sat down with a shrug.

I cleared my throat. "Yes."

"And you're a professor of history at the University of Cambridge, England, on secondment to Howard's Lake College for a year?"

"Yes."

"So at the time of the *alleged* attack, you had been in these United States of America for… how long?"

"Six weeks."

"Six weeks, and in those six weeks, had you met the defendant at all?"

"Yes."

"How many times?"

I swallowed, "Four – no, five times."

"Just five times, including the night on which you received your life-threatening injuries?"

"Yes."

The big man was on his feet again. "Your Honour, it is a matter of conjecture whether the injuries were life-threatening or not."

Duffy waved a finger at him, then addressed the bench. "Your Honour, I think I can show beyond reasonable doubt that the injuries received by Professor D'Eresby were indeed life-threatening, with the testimony of an expert witness."

Matthew, she meant Matthew. My pulse stuttered briefly. Duffy had asked another question; I must concentrate.

"Professor D'Eresby, on the night in question, you attended an event called the All Saints' dinner in the main hall of the college, is that right?" An image of the great dining hall flashed through my memory: crowded, hot, noisy.

"Yes."

"And all members of staff are expected at this event, is that not so?"

"Yes."

"Including Professor Staahl."

"Yes – but... but he wasn't there."

"He wasn't there? And how do you know that?"

"Because I looked for him and he wasn't there."

"*Why* did you look for him?"

My heart thundered, deafening me. "Because I didn't want to see him." Even to my ears that sounded pathetic.

"You *didn't* want to see him. Why was that, Professor D'Eresby?"

"He frightened me, he... he had been following me. I dreaded seeing him."

I knew this to be dodgy ground so I was surprised when she pushed the point.

"Professor Staahl had been following you?"

"Objection." The prosecution counsel rose again.

"I'm just trying to show the state of mind of this young lady on the night of the attack – my apologies – *alleged* attack, Your Honour."

The judge snuffled and blew her nose. "Overruled. Sit down, counsel."

Duffy directed another question at me. "Did you tell anyone else of your fears?"

"Only Professor Smalova and Professor Lidström."

"Your colleagues. No one else – you are sure of that?"

I sifted rapidly through my memory. "Yes, I'm sure."

"Now..." She took a step towards me and looked up

through her lashes, lowering her voice to a soothing tenor that warned me she was about to ask something I wouldn't like. "I'd like to take you back to the events surrounding that night."

She took me through the attack step by grinding step until I came to the point when Staahl had held the knife to my wrist and Matthew stood beyond the doorway.

"And at that time, did you believe that Professor Staahl intended to take your life?"

"Objection."

"Yes," I said, but so nervously that my voice came out more quietly than I intended.

"I'm sorry, Professor D'Eresby, will you repeat that?"

"*OB*-JECTION!"

Duffy rounded on Staahl's counsel. "There is no need to *shout*. Your Honour…"

The judge called both attorneys to the bench and the room descended into a hum. I had never felt so lonely, the sea of faces before me no more than a blur of shapes and colours, mouths opening and closing, eyes staring. Elena and Matias were in the row directly behind where I had been sitting. Elena clutched Matias's arm, her face pale as she whispered in short bursts to which he replied, the deep creases either side of his mouth moving shadows as he spoke. But near the front, a few rows behind my friends, one face stood apart from the others by its stillness. I focused – it was Henry. Calm and still, he fixed me with a steady gaze and I thanked him silently. He smiled as if he'd heard me.

"Professor D'Eresby, if you would?"

I blinked; I had missed a question. The counsels were back in position and the jury were looking expectant.

Duffy frowned slightly. "If you would please reply so that the court might hear it."

Reply? Blast – what had been the question? I opened my mouth but didn't know what to say.

"*Yes.*" I heard it quite distinctly – a voice from the very centre of me.

"Yes," I said firmly. She looked relieved.

She swung around to half-face the jury. "One last question, Professor D'Eresby – did you ever have sex with Kort Staahl?"

"*No!*" I was half out of the chair before I realized it, and if anyone had been in any doubt about how I felt regarding Staahl, they shouldn't be now. I sat down again.

She gave me a sideways, satisfied look. "Thank you, professor, that'll be all now."

She walked back to our table, leaving me stranded and numb.

The judge took off her glasses and proceeded to clean them on her gown as she peered at me short-sightedly. "You can go back to your seat now, professor."

I nodded and found my feet somewhere at the end of my legs, and made it back to my chair without collapsing and making a complete idiot of myself.

"The court will take recess and reconvene at fourteen hundred hours," the judge announced, and then stood up and left through a rear door. The jury filed out next and then the room burst into a hubbub behind us as people shuffled down the long benches and out of the room.

Duffy finished putting her sheaf of papers away in her bulging briefcase and said something to her clerk, who laughed and shook his head. She swivelled in her chair to face me. "Hun, I expect you could do with some R and R, couldn't you?"

I didn't look at her. "Has he gone?"

She looked mystified. "Who?"

"Staahl. Has Staahl gone?"

She stood up and pushed her chair back, the metal caps on each leg scraping unpleasantly on the scarred wooden floors. "He's gone. I think we'd better have a little downtime here. Come with me and we'll find somewhere quiet to talk."

The hall was almost empty but Elena and Matias were waiting on the bench opposite the door. At the far end of the hall a man talked on a mobile. His expression took on an alert interest when he saw us.

"Journalist," Duffy said loudly. "Best friend or vulture, remains to be seen," she added more quietly.

Matias had one leg crossed over the other and he tapped the toe of his shoe with his thumb like a drumstick on a tambour, *tap, tap, tap*, repeatedly. He stood up as he saw us, his combed hair already beginning to rebel into its normal unruly mass.

"How's it going?" he asked both of us at the same time, but Duffy answered.

"Emma's doing just fine; it's always a bit of a learning curve the first time. You her friend?"

"Yes – Matias Lidström, and this is Elena Smalova," he said, bringing Elena forward with his arm from where she hovered behind him.

"Can we take Emma out? Is it allowed?" Elena asked, looking as anxious as I felt.

"Sure you can, but I want to have a quiet few words with her first, so give us half an hour or so, if you would. I'll show you where my office is so you'll know."

Duffy led us down the back stairs and around to her office.

"Half an hour," Matias said, looking at me with a promise, and the door closed behind me.

Duffy went over to a door at the side of the room and stuck her head around it. "Leon, get us some coffee here and a bagel – the usual." She pulled back to look at me over her shoulder. "Emma, what will you have?"

I shook my head. "Nothing, thank you."

She raised her eyebrows and thrust her head back around the door frame. "Make that two, will you, honey? Sit down, Emma, you look as if you might fall down if you don't." She sat on the chair behind her desk, tilting it on to its back legs like we used to do at school. "Bet you're feeling a little raw now," she observed.

I grimaced. "That was… appalling."

"Now, don't you worry, you did OK. It always feels bad when you're not used to it. That last question took you by surprise, didn't it?"

"I think that's an understatement."

"But it did the trick, and it's something Staahl's counsel will want to come back to so don't let it bother you. We had to get in there first."

The door opened and the clerk brought in a tray with two small red cups that steamed seductively. The aroma of strong coffee filled the room, and I instantly felt a surge of nausea at the acrid smell.

Distaste must have shown on my face because Duffy slapped her thigh. "Dang, I went and forgot you don't drink coffee. Leon, can you go get a bottle of water if you would – thanks." She took a slug of coffee. "I take a double espresso myself during a trial; keeps me alert and frisky and on – their – *case*. All right, any questions?"

"What happens next? Do I have to go back on the stand after lunch?"

She finished her coffee and the cup rattled unevenly as she replaced it on its saucer. "Sure, you'll be up again, the prosecution'll want to ask you some questions in cross-examination. Then, we call our next witness; I expect you know who *that* is?"

I did, but I managed to sound tentative. "Dr Lynes?"

She eyed me speculatively. "Of course you do. He'd be a bit difficult to forget, I imagine – in the circumstances."

I was saved from having to say anything by the clerk coming in with a brown paper bag with "Nellie's Deli" written in red Italianate writing across the front.

The thin paper crackled like Christmas morning as Duffy took out a bagel in a film wrapper, and handed it to me. I wasn't hungry, but took a tentative bite.

"You know, I think we'll do something with your hair before you go back in," she said, wiping her mouth with her napkin. "Loosen it up a little maybe, just around the edges."

I put a hand to my hair defensively. "Why, what's wrong with it?"

"Wrong with it? Did I say there was anything *wrong* with it? Hang, I'd kill for hair like yours. No, at the moment it's a little tight – like a schoolmistress – and the light can't get to it. We want to play the jury a bit before the prosecution gets going, get them on your side."

"I had the impression they've already won them over."

"Hell no, we can do better than *that*. Horatio might be a hot-dog lawyer but this jury is local and I know these people, I've been here long enough."

"Horatio? His name's *Horatio*?" I almost laughed. Almost.

"Quaint, isn't it? You just keep thinking his name when he starts asking you those questions you won't like, that'll help keep it all in perspective." She reached for the second cup of coffee and raised it to her lips. "You sure you and Dr Lynes are just friends?" I nodded, thankful I could focus on eating the bagel rather than having to look at her directly. "I only ask because he's so darn good-looking, a girl'd have to be blind or gay – not that I have anything against gays or such – or lying, not to see it and *hell*, I see it and I'm a happily married woman."

I glanced at her obliquely and she looked at me over the edge of her cup, her eyes sharply enquiring despite the light tone she adopted. "Of course," she said slowly, "we wouldn't want Staahl's counsel thinking there's more to your friendship than just being *friends*, because that might just undermine the testimony and we wouldn't be wanting that, now, would we?" She tapped her finger on her cup, the pink-tipped nail *tinking* flatly on the porcelain.

I pretended to be eating, but in reality I frantically reviewed the past few months and whether we had been less discreet than we thought. I felt doubly thankful we hadn't gone public, but there had still been plenty of speculation. And then there was Sam. If Sam were questioned, would he say anything? I remembered the way he had looked at us at the New Year party as if puzzled why we were not together that evening. He obviously still bore a grudge; would he be willing to cement it by revealing to the prosecution what he knew of our relationship? I hadn't seen him in the courtroom, but then I hadn't looked, and it hadn't occurred to me until now that he might be there.

She stopped tapping. "You know, you'll have to answer counsel if he asks you a direct question, and if you seem evasive, he will keep digging until he finds dirt. So just you remember: keep your answers simple and keep them decisive – whatever they may be." She let the chair drop with a dogmatic thud and put the cup on the saucer. "You better go see your friends. You'll find this afternoon a little taxing so you might need their support. Come back here at a quarter to two and I'll fix your hair."

I stood up gratefully. "Thank you, Duffy, and thanks for the bagel."

"Sure, hun, and you're welcome. Go see your friends; I'll be here."

I welcomed the cold of the street after the stuffy, overheated air of the courthouse. We found the little café we last visited when Elena and I had come shopping for our evening clothes for the All Saints' dinner, a lifetime ago.

The bitter, stewed tea made a welcome change from water and it fed life into my veins. I asked for a second cup as Elena and Matias ate their lunch.

"So, how was it – really?" Matias asked between mouthfuls.

"Really? Pretty horrid. I can understand what it must have been like walking to a scaffold in front of a crowd. You have this ball of fear in the pit of your stomach that won't shift, and when you're up there, you don't see individual faces – people are just a blur – and you think they're all looking at you, and judging you. The worst thing is, when I was asked a question my mind went blank, and I forgot all the things I meant to say and the way I wanted to say them. I felt like such an idiot."

Elena finished her mouthful. "But you did not look it. You looked nervous, yes, but you should not worry about what people think of you – they are on your side." She licked her finger. "That man on the prosecution team is very good too."

I groaned.

"Well, he is," she said, surprised.

Matias shook his head. "Emma doesn't need to hear that, Elena, not now."

"Elena's right, Matias; the man has presence, we can't deny that. The jury lapped him up. He's so convincing."

Matias put his big hand over mine. "So, you'll have to convince them he's wrong, won't you? See it like a debate, not an interrogation, and that is not a scaffold you're on, it's a stage – and you're the main player – so play them."

I rotated my mug on the table in front of me gloomily. "That's what Duffy said, but for me to act the part I have to know my lines, and I keep forgetting them."

"Look, what did you do the first time you lectured to a room full of students?"

I thought back. "I told them what I knew."

"Well, then, that's all you have to do. You know what happened. Tell the truth."

I studiously ignored the black-coated counsel for the prosecution and his client, whose eyes followed me all the way from the door, down the side aisle to my chair next to Duffy, the hairs on the back of my neck prickling with remembrance.

"That's better," Duffy said, inspecting my hair as we sat down. "That makes you look less uptight and a lot more vulnerable." She sat back satisfied, and emptied the contents of her briefcase onto the table, selecting items from it and decking the papers into a pile. Her clerk handed her a piece of paper and they discussed it in subdued tones that I couldn't hear properly.

The loosened hair formed a wave around my head, the strands shining pink-copper in the afternoon sunlight, catching my eye when I least expected it. I resisted the temptation to scrape it all behind my ears and out of my line of sight, and concentrated on the voices around me. I could hear them more clearly than this morning, almost as if I had taken cotton wool from my ears. Snippets of comments – shades of meaning behind veiled words. Mostly innocuous, but odd words filtered through: *fetish, sadist, masochist. She led him on, I read it somewhere.*

I whipped my head around to be met by a dozen pairs of eyes staring back: Elena and Matias – hopeful and supportive, others patently hostile, or curious, suspicious, or indifferent. I found Henry's steady gaze through the wall of strangers, kind and affirming.

Duffy tapped my arm and I turned to face the front as the judge came in and sat down cumbersomely, balancing half-moon spectacles on her nose.

"Prosecution calls Emma D'Eresby."

My mouth went dry. I pressed my damp palms together and rose to my feet, willing my knees to stop shaking. I couldn't read the hazy faces of the jurors as I approached the stand.

"You are still under oath, Ms D'Eresby."

I wondered why the prosecution counsel didn't address me using my title, then realized he used it as a ploy to reduce my standing in front of the jurors. Great.

"Yes."

"I hope that you had a pleasant lunch?"

Pig. As if he cared.

"Yes, thank you."

"In your testimony, Ms D'Eresby, you said that the injury to your right arm was caused by my client bringing it sharply against the edge of the door. I suggest that this could equally have been caused by an accidental blow, perhaps when Dr Lynes *flung* himself with such heroism in order to *save* you."

"No."

"*No*, it wasn't an accidental blow or *no*, Dr Lynes didn't try to save you?"

Horatio Pig.

"Kort Staahl deliberately broke my arm to stop me from struggling and trying to escape."

"So you say…"

My skin flushed but I stuck my chin out stubbornly. "Yes, I do."

"Why were you in the atrium, Ms D'Eresby?"

"I had been told that there was a telephone call for me. I thought that it was an urgent call from England."

"How convenient," he almost sneered, "and was it?"

"No, there was no one there."

"That wasn't much of a surprise though, was it, because you had already arranged to meet my client by the porters' lodge, hadn't you?"

"No."

"Oh, I think you had, but we'll come back to that later."

What did he mean?

"You say that you were afraid of my client. What reason did you have to be afraid of him?"

"I thought he was following me."

"And you reported this to the police?"

"No."

"Why not, Ms D'Eresby? You thought you were being followed – he *frightened* you, you say – and yet you didn't do anything about it. Why not?"

"It would have been difficult to prove."

"You mean you had no *evidence* to support your so-called fears, no evidence – like the telephone call. The jury can only make up their minds if there is *evidence*, Ms D'Eresby. What evidence is there that Kort Staahl planned and carried out an attack on you?"

Duffy cut through his bludgeoning attack. "Objection, Your Honour. Counsel is bullying Professor D'Eresby."

Two tablets plinked and fizzed in the glass of water in the judge's hand. "I want you to reword your question, counsel, and refrain from browbeating the defendant." She drank half the contents in one gulp.

"Ms D'Eresby, tell the court, if you will, about the subject you have chosen to make your particular focus of interest."

"I – I'm a historian. I study late medieval and early modern English and European social and religious history."

"Yes, that's all very *interesting*, but that doesn't define your area of *special* interest, does it? Let me quote some of your more recent works by way of illustration – and this *is* relevant, before counsel for defense objects."

He held up a piece of paper in front of him like a herald reading out a proclamation. "'*Demons and Demonology in Medieval Society.*' '*The Tortured Soul: The Use of Torture in Religious Courts 1300–1500.*' '*Religion Persecuted: The Use of Torture in Religious Courts in the Counter-Reformation.*' '*Crossing the Line: From Sect to Sedition*'; and this one is my favourite: '*Myth, Magic, and Monsters*' – very catchy, I love the use of alliteration, Ms D'Eresby. I could go on, members of the jury, but I think you get the picture." They did; they looked at me in a new light and it wasn't favourable.

"You enjoy studying topics that involve pain and torture, don't you, Ms D'Eresby?"

"No."

"Oh? You were *forced* to research those areas and write papers on them?"

"No."

"Then please explain why a young woman of your obvious… *talent* would wish to focus on such unpleasant, violent subjects?"

A strand of hair strayed over my eyes; I twitched it out of the way. "Because they inform me of human behaviours that shape the history of that period."

"So you say."

I opened my mouth to reply, but he moved on.

"You indulge in fantasies about violence."

"No, I do not."

"You read and study acts of violence – some quite indescribably despicable acts – carried out on other human beings, is that not so?"

Duffy cut in. "Objection. Counsel cannot refer to acts in such general terms as it can lead to misinterpretation."

Horatio held up his hand as if accepting judgment. "Thank you, I am much obliged to the counsel for the defense for pointing that out and I will correct my error by being more specific. Ms D'Eresby, let me read from part of your own work, your paper on: '*The Tortured Soul: 1300 to 1500*'.

"'*Although Papal guidelines were in place, authority for the processing of inquisition was not centralized until the Reformation. Responsibility for the organization of inquisition therefore lay with local officials resulting in varying interpretation of the guidelines.*' Blargh, blargh, blargh – ah yes, here we are…"
A widespread snigger from around the room.

"'*Records from the Courts of Inquisition held locally recount the use of torture including: ripping out of teeth, hair or nail, beating, choking, bone-breaking, and cutting…*'

"Bone-breaking, choking, and cutting… and the list continues with some graphic descriptions and examples. So, I repeat, you read and study acts of violence, carried out by individuals on other human beings, is that not the case?"

I glared at him, but could not get around this one. "Yes."

"Yes – you do, and indeed only recently you read such a work, did you not?"

I frowned. "No."

"Oh, really? Then let me remind you. Do you recognize

this book?" The black cover with its red lettering shouted at me from where he waved it for everyone to see: it was a copy of Staahl's book Maggie gave me at Christmas. I paled. "I see that you do. Can you remind the court of its title?"

My lips were numb, my mouth refused to move. Maggie must have told Staahl's counsel about it, and if she had told him that, what else had she been prepared to say?

"Let me help you, Ms D'Eresby. The title of the book is: *The Devil's Whore: The Role of Women in Medieval & Early Modern Literature*, by Professor Kort Staahl. Do you recognize it?"

"Yes – yes, but…"

"And what is the main theme of the work?"

"I… I haven't read all of it."

"Let me remind you again. It is a book whose main theme postulates the theory that women are the willing sexual playthings of men. Were you aware of this?"

I bit my lip.

"Yes or no, Ms D'Eresby."

"Yes."

"And were you in receipt of a copy of this book recently?"

"Yes."

"And can you explain how it is that it cites in *specific* and *graphic* detail the cutting of a woman and the drawing of blood from the wound as part of a sadomasochistic act in *precisely* the same way as you described your alleged attack?"

"No, I don't know."

"Are you saying that you were not aware of this?"

I hadn't read enough of the blasted thing, had I? "I was not."

"Will members of the jury please look at the page marked with the blue tag and then at the page marked with the red tag and then at the date on the front page along with the dedication, marked in yellow. Court clerks, if you will assist the jurors. Ms D'Eresby, if you would care to look at this copy…"

He strode over to me where I sat as rigid as timber. He held out the book and I fumbled taking it from his hand. Turning to the page marked with a thin blue tab, I saw that a section had been underlined and highlighted. I recognized a direct quote from one of my own works with a reference number. I opened the page near the back marked with the red tab and saw the reference number next to my name and the piece of research from which the quote had been taken; it had been published in an obscure periodical years ago, but I remembered it well. Staahl had totally misrepresented what I had written, placing it within a context entirely suited to his own needs. I had no doubt how it would appear to anyone reading it here, outside the strict boundaries of historical reference in which I had confined it.

Hands shaking, I turned to the front page. My hand shot over my mouth and I bit the side of it as I read the dedication:

> *Dedicated to E. D'Eresby, without whose inspiration this book would never have been written.*

And the day and month.

"I don't understand…" I shook my head in disbelief, crushed by the weight of evidence so circumstantial that I would never have relied on it in my research. That wasn't the point; it was how it would look to the casual observer, how it could be *made* to look – manipulated, manoeuvred – until the abuser became the abused and the world turned upside down.

My voice rasped out thin and drawn and harsh. "This has *nothing* to do with me. This is a… corruption of my work."

"By your own admission, Ms D'Eresby, you had a copy of this book."

"Yes, I did, but…"

"Who gave it to you?"

"I… don't know."

"You don't *know*?" He made me sound like a liar. I *was* a liar.

"It could have been anyone."

"No, Ms D'Eresby, not *anyone*. Professor Staahl says that he had only *one* copy of his book and that he sent it to *you*."

"No!" I looked wildly around. Elena had her head turned away.

"Yes, Ms D'Eresby, only – *one* – copy."

"Someone else must have sent it," I said desperately.

"No, there were no other copies at that time. The book had not yet been distributed. You were in receipt of the only copy available in the world. These…" he indicated the books now being collected by the court clerks from the jurors, "… were advance copies obtained from the publishers for the purpose of this trial."

"That's impossible," I whispered.

"Where is the book now, Ms D'Eresby?"

I closed my eyes, hearing condemnation in my own words. "I burned it."

"How *convenient*," he dripped sarcasm. "Now, please tell the jury why you were in the atrium on the night of October 31st."

"There was a telephone call…"

"Which has not been traced. You were there to meet Kort Staahl for a specific, lewd purpose and, had you not been interrupted by Dr Lynes, your assignation might never have been discovered."

"He attacked me!"

"We have already seen your penchant for the macabre. Dr Lynes came upon a scene – perhaps by accident, perhaps not – he would naturally think bizarre and, in believing he was coming to your aid, only served to cause additional damage to a consensual act. The knife slipped, Ms D'Eresby. Caught in a compromising position, you decided to turn the tables to defend your own reputation using Dr Lynes as a witness. Thinking he was helping you, Dr Lynes forcibly restrained Kort Staahl and might have injured him had it not been for you calling to him to stop, and the arrival shortly afterwards of other members of college staff. And at – no – *point* did my client attempt to fight back." He beat out each word with the flat of his open hand on the blank, black face of the book.

"NO!"

"*Why* did you tell Dr Lynes to stop hurting the man you claim had been – only seconds before – trying to kill you? Surely that is inconsistent, Ms D'Eresby?"

"I didn't – he wasn't. I… I was losing consciousness, I was…"

"So you said, Ms D'Eresby, but the facts speak for themselves."

He cut short my stumbling explanation, leaving me high and dry like a stranded fish futilely flapping on the beach of his accusation. I could feel myself slipping beyond reason, his words blinding me. I wiped the perspiration from my forehead but found it to be dry and burning instead, and inside my chest, my fraught heart laboured heavily.

Duffy sprang to her feet, giving me a welcome reprieve. "Your Honour, I must protest at my client being subjected to this barrage of questioning."

The judge coughed gently, looked at me, and then squinted at her watch. "It's getting late. Court will adjourn for the day. Counsel for the prosecution can resume questions tomorrow."

Horatio threw a livid look at Duffy, who returned it.

I gathered my coat and bag and looked up as Elena and Matias joined me.

"You did well, Emma," Matias said quietly, as he helped Elena into her coat. "I don't think I could have been so cool on the witness stand in the circumstances. Would you like to come back with us?"

I barely listened. Elena weaved her arm through mine. "And when we get back, I will fix you some of that soup you like so much, yes?"

I hugged her arm and smiled thinly. "That'd be great, thanks."

We sidled past small clusters of people still talking in the aisles and resisting the attempts of the judicial marshal and court sergeant to move them on so they could lock up the room and go home for the night. One or two people looked at me curiously as we passed, and a figure blocked our exit. I did a double-take. "Dad!" I exclaimed. "What are you doing here?"

He wrapped me in a big embrace, his clothes smelling of home – of his potting shed and hyacinths, homemade marmalade, and old stone walls.

My first instinct was to cling to the father who had comforted and protected me when I was very little, and before I knew my own mind and he wanted to change it. But my next was to protect him from the full horror of the trial.

"Dad, why have you come? How did you kno…"

"Dr Lynes phoned me…"

"Shh," I hushed, throwing a look at Hart. "Wait until we get outside."

It was still light outside the courthouse and a small crowd lingered on the steps. As soon as they spotted us, they turned as one towards me.

The journalist I had seen earlier detached himself from the crowd and made a beeline for us. "Professor!" He shoved between my father and me. "Any comments? Why did you meet Kort Staahl that night?"

I started to respond, but my father stepped in front of him, shielding me from view. "Dr D'Eresby has no comments at the moment." He took my arm and walked us down the steps and along the pavement. The journalist started to follow, but a flurry of noise at the top of the steps captured his attention and he spun around and bounded back up them two at a time. I looked back and caught a glimpse of the prosecution team before we rounded the corner of the street and were out of sight.

We travelled back to college without speaking. When safely within the confines of my apartment, Dad took off his coat and folded it precisely, lining side out, the yellow silk gleaming in the last light of the sun.

"Dr Lynes thought we should know. I would have been here this morning, but we had fog at Heathrow and it delayed the flight for a couple of hours." He placed the coat over the back of a chair. "He shouldn't have been the one to tell us about the trial, Emma. This is not something you should go through alone."

"I'm not alone, I'll be fine." I pulled off my gloves and he helped me with my coat, running his eyes appreciatively over the fabric. "Matthew bought it for me," I said, taking it from him.

"He's looking after you," he stated.

I appreciated the effort he made to prevent it from

sounding like an accusation. We still had so many years of resentment to make up and it was early days yet.

"I didn't think it fair on you and Mum, not with Nanna so unwell. Besides, I didn't want you hearing all the details." I switched on the desk lamp. "Sit down, Dad; I'll make a cup of tea."

"Emma, you know I didn't come to interfere." He stood all stuffy and formal in his customary tweed jacket and heavy winter twill trousers and brown lace-up shoes. "Matthew told me what happened in quite some detail back in November. You don't have to protect me. I saw and heard things that were much worse when in the Army."

"Did you?" I drew my hand wearily over my eyes. "I didn't realize. But it's not the same when it's family, is it? And Staahl's team is putting a rather unpleasant twist on things."

My father regarded me from under his shrubby brow. "I gathered that."

"And I think it's going to get much worse."

"I expect it will." He changed tack. "I take it from what you said earlier that you are playing down your relationship with Matthew?" I nodded. "You don't want his – or your – evidence compromised?"

I nodded again. "Dad…" I hesitated. "You might hear me say things that you know are not… accurate. Please, *please* don't think that it makes what the prosecution says any more true. I have my reasons."

He mustered an interrogative eyebrow. "I'm sure you do," he said, but thankfully didn't ask me to explain.

18

The Trial – Day Two

Elena had been right about a change in the weather. Overnight, cloud had drifted in, obscuring the cold, blue sky, and bringing with it a warming wind. The snow still clinging to the branches of the cedar tree became increasingly translucent as, drop by drop, it began to melt.

Ready early, I phoned Matias before Hart arrived to collect me. "I don't want Elena sitting through the trial," I told him. "Please, Matias, I really appreciated you being there yesterday, but I saw Elena and she's finding it really difficult to cope."

He coughed, his voice still gruff with sleep. "Yes, she is – it reminds her of when she was attacked as a girl. You know how stubborn she is; I'll need a good reason for her not to go."

I had anticipated that. "I meant to meet with my students today; could she do that for me instead? We haven't that long before the conference and I could do with some help getting them prepared. Would that work?"

"It might," he said thoughtfully. "I'll give it a go. If it does and we don't see you there – good luck today."

"Thanks," I said. "I think I'm going to need it."

In the quiet moments as I waited for my father, I sought enough stillness within me to ask for the courage to do what was right in the day to come, and for forgiveness for failing the day before. I then checked my mobile for messages. There were two: one from Beth, wishing me luck, which meant that Dad had told her about the trial; the other from Matthew.

I opened it, read it and reread it to make sure. It was the last verse of a poem by George Herbert:

> *Onely a sweet and virtuous soul,*
> *Like season'd timber never gives:*
> *But though the whole world turn to coal.*
> *Then chiefly lives.*

I understood his message; he wanted me to follow my conscience before all else, before *him*, and that my soul was more important than all other worldly considerations.

I rapped the mobile against my chin, thinking of a reply. It wasn't great, but it would have to do:

> *Who is so safe as we? Where none can do*
> *Treason to us, except one of us two.*

It might be a bastardized version, but it was the best I could come up with at such short notice. I kissed the screen and pressed *send*, watching the little arrow pulse as the message transferred. Just in time; I heard noisy footsteps on the wooden floor outside my door and opened it before my father could raise his hand to knock.

The courtroom positively teemed as more people than yesterday tried to squeeze onto the benches. Harry also now sat behind me, and he had been joined by Pat. A place between them remained empty. She gave me an encouraging smile as she sat down, her coral jacket a splash of vibrant colour in the grey light of the morning. My father sat to the right, a stranger separating them. I hadn't introduced him to Matthew's family and I didn't indicate that I knew them except for the brief smile of gratitude I returned to Pat. The judicial marshal was trying to organize a small group of people who were arguing about seating arrangements. Several of them had notebooks in hand. Reporters. Outside in the hall, Matthew probably waited to be called as a witness later in the day, and as much as I longed to see him, I dreaded the thought of him up there on the witness stand in the eye of the world. The burgeoning audience made me nervous.

"Why are there so many people here today, Duffy?"

A clerk plomped into the chair beside Duffy, thrusting a newspaper in front of her.

Looking up from the paper, Duffy folded it and put it away.

"This is a little town, hun. Not much happens around here and people are interested. It gives them something to talk about."

I scanned the crowd. A number of people held newspapers in their hands, some being read, others rolled or folded as if they had been finished with, but not yet discarded.

"Is it in the press?"

Duffy busied herself arranging her files on the table. "Sure, honey."

"May I see?" I held out my hand. Reluctantly, she handed me her paper.

"College Don in Sex Fetish Trial"

I caught sight of my name in the piece that followed and hastily closed the newspaper. "It could be worse," I said, handing it back to Duffy.

"It probably will be – just so you're prepared," she warned.

A light movement of air brought change behind me, but I still started when I felt a hand on my shoulder. Henry smiled apologetically as I turned around. He lent close and took my hand and pressed something small and round and hard into it. "Matthew said this will mean something to you," he said quietly, and closed my hand around the object, keeping it hidden. "God bless, Emma."

"Thanks, Henry." I opened my hand slightly. There in my palm lay the russet nutmeg, worn smooth and glossy through all the long years that Matthew had kept it with him as a symbol of hope. I brought it to my lips, then clenched it tightly, its presence as staunch and unswerving as its owner.

Staahl's team sauntered in at the last minute and the drum of my heart stepped up a beat. They took their time to settle, taking centre stage from the moment they set foot through the door.

"All rise."

The courtroom hushed and rose as the small figure of the judge made her way to the bench and sat down, adjusting her glasses with one hand and her robes with the other. She had had her hair done since yesterday, and the grey curls that bloomed around her face, making her look like an aged Shirley Temple, were now neater and tighter and tamed.

She reminded us that witnesses were still under oath, and then the first witness of the day was called. I took a deep breath, held the nutmeg tightly in my fist, and walked as calmly as I could to the stand.

"I trust you had a pleasant evening, Ms D'Eresby," Horatio oozed, "and are feeling quite refreshed?"

I might still be under oath, but did he really want the truth? Sometimes history was best fudged.

"Thank you for your concern," I answered ambiguously. He looked a little nonplussed, but nonetheless continued to seamlessly recap his argument for the benefit of the jury. Many of their faces were now familiar: the tall man with the long, thin face and lantern jaw – like a Hapsburg – who must have had a hearing problem he hadn't declared because he leaned forward with his left ear to catch what counsel was saying. The woman with the blonde wig and big earrings, who tried to look forty but must have been at least fifteen years older. The younger woman sitting at the end nearest to the witness bench, who smiled all the time, but only with her mouth; the rest of her face never followed. And the little mouse-like man with small black eyes that darted to and fro restlessly. I tried to work out what they were all thinking, but their expressions changed depending on who presented the evidence, and I found myself relying more and more on guesswork and instinct.

Horatio wound himself and the jury up to an attack. He had patently disliked being interrupted yesterday and had lost momentum as well as his audience's interest. Now he had to recapture both.

"Are you promiscuous, Ms D'Eresby?"

Wow, that made some opening gambit, but it didn't shock me as much as it might have done a few days ago. It did the trick for the jury though; they craned forward to hear my reply.

"No, I am *not*."

They sat back almost with a sigh of disappointment. What on earth did they *think* I would say? I quelled the rising irritation I felt at his blatant attempt to discredit me.

"No? Is it not true that you had a relationship while at the University of Cambridge?" He had been doing his homework. Duffy had warned me he had been digging around in my past, but I hadn't thought he could make much of it. I was wrong.

"Yes."

"And it was a relationship prohibited by the university, but in which you blithely proceeded to indulge nonetheless, and one that nearly ended the career of your unfortunate lover, is that not the case?"

This was so embarrassing with my father sitting here listening to all this guff and worse – *blast*, it'd only just dawned on me – and worse still, so was Matthew's family. Talk about hanging out dirty washing for all to see. The media were lapping it up.

"Not exactly, no."

"But you knowingly flouted the rules of the university, did you not?"

"Yes, but…"

"So you think you are above the law, is that it, Ms D'Eresby? You knew the rules but chose to ignore them, intent only on indulging your own desires."

"No!"

He smirked, making his view on the matter clear to the jury. "By your own admission, *yes*, I think, Ms D'Eresby! No more questions at this point, Your Honour," he announced with a dismissive wave of his hand, intended to make me feel insignificant. It worked. He turned to go to his table.

"Can I have that in writing?" I muttered under my breath.

Duffy flashed me a look that warned me I should have stayed silent. Horatio hadn't yet reached his table and he swivelled on one foot to face me again.

"Did you *say* something, Ms D'Eresby?"

The judge leaned over the bench and looked down at me. "Repeat what you said for the jury please, professor."

Ugh! Humiliation or contempt of court? What a choice. Humiliation carried the lesser penalty.

"I said, 'Can I have that in writing?'"

The judge's mouth twitched as the room descended into laughter. She thwacked her gavel on the bench hard enough to dent the wood. "Counsel will *please* advise her client that such comments are not for this court."

"Thank you, Your Honour," Duffy admonished me with a look that was meant more for the judge's appeasement than for my contrition. "Professor D'Eresby, can you please tell the jury how old you were when you entered into the relationship you had while at Cambridge?"

"I was nineteen."

"*Only* nineteen. And how old was the man with whom you had this relationship?"

It seemed so seedy now that I looked back at it. "He was thirty-six."

A low murmur wove through the courtroom, but I couldn't tell whether from sympathy or disapproval.

"Let me get this straight: he was a 36-year-old senior lecturer and you were a nineteen-year-old student just out of school. That sounds more like an *abuse* of trust by a man who should have known better. Was it a serious relationship?"

"I thought so at the time; it lasted just under a year."

"And tell me if you will, professor, how many relationships have you had since then?"

My hand gripped the nutmeg. *Forgive me.* "None." I didn't waver as I answered, because what Matthew and I had didn't count – *couldn't* count – not if we wanted what we had to remain undisclosed for as long as possible.

"So much for promiscuity, hey, Horatio? Thank you, professor."

I felt like hugging her.

Staahl's counsel circled like a shark. He took his time until the judge began to shuffle impatiently. I peeked at my watch; it was already after eleven.

"Ms D'Eresby, yesterday you gave evidence about how you were allegedly saved by Dr Lynes, although you were unfortunately injured in the process as you were *thrown* to one side. What did you say when you saw Dr Lynes attack my client?"

"Objection!"

"Sustained. Do I even have to say *why*, counsel?"

He placed a hand over his heart. "My apologies, Your Honour. Ms D'Eresby, when you saw Dr Lynes with my client, whom he held by the throat against the back wall of the porters' lodge on the night of October 31st, what words did you use?"

"I said, '*No!* Matthew, *no!*'"

"That's all?"

"Yes."

"Are you *sure*, Ms D'Eresby? Because my client says that you said: '*No!* Matthew, *no!* You'll *kill* him.'"

"No."

"Oh, *yes*, ma'am. You saw Dr Lynes forcefully restrain my client and you told him to stop. Why?"

"No."

"Is it perhaps because you didn't want to see your lover, whom you had arranged to meet that night, hurt?"

"I was dying. I wasn't in any position to say anything to anyone."

"Ms D'Eresby…" he began, holding back to build up the tension. "How often did you meet Kort Staahl for sex?"

"Never!"

"Let me put it another way. How many times did you meet with my client?"

"Intentionally – none."

"That's a *lie*, isn't it, Ms D'Eresby?"

"Ob-jec-*tion!*" Duffy leapt to her feet, face scarlet. "Counsel is attacking my client, Your Honour."

"Yes, yes – counsel, might I remind you to try not to use such a contentious line with the defendant?"

He inclined his head to the judge in acknowledgment before turning back to me.

"I shall rephrase my question. That is *untrue*, isn't it, Ms D'Eresby? On at least one occasion – and we can only guess on how many others – you invited my client to meet with you."

"I did *not!*" I said vehemently.

"Oh, I think you will find I am perfectly correct in my assertion."

He held up something small and pale lilac in a little evidence bag; it looked familiar. "Have you seen this before?"

I squinted, but I couldn't make it out. He brought it closer so that I could see through the plastic film some elongated, sloping handwriting in blue. My stomach crunched: it was mine.

"If you would care to examine the exhibit, Ms D'Eresby."

I took it from him. Without opening the bag I smoothed the crinkles from the plastic until I could read what it said. I felt all colour drain from my face as I now realized its relevance.

"Ms D'Eresby, do you recognize this note?" A hush had descended on the entire room. "Well?"

"Yes," I whispered.

"Louder for the court, Ms D'Eresby."

I cleared my throat. "Yes."

"Read it out loud, if you will."

I continued to hold the bag with the lilac Post-it note in one hand, the nutmeg in the other.

"*Now*, if you please." Except for a ticking noise coming from one of the water-filled radiators, the room was silent.

I chewed my lip. "This wasn't meant for *him*," I said, too quietly.

"Read it to the jury, Ms D'Eresby."

"I did *not* write this for Kort Staahl." My voice had risen higher than I intended, making it sound shrill and defensive and *guilty*.

"Ms D'Eresby…"

"All *right!*" I snapped, feeling cornered and at bay with his teeth at my throat.

I heard Duffy's sharp intake of breath and the judge peered at me over her spectacles. "Read it as directed by counsel, professor."

I nodded mutely, miserably. "'Meet you at 10 at A re: S & M as promised.'"

I kept my eyes lowered and my head down, avoiding looking at people's faces in case I saw the condemnation I fully anticipated there. There were a few murmured remarks that sounded like questions, but nothing more.

"I'm sorry," Horatio swaggered, "some of the jury didn't quite catch what you said. Repeat it so that they can *all* hear it this time." The look of satisfaction on his face said it all, like a playground bully with his heel in his victim's face.

I slowly raised my head and turned to look directly at the jury, some of whose knowing, disgusted, *riveted* faces told me only too clearly that they had heard what I said perfectly well the first time. I rallied what courage I had left and, in a loud, slow clear voice that defied any of them to comment, I reread the note: "'Meet you at 10 at A re: S & M as promised.'"

I lowered the note and waited. First there were a few disbelieving gasps, then some sniggers, and finally – as one by one the audience worked out the significance of the note – the room broke down into a clamour of conjecture. Horatio cast a *told-you-so* look in Duffy's direction. Just behind her, my father sat forward on his seat with his head in his hands, and next to him, the Lynes family were stony-faced and completely still, neither looking in my direction nor at each other. There would be no point in trying to explain the note to them, to the court, the media – anyone. No point at all. They would all come to their own conclusions based on the evidence presented to them and the innate prejudices of the human condition. I hadn't a chance. I felt my skin blaze crimson under the lurid, sleazy eyes of the courtroom as they sat in judgment on me.

The judge hammered on her bench, but it took minutes for the racket to die down enough for her to make herself heard. "I will *not* have my court turned into a circus," she boomed across the heads of the crowd. "Any repeat of this behaviour and I will hear evidence in closed court." Silence fell as the room settled rapidly into order. "Now, counsel?"

"No more questions, Your Honour," he said with a self-satisfied smirk.

"Counsel for the defense?"

"Thank you, Your Honour." Duffy rose slowly, giving everyone time to adjust to her being there and for me to gather my wits. She retrieved the evidence wallet with the lilac Post-it note and held it up high. "Professor D'Eresby, counsel would have us believe that this note was sent by you to Kort Staahl as an invitation to meet him. Was this your intention?"

I swallowed to loosen vocal cords that were so tight they hurt.

"No."

She leaned forward slightly. "There was no name on this note; who did you intend it for?"

"I wrote the note for Professor Smalova. I left it in her pigeon-hole in the history faculty, but she didn't get it. The…" I stopped suddenly as I realized what must have happened. "*He* must have taken it," I accused Staahl, remembering how he had known where I would be when I went to collect the posters from the porters' lodge earlier in the term. Increasingly jittery as the lack of sleep began to take its toll, my raw nerves were made more ragged as they were dragged back and forth between prosecution and defense like a dry loaf of bread on a cheese grater.

"Please explain exactly what the note means, letter by letter," Duffy prompted me back into line.

"The note meant 'Meet me at 10 p.m. in my apartment to talk about Sam and…'" I barely paused, "'Matias', as we had promised."

"Please explain to the jury who the people you have referred to are."

"Professor Elena Smalova is a friend and colleague of mine from the history faculty, Professor Sam Wiesner was a mutual friend of ours, and Professor Matias Lidström is Professor Smalova's fiancé." All very normal, very respectable.

"And why were you going to meet to discuss Sam and Matias?"

I thought quickly. "It was just girls' talk – I can't really remember what about."

"Please try, professor."

Duffy was attempting to paint a different picture, one of an ordinary young woman doing ordinary things with ordinary people.

"I think that we were going to discuss them because Elena thought that we might all go out together and she wanted to know what I thought."

"About what, exactly?" she probed.

"Professor Wiesner."

"Was he your boyfriend?"

"No, but I think he wanted to be."

"Why do you believe that Professor Staahl took the note?"

"He had done something like that before."

"Is that one of the reasons why you thought he was following you?"

"Yes."

Such boring, mundane, everyday, *trivial* stuff. Who would want to believe it, when the spicy bits were so much more titillating?

"Professor D'Eresby, have you ever invited, agreed to meet, or have gone out of your way to meet Kort Staahl at *any* time since joining the college in September of last year?"

"*Never.*"

"Thank you, professor. I have no more questions for the defendant, Your Honour."

I hoped that a few of the faces looking at me from among the jurors might be less judgmental now that Duffy had given me a chance to explain the note, but nothing in their expressions made me think they viewed me as anything other than a black-hearted whore, and a perverted one at that.

My arm ached. Although the fracture had healed perfectly, just occasionally it throbbed where the bone had broken, reminding me – if ever I needed reminding – that the attack wasn't so very long ago, and that some of the scars I bore were still rough-edged and new, even if the physical ones had mended. I rubbed and kneaded the area, but it continued to niggle.

The judge finished conferring with the court clerk and announced an early break for lunch, and we let the room empty before making any attempt to leave. My father hung back but Henry, Pat, and Harry left as soon as they could without looking at me. I waited in abject misery, rolling the nutmeg between my palms.

Duffy didn't say anything until we were alone. "Emma, there's going to be reporters and such waiting for you out there, so use my office if you like and you can send out for some lunch."

"Thanks," I said quietly.

"Aw, don't take it so bad. Horatio's just clutching at straws to blacken your reputation. It's all in the game."

"Yes, well, he seems to be doing a pretty good job of it," my father groused, his jutting jaw making him look more like a bulldog than ever. Duffy didn't disagree.

"*You* believe me, don't you, Duffy?" I asked, watching her evasive movements as she sorted out papers before putting them into her briefcase.

She avoided looking at me. "It doesn't matter what I think, only what the jury believes."

"I know that, Duffy, but it matters to me what you think. How can you fight my corner if you don't trust that what I say is true?"

She stopped fiddling and swivelled to face me, one hand on her hip as she inclined her head to consider me thoughtfully. "Hun, I don't rightly know if everything you have told me *is* true, wait…" She held up her hand as I began to object. "Especially when it comes to Dr Lynes – you two look as if you should be together, if you get my drift. But Staahl is as guilty as a 'gator with its mouth full, and you sure don't strike me as a kinky type, so, whatever you're not telling me, I don't think it's relevant to this trial. Now, go get some lunch and some rest before this afternoon. The judge is real eager to wrap this up and ship it out, so you'll need to be on your toes in case you're called again. You want me to take you to my office, or can you find it by yourselves? No, scratch that, I'll take you round the back way so you'll avoid them flesh-stripping vultures out there."

She took us via the door to the courtroom that the judge used though the various offices until we came to her own. She left us there in the comparative peace of the empty room. I slumped into the chair behind her desk.

"Emma…?" Dad said tentatively. I glanced up and my heart tugged. He looked so miserable, his shoulders sagging and his gruff face worn and despondent. "I know what was said was untrue – every last, sick, twisted word of it – and it doesn't matter what anybody else says about you, you're still my little girl, and I'll defend your reputation to the grave, if that's what it'll take."

I sprang out of the chair and hugged him hard until I could speak without my voice wobbling.

"Thanks, Dad. Don't worry about my reputation. I reckon I'll be able to sell a few more books with all the attention this will bring me; just think of the royalties."

He gave a little *hurrumph* of a laugh, more, I thought, because of the sheer ridiculousness of what I had said than because he found it funny. My tummy rumbled unexpectedly, and he smiled fondly. "Well, *that's* a good sign. Let me get you some lunch before we have to face the enemy again, shall we?"

Lunch was a hurried, silent, and tasteless affair, washed down by the deli's approximation of tea. We returned to the courtroom as sleet started to fall sullenly from the sky.

"I don't know what he's at," Duffy said as we finally resumed our places, "but Horatio's sure playing unconventional." She wouldn't be drawn further, except to say that we were up next, and the general shuffling of feet and of comments exchanged ensured I didn't hear her murmured afterthought, as the courtroom prepared for the next player.

Now mid-afternoon, the room had become overly warm. With their stomachs still full after lunch, time began to drag and the onlookers were getting bored. A juror – the woman in her fifties with cheeks made of gently sagging skin – yawned. As her mouth opened wider, her hand barely covering the aperture, she suddenly stopped and nudged the younger woman sitting next to her. Together they stared as an awed hush flowed through the room. Duffy turned and winked at me as Matthew walked with lithe grace to the witness stand to take the oath. He passed within a foot of where I sat, the movement of air he caused brushing my skin. He could have been on the other side of the planet for all the comfort it gave me, and I didn't dare give him more than a cursory glance in case our bond showed on my face.

I felt the surge of electric interest sweeping through the watching crowd. Briefly, Ellen's words about the effect he had on people came back to me. Sitting there, I wondered whether it was entirely to do with his looks, or more the energy he exuded, as if he brought light with him into the room. If aware, he didn't show it as he took the oath.

Duffy stood to one side, making sure she didn't obscure him from the jury.

"Dr Lynes, you are in the unique position of being the first at the scene of the event as well as the medical practitioner who treated Emma D'Eresby immediately after the incident took place. Can you please tell the jury in what capacity it was that led you to be at the scene of the alleged – I struggle to find another word for it – crime?"

I thought it an oddly worded question.

"I had been at the All Saints' dinner when I received a call to attend an emergency at the Memorial Hospital here in town, and was returning when I heard noises in the atrium. I went to investigate."

"Forgive me, doctor, but why interrupt your evening by going all the way to town to attend a medical emergency? Surely the hospital here has its own medical staff without having to call on your services?"

"I am able to help out when the hospital is short-staffed, as it had been because of the seasonal flu outbreak."

"Yes, but on the night in question there had been no further admissions for flu, had there, so the staff were not so hard-pressed?"

"Yes, that is so. However, the nature of the emergency required specific intervention…"

"That only you were able to perform?"

"In this case, yes."

His modesty only served to fuel the impression he gave of altruism. The crowd were rapidly warming to him.

"Can I bring you back to when you discovered the incident – you heard noises in the atrium; what sort of noises?"

"I heard a woman scream."

"What did you do then?"

"I went to investigate and I saw Professor D'Eresby and Professor Staahl in the porters' lodge. The door was ajar."

"Can you describe for us exactly what you saw, doctor?"

"Professor Staahl was standing behind Professor D'Eresby, gripping her left arm with his left hand and with his right arm across the front of her body, trapping her. He held a knife against the inside of her left wrist."

"Did Professor D'Eresby look as if she was enjoying herself?"

"Objection!"

The judge must have been suffering with her cold. She took out a man-sized hankie and blew her nose on it noisily, before regarding Horatio with baggy eyes.

"Sustained."

"Can you tell the jury of your impression of Professor D'Eresby's demeanour at the time, Dr Lynes?"

"She looked terrified."

The room echoed to a low murmur. I didn't dare look at Matthew because I could feel what he saw in his mind's eye – my ashen face, screwed with fear and pain – and I knew how it hurt him although it wasn't reflected in his face.

"And at that point did Professor D'Eresby struggle or try to fight back?"

"She was on the verge of losing consciousness, and her right arm had been fractured, so she couldn't move without great pain."

"And you could see that her arm was broken from where you were standing, even through you were some way away? How?"

"I have seen many broken arms in my career."

"At this juncture, what did you do?"

"I challenged Professor Staahl; I told him to let her go."

"And did he?"

"No, he did not. He pressed the knife into her wrist, causing it to bleed."

"He slashed her wrist?"

"No, not at that point. Professor Staahl used the point of the knife to make an incision in Professor D'Eresby's inside wrist." From somewhere outside in the street, a car blared its horn and another answered, shrilly.

"What happened then, Dr Lynes?" Duffy asked.

"I repeated that he should let Professor D'Eresby go, but he used the knife to cut her wrist."

"From side to side?"

"No, longitudinally."

"In your opinion and from what you witnessed that night, could the cutting of Professor D'Eresby's wrist have been an accident?"

Matthew turned on Staahl, his eyes as hollow and black as I knew he felt inside. "No, I believe it was an act calculated to cause pain and massive loss of blood."

Duffy let the enormity of what he said sink in. The jurors' faces spoke volumes. Near the middle of the room, a sudden commotion broke out as a young man pushed past the legs of people seated next to him on the bench, his hand clamped over his mouth as he made for the door.

"Did Professor D'Eresby at any point assent to what was being done to her?"

"No."

"How did you react to what he was doing?"

"I intervened to prevent him from killing her."

"Shouldn't you have waited for the police?"

"No, Professor Staahl still had the knife. I didn't know what he was going to do next and Professor D'Eresby was losing too much blood to wait. I had no choice but to act."

"So you prevented him from hurting her any further. What then?"

"He dropped the knife and I went to Professor D'Eresby. I had to stop the bleeding." His brow creased as he remembered.

"And what was Kort Staahl doing at this time?"

Matthew raised his eyebrows. "I believe he was unconscious."

"You *believe* he was unconscious. Didn't you know? He might have attacked again."

"I was more concerned with controlling the bleeding than anything else. People were arriving and I left them to deal with him. I took Professor D'Eresby to the medical centre."

"You didn't wait for paramedics – you took her yourself – you carried her?"

"Yes, there wasn't time to wait. She was dying."

Duffy let his last words hang in the air. "Thank you, Dr Lynes. I will be calling you again for your expert testimony and medical opinion."

Matthew remained as outwardly self-possessed and calm as when he came in, but inside he seethed in a coiling mass of conflicting emotions. I reached out to him, trying to make a connection, but he avoided me and I realized he only just maintained his composure. It's strange, sometimes, how it's easier to cope with your own pain than to watch someone else go through it. Although it made me queasy listening to Matthew's account, there was nothing that I didn't already know. There was nothing in *how* he recounted what he had seen – precise, factual, detached – that could possibly indicate what he went through inside and what, until now, I had never fully appreciated: it was as if a part of him had died that night.

I looked away and found myself facing Staahl's grey eyes. He smiled – a knowing, sly smile – and slowly licked his thin lips, leaving a trail of spittle at the side of his mouth.

Counsel for the prosecution took his time approaching the witness stand. When at last he looked at Matthew he dropped any pretence at pleasantries, his face rock, and as cold. "I'd like to remind you that you are still under oath, Dr Lynes."

"I am aware of that."

"Dr Lynes, how did you come to be passing the atrium at that time of night?"

"I was returning from a medical emergency at the hospital."

"So you said, but why go past the atrium? If I understand correctly, that is the long way round to get to the dining hall from the staff car lot, is that not so?"

"It is, but I went to change first and my office is next to the medical centre. There is a short cut from that side of the quadrangle to the main building though the cloister."

"The cloister? Is that not separated from the atrium by walls and a glass door?"

"Yes."

"Then tell me, doctor, how is it you heard *noises*, as you put it, through a wall and a heavy door?"

"I heard Professor D'Eresby scream. A scream can carry further than many other sounds because of the frequency at which it is pitched."

"Thank you for the lecture, doctor..."

"I also have excellent hearing," Matthew added. A murmur of laughter ran across the room, but he remained watchful.

"Did you try to strangle Kort Staahl, Dr Lynes?"

"I had to get him away from Professor D'Eresby."

"Professor Staahl states that you held him off the ground with phenomenal strength and tried to strangle him."

"He would have killed her."

"You rendered him unconscious, Dr Lynes. How did you

manage that if you didn't attempt to strangle him? There were no blows to his head…"

Duffy jumped to her feet, fuming. "Objection, Your Honour – Dr Lynes is not the subject of this trial here."

Horatio pursed his mouth. "Your Honour, I'm trying to establish a point."

The judge's cold seemed worse; she coughed and sniffed and coughed again. "Get on with it, counsel. Objection overruled."

"Dr Lynes, I suggest that you misjudged the situation and overreacted, strangling Kort Staahl in your enthusiasm to act the hero and causing bodily harm to Ms D'Eresby in the process. You only ceased when Ms D'Eresby implored you to stop hurting her lover."

From where I sat, Matthew's eyes appeared black.

"No."

"There *was* no attack on Ms D'Eresby and you did not *save* her from a despicable act. Indeed, Ms D'Eresby was there of her own volition and it was you, by your own admission, who inflicted injury on her person by your untimely intervention."

Anger flashed across Matthew's face, instantly veiled as he brought his temper under control, but Horatio had been playing to the jury and had missed the telltale signs.

"No."

"No witnesses, Dr Lynes, *no – other – witnesses.*" He paused, gathered himself and the jury, and continued. "After the incident, you took Ms D'Eresby to the medical centre, where you treated her injuries, which you state were life-threatening. Given the nature of the injuries, I take it you had medical assistance?"

"I did not."

"But surely nursing staff were on hand to assist you, even at that late hour?"

"Yes, but I preferred to work alone; I needed to concentrate."

"A little unorthodox, Dr Lynes, wouldn't you say?" He didn't wait for Matthew to reply. "Isn't it true that there were no other members of the medical staff to corroborate your claim as to the extent of Ms D'Eresby's injuries?"

"The police saw the injuries shortly after the attack, and the photographs you have seen were taken at that time."

"*Alleged* attack, Dr Lynes, the subject of which is yet to be established and is not for this court. As for the so-called *injuries*, the police were not medically qualified to make a judgment, were they? And you seem to be the only medical practitioner to have treated her."

"What are you implying?"

"You seemed very keen to keep Ms D'Eresby away from other people. I mean, you send nursing staff away, you refuse to admit her to the Memorial Hospital, and then you remove her from the medical centre to your own rooms despite her serious condition. Why were you so keen to have her in your control, Dr Lynes?"

"I saw no need to send Professor D'Eresby to the Memorial Hospital. All the facilities required to treat her were contained in the medical centre and she was frightened to stay in the centre itself. She was too unwell to be taken back to her own apartment, so I took her to my rooms next to the medical centre, where she would feel safe and have medical supervision."

"Which you undertook when nursing staff could just as well have looked after her in the centre with some medical supervision from yourself – or from any *other* qualified practitioner, for that matter. How noble of you to give up your time like that for a patient. Is this something you make a habit of, doctor?"

"No."

"No, well – you wouldn't, would you, because removing a patient from a medical facility to your own rooms would be considered highly unethical. Why did you really do it, Dr Lynes?"

"Professor D'Eresby was terrified and in a state of shock. Once her condition had stabilized, I took her where she would feel safe."

"And that was with *you*, was it?"

"Yes."

"What is the nature of your relationship with Ms D'Eresby, Dr Lynes?"

"We are friends."

"Just *friends*," Horatio echoed. "And would you have liked it to be more than a *friendship*, Dr Lynes? After all, Ms D'Eresby is a very attractive young woman, which I'm sure you would have not failed to notice."

"We are friends."

"Or was it that it suited you to have Ms D'Eresby under your control, where you could perhaps suggest to her a particular line to take when giving evidence to the police that might place you in a more favourable light given your misguidedly overenthusiastic response to what you saw? She was very vulnerable, Dr Lynes, and, given her distressed and weakened state, I suggest easily manipulated."

"That was not the case."

Duffy was beside herself. Facing Horatio, she more than made up for her lack of stature as she faced him down, but it was the judge she addressed. "Your Honour, my witness should not be subject to such an aggressive approach. Dr Lynes is not facing a charge here."

"That will be for the DA to decide," Horatio slipped in

as he passed close by her on his way to the prosecution table. "No other questions at this time, Your Honour."

My hackles rose, forgetting my own predicament in the greater anxiety of his. Despite the judge's subsequent reprimand, Horatio had planted seeds of doubt about Matthew's actions that evening. Would they germinate? Would they grow and flourish in the torpid imagination of some enthusiastic DA until they blossomed into a full-blown court case where he would be torn to shreds? I was given no time to dwell before it was Duffy's turn to try to rescue the situation.

She swung her high ponytail off her shoulder and levelled her eyes at the jury. "You have heard the evidence of Dr Lynes as the witness who discovered this young woman being allegedly attacked by Kort Staahl in a small room at the college where they work. Now Dr Lynes will give testimony in his capacity as a doctor of medicine who treated Professor D'Eresby immediately after the incident. I want to show you the severity of the damage inflicted on Professor D'Eresby. Dr Lynes…" She turned to face him. "You have given evidence that the injuries sustained by Professor D'Eresby were life-threatening. Will you please explain to the jury what happened when you reached the medical centre and the extent of the injuries you found, and why you came to such a conclusion."

A flip chart had been set up between the jury and the judge where both could clearly see it, and Matthew walked towards it. Several of the female jurors followed his movements from under their eyelashes. As he undid the buttons of his jacket to point to the chart more easily, one of the younger women suppressed a giggle behind her hand.

"Professor D'Eresby sustained a significant deep laceration to the inside of her left arm, extending from her wrist here..." he pointed to the diagram, "... to near the crease of her elbow here, severing the radial artery and causing immediate and rapid blood loss. Despite reducing the flow of blood at the scene of the incident, trauma to the area was sufficient to cause continued blood loss requiring emergency surgical intervention." My scar itched and stung under my jacket and I put my hand over it to soothe the irritation as he continued calmly, professionally. "I managed to stop the flow of blood and repaired the damage to the arterial walls. Despite replacing fluids intravenously, however, blood loss was critical at this point and Professor D'Eresby was at risk of hypovolemic shock. This occurs when there is reduced blood flow to the organs, a rapid heartbeat, and blood pressure plummets, resulting in death in one or two hours."

I could see Staahl from the corner of my eye. He sat very still, his mouth pinched thin with morbid curiosity, yet it didn't seem as if he felt any connection with what was being described at all, as if he had nothing to do with it.

Duffy took a step closer to Matthew. "So at this point, Dr Lynes, was Professor D'Eresby's condition critical?"

"Yes. She had a less than 30 per cent chance of survival. I thought I was too late."

His distress was palpable. Surely it must be as clear to everyone else as it was to me? But I saw nothing in their expressions other than curiosity or admiration, even desire, and I realized with a jolt that it wasn't his face I read, but the colours of his emotions radiating from inside him.

"However, due to your considerable skill as a surgeon and the proximity of the medical centre, you were able to save her. Can you please describe her other injuries?"

"Professor D'Eresby sustained a distal fracture to the radius of her right arm with substantial tissue trauma to the area surrounding the fracture. She had a puncture wound to her neck, and bruising to her throat."

"Do you know how she obtained the fracture?"

"It was consistent with a sharp blow to her forearm with – or against – a hard linear object with an edge."

I gripped the table as the faces of the jury looked blankly at the chart. They couldn't make the connection between the illustration and a living, breathing being.

Use me. *Use me, Matthew – show them – they can't visualize it. Matthew…!* I called to him silently, but he frowned and didn't look at me. I leaned over to the clerk next to me. "Get Duffy to use me – *show* them."

The girl caught Duffy's eye. Duffy stopped, raised a hand as if for permission. "Your Honour, if I may have a moment…?"

"Make it quick," the judge said, watching as Duffy came over to our table. The clerk spoke rapidly to her.

"Are you sure?" Duffy asked me. I nodded. She turned back to the judge. "Your Honour, to enable the jury to understand the mechanics of the injuries, I'd like Dr Lynes to illustrate using Professor D'Eresby."

Matthew flashed me an angry look, and my father shunted forward in his seat with a grunt of disbelief. The judge peered at me down the length of her nose and then at Horatio, who shrugged. "A little unorthodox perhaps, but if you wish, counsel, you may."

Walking self-consciously towards Matthew, I sensed his displeasure before I reached him and avoided his eyes, feeling awkward suddenly, and shy.

Duffy raised her hand towards me. "Could you remind the court what you were wearing at the time of the attack, professor?"

"I was wearing a sleeveless top, like a camisole, and a long-sleeved jacket and evening skirt. Wait…" I said, and slipped off my jacket as an afterthought. Underneath, I wore a short-sleeved shirt that exposed my scar.

"Dr Lynes?" Duffy urged. I held out my right arm. With a degree of reluctance he took it.

"The fracture to the radius was here…" he drew his finger in an arc around the outside edge of my arm, "… consistent with an injury caused thus…" and he drew my arm back sharply towards the edge of the judge's bench, stopping before it hit.

The jurors murmured among themselves.

"What other injuries did you observe, Dr Lynes?"

"Professor D'Eresby had a knife wound to her neck, here." He lifted my chin and turned my head gently so that they could see. "And extensive bruising to her left arm around her wrist with evident marks caused by fingernails digging into her wrist, like so." He wrapped his hand around my arm, placing his fingers exactly where Staahl held me and extended my arm, the long scar clearly visible.

A sigh of displeasure floated from the court as Horatio interrupted. "Objection, Your Honour. It is a matter of speculation what caused the marks on Ms D'Eresby's wrist."

Matthew shot him a withering look as he addressed the judge. "No, Your Honour, DNA testing of samples taken from under Professor Staahl's fingernails of his left hand clearly show he had broken Professor D'Eresby's skin with his nails and the pattern of those wounds corresponds *exactly* with his digits."

The judge nodded. "Overruled. Please continue, Dr Lynes."

"Professor D'Eresby also had bruising and friction burns across her throat here, having been held forcibly, like so…" He stood behind me, his body just touching, bringing his arm around my neck.

I began to feel dizzy as he trapped my right arm beneath his. I took a breath to quell the encroaching sense of rising alarm, but as Matthew gripped my left wrist in his fingers, totally immobilizing me, I began to breathe rapidly, sweat breaking out around my neck and under my arms, and I stifled an urge to scream.

Panic.

Blind panic they call it, when there is no sense or reason to your actions but you react out of fear and an instinct for survival. I struggled against him.

"Let – me – *go!*"

He released me immediately, shock on his face as I broke away from him. The courtroom emptied of sound except for my rapid, rough breaths.

Swiftly coming to the rescue, Duffy threw my jacket around my shoulders and led me back towards our table, where I sat down, shaking.

"I'm fine," I said. "I'm all right. Sorry… I'm sorry." But my apology was not for Duffy or anyone else watching, but for Matthew, who emitted unspoken anguish from every pore.

"You did just great, hun, couldn't be better," she whispered, quickly curving around and returning to where Matthew still stood, his mouth a grim line.

"To continue, Dr Lynes," she said, maintaining momentum, "were any other injuries noted by you on that night?"

Matthew managed to focus on her again. "Professor D'Eresby also sustained two broken ribs."

"And how did these injuries occur?"

He looked uncomfortable. "When I tackled Staahl, Professor D'Eresby was knocked out of the way. *I* knocked her out of the way."

What the hell did she think she was doing? I scowled at her, not caring who saw me.

"So you *inadvertently* caused the fractures to her ribs?"

"Yes, I did."

"If you had not acted as you did at that moment, what – *in your opinion* – do you think would have happened?"

He answered without a moment's hesitation. "He would have killed her."

The door at the back of the courtroom suddenly opened and rapid footsteps of hard-soled shoes on the wooden floor broke through the absolute hush that gripped the room. The judge removed her spectacles as the man approached her. He bent low, his mouth to her ear. She nodded and looked over at Duffy.

"Counsel, please approach the bench."

She whispered something to Duffy, glancing towards Matthew before calling Horatio and the clerk of the court to join them. Duffy hurried back towards Matthew and spoke rapidly.

I felt it before he raised his eyes and looked at me, an age of time within a fleeting tremor, a melting grief. Then he was moving towards his son and family, who were already halfway along the bench, pulling coats over their shoulders.

The eyes of the courtroom tracked them as they crossed the room towards the exit, where they were joined by Maggie at the door, her face bleached white.

The room erupted as the door closed and the judge hammered on her bench calling for quiet, and everyone rotated to face her. All except one – an elderly woman seated at the far back of the room, whose face remained directed towards the door as if she were following the retreating footsteps down the hall. Then she turned and in the brief moment our eyes met, I saw *cognition*. Her mouth tweaked, she looked away, my querying glance unanswered.

The court clerk coughed roughly. "Court will adjourn until Monday morning at O-ten hundred hours. All rise." I heard him but my body wouldn't respond.

"Emma, stand up," Duffy whispered, pulling me. I stared at her blankly, then came to my senses and did as bidden. The judge left the room and the courtroom began to empty.

"That went very well," Duffy said with evident satisfaction. "That doctor is just so unbelievable. If I had to be rescued by anyone, it would have to be by him – on a horse *and* in shining armour. I can't believe he carried you all that way."

If I had my way, that's exactly what he would be doing at this precise moment, and he would be taking me away – a long, long way away where there were no Staahls, no judges, and no counsels.

Still talking, Duffy flopped back into her chair in triumph. "And that was darned brilliant, Emma. I would have suggested using you as a dummy if I thought it were ethical. The jury just *lo-ve* a bit of drama." When I didn't answer, stock-still and frozen, she peered up at me. "Horatio's really put you through the grinder today, hun, but that adjournment came just in time, although I'm sorry for the family, of course. Did you hear what's happened?"

She didn't need to tell me, I already knew: Ellen was dead.

Outside the courthouse, the space was crammed with people aimlessly intent, hands in pockets and collars pulled up against the driving sleet. With no room for umbrellas, several people used their folded newspapers to keep their heads dry. They were a patient people, stamping their feet and flexing their hands to keep warm, exchanging comments – young, old, and middle-aged – a throng, a crowd, a community.

By the time we left, a premature gloaming pursued the cloud, and the street lamps had come on early, reflecting orange pools of light off the cars parked underneath.

Duffy drew air through her teeth as Hart opened the wide door for us to pass through. "Hang on to your hats, this is going to get rough."

"There she is!" an overexcited voice yelled. As one, the mass of bodies came alive, converging like a swarm around us, animated faces mouthing questions, comments, insults – a frenzy of voices; and eyes – wide and staring – their whites showing like cattle about to stampede.

"Keep back!" Hart ordered, using his shoulders to control the heaving flank of bodies as we tried to push our way through the mob, but he was short, and arms waved and reached around and above him, newspapers thrust at us, jabbing, accusing.

"No comment, no comment," Duffy pushed voice recorders out of her face.

My father elbowed his way forward and all I wanted to do was cut and run, but they mirrored my moves like a rugby scrum with me as the ball.

We reached the pavement where the car waited. Hart wrenched open the door and pushed me inside. "Monday," Duffy said and slammed the door shut between us and the disappointed crowd. My father slid into the seat next to me, sweat standing on his brow, and we left the herd behind.

Dad mopped his forehead, breathing heavily.

"Are you all right?" I asked, concerned. It took him a moment to catch his breath.

"They were behaving like a pack of damned hyenas..."

"I know."

"What did Staahl's barrister think he was doing asking all those questions, making you out to be some sort of cheap slut? Damn and blast him! And what about Ma... Dr Lynes? Where did he go, all of a sudden?" It sounded like an accusation.

I watched sleet hit the window and slide diagonally in a melting stream down the glass, but all I could see was Matthew's shocked face mirrored in it.

"His grandmother has just died."

"Oh – I'm sorry to hear that. Those people I sat next to, are they his family, his parents?"

I traced a piece of sleet with my finger all the way down the window until I could go no further. "His family. Yes."

He didn't pursue the subject any further, aware that Hart listened with his head inclined to catch the conversation.

"Isn't there a law about defamation of character in court?" Dad grumbled instead.

I sighed. "They don't have much to go on. They're allowed a certain degree of character assassination as part of the prosecution."

"Damn fool system. And why *did* Dr Lynes take you to his rooms, anyway?"

"You see, Dad? That's how it works. The prosecution has you wondering whether Dr Lynes is what he seems, sowing seeds of doubt, little niggles that will work their way into your thought processes until you don't know what's fact and what's fiction. That's how it works," I said again, more quietly this time and almost to myself. Hart's eyes reflected briefly in the rear-view mirror. "Even Mr Hart here is wondering whether any of what was said about me is true, aren't you?" I addressed the mirror.

"I'm sorry, ma'am, it's not my place to say."

"No, but it doesn't stop you thinking, all the same, does it?" He didn't deny it. The car slowed to round a corner, and I recognized the highway that took us back towards the college. "And just so that you know, Dad, whether you choose to believe it or not, Dr Lynes took me to his rooms for the very reason he gave: I was petrified. He made me feel safe."

My father brushed drops of water from his coat and undid the buttons. "But that disgusting man was in custody. He couldn't have hurt you any more."

"No, but fear isn't rational – I couldn't think straight. I saw Staahl in every shadow and every time the door opened I thought it would be him. Sometimes… sometimes I think I still do."

Enough was enough for one day. I placed my cheek against the cold window and closed my eyes, letting the rocking motion of the car replace the tremors – like the vibration of an oncoming train – running through me.

By the time we reached the college, it had become fully dark. Hart walked with us back to my apartment, but nobody asked questions or bothered us. The college still represented a sanctuary until the evening newspapers were published.

"You didn't tell the truth – neither of you did – about your relationship." Dad placed his fork on his empty plate and it slithered to one side on his uneven knees. He leaned forward to put it on the coffee table. I had hardly touched my food, although Elena had made me promise on all that was holy in Russia that I would. I felt unspeakably tired and I didn't need the third degree from him this evening. He looked as if he could do with an early night as well. Dark circles, the colour of an overripe fig, lay in the recesses under his eyes, and the pouches of his jowls sagged like a basset hound. But he wanted an answer.

"Dad, I said that you might hear things you didn't like. You see how they twist the truth? We wouldn't lie if we didn't have to, please believe that."

"I do – at least I think I do, Emma, but it's always more difficult when you hear it from your own child. Tell me though, just one thing – did Matthew try to kill Staahl?"

"Don't be silly, Dad."

"Pity. *I* would have done, if I were him."

I went over and gave him a long hug then kissed his weathered cheek. "You surprise me sometimes, you really do; what would Mum say?"

"Your mother? She wouldn't have hesitated, she would have shot him weeks ago." He rumbled a laugh. "I think it's time I gave her a call and told a few lies myself." He patted his pocket for his mobile and I left him to it so that I wouldn't have to hear my father play dirty with the truth, and went to get ready for bed.

I wasn't thinking about sleep, but about Matthew. I thought about the evidence he had given as he had recounted the events of the night I had come so close to death, and the pain he had expressed without knowing he did so. I hadn't been aware of it after the attack, of course, but I had seen a glimpse of it today like an unbidden, hidden memory engraved on his emotions as surely as a name is recorded on a grave.

The last thing I saw before my eyes closed for the final time that night was my little triptych silhouetted against the distilled light of the window, and the last thing that floated through my drifting mind was what Matthew would be going through right now as he came to terms with his wife's death. And I wondered – a little, *tiny* part of me wondered – whether he might ask himself: *Is all this loss worth it?*

CHAPTER 19

Uninvited Guest

Sleep on my Love in thy cold bed
Never to be disquieted!
My last good night! Thou wilt not wake
Till I thy fate shall overtake...
HENRY KING (1592–1669)

A sense of change magnetized the air, and I threw open the windows to let the cold, light wind stream through the apartment, lifting the papers on my desk and sending a stray white feather scurrying across the room. Snow thinned on the ground and, here and there, browned patches of grass waited for spring to green them. While all the snow had gone from the cedar tree, a faint mist clung to its branches.

I checked my mobile first thing in the morning, but Matthew hadn't left a message. I didn't have to wait long to hear from him. I heard a quiet knock at my door.

"Harry!" A combination of relief and delight in my voice brought a wan smile to his face. He returned my embrace, his clothes smelling fresh and cold from the air outside. I ushered him to the sofa. "How is he?"

"Well, you know…"

I rocked my head back and forth. "I'm sorry, that was a stupid, asinine question…"

"I was going to say that he's OK, Emma, in the circumstances."

"Oh. And the rest of you? What about Henry?"

"Yeah, well, we were expecting it. Ellen died peacefully."

"I'm glad about that at least. And Maggie?" He grimaced and shrugged. "You look exhausted. I'll get you some tea. I don't have any coffee, sorry."

He raised a wry smile. "That's probably a good thing, remembering what happened last time, right? Don't worry about it; I had a drink at home before I came. I forgot to shave though." He rubbed his chin where faint, fair stubble just pushed through, reminding me he was older than the seventeen years he appeared. "Look, Emma, Matthew wanted me to give you this." He reached into a side pocket of his jacket and pulled out a cream envelope. "I would have brought it over sooner, but I had to help Dad with Maggie."

So it must be urgent.

I sat down on the edge of the coffee table opposite him, and turned the envelope over in my hands and saw my name written in Matthew's distinctive script. I looked, but did not open it.

"That reminds me," Harry said. "Matthew said to ask if you've had breakfast."

I gave a short laugh. I had reheated the food I hadn't eaten last night, but too long in the microwave had resulted in vulcanized rubber, which had been barely edible.

"Tell him I have, will you, please?"

"Yeah, sure." He glanced at me and then at the envelope still unopened in my hand, and his young, unlined face crinkled into unaccustomed furrows. "Matthew would've brought it himself, but there's so much to do, you know?"

"Oh, I wouldn't expect him to, Harry."

I knew why I didn't open it. There were some things that were better written than said, and part of me had always expected a change, one way or another, when Ellen finally died. After all the trauma of yesterday with the trial, the accusations, the news of her death, I couldn't be sure how Matthew might react.

Harry regarded me with eyes older than his years. "Matthew asked if you would mind reading it now; it's from Ellen."

From Ellen? *Ellen!*

I wondered whether my relief showed. "Yes, of course, sorry."

The letter was short, dictated to Matthew, and written on the same heavy paper as the envelope.

> *Valmont*
> *6ʰ February*

Emma,

I have little time left and I want to thank you for the service you have done me in the ways we discussed. I can rest easy now, and Matthew, too.
I am asking you to go to my funeral. I know this will be difficult but it is the last thing I will ask you to do. Look after Matthew and my family. I have always loved him.

Your friend

Ellen Lynes

She spoke of her love for Matthew, but I thought there was something defensive in the way she said it. It must have been a painful letter for her to dictate as she relinquished him to me, and equally difficult for Matthew to write. Her use of language might well be colloquial, but it spoke eloquently enough of the things that concerned her most in her last days, and I wiped my eyes quickly and folded the letter, sliding it back into its envelope.

Harry looked at me quizzically and I smiled so that he could see that I was all right, and so that he wouldn't need to ask, and I wouldn't have to lie.

"Please will you tell Matthew 'yes' from me; he'll know what it refers to. Do you know when the funeral will be, and where?"

"Yeah, that was all arranged some time ago. Ellen wanted it sorted out so there wasn't much for the family to do. The funeral's on Sunday at eleven. It's a small chapel up near Valmont."

So soon. I considered how I would get there and whether a taxi – if prepared to take me that far – would wait.

"How many people are going?"

"Only the family and Dr DaCruz. And Eli, of course."

Bother, that would make blending in with the crowd a little difficult.

I hoped that there would be some sun for Ellen as her family said goodbye. Rain at a funeral seemed a little clichéd but, judging by the clouds that greeted me as I drew the curtains the following morning, we would have rain. Or more sleet.

I spent some time thinking about how I could make my presence inconspicuous. I hardly thought that standing by the graveside with Matthew would be appropriate, despite Ellen's wishes.

I stood on the path above the steps in the staff car park waiting for the taxi. It was late. I checked my watch for the fifth time, and writhed in irritation. I thought it bad enough to be going to the funeral where my presence might not be welcome, especially by Maggie, but to be late would be unforgivable. At least my father would have a quiet day resting in my apartment. He needed it if tomorrow proved to be as bad as Friday.

I started to walk along the path, up and down, backward and forward, grit grating under my feet and my eyes fixed firmly on the ground so that I wouldn't distract myself with the view, and went through what Duffy said was likely to happen.

Horatio seemed to be pitching his argument at several main areas: by asserting that in arranging to meet Staahl to indulge a masochistic fetish, I somehow made what he did *consensual*, and that in rescuing me, Matthew had aggravated the situation and made it public. If I had consented, then, by definition, my claiming it to be otherwise made that claim malicious and the case against me proved.

Then, he intimated that Matthew had intervened, perhaps out of jealousy, and somehow persuaded me to change my story to prevent his own prosecution. Surely that was a mere step away from him being hauled up in court on charges of perversion of justice?

My head swam with the tortured arguments. I had the scars to prove an assault had taken place whether I consented to it or not, and Duffy had made it clear that what had happened was indeed a criminal offence; but that in itself was not enough of a defence against a lawsuit for defamation. Could anyone in their right mind believe I had consented to this bizarre act with Staahl? Could they? *Did* they?

Ridiculous as Staahl's assertions might seem to me as I stood under an overcast February sky, to the jury in the overheated atmosphere of the courtroom with a silver-tongued counsel feeding them an alternative truth, anything might be possible. The point was: did they think it *probable*?

The smooth note of a car engine interrupted my reverie. I walked back along the path, bent down to pick up my bag, and turned around, nearly colliding with Matthew.

I had thrown my arms around him before I remembered that we were only supposed to be friends, but he didn't seem to care if anyone saw us either.

"I'm so, so sorry about Ellen."

His face showed the strain of the last forty-eight hours and he looked drawn and taut, but his mouth loosened into a subdued smile.

"Thank you for saying you would come."

I smiled in return. "Ellen knew I would if she asked, and I'm glad she did."

A door slammed somewhere close by and someone called a name.

"We'd better go," he said, putting out a hand to me to help me down the steps where patches of ice still clung stubbornly at the sides. "I've cancelled the taxi. You didn't think I would let you come alone, did you? I'm sorry, I forgot to say to Harry yesterday."

We reached his car. "Would you like me to drive?" I asked.

His answering glance had humour in it. "Please don't take this the wrong way, but we'll be late if I don't." He had a point.

I buckled my seatbelt. "I thought that you had enough to think about without arranging transport for me."

He started the engine and the car moved smoothly away. "And you don't?"

I shook my head. "That's different. This is more important – this is real."

"The trial isn't real to you?" I could hear the note of disbelief.

"It doesn't seem like it at times."

We were quiet for the time it took to reach the bridge before we joined the main road. We drove parallel to the river, which was running riot with meltwater. Rising sap in the trees growing close to the water's edge tipped their branches lime or cardinal, and foaming water chopped at the banks. Darkly menacing and laced with brown, the river parted around boulders as they clung stubbornly to the riverbed like trolls wading a stream. I looked away from the churning waters and struggled out of my coat. Matthew turned the heating up a notch and warming air circulated.

"Harry said Henry's coping," I said.

"He is."

"But that Maggie's finding it difficult?"

"As you would expect."

"And what about you, Matthew?"

Soft, blunt sleet began to fall against the windscreen, rapidly obscuring it, and Matthew set the wipers onto a slow beat, the slush gathering in ridges at the edge of the screen.

"All things pass, Emma." His face betrayed no emotion, but grief seeped out of him, and I reached for his hand and held it, our fingers knotted as the miles were consumed by the speed of the car. Finally, he brought my hand to his lips and held it there briefly.

"Do the family know I'm coming and that Ellen wanted me to be there?" I asked, suddenly conscious, in a flutter of nerves, that we must be near our destination.

"Yes, of course; they'll be pleased to see you, only don't

expect too much from Maggie. We've told her to keep away from you but she's very fragile at the moment."

I remembered her pale face at the courtroom door on Friday. This wasn't the time for me to hold grudges. "This is it," he said, as he turned the car down a short drive and through some ornate wrought-iron gates painted black.

He pulled up by the side of a pretty church. Clad in white clapperboard with a steeply roofed belfry to cast the snow, a simple cross declared the faith of the interred, and a blue clock over the door marked time. A hearse already waited by the entrance, with Dan's car parked to one side.

Matthew opened the car door, but I stopped him before he climbed out.

"I'm going to stay here until everyone's inside, and then I will be in the back of the church. Whatever Ellen wanted, I think that it will be more appropriate."

Subdued, he nodded. "You're probably right."

"God speed," I whispered and he gave me a thin smile, looking up as the sound of several other cars reached us as they drew into the parking area. He retrieved his coat from the back seat and climbed out.

Her eyes downcast, Maggie looked ghastly. As Matthew joined them, he embraced his son and spoke to her, but she didn't respond. Together, they went into the church, followed by Charles DaCruz with Eli, shambling and uncertain, next to him, as if Ellen's death had left him devoid of purpose.

I waited for a further minute to let everyone settle, and then picked up my bag and coat in readiness to leave the car. As I placed my hand on the handle, a taxi drove up beside me and stopped so close that if we'd opened the doors at the same time, damage to the cars' paintwork would have been inevitable. I waited, but no one climbed out and the reflection of the glass made it impossible to see if anyone other than the driver were inside. The bell began to toll, and I inched hurriedly from the car feeling nervy, gathering my coat around my shoulders as I made my way across the melting ice to the church door.

The small building smelled of flowers and floor polish, and it felt warm and welcoming inside. What daylight there was filtered through the high arched windows. Either side of the broad aisle ranged rows of comfortable chairs, but no amount of care could disguise the pervasive scent of lilies and death. When full, the church could take perhaps a hundred people at most, but the little family occupied no more than a handful of chairs, making them look vulnerable in their isolation.

Dr DaCruz and Eli had placed themselves to one side, but as I entered the church, Dan was inviting them to join the rest of the family, shifting along two spaces to make room. I slipped quietly into a chair at the back.

The minister wore a white surplus over a plain, dark suit, making his denomination unclear. Tall and skinny, he stooped slightly, and his sandy greying hair and long sideburns made him look like a Victorian gentleman. His expression was lugubrious and well-meaning, and he spoke for a few moments with Henry. Taken aback at first, I then remembered that here, in a public place, Henry was the chief mourner and Matthew but the youngest of Ellen's grandchildren.

Matthew stood with Henry on one side, and Pat on the other, his back straight but head bowed. Despite his family, he seemed alone, with memories of centuries of death of which they were unaware and at which I could only guess.

I wanted to be there, not in this form of self-imposed banishment, and I had almost made up my mind to go to him and risk upsetting the others, when a cold rush of air chilled my legs as the door opened with a thin squeal behind me.

I looked up to see a slight figure, opulently dressed in full mourning, slide through the narrow gap she made for herself between the two doors. I couldn't see her clearly – she wore a hat that threw a deep shadow over her face – but her hair was pewter and tied in a swathe at the back of her neck, held in a luminous black bow.

The minister addressed the little congregation, and the opportunity to join Matthew passed. We all stood and prayers were said and the service began.

The woman sat stiffly on the opposite side to me, and whether she noticed my presence I couldn't say. I thought there was something familiar about her, but when I took the chance to look at her again, her chair was empty, leaving only a faint scent of expensive perfume and mothballs lingering in the air.

We sang a sad hymn of farewell to Ellen, each voice distinct. Only Maggie didn't sing. She stared straight ahead, unseeing, her hands clasped in front of her, Jeannie giving her nervous little glances every now and again as she held her hymn book out between them.

I couldn't listen to the address. I could sense Matthew's grief in undulating waves the colour of bruises, and I reached out, feeling the force of his desolation as I pulled it, like strings of glue, away from him so that I could feed in its place some semblance of peace. This fear he had to endure: not the horror of discovery I felt for him, but the dread of being left behind in the shattering aloneness that death brought in the sure and certain knowledge that he could not follow.

The family followed the coffin down the central aisle towards the door. They had almost passed when Henry broke away from the group and came towards me. He showed no sign of resentment as I returned his fatherly hug.

"I know it was expected, but I'm still so sorry, Henry."

"Well, yes, I suppose loss is always a shock even when you're prepared, but thank you, Emma, and thank you for coming. Dad said it was at Ellen's request, but it isn't pleasant for you, especially with everything else that's going on." It took me a second to remember to what he referred. I had more or less successfully managed to push the trial to one side for the day. "Emma, I appreciate your sensitivity towards the rest of the family, but this can hardly be described as a normal situation, so please, come and join us. My father won't ask you for himself, and he needs you with him. Besides…" he added with a hint of poignancy, "… you are one of the family now and you should be with us."

I didn't know what to say, so I just hugged him again, and together we tagged onto the end of the little group of mourners as we crossed the rough ground still smudged in snow.

A mound of bare, brown earth and an empty coffin-shaped hole at the edge of the cemetery where the ground fell away steeply marked his mother's grave. Trees, shapely in naked winter form, framed a view to a deep valley filled with the seal-grey waters of a velvet lake. Winter or summer, on a fine day or foul, serenity and beauty lay in this land of which Ellen would now be part.

Henry left me with Matthew, our arms almost touching, and went to join Pat as the pallbearers placed the coffin on a platform beside the grave. As the earnest minister read a final prayer, and the coffin lowered slowly into the ground, I felt Matthew's gloved hand seek mine and I risked a glance at him. He saw not the coffin but the future and, with a jolt,

I realized that he pictured the day he would be standing by my grave and burying me. In that instant he saw that I understood, and looked away in agony. The coffin grounded with a definitive thud and Matthew shuddered slightly. I gripped his hand tightly.

Movement caught my attention, so fleeting it could have been a branch brushed by the wind, and unease raised the fine hairs on my arms. I stared at the nearby small group of trees bunched in whispering conversation, but the scattering of sleet driven by the light breeze made every shadow dance uncertainly in the dim light, and no form materialized from the shapes. Nobody else seemed to have noticed as they looked at the coffin now deeply snug within the grave. Sleet ghosted into snow and back again, phasing dark silhouettes into restless grey as the minister invited Henry to cast the first fistful of earth. Henry turned wordlessly to his father, and Matthew stepped towards the open grave to enclose the soft, fine earth in his gloveless hand, and let it fall, softly rattling, onto the wooden surface of the coffin.

Disguising his surprise at the change in precedence, the minister continued with the rites of interment as, one by one, the family scattered the soil until it was my turn to let the dry dust crumble between my fingers. I held back the inevitable emotion that such a final act was bound to evoke and silently voiced my own prayer. Sleet settled on my cheeks and I brushed it away along with tears.

Something felt wrong.

The sense of foreboding suddenly intensified, becoming so physical it became almost a presence. As the minister took his leave of Henry, I searched the face of each person around the grave, but all I could feel from them was sadness, emptiness, but not this overwhelming resentment, this *hate*. Matthew saw me look, and his expression turned to disquiet as he read my face. "What is it?" he asked quietly.

I shook my head. "I don't know, something... someone's wrong."

"Some*one*?" he instinctively looked over to Maggie, but she remained blank and disengaged, lost in a wilderness beyond reach.

He ran his eyes over the rest of his family, then to the minister talking to Eli, whose round face looked pale and blotched from crying. "Is it anyone here?"

I shook my head. "It's not one of us, but he's close."

He didn't question my judgment; instead his body tensed and his eyes pierced the recesses of the cemetery where the deepest shadows lay. On the other side of the grave, first Joel then Dan became alert. Ellie stopped crying. The minister had taken his leave, and Henry quickly thanked Eli and the doctor for attending before they too left, and he rejoined the watchful, waiting family.

Without taking his eyes off the perimeter, Matthew leaned down, keeping his voice low. "What do you sense?"

I closed my eyes and concentrated, letting the impression deepen into a shifting of colours and half-formed shapes that changed like a mirage even as I tried to grasp them.

"He's angry – no, resentful, bitter – it's unclear, there's so much emotion... but he's very close."

A dead branch cracked as it broke.

"Hello, Henry." A voice deeper than feminine accompanied a figure malevolent in black as it disgorged itself from the dark bowels by a tall tree. "It's been a long time."

Disbelieving, Henry turned slowly until he faced the old woman I had seen earlier in the church. Face on and swathed in darkness, I recognized her from the trial.

Pat grasped his arm. "Henry, who is this?"

The woman came closer, and Dan stepped back as if she repulsed him like the negative force of a magnet. Still very handsome, high cheekbones in a feline face had helped her wear well, her skin still soft but tautened through the clever application of a surgeon's knife, and her eyes – elongated and rich brown – were fire and honey. She would have been beautiful, but the set of her mouth and the fine down-turned lines around it betrayed a sour pleasure in the discomfort of others, and an arrogance that ran hard like a seam of quartz though her. And she was pale – too pale – with an unhealthy pallor that careful make-up could not entirely disguise.

"Why, Henry, aren't you going to introduce me to your family? This must be your wife." She looked Pat up and down with barely disguised disdain, and summarily dismissed her.

Matthew unclenched his jaw enough to be able to speak. "What are you doing here, Monica?"

She looked at him as if she had only just noticed, but her surprise seemed staged.

"Matthew! I came to pay my respects to Ellen, of course." She openly gazed at him, a long, salacious look as if he could satiate her hunger. "Look at you," she purred, "after all these years and you're still as handsome as ever. What I wouldn't do to know your secret of eternal youth."

"You are not welcome here. What do you want?"

She disregarded his question and instead shifted her gaze, letting her barbed, greedy eyes roll down and then up my body, making me feel exposed. Resting on my hair, they burned, envy oozing out of her like larva.

"I see you've brought someone to comfort you in your grief and with your *wife* no sooner than in the ground. Matthew, I'm surprised at you. How did Ellen take it when she found out you had already replaced her with a younger model? Does this girl know your secret, I wonder? Well, *do* you, my dear?" She paused, and when I didn't answer, gave a little dismissive shrug. "It doesn't matter. I did enjoy your performance on Friday, by the way; it was surprisingly entertaining and I'm *so* looking forward to tomorrow – who knows what a new day might bring?"

Matthew emitted a low, threatening noise deep in the back of his throat and she took a rapid step back, her high, black-heeled shoes sinking into the thawing earth.

"You haven't answered my question, Monica. You long since relinquished the right to comment on my family."

Her gloved hand patted her chest in a dramatic flurry. "Don't forget, Matthew, that I still have an interest in part of it." She looked meaningfully at Maggie, who stared at her mother with the round eyes of a startled child. "When you came to see me after the accident, I really thought you were going to kill me – oh, you looked so *angry*; but really, you've been perfectly sweet all these years, keeping me in a manner to which I have grown very accustomed."

Henry shot a puzzled glance at his father, and Monica turned her attention to him. "Didn't you know, darling? Matthew's been keeping me quiet. He's been paying me all these years to keep me away from you all – especially from *you*, darling," and she held out her hand to Maggie. "Margaret, come and say *hello* to Mommy."

Maggie focused unsteadily on her mother, and her mouth slackened but no sound came. Placing himself directly between his daughter and her mother, Henry's brow drew into deep, angry ridges. "Keep away from her, Monica. You are nothing but poison. You always were, and you always will be. I wish to God I'd killed you."

The boys had taken up defensive positions but shifted uneasily, apparently sensing the threat this stranger brought to the family, although it seemed unequal to the frail, willowy stature of the old woman before them. They might underestimate the damage she could do, but Matthew and Henry obviously didn't.

"Oh, Henry, you always were too soft; you need some of your father's steel. Nobody would ever believe you capable of murder. Not like you, Matthew; who knows what *you* might do! Nearly strangled the man, didn't they say in court? What stopped you? Why didn't you finish him?" She placed her hand against her mouth in a mockery of surprise. "Could it have been this girl, possibly? '*No!* Matthew, *no!* You'll *kill* him,'" she mimicked in a high-pitched wail. "Did this girl stop you, Matthew? Is she your *conscience?* You surely don't still believe in that *talisman* – that *institutionalized relic of a superstitious age* she wears around her neck, do you?" My hand found my cross beneath my coat as she echoed the words I last heard from Staahl's mouth that night in the porters' lodge.

Matthew's muscles contracted under my restraining hand, but I was equally angry. "How do you know what Staahl said?" I spat. "I've told nobody."

Monica bathed in my reaction, slight colour in her pallid cheeks. "She speaks! How delightful. How do you think?" A slow smile of satisfaction spread across her face as realization dawned on mine. "That's right – Kort Staahl. Where do you think he's managed to get the money to pay for his legal team? Cost me – actually, cost *you* – top dollar, Matthew. It didn't cost me much more than a phone call, but you've been so generous over the years."

"We thought you were dead," Pat said.

"Thought? Or hoped?" Monica's voice cut like razor blades. Then she snickered, a high, unappealing sound. "Oh, and you *children*, all so *handsome*, so very like you, Matthew. You must be so proud." She reached out and lightly touched Harry's face before he knew what she was doing. He shrank back as if struck, wiping the memory of her from his skin with the sleeve of his coat. She didn't like that. She lost any pretence of conviviality, her face stony, her eyes the colour of flints.

"It's time you left," Dan said, stepping between her and his children.

"And you must be Henry's son. Dan, is it? I'm not ready to leave just yet, not until I get what I came for."

"What *do* you want?" Dan asked, lowering. "More money?"

Monica ignored him and turned to Matthew. "*Money?*" she sneered, reminding me acutely of Maggie at Christmas. "Oh, I don't need your money. I have more than enough from my late husband. He was a fool as well. I seem only to have married fools, Matthew – rich, but so impotent. I almost wished Henry had tried to kill me, it would have been a little more *exciting*. No, money doesn't interest me any more. I want to see you suffer, Matthew, it's as simple as that." Henry cursed under his breath. "Not you, Henry dear, don't worry. I forgot all about *you* a long time ago. It is your father I blame. Matthew, you drove me out and kept me away for all these years. Had it not been for that little snippet in *The Times* I might never have known what you were up to and, who knows, I might have let sleeping dogs lie. But there you were coming to the rescue of this girl, and I just had to make a few enquiries. I was always good at that, wasn't I? Making enquiries, getting to the bottom of things. It didn't take much to find out where they were keeping dear Kort, and then, such a *gift* to find my own clever little Margaret in charge of his care." She clasped her gloved hands, her translucent eyelids fluttering at the memory of fate playing so neatly into her hands. Pat could hardly keep her revulsion from showing. Monica gloated openly.

"Kort and I have kept up our correspondence ever since. He is such an interesting man, so full of intuition and novel ideas. I think if I were a few years younger, I might have found him quite... entertaining. Anyway, I was able to help my own sweet child at the same time as encouraging Kort to fight for his rights and humiliating *you*, Matthew." A gust of wind lifted the edge of her short veil and she patted it delicately back in place. "All those little titbits of information I fed Staahl that he gave to you, Margaret, to help you reach your conclusions. Nobody will forget this trial; you will be *famous*, darling." She pursed her lips as she regarded her daughter. "Of course, we must buy you some new clothes; the ones you wear are so unbecoming, but then you obviously haven't had any guidance in that quarter." She flashed a contemptuous glance at Pat. "Perhaps you would like to come and stay with Mommy, darling? We could have such fun; we could go shopping at Saks."

Henry bled rage. "Don't even begin to pretend you did this for anyone else but yourself, and certainly not for Maggie. What have you told Staahl about my father?"

Monica briefly adopted a coy expression, smiling up from under her lashes in a way that men might once have found appealing, but now looked pitiable and sleazy, like a worn-out whore in a side-street brothel.

"Oh Henry, you are just so *sweet* when you get cross. I haven't told Kort anything – yet. You don't think I would give him my ace card just like that, do you? Not that *little* man. No, I don't need to tell the world about Matthew's secret, not until I'm ready. I want to make him pay first. I want to make him suffer and squirm for all those years he deprived me of my daughter when she needed her mother most. Look at her, what have you done to her?" She pulled her face into an imitation of an agonized Madonna and held out her hand to Maggie, who moaned and put a hand to her head, closing her eyes in confusion.

"You are *pathetic*," Pat flung at her. "Have you any idea of the damage you have done, and what it has taken to help Maggie through it?

"*I* should have been the one to help her." Monica's façade of civility slipped, her breath escaping in an unpleasant rasp as she thrust her head forward, forcing the thin, tautened skin of her neck into ridges over her throat muscles like a tortoise stretching for a leaf.

Matthew had been examining her carefully and now he moved silently until he stood barely three feet away from her, so that she started when she looked around and saw how close he had come. When he spoke, he had assumed complete control of his anger, but the calm was more intimidating. It hung between them and she recognized the threat within it.

"Don't delude yourself, Monica, it was you who left – no one drove you away – and you were only too eager to take the money you were offered to stay that way. Not once in all these years have you asked to see Maggie, or even enquired after her. Your only interest in her has been in what you could squeeze out of me."

Monica stabbed a finger at him. "My daughter died in that crash. I was in mourning…"

"For forty-six years?" Henry said caustically. "Ellen was my daughter too. We had two children, Monica; you effectively abandoned one of them."

Her mouth slithered into a sneer. "You blame me for the crash, but it wasn't my fault – Margaret was crying…"

"Mommy," Maggie stumbled forward between Henry and Dan, the remorse in her face heartbreaking. "You were so angry. I didn't mean to cry."

Henry held onto her arm. "It was an accident, Maggie."

"It was my fault – it is always my fault. Ellen and Grams…" Maggie pulled, trying to free herself as she became increasingly distressed and working herself into a frenzy.

Matthew turned his back on Monica so that his granddaughter could see only him. He didn't try to stop her, he didn't try to touch her, but his voice dropped, taking on the mesmerizing cadence he used when he wanted to calm me.

"No, Maggie, there was ice on the road. Remember the ice in the yard at home, how you had been playing on the frozen puddles that morning with little Ellen, how you slid into each other…"

"… And I fell over and I cried and Ellen said it was just an accident. I remember – she couldn't stop."

"And the car couldn't stop, Maggie. It slid on the ice and it couldn't stop. It was just an accident."

She looked up at him, and her expression changed from bewildered child to one of growing acceptance. "An *accident*?" she whispered.

"Yes," he said gently.

"But Mommy was angry with me and then she left."

"She didn't leave because of you."

"I was frightened and there was shouting and then she was angry with me and then she left."

"You were not in control, Maggie, you were just a little girl. You were not the adult, you were not responsible."

The conversation ran between the two of them, Matthew holding her attention as he wound his way through her tortured thought processes, leading her towards comprehension now that her lifetime of defences were down.

What had been a light breeze became a fretting wind in the cooling air, and the intermittent sleet now became a steady, light snowfall that lay on our shoulders without melting.

"Mommy was driving."

Monica's face warped into ugly resentment. "I couldn't hear myself *think* over the racket she made; she distracted me."

"Shut *up!*" I heard myself hiss at her without thinking, the image of the frightened child vivid in my mind.

"Mommy was driving and there was shouting and then we crashed."

"Yes," said Matthew.

"It *was* an accident."

"Yes, Maggie, just an accident."

She didn't faint as such, just became limp, like a rag doll whose stuffing has lost its vitality. Matthew caught her as she sagged, and whispered something to her. He looked over to Harry and Joel. "Boys, take Maggie to the church. This won't take long."

Maggie came to life again as Joel helped support her, trying to push him away although it made no impression on him. "I want to stay," she said more strongly, and there was determination in it. Matthew nodded and Joel let go of her, but they stood protectively close and she let them, without further protest.

An old crow barked balefully from a gnarled tree close by. Matthew turned to Monica, who seemed almost to have diminished and aged within the time it took for the bird to rise heavily and fly to the belfry of the church. I heard sadness in his voice as he spoke. "What have the years done to you, Monica, that you should be so filled with hate; to what end?"

But as she shrunk, her bile concentrated. "*Yours*, Matthew," she spat. "For every time I looked at you and you taunted me with your looks and your agelessness. For everything you were that I wanted. For everything I could see in Henry and the girls, but I couldn't be. Ellen might have accepted she would get old and ugly, but I didn't. She couldn't understand why I had to know your secret, and she tried to stop me from finding out."

Henry could hardly contain himself as he stared at the woman in front of him. "So all the tests, the doctors – you weren't even trying to find out for the girls' sakes? It was always for you, what *you* wanted. Their happiness didn't figure at all?"

Monica raised one eyebrow as if it were obvious and he unreasonable to expect anything else. "Why would it? They already benefited from whatever it was Matthew has passed on to you, and it was unfair that I should miss out. Anyway, I knew they would understand when they grew up, although, as they didn't have my beauty, how could they even *begin* to know what it was like finding the first lines around my eyes, watching my skin begin to sag, the first grey hairs?" She touched her fingers to her face as if she could erase the memories along with the lines.

Ellie circled the grave and came to stand next to me. Stiffly alert, she stood so close that I felt the guarded fearfulness as her eyes flicked between Monica and Matthew.

Monica looked towards me. "I must have been only a little older than you when I noticed." Her eyes roamed longingly over me, and had she been a man, I would have described her desire in terms of lust. But she didn't see me, she saw my youth. "Have you seen your creeping age yet? Have you looked in the mirror and wondered what you will be like in ten years' time surrounded by all his *radiance*? If it hadn't been for the crash, I would have found out what it is that preserves him. Someone would have known."

"Leave Emma out of it, Monica; this has nothing to do with her."

"Don't be so naïve, Matthew – of course it has. I learned a long time ago that if I couldn't get at you directly, I would find your Achilles' heel and all I would need to do is prick it to watch you bleed. Kort had such an intuitive understanding of your relationship it wasn't hard to plant some tiny suggestions and watch them grow. The book was *my* idea," she crooned. "Staahl nurtured it, and dearest, darling Margaret delivered it *perfectly*. It wasn't difficult to persuade Kort to play sane. It's remarkably simple when you know what buttons to push, and he has certain… incentives. He so looks forward to seeing you again, my dear; he genuinely believes you are meant for him. He is such a hopeless *romantic*."

My churning stomach rebelled at the thought of Staahl's dead eyes, devoid of all compassion. "You're wasting your time. I don't give a damn what happens to me."

"How noble of you, my dear. You might not, but Matthew does. The Lynes men are such chivalrous fools. It makes them so tediously predictable and therefore vulnerable."

Matthew's reactions were instantaneous as he intercepted Ellie's hand as it fell slicing towards the woman's neck. He held on to her raised arm firmly.

"Ellie, no, she's not worth it."

Her eyes flared. "But *you* are. This is so *wrong*."

"You're hearing the bitter thoughts of a mind intent on destruction. There is no substance to them."

Her face crumpled and he let go of her hand, and she scrubbed angrily at the tears beginning to creep down her cheeks.

"I want to *kill* her."

"There's no need." He turned to Monica. "How long have they given you?"

She screwed her eyes in disbelief, the words escaping through her grid of teeth.

"*How* do you know?"

"You reek of death. The malice of your life is eating you from within. Whatever you have been told, you haven't long."

"Long enough to destroy you."

"I think not."

The clock tolled a mournful hour from the church, setting the crow cawing as it rose into the air in uneven spirals.

Henry broke the stunned silence. "She's dying?"

Ellie crossed her arms over her chest. "Good."

Monica faced Matthew, her expression no longer sly, but pleading. She grabbed at his arm, fingers biting into the fabric of his coat like claws as she clung to hope.

"You can help me, Matthew, I know you can. Whatever it is that has left you unchanged…"

He removed her hand. "There is nothing I can do."

All her arrogance and bravado slipped away, her handsome features dissolving into those of a haggard, worn out, and sick old woman.

Matthew looked at his family and Henry nodded. "Yes, it's time to go. Goodbye, Monica."

He led the way with Pat over the tumbled soil towards the cars, picking the smoothest path and leaving dark footprints in the thin, wet snow. Maggie looked back at her mother, once, and the rest of the family disappeared into the encroaching snow-laden gloom as Matthew stood by the grave of his wife for a few moments more. Then, joining me, he took my arm and wove it through his.

As we passed, I swiftly glanced at Monica, only to be met by contempt, and I saw in that look how consumed by her own mortality she had become. She read my face with a shocking degree of accuracy, for out of the falling snow her voice rang piercing and shrill, "Don't you pity me. Don't you *dare* pity *me!*"

The windscreen wipers played a guessing game with the snow, the haphazard flurries causing the automatic sensors to switch off and on with annoying unpredictability like the intermittent drip of a tap. I gritted my teeth as the wiper blades chased another scum of oily snow off the glass, then hesitated several seconds longer than previously, before sweeping their wide arc once again.

Matthew flicked onto manual and the blades became still. "We'd better find you somewhere to eat," he observed, the first thing he had said since we left the church. It was well past lunchtime.

"I can wait until we get back." The windscreen clouded with snow again, forcing him to switch the wipers back on. I scowled at them.

"I don't think you can."

We drove on. I couldn't remember seeing much in the way of roadside cafés on the way there, and I didn't want him wasting time with a diversion to a town. But he was right, I was becoming increasingly short-tempered as hunger bit, and I could have murdered a mug of tea at the very least.

We passed the trailer, like a long silver tube abandoned

by the roadside, before I registered it as a diner. Windows obscured by condensation declared it to be open.

"Stop! We've just passed one."

"*That*? When I said you needed to eat I meant food, not pathogens."

"Matthew, it'll do," I insisted, and he took a deep breath and swung the car in a tight circle without warning, and headed back the way we had come until we drew up in front of the diner. He peered dubiously at it through the windscreen. I didn't give him any choice. Huddling into the raised collar of my coat, I climbed out and located the metal steps to the door.

We weren't the only customers, but given that there wasn't much in the way of choice along this stretch of the highway, perhaps that wasn't so surprising.

In a uniform of red shirt and black skirt, the waitress perked up visibly when Matthew walked in, but no one else bothered looking up. Preserving anonymity could be difficult sometimes, but we had as good a chance as any in here.

We went to the opposite end of the diner, as far away from ears and eyes as possible. Matthew helped me out of my coat and I smiled up at him, but he avoided my eyes. I bottom-shuffled along the padded bench seat to be near the window, my shoulder brushing against the glass and leaving a bald patch in the condensation.

"What's the matter?"

"Don't have anything with meat," he muttered, "or eggs."

"It's not as bad as that."

He didn't answer.

The waitress bounced up and I ordered tea and toast.

"I can do you coffee and pie?" she offered. Matthew groaned and I kicked him under the table.

"Toast and… what else do you have to drink, please?" She ran through a list of alternatives, adding, "… and coffee."

"Toast and cola, thank you."

She looked expectantly at Matthew, the tip of her tongue playing against the end of her pencil as she waited for his order. He stared morosely out of the window. "Nothing else, thanks," I told her, and she swung away in her purple trainers and short socks like a thwarted cheerleader.

I reached across the table to where Matthew's hand rested on the worn red melamine, his fingers drumming a relentless beat against the aluminium trim, and curled my hand over his. His fingers twitched under mine.

"Matthew, please – what is it?"

If he had been me I would have said he must be tired and hungry, but neither could be true in his case. He continued to drum.

"I wanted you to eat, not scavenge for scraps."

"Oh, come on, give me some credit, and I know it isn't the funeral." *Although Heaven knows, that would surely have been enough.* As I said it, I knew it to be true. His moods were becoming colours to me, and I began to recognize the shades in between sad and happy, rage and calm.

He loosened his tie and shrugged off his coat, and finally met my gaze. "I don't understand why you're not angry with me, or at least resent me."

That took me by surprise. "Why should I?"

"You were there, Emma – you heard what the woman said."

"Of course I did. What of it?"

His eyes suddenly blazed and he whacked the table, making the sugar dispenser jump and fall over.

"If it were not for me, you wouldn't be going through hell in that *bloody* trial."

I sat back against the upholstered seat, thankful he had his back turned to the rest of the trailer's occupants. A moment later, I registered what he had said, and my temper flared in response.

"You're right, if it weren't for you I *wouldn't* be there, would I? I'd be dead!"

"I meant…" he ground his teeth in frustration, "… that Staahl would still be banged up in a mental institution for the criminally insane and you would not be being crucified for the entertainment of that *bitch*."

"I *know* what you meant," I shot back at him, aware that everybody now watched us with open mouths, "but you weren't to know, and you are *not* responsible for her behaviour any more than Maggie was responsible for that crash. Perhaps you should have killed her, and put her out of our misery."

"You really think I should have? Do you think I'm soft, no – *impotent* – as she so delicately put it?"

"Don't be ridiculous, of course not. Anyway, I thought she was already dea…" my hand shot over my mouth. "*Blow*."

Matthew's eyes narrowed. "You thought she was already dead. Why?"

I faltered. "It is only that nobody seemed to know where she was, or even if she were alive."

"I see," he said slowly, "and you thought that I had killed her?"

I squirmed under the full force of his gaze, pinned like an ant under a microscope.

"No. Well, yes – all right, it did cross my mind at first, but not recently."

"Why not *recently*?"

"Because I know you better. I think *I* would have been tempted to kill her, but not you."

"I say again, why not?"

"Because you are a better, *stronger* person than I am, Matthew, and it takes strength and conviction not to give in to your base instincts, that's why not."

He leaned back and observed me through half-closed eyes, then straightened his back and gave a grunted laugh.

"Mmm, well, we'll see. At least there's one thing for which we can be thankful – Maggie's in no fit state to stand as prosecution witness tomorrow; her mother's seen to *that*."

The girl had been hovering by the till with my order, apparently unsure whether to bring it over.

"Matthew, we're making everyone nervous – be nice," I indicated the waitress and he frowned then nodded.

She eyed him warily as she put the cola and toast on the table. "Will that be all, folks?"

Matthew gave her one of his dazzling smiles along with a very generous tip, which she didn't even look at. "Thank you, you have been most kind."

"You're welcome," she stammered, blushing the same colour as her top as she went away, happy.

The smile dropped from his face. "That good enough?"

"Oh yes, very charming, very smooth."

"I feel neither charming nor smooth at this minute. What a bloody awful day; I'm so sorry you had to be there."

I frowned a warning at him. "Don't start that again. I'm glad I could be, even if I couldn't exactly do anything."

He reached across the table and took both of my hands in his. "But you did, more than you can ever know." He kissed first one hand and then the other. "Look, can you eat that in the car? It's going to be long day tomorrow and I want to get you back to some degree of normality before you have to face it. Besides, you need a proper meal – that won't do."

Tomorrow.

Even the mere mention of it caused dread panic to surge from the pit of my gut to lodge in the base of my throat. When Monica said she was looking forward to what tomorrow might bring she had been gloating, as if holding all the cards in a game of poker she knew she had already won.

Once we reached the campus, I tried to persuade Matthew to go home to be with his family, but he wouldn't leave until he had placed an order with the restaurant and made me promise that I would eat it. My father assured him that I wouldn't be allowed to leave until I had, and I made a feeble joke about being a martyr for my cause like a suffragette; but really Matthew and I were aching to be alone without the weight of grief and responsibility and the fear of what tomorrow might bring. In the few minutes we had alone together while my father answered the door, I wrapped my arms around Matthew's waist and we melded until there seemed to be no semblance of self, but one entity – just briefly – for that fleeting moment, and then consciousness intervened driving reality, like a wedge, between us.

Judgment Day

Sleep came late.

I had eaten the prepared meal dutifully, but with neither hunger nor relish, and felt too full for hours afterwards. I took a bath, going over and over the day's events and my predictions for tomorrow, until the two became a jumble and I gave up and washed my hair. By the time I climbed out, I felt no more relaxed than when I had started.

I lay awake for hours in the certain knowledge that Matthew would be too, and it seemed wrong that I should sleep and escape when he could not, but my body defeated me and, by dawn, I drifted into a dreamless slumber.

It hadn't snowed for very long during the night, and by morning the sun shone strong and vital. The early air was still cold, and the new, thin snow had refrozen into a hard crust over which the students now skidded on their way to class. That was where I should have been going now, instead of sitting and waiting for Hart to come and collect me.

I viewed Elena's bag of students' texts enviously when she popped in to wish me luck for the day.

"It will all be over this time tomorrow, and you can return to your normal life," she predicted in an attempt to cheer me up. Hard as I tried to imagine it, I couldn't see beyond today, and normality – such as I had grown accustomed to with Matthew – seemed as remote now as when I had been back in Stamford in the days when each minute ran into the next without being marked with hope. She was right, of course – this day would pass. All things pass, one way or another.

Hart was out of breath when Dad answered the door to his knock. He hurried us without explanation down the back flight of stairs to the car waiting with its engine running in the Dean's private car park. The car pulled away as Hart's door slammed shut and the security locks fired.

He swivelled in his seat. "Now, Miss D'Eresby…"

"*Dr* D'Eresby," my father corrected him, still breathing heavily from the unexpected haste of our departure.

"Sorry – Dr D'Eresby – you might find that there is more media attention than on Friday…" As he spoke, the car rounded the side of the building and almost ran into a group of people wielding cameras, all watching the front entrance to the atrium. They saw the car as it swerved to avoid them. It left me speechless.

"As I was saying," Hart continued as the car left the college behind, "there'll be more interest from the media and the public, just so you know. There's quite a crowd at the courthouse."

It was an understatement, and not even my imagination prepared me for what waited for us. The steps, the pavement, even parts of the road were teeming with people. Uniformed officers from the Sheriff's Department fought to keep the crowd under some sort of control, but they were heavily outnumbered. The mass turned as we approached, and began to press forward. At this distance, the hybrid collection of moving colours were not human at all, but a ravenous animal waiting to feed.

Hart tapped the driver on the shoulder and he took us straight past without slowing. "We'll go in round the back."

"Don't they have jobs to go to?" I snapped, tired and stressed.

"A lot of them have taken the day off to be here; my cousin's one of them. The national media's in on it. Wouldn't surprise me if some of the internationals were here, too. Not much else is happening, so you'll get plenty of column inches I guess."

The car swung around the side of the courthouse without indicating, and came to an abrupt halt. Journalists and onlookers were already swarming around the side of the building from the front.

Hart sucked air as he contemplated the best course of action. "OK," he said. "Here, put this over your head and we'll make a run for it." He began to take off his coat, but I recalled the countless images of individuals on trial at the Old Bailey, their heads covered with a blanket as they raced from prison van to the court. They had always looked guilty, whether that proved to be the case or not, and I was blowed if I would hide my face when I had done nothing wrong. Let them stare.

"No, thank you, I have nothing to hide."

"If you're sure..." he said doubtfully, his hand hesitating on the door catch.

"I am," I said with more assurance than I felt. "Ready, Dad?"

He didn't reply. He looked at me with such pride. "That's my girl," he said.

The space between the car and the courthouse door had already filled with bodies, and the car began to rock slightly as the crowd pulsed around it.

Hart and the driver climbed out first and formed a bubble of space around my door. If I hadn't been prepared for the number of people before, I certainly wasn't now, for the conflict of noise and movement and the smell of hot armpits and agitated expectancy brought instant confusion. "It's her!" a man stinking of stale cigarettes in a big coat yelled over the heads of those nearby. The mob lunged forward despite the best efforts of the police, hands pushing through the cordon, grasping and pulling. One landed a punch on my arm. My father hit back but there were too many people and we were at risk of being engulfed.

A soldier in uniform shoved determinedly through the crowd towards us, materializing into Joel, followed by Harry. He raised his voice above the lumpen throng. "In need of assistance, ma'am?"

"Let them through," I shouted across to the officers as someone grabbed my arm from behind and tried to pull me backward. Dad did his best but he was becoming overwhelmed as we fought towards the door, where Duffy was waiting with two court sergeants.

"Geesh, Emma, you sure can pull a crowd," Joel grinned, elbowing someone out of the way. "The old man sent us. He seemed to think you might need some help. Don't know why." He put his arm around me, using his body as a shield as a man, old enough to be my father, aimed a punch at my back. "Sorry we're late, the cops wouldn't let us through at first." He craned his neck to judge the distance we had to cover. "It'd be quicker if I carried you," he said cheerfully.

"Leave me some dignity, please," I puffed.

The jostling lessened considerably as those intent on reaching me found their way blocked by the boys' immovable frames.

"Need a hand, sir?" Harry asked Dad over his shoulder.

My father grunted. "Just get my daughter through, young man. I'll be fine."

"*Bitch*," a woman screamed at me from somewhere behind us, repeated by a number of voices, thick with vitriol.

"Come on, you don't need to hear this," Harry muttered and picked up the pace, ploughing a clear path for us to follow. Once safely inside, Joel blocked the entrance behind us like a rock in the mouth of a cave. The noisiest thing in the peace of the rear hall was the sound of our breathing.

Duffy looked concerned. "You all right, hun? That sure is some crowd today."

"Morning, Duffy," I panted.

"Yes, well, let's get you upstairs and sorted out. You look as if you've been used to comb cotton. Come on, now, we need to hurry."

She ushered me into her office to tidy up. My arm hurt where I had been viciously pinched, but it was nothing compared to what scared me witless: with all the media attention, Matthew's relative obscurity had been blown out of the water.

I combed my hair and began to plait it. "Duffy, Hart said there's a lot of media here today."

"Sure is. Here, let me do that for you." She took the comb from my hand and started again.

"And the national press?" I asked, feeling powerless against the forthcoming blitz.

She finished the long plait and wound a securing band around the tail end. She curled it around my head, pinning it into place. The style felt alien. "Hell, yes, and the networks. Now you go into the bathroom and tidy yourself up, and then we can run through a few things before we go in."

Standing in front of the mirror in the cramped staff bathroom, I took in my shambolic state. My collar had been yanked sideways and a button had disappeared altogether from my jacket. My face went beyond pale, the freckles less gold and more grey in the artificial light. Bleak eyes stared back at me, the clear blue dulled, and with dark purple rings underneath. I pinched my cheeks and pressed my lips together to bring up some colour, but even my old pearl studs looked more luminous.

Duffy came in as I neatened the revers, my hand automatically reaching to pull my cross around to sit straight in the dip of my throat. I felt for the chain but where the warmed metal usually lay was cold, bare skin. I looked down and then patted my jacket and shook my shirt, but heard no responding tinkle of metal on tiles as it fell to the ground. I bent hurriedly to look under the basins.

"What's the matter, honey?" Duffy asked, responding to my increasingly frantic search.

"My cross, it's gone!"

"Did you forget to put it on this morning?"

"No, I never do." My voice caught. "*Never.*"

The courtroom buzzed with the intensity of a June swarm, and it was already hot from the press of bodies squeezed inside it. My hands were damp with nerves, darkening the nutmeg as I rolled it back and forth between my palms, feeling it rattle in its hard outer shell.

Henry and Pat had not yet arrived, but Harry and Joel were in the next row with Dad near them, so close that I could hear his short, husky breaths as I approached. He gave me an encouraging smile but was clearly anxious, despite his best efforts to hide it. I wanted to tell him I had lost my cross and how much it mattered, but I thought I would cry if I tried to explain it to him, so instead kept quiet.

I was thankful we had beaten Staahl's team to it and his chair sat empty as we passed. One of the junior defense clerks was reading the morning edition of the local paper, hurriedly folding it out of sight as I sat down. Quick she might have been, but not so quick that I hadn't seen the headline:

Revelations As
Kinky S & M Sex Scandal Trial Continues

Duffy shrugged apologetically.

I turned away and searched the room, purposefully avoiding the eyes of any of those who tried to engage with mine. Monica was not where she had been on Friday but sitting in the third row from the front, so carefully positioned it could hardly have been coincidental. I had hoped she wouldn't appear, thwarted as she had been yesterday, but she saw me and smiled, raising the tips of her fingers in a wave that might as well have been an obscene gesture, because that was exactly what she meant by it. I looked down at my hands on the edge of the table and contemplated murder. Everything I had heard about Monica – from her own lips or from others – pointed towards a narcissistic, self-obsessed woman. Unable or unwilling to look beyond her own desires, her manipulation of Maggie bordered on abusive, and that she delighted in the chaos she caused others I considered out-and-out perverse.

After a few minutes of trying in vain to evoke a reaction from me, she gave up and instead made a fuss of unfolding a newspaper and holding it in front of her with the headline prominently displayed.

Staahl arrived, flanked by two sergeants, and I fought the familiar pall of revulsion. Yet, in the longing look he gave me as he passed, I thought I detected something else: a corrupted delusion that somehow what he had done was *right*. Staahl was dangerous because he believed he was right, but he wasn't evil. What he had done was evil, but the rest was just madness and somehow, in all of this stuff we were dealing with, we had lost sight of that fact. He wasn't controlling this game any more than I was. Staahl was dangerous because he could be manipulated by someone more cunning and devious than he was. But there was one facet of his personality I wondered if Monica had overlooked. While she was cold, calculating, and consistent, he had that one element insanity conveyed that she lacked: he was unpredictable. I still feared him, of course – the lingering memory of his brutality caused fissures of terror to surface like burning magma through a fault – yet he was weak because he was as much a victim of his desire as I had been to his knife. I put my hand to my throat where he had held the cold blade, finding the empty space where my cross had been, and instantly regretted the action.

It was the turn of the Staahl's team to produce witnesses. I tensed in anticipation.

Horatio straightened his broad silk tie and approached the bench, turning neatly on one heel to face both the waiting crowd and the jury, measuring time, using all the space available to him to make his presence felt. He smiled a lot; in fact, I realized, he smiled all the time. His mouth lifted where it should but his eyes remained the same – expressionless, blank – like a shark.

"Your Honour, ladies and gentlemen, prosecution calls Dr Margaret Lynes."

Behind me I heard an exclamation. Henry hadn't anticipated her being fit to take the stand, which meant Matthew didn't know either. Horatio must have worked some magic to get her this far; how much further was he prepared to go? Maggie knew everything needed to discredit our testimony, and she could expose Matthew to the world.

He had always maintained she wouldn't, but who knew what lengths she might be prepared to go to since our confrontation at Christmas, and with the manipulation of her mother and the ruthless counsel? After what had happened at the funeral and Monica's revelation, Maggie was as about as reliable as fractured ice on a pond.

I started to reach out to gain Duffy's attention, but stopped. If Duffy knew of Maggie's instability she would use it to undermine her credibility as a witness, but it might also reveal Monica's involvement and my prior knowledge. Questions would reveal cracks in our story, and begin investigations that would lead goodness only knew where. Ultimately there was so much more at stake than my losing this case.

I watched Maggie curiously as she took the oath and sat down. Her movements were efficient, as smooth as Matthew's and almost as elegant. Her silver-white hair had grown since Christmas, and it looked softer, more becoming, as it framed her pale face. She no longer wore solid black, but a well-cut, flattering dark grey dress suit that made her look professional without being too severe. Staahl's bunch had done a good job. Despite all that had happened yesterday, today she appeared to be self-possessed and in control.

"Are you OK, hun?" Duffy whispered. I unclenched my fists and forced my fingers to relax.

"Yes, thanks."

Horatio looked particularly smug as he approached her. "Dr Lynes, before we begin examining the evidence, the jury might be wondering if there is a familial connection between you and Dr Matthew Lynes, so for the sake of clarity, please explain the nature of your relationship."

Staring at the wavy dark grain running through the light wood of the table, I waited. A movement behind me, and a quiet word spoken quickly, told me Henry and Pat were also acutely aware of the potential danger.

"I am Dr Lynes' older sister."

I exhaled and dared to look at her. She flicked a glance in my direction and beyond to her family.

"Thank you. You are chief clinical psychiatrist in charge of the psychiatric unit at the Memorial Hospital, where Kort Staahl was taken shortly after his arrest. In your capacity as clinical psychiatrist, please explain what you were required to do by the Superior Court."

"It was my role to assess Professor Staahl's mental state during the commitment period and to report to the Commissioner of Health and Human Services on his competency to stand trial."

"And what were your conclusions, Dr Lynes?"

Although she continued to address the counsel, her eyes briefly met those of Staahl and his mouth twitched in what might have been a smile. "That Professor Staahl is competent to stand trial."

What was she playing at? Had she not understood what Monica had done to sabotage the evidence? Surely she wasn't going to sit there and tell the court that Staahl was sane? Surely she wasn't going to lie? *Or was she as delusional as the man she had assessed? Did she believe the fabrication her mother had woven between them?*

"Forgive my ignorance, Dr Lynes, but what does that mean in layman's terms?"

"It means that Kort Staahl was aware of what he did and in control of his actions."

I looked swiftly at Duffy, but her face told me nothing.

"When you assessed Professor Staahl, what explanation did he give you for what happened on the evening of October 31st?"

"He said that he met Professor D'Eresby in the atrium."

"*Met* Professor D'Eresby – by accident, do you mean?"

"No, he said that they arranged to meet."

I sat forward abruptly, my teeth clenched. Duffy put a restraining hand on my arm. From his place between two clerks of his team, Staahl listened motionless and impassive.

"Now, let me get this straight. Kort Staahl told you that he had prearranged to meet with Ms D'Eresby at the atrium on that evening? So she was aware that he would be there?"

"That is what he said, yes."

"I think that members of the jury might be wondering what this attractive young woman was doing meeting a colleague in somewhat odd circumstances when she was supposed to be at the college dinner. Did Professor Staahl say *why* they had arranged to meet?"

Maggie's eyes slid towards me as she spoke. "Professor Staahl said that Professor D'Eresby wanted to meet to enact a fantasy."

"Can you be more precise, Dr Lynes?"

"He said that Professor D'Eresby had a sadomasochistic fetish she wanted to explore with him. Meeting in a public place when she should have been at the dinner was part of that fantasy, and the illicit nature of the meeting intensified the sexual tension they would have experienced."

I clasped a hand over my mouth, fighting the urge to cry out in protest.

Duffy spoke softly, hardly moving her lips. "It's just part of the game, Emma – don't let it get to you."

Horatio went into full swing. "And Professor Staahl was willing to go along with her wishes?"

"Yes, Kort Staahl freely admitted taking part in sadomasochistic sexual fantasies on previous occasions."

"With Ms D'Eresby?"

"No, with other willing participants."

"Has Professor Staahl a history of mental health illness, Dr Lynes?"

"No, none on record."

"So from a clinical point of view, Kort Staahl's behaviour was *deviant* but not *criminal*?"

"Objection!" Duffy sprang to her feet, hands flat on the table in front of her. "Your Honour, the witness is not in a position to make judgment on a point of law which is beyond her professional knowledge."

"Sustained," the judge said dryly. "Rephrase your question, counsel."

Horatio smiled. "Dr Lynes, in your capacity as a *senior* clinical psychiatrist of many years standing, in your *opinion*, was the defendant acting with criminal intent?"

"No, Professor Staahl understood Professor D'Eresby to be a fully cognisant and consenting partner. While Kort Staahl describes himself as needing to dominate in any partnership, he feels dependent on the submissive element's willing participation. There would be no gratification without this. He is... besotted with her."

"Thank you, Dr Lynes. Please remain on the witness stand. My colleague might have some questions for you."

"Darn right I do," Duffy muttered and made to rise, but Horatio waved her back.

"If counsel for the defense would indulge me for a moment?" She sat down again, slowly, and he raised a lofty hand. "Thank you, ma'am. For the benefit of the jury, let me clarify that an act that is repugnant to many people does not necessarily constitute a crime if there is no criminal intent on the part of the individual. Let me be clear about this point.

Kort Staahl openly admits taking part in sadomasochistic acts that were agreed beforehand and consensual in nature. That is, he had no intent of causing grievous harm to another, and that Ms D'Eresby suffered hurt was entirely accidental and aggravated by the intervention of Dr Lynes. This was a private matter between the individuals concerned. We are in this court today because one of those individuals…" he raised his finger and directed the jury's attention towards me, "… caught *in – the – act* by Dr Lynes, chose to defend her reputation by accusing her lover – my client – of criminal intent, thus robbing him of his livelihood and his reputation." He circled the air with his finger and let the accusation settle like dust upon the room. "My client, formally of sound mind and blameless repute, suffered months of mental anguish as a result. As you have heard from Dr Margaret Lynes, Kort Staahl is not mentally ill. His is a lifestyle choice, conducted in seclusion for the mutual entertainment of him and his partner. What, ladies and gentlemen, are we to think if such private matters are made public? How many people here have individual pleasures that involve none other than the couple, but who wish them to remain private for fear their reputation might be called into question? I, for one, have a passion for ice cream." He let the laughter subside before continuing. "Make no mistake, ladies and gentlemen, reputation is no laughing matter, as my client has found to his cost." He bowed his head in momentary reflection. "Your witness, counsel."

Duffy didn't rise immediately, but sucked her teeth thoughtfully for a few seconds until the judge squinted at us. "Your witness, counsel?"

"Thank you, Your Honour," she said, rising and approaching Maggie. "Dr Lynes, can you describe the defendant's mental state at, or as near to, the time at which he was committed for observation and assessment to your care?"

"He was very calm."

"That was not what I asked. What was his *mental* state, Dr Lynes?"

Maggie shot her an acid look that would have dissolved carbon.

"Professor Staahl appeared to be in control and without evident psychosis."

"But looks can be deceiving, can't they, Dr Lynes? Is this what you would normally expect when a person has been placed under arrest for a serious and aggravated assault on another person?"

"It can be a shock reaction to extreme events, yes."

"But would you describe it as *normal* behaviour?"

"I don't follow."

"Isn't it also the case that persons with certain mental health issues might also display calmness – or a lack of compassion – towards a victim, let's say, indicative of a dissociative disorder?"

Horatio waved his notes in the air. "Objection. The witness has already testified to the defendant's mental state. This is a waste of court time."

The judge had been taking notes; her pen hovered over the paper. "Is there a point to this question, defense counsel?"

"Yes, there is, Your Honour, and if counsel for the prosecution will return the favour and be a little patient here, I will allude to it in due course."

The judge's sigh ended in a compact cough. "I'll allow it."

Duffy persevered. "Dr Lynes, you stated that Kort Staahl said he believed that Emma D'Eresby had consented to – *instigated* – sadomasochistic acts, did you not?"

"Yes, he did."

"And why did you believe him?"

Maggie blinked. She wavered, trying to formulate an answer, but Duffy didn't give her the chance. "I mean, what made you think he told you the truth? Why couldn't he be lying?"

"He… had no reason to lie. Professor Staahl was open and honest about his sexual preferences. He regarded them as normal behaviour, he had nothing to hide. Over a lengthy period I was able to form an accurate profile of my client and, given my extensive experience, I had no reason to believe he told me anything other than the truth. I am rarely incorrect in the assessment of my patients." There – the touch of arrogance slipping in again, just as it had in Matthew's study at Christmas. Two of the jury members exchanged glances.

Duffy wasn't impressed. "Unless, of course he is mentally delusional, or guilty of a serious assault with a deadly weapon that would have cost the life of this young woman, and he manipulated you into thinking otherwise, Dr Lynes?"

Maggie's leg twitched, not so much as to be noticeable but enough to tell me that whatever was holding her together was beginning to come unstuck.

The judge cleared her throat and took a sip of water from the glass beside her.

"Please answer the question put to you by counsel, doctor."

"It is possible he lied, yes; but I don't believe it to be so," she added defiantly.

Duffy smiled. "Thank you, Dr Lynes. No more questions – for now."

People stretched and yawned and blinked, exchanging comments with their neighbours as they eased their bones. It neared midday but the sullen light had intensified, and someone switched on the overhead lamps. The judge called

Horatio Pig to her bench and, after a moment, the court clerk announced early recess for lunch.

Dad leaned over the back of my chair. "Emma, would you like some fresh air?"

Duffy fastened the clasp on her briefcase and swung it onto her shoulder. "I don't think it advisable, not after this morning's brouhaha. Use my office – Leon'll fetch whatever you need."

Dad heaved on his heavy winter coat and pulled his brown leather gloves over his stubby fingers. He looked absurdly military and utterly British. "I'll take a stroll, Em. Don't worry, I know what you'll want to eat. I won't be long."

Once in her office, I collapsed into the chair behind Duffy's desk. Pushing an empty coffee cup out of the way, I rested my head on my folded arms and closed my eyes. This morning had been a nightmare not helped by my lack of sleep. I didn't hear the door open.

"Hello."

I was halfway across the room before I stopped abruptly. "You didn't believe any of that, did you?"

It took just two of Matthew's strides to reach me, and he lifted me off the ground, leaving my feet dangling. "You should know me better than to ask that," he chided gently into my hair. I inhaled deep lungfuls of his wholesome, outdoor scent, my face crammed into his neck. He held me for a few seconds more. "Emma – listen to me…" He put me back on my feet and looked into my face gravely. "You must tell Duffy what Maggie told you at Christmas about Staahl, and about the book. You have to tell her she said he is insane."

"I can't do that!"

"You have to – it's the only way you'll get some sort of justice and put Staahl away where he can't hurt you."

"Matthew, if I tell Duffy she'll want to know why I didn't say anything before, and she'll ask how I came to meet Maggie. It'll open a can of worms and I can't have Duffy asking questions that might reveal our relationship or *anything* about you. Besides, it could ruin Maggie's career if it exposes her to accusations of either perjury or incompetence, and she couldn't cope with that now."

He looked as if he was silently counting to ten before he spoke again. "This trial isn't about Staahl's reputation now any more than it is about yours, Monica made that clear. Whatever the outcome, I think that there is a good chance that Staahl will be ultimately released, given Maggie's testimony. We know now that her evidence is based on false assumptions. If that is the case, Staahl could be back at college in a matter of days and he won't hesitate to come after you again, and if I don't kill him first, God alone knows what other women he will mutilate or murder before he's caught."

"Don't! Don't talk about killing – not even in jest. There has to be some way other than telling Duffy." I wasn't at all certain that he had been joking; his eyes blazed with tension.

"There isn't. Tell Duffy and get her to push Maggie to her limits; she has to retract her statement. She is forsworn, Emma – she has deceived us all."

"She's as much a victim as I am, Matthew. Look at what we've been prepared to do to protect ourselves."

"That's precisely it – to *protect* ourselves. What we have done injures no one. Maggie's perversion of the truth harms not only you, but might allow a guilty man – a *dangerous* guilty man – to go free." I must have looked shocked because he went on grimly. "I won't stand you being hounded like this. Maggie made her choice when she gave you that book from Staahl and when she decided to give evidence for the prosecution, knowing what it would mean for you. I know she's ill, Emma, but I also know her well enough to see that she is complicit in all this even if she didn't know Monica was pulling the strings. Henry and I haven't been able to dissuade her to change her evidence, so if you won't tell Duffy, I will."

The consequences of such an action were all too clear. My skin flushed hot. "Matthew, you mustn't. If Duffy puts Maggie under pressure on the stand, who knows what she might say about you, about Monica – *anything*. She might not mean to hurt you, but Maggie's only just in control now. Have you seen her today? If she breaks down under cross-examination, the damage she could do to you and the family is… unthinkable, let alone what it'll do to her. It's not worth the risk."

His mouth set in a stubborn line. "Yes, *you* are."

"No, I'm *not*. My reputation is expendable and you can protect me from Staahl. He might still be put away; you never know, miracles do happen." I didn't sound very convinced and he certainly didn't look it, but he was intractable, the muscles along his jaw as rigid and unyielding as his decision.

"Nonetheless…"

I could see that I wasn't going to dissuade him. "All right, I will do something, but just promise me that you *won't*. Please, Matthew, keep a low profile. Duffy already suspects I've been lying to her about us."

Immediately wary, he asked, "Why, what has she said?"

"She said we looked as if we '*should be together*'."

A smile lifted the tenor of his voice and he briefly caressed my cheek with his. "Mmm, well, she is right about that at least." He frowned suddenly. "Where's your cross?"

"I lost it when we were trying to get through the crowds from the car. They were grabbing at me."

His frown deepened. "I know how much it meant to you. If only I'd been there, I would have been able to protect..." I put my finger on his lips, aware that only a door stood between us and the clerks' office, where I could hear a constant murmur of voices interspersed by the occasional raw, ribald laugh.

"Shh, I know you would. The boys stopped it from being any worse than it was. Thank you for sending them, and thank you for this – it made all the difference." I held out my hand, and the nutmeg rolled back and forth in my palm.

He folded my fingers over it. "Keep it if it helps. It's hardly your cross and it holds no religious significance, and if I could endow it with any powers to help you I would, but I kept it with me through some very difficult times and it was a constant in a changing world..." He halted with a hint of awkwardness and looked at me from beneath dark lashes, for once lost for words. "Your arm's bothering you," he stated, laying his hand over the area. The ache subsided almost immediately to a background throb and his expression relaxed. "I wish I could do the same for what's happening in court. I would that I were able to reach inside people and draw off all the poison that has led to the corruption of their conscience – led to all *this*. I wish..." He paused, his eyes on the door from the interconnecting office. "I'd better go, my love." He bent swiftly to kiss me, his lips so briefly on mine yet his touch lingered even as he crossed the room to leave. He turned once with a look of regret at parting. "I love you, Emma D'Eresby," he said, and left before the handle of the door had finished turning and Duffy came in backward, still talking to someone in the other room.

"All alone?" She put a block of papers down on the desk with a thump, pushing the empty cup still further to one side. "Damnation, I knew I forgot something. Leon, honey..."

she called, and the cheerful face of the junior clerk appeared around the edge of the door, framed by his mass of tight, black curls. "Go fetch me a double espresso, will you? I clear forgot." The face disappeared. "No, wait…" she yelled after him. "Make that a *double*-double espresso, I'm in dire need of coffee. Thanks." She became briskly purposeful. "Had any lunch yet?"

"My father's getting some." I fiddled with the nutmeg and then put it in my pocket. "Duffy, what happens next?"

"If there's no more cross-examination, we'll sum up with our closing speeches and then the judge'll say her piece and the jury will retire to find a verdict."

"And in your experience, what is the likely outcome of this trial going to be?" On the surface I might have appeared calm, composed, reasonable, but beneath, the muscles of my stomach were so tightly clenched they hurt, and I felt sick with fear.

"Well… you know, we have a pretty good chance…" she began, then sighed in resignation at the look on my face. "OK, OK, let's cut the bull crap here. I'd say the jury's split pretty evenly between the acquittals and the don't knows – with a few guiltys, perhaps. The problem is in persuading them that this was an act of violence against an *unwilling* victim, giving you reason to report it as such. If he'd raped you, it would've been easier to prove."

"Gee, thanks," I muttered.

"As it is, if I'm honest, that looks less and less likely. I think you might have to face facts here, hun. With no other witnesses to the attack and Dr Lynes' evidence stymied by his taking you to his rooms, Staahl has a chance of pushing this through."

"I don't care whether he wins, Duffy – in the eye of the public I'm already guilty. What worries me, frankly, *terrifies* me, is that Staahl might one day be free to come after me again. Or anyone else, for that matter."

"There'll be his own trial, don't forget, though Heaven knows how that'll work after all the shenanigans in this one. But I'm sorry, that's the way the system works. Of course, if he attacks you again, then…" She lifted her shoulders in a brief upward motion and let me fill in the rest.

I studied my shoes, weighing up my choices. As Matthew had said, it didn't seem as if I had many.

"What if… what if he *were* found to be insane, what then?"

"Aw, hun, that would mean Dr Lynes – Dr Margaret Lynes, that is – would have to change her evidence, and at this stage that isn't very likely, now, is it?"

I felt like a condemned prisoner clutching at straws until the very last moment before she felt the noose tighten around her neck. "Yes, but what if she *did* change her evidence, Duffy?"

She came and perched on the edge of her desk and scratched at a place on her arm, thinking. "If Dr Lynes changes her evidence," she said slowly, "it would undermine the prosecution case to such an extent that the case would probably collapse, there being doubt about Staahl's claims that you consented, due to his possible mental state and such. The judge'll probably call for a halt to the trial for further reports and verification to corroborate the statement of fact."

"And if that were done and he *is* found to be insane?"

"Well, then either he is held for a further period for observation and treatment or, if the evidence is compelling, the judge can have him committed to a secure institution indefinitely. But, in order for that to happen, it would have to be shown that he was a continuing danger to the public. Now *that* would explain why they didn't want him on the stand."

She screwed her eyes, assessing me. "Do you know something that I need to know?"

I fixed her with a steady look. "Yes," I said. "I know that Kort Staahl is insane."

Duffy's eyes widened slightly, then she nodded and hopped off her desk. "I reckon you're right, hun, but proving it is another matter."

Matthew waited outside the courtroom, the set of his shoulders betraying the tension I could feel flowing from him as I passed to enter the room. He held my eye with a question, but I gave only a fleeting, evasive smile in response. His brow knitted in frustration and concern and I realized that, even from this distance, he could sense the sporadic hammering of my heart.

The room felt fuggy with the heat of anticipation. Duffy placed her steaming quadruple espresso on the floor between our chairs with a conspiratorial wink. "Don't say a word. The judge won't take kindly to me bringing it in, but I need my caffeine fix if I want all my wits about me and more."

The acrid steam rose in a silent, pungent column, making my empty gut heave, so it was probably a good thing that I'd only managed a few mouthfuls of food before my stomach rebelled at lunch. Only the tea that my father insisted I drank kept it all where it should be. I held my breath and turned away from the smell until the nausea passed.

"Defense calls Dr Matthew Lynes."

Startled to hear him called again, for a horrible moment I wondered if he had already spoken to Duffy.

A little quiver of expectation rose from some of the women seated nearby as he walked down the central aisle to the stand, where Duffy waited.

"Dr Lynes, in your testimony as an expert witness, you described to the court your medical qualifications in relation to your extensive surgical experience. Do you not also have qualifications in the field of psychiatry, including forensic psychiatry?"

"Yes, I do."

"And do these qualifications not only equal but surpass those of Dr Margaret Lynes?"

Matthew wasn't comfortable but I knew he could see as well as I could where Duffy wanted to go with this. "They do," he said quietly. I took a furtive glance at Monica. She stared at Matthew but I couldn't see if she was resentful or fearful.

"Dr Lynes, in your *qualified* professional opinion, were the actions of Kort Staahl on the night of the alleged attack on Professor D'Eresby those of a rational, clear-thinking individual in his right mind?"

Horatio raised his voice before she had finished her question. "Objection, Your Honour – counsel knows that my client's sanity is not in question here."

The judge pushed her glasses up to the bridge of her nose and held them there for a second. She reviewed Duffy, who waited for her judgment with the tip of her toe tapping out her nervous tension.

"Counsel, I take it that there is a point to your line of questioning?"

"Why, yes, Your Honour, I am trying to establish an expert witness's *opinion* on Kort Staahl's behaviour as it pertains to his actions on the night of the incident." Her Southern twang lent a strange emphasis to the formality of her words.

"I'll allow it, counsel. This time."

Duffy grinned. "Thank you, Your Honour. Dr Lynes, answer the question, if you will."

Matthew's stillness was both compelling and disquieting, like waiting for the ticking of a bomb to stop. "From the evidence gained from my observation of Professor Staahl's behaviour, and the nature of the severe physical trauma inflicted by him on Professor D'Eresby, Kort Staahl displays behaviours consistent with a diagnosis of dysfunctional schema – or fixed fantasies – indicative of a long-standing egosyntonic sociopathic personality disorder."

"In your opinion, then, Dr Lynes, is he – how shall I put it – *aware* that he has caused physical injury to this young woman?"

"He is not only aware of it but believes it to be a normal and acceptable pattern of behaviour in his belief that his fantasies are shared by the victim. In line with a diagnosis of a sociopathic disorder, he is unaware of the needs of others and as such is a continuing danger to the public."

Horatio hauled his big frame to his feet again, this time more slowly and with a measured air. "Objection – the witness cannot testify with respect to the mental state or condition of my client as to whether, in his opinion, my client did or did not have the mental state or condition constituting an element of this act. That is one of ultimate fact for the trier of fact alone."

Duffy spun around to face Horatio, waving a cautionary finger at him. "I am aware of Rule 704 of Article Seven, counsel, but the witness is not giving an opinion as to whether Kort Staahl did, on the night in question, have such a mental state as have him cause Professor D'Eresby harm, only that he believes him to have a mental condition *per se*, from the evidence he has seen. Be fair, now, Horatio, at least *my* witness was actually present at the incident." Laughter rippled through the room as Duffy sat down, interlacing her fingers in front of her. "Your witness, counsel," she said as if bestowing a great honour.

Horatio purposefully strode towards Matthew with a businesslike air intended to intimidate, taking with him a sheet of printed paper, which he proceeded to flick with the end of his finger, *thrwat, thrwat*. It was already irritating.

"Dr Lynes, you state that your qualifications in psychiatry surpass those of your older sister."

"Yes."

"How important is *experience* in honing the skills first obtained through paper qualifications?"

"I should say that it is vital."

"Dr Margaret Lynes is a senior clinical psychiatrist whose daily practice it is to evaluate the mental state of patients in her care, is it not?"

"Yes, it is."

"She is also – and I beg her forgiveness for this lack of gallantry – quite a few years older than you are, Dr Lynes, and therefore has considerably greater experience, would you not say?" Thankfully he meant it as a rhetorical question, saving Matthew from having to lie to answer it. "So why do you believe that *your* evaluation of my client should be more accurate than that of a senior clinical psychiatrist in charge of a mental health unit with many years more experience than you have, and who spent dedicated time in observation and assessment of my client?"

Matthew's gaze fell upon Monica, and it was clear to me what he contemplated. I closed my eyes and tried to reach him but I couldn't focus long enough through all the distractions of the courtroom. *Please, Matthew, you promised.* I willed him to silence.

"I'm waiting, Dr Lynes."

"I can only state my opinion based on my observations, qualifications, and experience. I cannot comment on the reasons for the decisions reached by another professional – no matter how learned or experienced."

I let out a long breath I hadn't realized I had been holding.

"So you fully admit, Dr Lynes, that your sister is highly qualified and experienced in this field?"

Matthew looked directly at Staahl, who visibly blanched under his gaze. "Yes, she is, and she has a reputation for *complete* professional integrity."

Horatio smiled broadly, obviously pleasantly surprised by Matthew's assertion.

"Well, thank you for your comments, doctor. I have no more questions for this witness, Your Honour."

Duffy had been scribing notes in swift, illegible strokes, and she now sprang from her chair before Horatio had time to carefully settle back into his.

"Defense calls Dr Margaret Lynes to the stand."

My pulse quickened. This was exactly what I had dreaded.

Duffy spoke quickly with Matthew. He nodded, and instead of leaving the room as I expected, went to an empty seat nearby and sat down.

Maggie approached the witness stand stiffly. Squeezing her legs together, she clasped her hands tightly, and an undercurrent of stress rippled through her. Still as pale as she had been in the morning, now I saw a fire in her eyes that spoke of defiance, and a matter of professional and personal honour to defend. Maggie might be damaged and fragile, but she still had a ribbon of iron running through her core, welding her together. How far would she be prepared to go to defend herself, and at what cost?

Monica leaned forward, her claw-like hands grasping the padded back of the bench in front of her. Maggie gave her a hasty glance, then looked away.

Duffy read from a venerable tome she had elicited from somewhere. "Dr Lynes, you are a renowned expert in psychopathology, which is, and I quote, '*The study of the manifestation of behaviours and experiences indicative of mental illness, or the description of the manifestation of abnormal, maladaptive behaviour*', is that correct?"

Maggie lifted her chin with an allusion to the haughtiness we had seen earlier in the day. "I am."

"Do you ever discuss your cases with your brother, Dr Matthew Lynes?"

Immediately prickly and on the defensive, Maggie replied, "Only on a completely confidential and professional basis, yes."

Duffy remained straight-faced. "That is understood. Did you discuss *this* case with Dr Lynes?"

"No, I did not."

"Oh... and why not?"

"I didn't think it necessary and he was... preoccupied."

Duffy handed the book to her waiting clerk and exchanged it for a blue cardboard file, which she opened. "I see. In your original report to the Commissioners of Health and Human Services, you stated that Kort Staahl demonstrated patterns of behaviour associated with psychopathic disorder such as – and I quote here from your own report – '*dysfunctional schema*'. That is the exact term used by Dr Matthew Lynes just a few minutes ago to describe his assessment of Professor Staahl's mental condition. Did you not use that term to describe Kort Staahl's mental condition in your initial assessment, Dr Lynes?"

Clearly rattled, Maggie threw a harried look at the prosecution team. "I thought that Professor Staahl's mental state was not in question here?"

"It isn't at present, Dr Lynes. Please answer the question."

Maggie's answer bordered on surly. "Yes."

"It would appear that both of you, at some point, came independently to the same conclusion, wouldn't it, doctor?"

Reluctantly, she nodded.

"Out loud for the court, if you will."

Two bright points of colour had appeared in the confines of Maggie's hollow cheeks. "Yes," she said, terse to the point of rudeness, and in her lap her hands twisted convulsively.

"Can you tell the court why it is, then, that in your *second* report you conclude, and I quote: '*The patient shows no signs of sociopathic tendencies or personality disorder that constitutes a psychological problem or a danger to himself or to those around him*', end quote. Dr Lynes, why did you change your mind so radically?"

Maggie half-lifted herself out of the chair and then sat back down again. A small spot of blood formed on her bottom lip, glistening red, where she had bitten hard. She touched it, surprise in her eyes as she looked at her finger.

Duffy could obviously sense she was breaking. "Dr Lynes?"

Maggie licked at her lip with the tip of her tongue, her eyes flicking first to Matthew, then to Monica, as if trying to make a decision. Staahl slid to the edge of his chair, leaning forward as far as he could, an expression of deep concentration frozen on his face. Not a whisper lifted the tension of the room.

The judge's forehead became a series of horizontal creases that matched the line of her spectacles. "Dr Lynes, you must answer counsel."

Maggie stuttered back to life. "It… it is accepted that in the case of a sadomasochistic relationship, as long as it is consensual, it is not deemed to be a psychological problem…"

I heard a low sound behind me. Turning, I saw Matthew glaring at Maggie with an intensity that made me shudder.

She looked nervously towards him, then back at Duffy, caught between the interrogative onslaught of them both.

"You haven't answered my question, Dr Lynes. *Why* did you change your mind? Did *you* change it, or was it changed for you? Did you perhaps make a wrong assessment in the first place? Are you incompetent, Dr Lynes, or have you chosen not to tell the *truth*?" Duffy had found Maggie's weakness and she would exploit it to its natural conclusion, wringing every last drop of mental reserve from her. I realized that this was going to push Maggie over the edge into goodness only knew what chasm, and take Matthew with her. She had to be brought back before the gulf opened too far and it was too late.

The forgotten coffee reeked on the floor next to me, still and rank and bitter. Something Matthew had said when we were in Duffy's office came back to me with all the resounding force of a blow.

Throwing a cautious look at the judge, in a movement so quick I hardly knew what I was doing until I did it, I leaned down, picked up the cup of espresso, and drained it in one continuous stream. I nearly gagged. The empty cup fell with an accusingly hollow *tok* on the scuffed wooden boards, and I waited, wiping my mouth with the back of my hand. Nobody had seen me.

Nothing happened.

Maggie still struggled to maintain her composure, but she was losing control fast and the wretched coffee wasn't working. Sure, I felt the stuff hit my stomach like a cannonball, making me curl up on my chair with my arms clasped around me momentarily until the spasm passed, but I had no clarity of thought, no inspiration, no *insight*.

Duffy's voice carved through the hushed suspense in the room. "*Incompetent* or *liar*, Dr Lynes? The court is waiting..."

"I… wh… when I spoke to Professor Staahl, he said that she consented to the act and that she… invited him to… meet her." Maggie's speech became halting and a muscle in her temple began to twitch. She put up a shaking hand to stop it.

My fingers were beginning to tingle and my tongue had gone numb. It was a reaction of sorts, but it wasn't what I wanted. I closed my eyes and tried to focus on Maggie. Nothing. No connection. Damn it, *work*.

I opened my eyes again as my pulse became increasingly erratic, the blood pounding insistently in my ears, hammering away at my consciousness. I tried again, not entirely certain what I looked for. I found it so much easier with Matthew, and even Monica had made her presence palpable with her malevolence; but Maggie was surrounded by so many confusing signals and conflicting information that I couldn't gain a clear picture of her emotional state even if I had known what I was doing. Cold sweat forced beads of moisture to sit uncomfortably on my brow. I scrubbed at them and attempted to concentrate.

Duffy upped the pressure. "And when you refer to '*she*', do you mean Professor D'Eresby?"

"*Yes*," Maggie almost spat the word out in a demonstration bordering on contempt.

"Let me get this straight, Dr Lynes. On the basis of what the defendant *told* you, you changed the conclusion of your report?" Duffy made no attempt to hide her disbelief.

Maggie said something else, but I didn't hear as a sudden rush of feelings crowded my senses, almost overpowering me with their unexpected intensity. I gasped. The door opened and closed at the back of the room and high up, a bird flew into the glass of the window, its soft impact ricocheting inside my head. I lost sight of Maggie and searched desperately for her again amid the encroaching anarchy of sensory overload.

In all the maelstrom, I had to find her – *fast*.

Maggie began to panic, her voice rising with hysteria. "No! No – you don't understand, it was *her*…" She jabbed a vicious finger in Monica's direction and heads turned to stare at the old woman. "*She* did it! She made me do it. She wanted to destroy my grandfather – she wanted to destroy *him!*" She swivelled in her chair and pointed wildly in Matthew's direction. The room erupted into frenzy.

"*No, Maggie, STOP!*" I yelled inside my head, still fumbling blindly for her in a sea of sensations in which I rapidly drowned. Lights dazzled and Duffy moved with exaggerated jerks on the dais, and the stench of cheap washing powder clashed with an expensive perfume from somewhere behind me. I felt sick again, and my collar rubbed raw against my neck. I used my hand to ease the fabric from my skin but I couldn't feel my fingers any more. My pulse raced to escape my body.

And then everything slowed and came to a standstill as if someone had put their foot on the brake. Although still acutely aware of every sound and smell and taste, each stretched into a tangible and continuous stream of consciousness so that if I reached out I could touch them, and take each one within my hand and change it.

Time dawdled like a film divided into individual frames, and I could move between each one at will. The frames dissolved into a movement of colour – all shades – dark and light, fat and thin, dense and so fragile that I could push myself through their luminosity. People became colours. I could no longer see their faces and their arms and legs, but their emotions – pulsating, vibrating – changing colour constantly, all clamouring to be heard, all wanting my attention, barely aware that I fought for each breath I took, nor of the tightening band in my chest.

The press of emotion was becoming too much, and I felt myself slipping away into the mass of them, beleaguered by their hopes and joys and spite and grief. But I found Maggie there too. She stood on the precipice of a pit of darkness, a writhing, coiling mass of blacks and deepest purples that were drawing her closer and closer to the edge of despair.

"*Maggie!*" I called in desperation. "*No, don't go, not that way!*"

She couldn't hear me. The darkness was defeating her and I couldn't fight against it, she had to do it herself. "*Maggie, come back to the light. I know you can hear me. Come back to your family, Maggie, don't leave them, don't go.*" With supreme effort, I gathered all my emotional strength and flung it towards her across the void like a rope to a man as he sinks beneath the surface.

Several things happened at once. I distinctly heard Matthew swear behind me at the same time as I opened my eyes and saw Maggie staring at me with her mouth slack in astonishment. She had heard me. I smiled at her.

The room became very still, and the only sound I could hear in it was a slowing, ragged *thump, thump, thump* like the faltering mechanism of a clockwork toy as it unwinds. And then it, too, stopped.

Matthew caught me as I fell forward, the table crashing against the dais as he kicked it away. "Emma!" he called and I tried to answer but the voices of the emotions kept pulling at me, greedy for my attention, weaving in and out and around me like spectres in a mist. "*Emma!*" Matthew's desperate voice called me back through the clamour. He looked up. "Harry..."

The light current of air he stirred as Harry moved towards us sent a spasm of shivers through me, but increasingly I was losing touch with my body and I soon stopped shaking.

"I've called 911, Matthew; what do you need?"

So much doubt and fear within the colours, all vying with each other for some part of me – plucking at me, feeding – but I had nothing more to give them. "*What do you want?*" I cried out, although no sound left my lips.

"I'm not getting a pulse." I felt Henry's growing apprehension through all the others. "It's happening again; did she drink coffee?"

I turned against the surge of people to reach Matthew but it was like swimming against a torrent and I couldn't make headway, and the effort it took drew on my rapidly ebbing reserves.

Henry counted beneath his breath. "It's been two minutes, Matthew."

"Epinephrine – *now*, Harry," Matthew said, and the boy moved rapidly beyond my sight. I sensed his urgency, felt the rising panic he fought to control.

Somewhere, further into the courtroom, I heard a call to clear the court. My detachment grew as the crowd began to thin, as if they were taking away some part of me.

Close by, frantic and frightened, Dad barked, "What's wrong? Do something!"

I wanted to tell him that there was nothing to be afraid of as colours – so beautiful that they sparkled like sun on flowing water – held me in suspension between two worlds, and I wanted to run with them.

"Emma…" Next to me, so close he was in my head, Matthew wound himself into my heart, calling to me, pulling me back towards him, not letting me follow, not letting me go. "… Emma, don't leave me." And in silent despair, *I can't face time without you.*

I clung to the bright light of his life as he drove all the ravenous colours away until only he surrounded me, keeping them at bay. He reached inside me, but it hurt where he touched my heart and I wanted him to stop.

Henry's voice hovered close, more pressing now. "Pupils not responding. We're up to four minutes, Matthew; she's at risk of hypoxia. Joel, keep them *back*, we need room!"

I heard the sound of shouting and people pushing and running feet, but the world felt remote and nothing made sense. I thought my chest hurt because it felt so heavy, although I couldn't be sure any more, and I drifted, sliding away, my colours almost gone behind dark shutters as they closed. *Don't take my colours away.*

Cold air touched my neck, my breast. Matthew's voice cried out in my head again. "*Emma, I've just buried my wife and I'm not going to lose you as well. Damn it, Emma, fight!*"

Why did his voice hurt so much? There's too much pain in it. I can't bear to feel his pain.

"We're losing her, Matthew – there's no response."

"No, I'm damn well *not!*"

"Matthew, we're over six minutes…"

Running feet again. Someone cursed as they were knocked to one side and Harry's voice carried across the room. "Matthew! Here – catch."

A small sound, tiny, the tip of a top being flicked off and then… oh, *agony*!

The pain in my chest bore into me, shattering the remnants of my colours into a million tiny shards and scattering them into oblivion. The pain went on and on, building into an excruciating peak, and then it stopped as a searing sensation replaced it. Starting around my heart it built and spread and seeped into my arteries like the encroaching tide over flat sand. I gasped and flailed, powerless in the face of such relentlessness. Someone had wound up the toy – *thump,*

thump, thump – soft and tired at first, then louder and stronger, and beside me, Matthew's quiet and steady voice, warm and comforting, reaching through the drumbeat. "I've got you, Emma; I have you, my love."

"OK, we have a pulse." Relief drenched Henry's voice.

In the near-empty courtroom, a dense, dark shape – confused and colourless – remained. Separate from the rest of the hues that surrounded it, I thought it was lost. I tried to see it more clearly, its significance uncertain, and I pushed out towards it beyond the spectrum of shades around me. It recoiled.

I recognized Staahl at once. His shape writhed and struggled to escape from me, in torment because he knew no colour, had no body of emotion. I had all colour and he had none, and there was no fear for me any more. I was free of him. I was triumphant.

I reached out and trapped him in my gaze. I searched his heart and found nothing but an empty hole that life and hope had once filled. He had sold his soul a long time ago.

"*I see you and you are* nothing *to me*," I told him. His hollow image shank before me.

Voices rang out with alarm. "Watch out!" "What's wrong with him?" Chairs clattered as they tumbled against the floor, and somewhere close by, a glass smashed.

Over the other voices, the judicial marshal bellowed, "Restrain him! Get him out of here!" They were taking Staahl away; I could sense him no longer; he was gone.

I heard Harry call out from some way across the room near the door, "Paramedics are here."

Joel answered close by me, his tone deeper than his brother's. "They took their bloody time. Geesh, we could have got her there quicker if we'd walked."

"Said they couldn't get through the traffic and the crowd."

Harry had moved next to his brother, but their colours faded into translucence and then I could no longer see, so I opened my eyes.

Matthew leaned so close that his face filled my vision and I couldn't look anywhere else but into the depths in which I could find peace.

"Hello again," he said softly.

I hurt. "Ow."

He smiled.

Someone put something heavy and scratchy over me and I recognized my father's coat from his aftershave. I remembered I had a body and that my body was cold. Through the opening doors, harsh, metallic rattling and new voices infiltrated the room, but I couldn't look at anything or anyone else.

"Will she be all right?" Dad's voice shook.

"Dad?" I whispered, as a different sort of reality imposed itself on my perception as I was drawn inexorably back into the world. I could feel Matthew's hand resting between my breasts beneath the coat.

"Henry will look after him, Emma; I'm taking you to the hospital."

Confused, my shrunken voice sounded alien to my ears. "Why?"

Matthew removed his hand briefly, and a swell of pain took me by surprise. He replaced his hand and the pain became mere discomfort again, and he kept it there as I was wheeled towards the door. The cold was becoming intolerable, but shock-induced sleep invited unconsciousness and, rocked by the motion of the gurney, I resisted it no longer.

And Spring Shall Come Again

My eyes were still heavy, so I kept them shut while I accommodated all the sounds around me. The intrusive bleep of a machine hammered my ears, insistent and repetitive but strangely comforting, and beneath it, matching stroke for stroke, the low, slow beat of my heart. A humming, so soft as to be almost not there, resonated within the metal frame of the bed, lulling me back into sleep but for the voices that held my attention. They came with colours, but not like before. These hues were weaker, almost transparent, but they carried the same tenor of emotions that I could read as easily as words. And sometimes the words used did not chime with the emotion that bore them.

Henry was explaining something to my father. His tone might have been tranquil, but he did not feel it.

"It's not straightforward, Hugh. There can be complications associated with the administration of adrenaline, including tachycardia, hypertension, arrhythmia – a bad headache would be the least we could expect. I think you need to be prepared – it's possible that Emma could suffer a further heart attack." Silence, broken only by the pulse of the machine.

Dad choked. "Are you saying she could still die?"

"It is a possibility, yes." Henry paused and I could sense his uncertainty. "Look, there is one other complication of which I think you should be aware." Dad's colour flowed from brown to black and back again. "Emma's heart failed to beat for over seven – nearly eight minutes, resulting in a lack of oxygen to her brain during that time…"

"But she spoke afterwards, I heard her," Dad interrupted in desperation.

I wanted to say something but my mouth felt like glue and the muscles refused to work in conjunction with my brain. I knew they were discussing me but somehow it seemed like someone else, and I couldn't make what they were saying real.

Henry continued. "It's too early to tell. If she survives the next twenty-four hours we'll run scans to measure the extent of the damage and, with therapy, some of it might be reversed in time."

I heard my father slump into a chair. "What am I going to tell her mother?" I had never heard him defeated like this, not even when his own parents died. His entire being became enveloped in a suffocating film of black.

I strove to speak again but my mouth would have none of it. I tried my eyes instead and they opened a fraction, but not enough to see.

"You're going to tell her mother that she'll be fine." Matthew shifted slightly as he turned to speak from where he stood at the end of my hospital bed. I read no darkness in him at all, his colours bright and vital. "There's nothing wrong with either her heart or her brain, except for her stubbornness, and that, I'm afraid, is incurable. You should have beaten her more as a child, colonel."

My mouth twitched involuntarily. I watched from behind my eyelids as hope coursed through my father. "Are you saying she *is* going to be all right? But surely, from what your father said a moment ago..."

As confused as Dad, Henry said, "Matthew?"

"Have a look at the readout, Henry." I heard footsteps cross the floor. "No arrhythmia, no palpitations, no indication of any electrical or mechanical disturbance or cardiac irritability at all. Perfectly steady and regular and *strong*."

"That's remarkable," Henry muttered as he studied the display, the paper creaking in his hands.

"What is more," Matthew continued, "there's been no change in the rhythm of Emma's heart for the last forty minutes or so." Something in his voice said there might be more to this than he stated.

Henry sounded doubtful. "Could there be a fault with the machine?"

"No, I've checked it – it's working perfectly. There's been no fluctuation, despite the nature of your conversation. Or mine," he added dryly.

Henry's mood responded, becoming brighter despite his misgivings. "The damage must be worse that we thought, or she couldn't have heard us. She's still unconscious, she..."

Matthew broke in. "No, she isn't, are you, Emma? Tired perhaps, which is not surprising, but certainly not unconscious. She's listening to everything we're saying."

"But does she understand?" Dad asked.

"Oh, yes, I think so; so we'd better watch what we're saying if we're not to get it in the neck later on. We need to push those bloods through though, Henry."

"I'll deal with that myself," Henry said, still in contemplation.

"Will you *please* explain what is happening?" Dad spluttered. "I don't know whether I'm supposed to be celebrating or mourning. Why won't she wake up if she's going to be all right?"

Matthew adopted the tone I recognized when he wanted to comfort and reassure. "Emma is going to be fine, colonel. She's very tired and her reactions are a bit sluggish, but I can assure you, she's largely undamaged."

I grunted silently at his quaint use of the word *undamaged* as well as at his cautionary use of *largely*. My chest felt pummelled like kneaded dough.

"And are you in agreement with your son's prognosis, Henry?" I heard my father ask, a little of the bullish mannerism surfacing as he struggled to comprehend the enormity of what had happened, and the narrow escape from death or a vegetative state I seemed to have miraculously achieved.

I wrenched my eyes open at last. Still standing at the end of my bed, his arms folded across his chest, Matthew watched me closely, as I guessed he had been all along. Standing next to the monitor, Henry had his back towards me. With a degree of resignation, he said, "Well, you know, youth must prevail in this case, Hugh. I defer to my son's greater knowledge."

Matthew raised an eyebrow at me and then grinned and I felt my mouth lift in response.

Still uncertain, my father sounded as if he intended pushing the point. "Well, if you're sure, but I would have thought…"

"Dad!" I coughed as my vocal chords vibrated and set up an irritating tickle. "Stop *arguing*."

"Emma?" his voice broke uncertainly. "Dear Lord, you're awake!"

I smiled weakly. "Hi, Dad."

Henry shook his head slowly from side to side as first he looked at me and then at Matthew. "Well, well, you never cease to amaze me – both of you. Welcome back, Emma; you had us all worried there for a while."

"Sorry, Henry," I murmured foggily.

"There's nothing to be sorry for, Emma, just *please* – for the sake of all our sanity – stay away from coffee in future." He glanced at Matthew, who hadn't moved. "I'll chase the bloods, Matthew, and I'll see *you* later, young lady," he said to me in a fatherly way, then nodded to my father. "Hugh."

Dad picked up my free hand and cradled it in his big, broad paw. "Henry said you had a reaction to coffee, Em. Sounds a bit extreme to me, but you never really touch the stuff normally, do you? You probably remember it didn't suit your grandfather either."

I didn't.

Matthew uncrossed his arms. "Oh?"

"Yes, my father couldn't stand it, said it made everything too noisy, too bright, whatever that means. But it didn't do *this* to him." He cast a baleful look at the equipment beeping and humming around me like a trapped bluebottle.

Matthew undid his jacket and took it off, slinging it over the back of a chair. "Did your father have a history of heart problems?" he asked casually.

"No, not a *history* of them, or none that I'm aware. He died after a massive coronary though; it came out of the blue after he'd returned from a Royal Engineers' reunion. Said he felt odd, keeled over, and that was it. Now I come to think of it, he did say something about the lights, said we should change the bulbs – too high a wattage, he said – and that the television was too loud. Strange I'd never thought of it before." It was the most I had ever heard Dad say about his father. His hand suddenly tightened on mine. "You don't think there's a connection between what happened to my father and this *thing* with Emma, do you?"

Matthew loosened his tie with his finger and thumb, and undid the top button of his shirt. "No, I shouldn't think so," he smiled reassuringly, but the little tight line to his mouth that I hadn't seen for some time reappeared.

"Why did you drink coffee when you know it doesn't suit you, Em? Look how ill it's made you." Dad sounded more aggrieved than worried now. Next his face would take on a reproachful look and I would be eleven years old again and being dressed down in his study like one of his cadets.

"I needed a caffeine boost, Dad."

"Now, you won't do that again in a hurry, will you?" he said in his best indulgently paternal manner.

"No – she won't," Matthew muttered.

I primped my lips at his tone, glad that I could feel them again, and raised my arm to look at the object attached to my finger monitoring my heartbeat. I wondered – if I tugged hard enough – whether it would come off, and then thought it would be better left, just in case. "Can I go home now?" I asked.

"No!" they both said at once.

"But I feel fine," I implored, "and, Matthew, you said…"

"No, Emma," he repeated, with a cautionary note that reminded me I wasn't in any position to argue. "You'll just have to be patient."

Dad rumbled a laugh deep in his chest, relief making him more loquacious than usual. "*Im*patient, more like. You always were a terrible patient, Emma. Your mother would be quite beside herself at times. Do you remember when you broke your leg and Nanna found you trying to get on your bicycle with the plaster barely set? You were only six and you made such a fuss. It took both your grandmother and your mother to get you back indoors."

I remembered it well. I felt very tired all of a sudden, and the thought of my mother and home and Nanna, and all the years spent without Matthew, expanded into an eternity of loneliness that caught me unawares. I choked back tears, silently cursing myself as they kept pushing out from between my lashes. I yanked my hand free from my father's, but too late – he saw them before I could wipe away the evidence.

"Emma… darling, I didn't mean it! I was joking, please don't cry." He began to flounder, because in all the years at home when at war with each other, I had endeavoured to hide my tears of anger and frustration from him. He wasn't used to seeing me cry, and his own face rumpled with distress.

Matthew tucked his arm around my shoulders, and I buried my face in his chest and sobbed as he stroked my tangled hair until the anguish eased and I stopped shaking.

"She'll be all right in a moment, colonel, don't worry," he said over the top of my head.

"I didn't mean to upset her." Dad sounded guilty and almost as upset as I felt, but it came tinged with something else, envious, perhaps, that another man comforted his daughter. I castigated myself for being so feeble. Matthew's voice reverberated against my cheek, soothing and reassuring. "Emma's exhausted, and she's reacting to both the physical and emotional stress she's been put through. There's no reason to reproach yourself. You must be tired as well. Perhaps you both should rest now." His velvet voice dropped, the suggestion laced with sedation. It was very effective and I snuggled into him, sniffling.

"I am feeling rather fatigued," Dad admitted.

I raised my head, feeling drained and blotchy, but less inclined to cry. "Dad, get some rest. I'll be all right here. Nothing's going to happen to me now."

"You can be assured of *that*." An ominous edge crept into Matthew's tone again.

"Well, if you're sure…" Dad kissed my forehead, his chin already scratchy after our early morning start. "Just don't do anything silly while I'm gone, Em, promise me."

As the door closed after him, Matthew rose from the bed and went over to the other side of the room, returning a moment later with a glass of water and two capsules. "For your headache," he said flatly.

I took them from him, not needing to ask how he knew that my head felt as if it were a log being split by an axe. "Thanks."

He waited until I had taken them, took the glass from my hand, deposited it on the table by the window, and then rounded on me. "What possessed you to be so totally *reckless*?" he thundered, eyes burning. I'd been expecting something like this. He held up his thumb and forefinger with barely a gap between them. "You were that close, Emma – *that* close – to dying. God alone knows why you're still here. What did you think you were doing?" A nurse stuck her head around the edge of the door with a worried expression. "Out!" Matthew fired at the poor woman and she hastily retreated. He strode halfway to the window, spun around as if he'd changed his mind, and came storming back towards me. "Well?" he demanded.

"I had to do *something*. Maggie was right on the edge, you heard what she said…"

"So you thought you would try to kill yourself as a *distraction*, is that it? Well, it certainly worked." He began pacing up and down, throwing me furious looks as he did so. I refused to be browbeaten. He might be older than me but that didn't always make him right, and this was something about which I felt absolutely certain.

"Matthew, putting her under pressure like that was wrong. It was always going to be counterproductive."

"And killing yourself wasn't? Come on, Emma, what did you think you were going to achieve?"

I stuck my chin out obstinately, wishing the pain relief would hurry up and work so that I could think more clearly. "You gave me the idea," I said more calmly than I felt.

"*What?*"

"You said that if you could reach inside people and remove the poison that made them do what they do, you would. But you can't – and I can – so I did."

"What the *hell* are you talking about?" Each angry step he took jarred my head, making it increasingly difficult to think. I put my free hand to my temple, and rubbed it.

"Well, if you'd just stop that pacing for one moment and give me a chance to explain rather than ranting like a… a deranged mongoose…"

He halted abruptly, his hands on his hips and clearly seething, but at least he remained still. "All right, I've stopped. Explain."

"You remember at Christmas I said that the coffee made everything clearer and that I could somehow feel Ellie's emotions?" He nodded tersely. "I thought that if I tried that again, I might be able to reach Maggie and stop her from saying something about you or the family." I stopped rubbing and instead put the heel of my hand to my throbbing head and tried to drive the pain away.

Still angry, at least he listened now. "And did you?"

"Did I what? Oh – reach Maggie? Yes, I did. It worked from that point of view; but I don't know how effective it was in getting her to change her mind or anything like that. Have you heard how she is, by the way?"

"Oddly enough I have been somewhat preoccupied," he replied caustically. I flinched at his tone and he moderated it. "So you reached her, and then what? You spoke to her?"

"Well, no, not exactly – it was more like I called to her emotionally, and I'm sure she heard me, but it was so crowded and they all wanted my attention at once, so I can only hope that she got the message."

Matthew looked at me with a mixture of curiosity and exasperation. "Emma, you're doing it again; stop talking in riddles. *Who* wanted your attention?"

My head still hurt, but there were lapses in the intensity of the pain like patches of blue on a cloudy day. I laid it gratefully on the pillows and found it even better if I closed my eyes. "The colours did, people. There were so many of them at first – it was confusing." I felt sleepy.

He almost contained the snort of frustration, but not quite. I smiled. I wasn't used to him behaving like this; I found it terribly *normal*.

When he spoke again I opened my eyes to find him looking down on me, and was relieved to see he wasn't cross any more. "I told your father you didn't sustain any brain damage. What am I going to tell him if you go around talking about colours wanting your attention?"

"It would only confirm what he's known about me all my life."

"Mmm." He balanced on the end of my bed. "I suppose I'm going to have to forgive you your lapse in self-preservation."

"It would be more peaceful," I agreed, stretching my legs out past him under the covers, and feeling multiple wires tug at sticky patches on my skin. "I didn't know I would have such a strong reaction to the coffee. I thought that perhaps I could control it better than I did; it was a calculated risk."

"Huh! Calculated on what?" He stared at the wall above my bed for what seemed like ages; then, when he looked at me, the fire had gone from his eyes and they were clear blue again. "At the funeral yesterday, you did something similar to me, didn't you? And then again when you sensed Monica?"

I closed my eyes and recalled. "I seem to be able to feel you more easily than anyone else in the same way you can sense my pain more intensely, but Monica was different – she imposed herself on me like a… violation." I pulled a face and opened my eyes. His hand found my shin and rubbed it in the way he often did when thinking. "But today there were too many distractions. I thought the coffee might help to boost the effect."

"It certainly did that. I suppose I only have myself to blame. I shouldn't have put you under pressure to speak to Duffy."

"Oh, I don't know, Matthew. I still think I would have taken the opportunity if the circumstances were right. Maggie was breaking, and the coffee was there for the drinking. I'm quite capable of making my own decisions, you know."

"Yes, and killing yourself."

"But I didn't, thanks to you, and it all still might have been worth it."

"It might," he said, but without conviction. He leaned over the bed and pressed a couple of the buttons on the heart monitor, concentrating as he read the display.

"What is it?"

Sliding off the bed, he went around to the machine, checking the lines running from the monitor to various parts of my body like wires from a telegraph pole. "If this is reading you correctly, there's still no change in the output of your heart."

I peered at the screen's flat face. "Is that bad?"

"No, not at all, just unusual. In the last half hour you've woken up, cried, and had me ranting like a 'deranged mongoose', I think you said – not withstanding your headache. I would have expected all that to have shown up on this," he tapped the top of the machine, "but it hasn't."

"And the significance of it is…?" I prompted him.

He shook his head. "I don't know. I'll wait and see what the blood test results are like and compare them with the ones we took at Christmas." He lifted my hand and, holding it against his face, breathed in the scent of my skin.

I stretched my fingers to stroke the crease between his eyes and smooth it, but it deepened at my touch, and he sighed. "I couldn't bear the thought of losing you. It was bad enough after Staahl attacked you, but now…" He drew a jagged, painful breath. "Emma, if you had died today, I would have lost my reason for being."

I didn't need to see his colours to know what I had put him through. For all that had happened to me, it was still Matthew who had just lost his wife and had buried her only yesterday, and yet here I lay – with what amounted to a self-inflicted injury – when I should be looking after him, not the other way around.

I inched forward and took my hand away from his face, and put my arms around him as far as I could without dragging the wires out of place. "I'm sorry," I whispered. "I only did it to protect you. I didn't mean to hurt you or anyone else."

He stared straight into my eyes, and at that distance the full impact of his gaze hit me like a taser. "*Hurt* me? Hurt doesn't even begin to come close. You have no idea what it did to me."

I withdrew against the pillow, annoyance fuelled by guilt. "Yes, I do, I know *exactly* what it's like, Matthew. I feel it every time I think of losing you. You don't have a monopoly on hurt, you know."

It was a stupid thing to say – a stupid, insensitive thing. He looked away. The axe man in my head began to split lumber again, blow after blow, pounding away relentlessly. I welcomed the pain – I deserved it – but he turned back to me, and positioned his hand over my temple, lifting the fire from my head as he did so.

"No… don't." I pushed his hand away. He smiled sadly and replaced his hand.

"Emma, your pain won't make mine any better."

"I didn't mean how it sounded," I murmured mournfully.

"I know you didn't." He looked at his watch. "It's time you had something to eat; it'll help your head." I thought he was about to say something else, but he appeared to think better of it. "I have some things to sort out. I won't be very long. Think you can avoid coffee for the next half an hour or so if I leave you alone?"

I didn't want him to leave, but he picked his jacket off the back of the chair and made for the door. "On second thoughts," he said, turning back briefly as he slung his jacket over his shoulder, "I don't think we'll take the risk. I'll get someone to sit with you, just in case."

I must have slept because it was dark outside when I opened my eyes again, and the only light in the room came from a side lamp and the glow from the machines by the bed. The attachment monitoring my heart pinched my skin and in my stupor, I put out a hand to ease it.

"Don't touch it," a voice ordered, then more gently, "I'll look at it for you."

I sat up. "Ellie, what are you doing here?"

She bent over the attachment and moved it millimetres so that it no longer nipped my skin, watching the monitor all the while. "There," she said, "that should do it." She smiled cheerfully. "Matthew's been in several times but you were asleep and he didn't want to wake you. He said you'll need to eat." She withdrew a mobile from her pocket, rattled a text off at an alarming speed, and replaced it.

"I see. So Matthew thought I needed babysitting, did he? What on earth did he think I could do, strapped up to this thing?" I waved my finger in the air and the line flopped with it.

She sat down, crossing her long legs, and untangled the end of her stethoscope from her hair. Unaccustomedly shy, she hesitated before saying, "Emma, I'm sorry I wasn't at the trial. I would have been there, but I had some medical assignments to complete and then I... well, I'm just sorry, that's all."

"I didn't expect you to be there, Ellie – any of you. It's good to see you now, though – you look very well. I love the boots."

"Thanks," she looked pleased. "Can I ask you something? What happened on Christmas Eve, what I did to you with the coffee – all *this*..." She looked at the machines and wires as if they were an accusation in themselves. "You know why I did it, don't you? You saw into me. I... I wanted to ask you about it before, but... well..." Brass buckles on her boots jingled as she shifted her position awkwardly.

"Yes, Ellie, I know and I do understand. I'm immensely grateful to you."

She jangled again and this time met my eyes directly. "You are?"

"I found it scary, yes, but without you I would never have known that I could do what I did."

Confused but evidently relieved, she unwound the stethoscope and put it on top of the monitor, where the end swung to a restful full stop.

"These can come off now." She started peeling off the sticky pads and lines dotting my body. "I didn't understand what Maggie wanted, Emma. I knew she didn't like you, but then she doesn't like many people, and she never said why. And I didn't know anything about… Monica." At the mention of the woman's name, we both grimaced spontaneously. "I never meant to hurt you. It's dumb, I know, but I get so… jealous." She stared at the monitor's blinking eye, not able to meet my own. "That sounds so gross, doesn't it? He's my great-grandfather. You must think I'm sick or something." She chanced a look at me.

"But you're not *in* love with him, are you?" I asked quietly.

She shook her head vehemently, pulling a face at the same time. "No-*o* way, it's not like *that!*"

"I don't know if it's the same with you, Ellie, but my grandfather helped bring me up. He meant everything to me: my father, my teacher, my best friend. If it weren't for him I wouldn't have become a historian or gone to university. He was my inspiration and my life. I loved and respected him more than anyone else in my family. I loved him, but only as my grandfather, and nothing more than that. I thought I would never find anyone else I could love as much when he died."

She picked at a loose thread on her trousers, winding it around her index finger and snapping it off before she spoke. "Yes, that's how it is with me, but then you *did* find someone – you found Matthew."

"But not before I made a mistake with someone else." She might as well know about Guy from me than learn about it in the local rag. "My mistake wasn't much in the grand scheme of things, but I regret it now."

She stopped fiddling and leaned forward. "What happened?"

"I let someone flatter me into making me think that I meant something to him. But I was younger than you are now, and much more foolish."

She smiled, the corners of her mouth tipping into an attractive bow, making her pretty in a strong, feline way, and I remembered Matthew saying that she had never met anybody significant enough to bring home and introduce to the family, and that seemed a shame.

A robust knock on the door had her tutting and rising to answer it. After a short word, she came back with a tray.

"Who's out there?" I asked.

"Oh, that's Joel. He makes so much noise."

"What's he doing outside my door?" I asked, nonplussed.

She shrugged, putting the plate down on the wheeled bed tray so I could reach. "He's just making sure you're not disturbed."

"By whom?"

"Anyone."

"*Blow this…*" I struggled upright, pushing the bed tray out of the way and swinging my legs over the side of the bed. "For goodness' sake, I bet neither of you have eaten. Joel…!" I called.

Ellie flustered, "Don't, Emma, you'll pull the line."

"I don't need it – there's nothing wrong with me." I gave a sharp tug and the device clamped to my skin came away with a satisfying *slup*. The monitor hesitated for a second while it registered the change, then an ear-piercing wail like a lonely calf filled the room, escaping into the corridor.

"Oops," I said, guiltily.

The door was flung open, hitting the wall with a resounding crash as Joel shot through, followed seconds later by Matthew, who took one look at me, his expression changing from apprehension to exasperation. He pressed a switch on the machine and the room fell into silence. All three looked at me.

"It sort of fell off," I muttered.

He viewed me disbelievingly. "Hardly, I put it on."

"Well, I might have encouraged it a *little*."

He picked up the beleaguered end from where it dangled and held out his hand for mine. I gave it to him meekly and he reattached it and reset the machine. "It's there for a purpose – leave it alone. Ellie, you have to watch Emma like a hawk."

"It's not Ellie's fault," I objected.

"I didn't think it was," he said.

"Well, how long *do* I have to be strapped to this machine for, Matthew? I thought you said it wasn't showing anything?"

"But it might do, and I want a clear run without any interruptions from you, so *leave it alone*. Look at it this way: as long as you're in here being monitored, you won't be in that courtroom being cross-examined, right?"

"OK."

"Got the message?"

"Uh huh." I twiddled with the lead. "So when do I get out?"

"When I say." Despite the hint of a growl, he fought the

impulse to laugh so I couldn't take it very seriously, especially as Joel loitered behind him with a grin the size of Marble Arch.

"Hey, Joel," I greeted him around Matthew's back.

He raised a hand in response. "Yo, Emma. You're looking pretty good for a corpse. Didn't think you'd make it this time." He scrabbled through the cornfield of his hair. "And you don't want to leave just yet – the press are outside waiting for blood. Seem to think you're a meal ticket: *Brit Chick Confesses All-*type stuff. Great."

"Thank you, Joel. The boy has his uses," Matthew said dryly, "but diplomacy isn't one of them. You'd better eat while that is still palatable." He nodded towards the food. I curled my legs under the bedcovers, and took a mouthful to appease him. "Why were you trying to escape?"

The now lukewarm food instantly eased the corrosion in my hollow, raw stomach.

"I wasn't, I just thought that Ellie and Joel might need something to eat – it's so late."

His expression softened. "Don't worry about these two. They're more resilient than they look."

To me, Ellie looked as if she could do with a square meal, and Joel always looked as if he needed a nuclear reactor of food to keep him going.

"They still need to eat, Matthew," I pointed out, reasonably, I thought.

He raised an asymmetrical smile in response. "Not as much as you might think."

Ellie nodded. "It's true, Emma. We don't need as much as you – our metabolism's much slower than yours."

"Yeah, sure, we *like* food, but we don't *need* to eat as much as we choose to." Joel leaned across my bed and pinched a disc of fried potato off my plate to illustrate. "Pretty cool, huh?"

"The Lynes gene again, I take it?" I asked Matthew.

"Yeah, *fre-ak* show," Joel mused. "Hey, Emma, how's it feel, joining the circus as one of the acts?" In answer, I held out my plate and he snaffled a few more potatoes.

Matthew took my plate from my outstretched hand and put it back on the tray in front of me. "As I said, they don't need to eat as much as you do, so, Joel – outside if you please; Emma doesn't need any unwelcome visitors. Ellie, please see if your grandfather has had any luck with those bloods yet. And you," he said, lifting my chin with one finger so that I had the full impact of his eyes, "eat."

"So you can read people's emotions?" Matthew took my empty plate away and balanced along the length of the bed with his arm behind me; it was so good to feel him close again. "The scientist in me would very much like to know how this has developed, unless, of course, it's been latent. You said to me – it seems like a lifetime ago – that you understand people's motives."

"I thought I did, but I'm not so sure now. Anyway, they were always dead so they couldn't contradict."

"That has its advantages," he said in an undertone.

"But what happened in court is different and all so new I can't quite get my head around it. I found it frightening at first because I couldn't control it – like being on a bolting horse: exhilarating but out of control. I think there were just too many people. They seemed to have an ambient consciousness and were aware of me emotionally, and they all wanted something *from* me. They weren't being aggressive or anything like that, more that they yearned for comfort and reassurance. I couldn't help them though; I had to look after Maggie. Like a black hole, she took just about everything I could throw at her," I wavered, wondering if this sounded like the ramblings of a mad woman. "Does any of this make sense to you?" I found a comfortable spot between his shoulder and his chest on which to rest my cheek and he adjusted his posture to accommodate me accordingly.

"I'm not sure about making sense, but it sounds very familiar. It took me years to be able to resist the pain of others so that I wasn't consumed by it. My ability has never sat easily with science, but I've had to accept it as real, and yours appears to be quite similar. I think the closest we can come to giving it a name is calling it a form of synesthesia. " He tightened his grasp of my hand where it lay against his chest, and I welcomed the insistent reassurance of the pressure, and the unbroken beat of his heart against my open palm.

"You know what would have happened to us if we were suspected of having these *abilities*, as you call them, four hundred years ago?" I said.

"Of course; I saw it often enough. Witch trials were a pathetic, ugly affair; it's a good thing we live when we do."

I wasn't sure if I could agree, and I played with the buttons of his shirt thoughtfully. "I don't know. Judging by what we've been through recently, I wonder if very much has changed – trial by innuendo and public opinion and all that. I suppose that at least now we won't end by being strung up outside the courthouse. They would have a terrible shock when you didn't die."

He winced. "What a cheerful thought, and I wouldn't want to put it to the test."

I yawned, sleepy again, and he smiled, hugging me close. "Once this is all over, whatever the outcome, I'm going to take you away – somewhere we can be together and you can rest with no expectations and no questions."

"And no bears?" I murmured.

He kissed me softly. "And no bears," he confirmed.

A strange, half-light filtered through the blinds, and the road noise, which had been clearly audible yesterday, sounded muffled as if I were hearing it through cotton wool.

I leaned sleepily on one elbow and attempted to see through the crack in the blind where it didn't quite meet the edge of the window. The sound of a book being closed and a pen lid replaced came from behind me.

"It's snowing."

I turned over and my chest twinged sharply inside and out, reminiscent of yesterday's battering. Matthew glanced at the monitor, but the bleep remained monotonously regular.

"What did Joel mean about me being a freak last night?"

He kept his eyes on the machine. "Apart from the bruising, how do you feel?"

I concentrated on my body, trying to pick up further signs of discomfort, but there were none. "Fine. I could run a marathon if the mood so took me."

"That's what Joel was referring to. You shouldn't, you should feel appalling. Even your chest isn't too bad, is it? You're still just a bit bruised and tired."

I blinked, nodded and stretched my legs and back until my toes touched the end of the bed frame. "Did the blood tests show anything?"

"No, they didn't, but they should have done. There were no telltale signs of heart disturbance at all."

"So is that it? Can I leave *now*?"

"We'll wait and see what Eve shows up first just in case, and play it out a little longer. Duffy wants to see you. I wouldn't let her in yesterday. Remember, you've had a major heart incident and you were on the verge of death so, for appearances sake and even if you feel as fit as a flea, act it up a bit."

He went over to the window and pulled up the blind. Snow beat against the glass, faltered, then slowed. I lay there, quite content to watch him move around the room.

"I suppose this is what you have to do, isn't it? Pretend to be something you're not?"

"All the time; which reminds me, it's time I caught another cold." I laughed and his eyes gleamed briefly. "It's so good to hear you laugh. I think, after all this is over, we'd better…" A soft knock at the door stopped him from finishing his sentence, and there were so many ways I could have finished it for him. "It'll be Duffy. Remember what I said." He went to open the door and I closed my eyes.

"How is she? Will she be all right?" Concern tinted Duffy's voice and I felt like a total fraud. "Was it the stress of the trial, and all, that caused it?"

Matthew stood guard by my bed. I found I could still see him even though my eyes were shut, a shape defined by his movement and colour.

"I think it pushed her right to the edge. She's lucky to be alive, but she'll pull through with plenty of rest and no further stress."

Duffy took the hint. She removed something, rustling like paper, from her bag.

"That's why I came. I wanted to tell Emma what's happening with the trial, you know? It might help a little."

I sighed and rolled slightly as if on the verge of waking, and opened my eyes.

Matthew stood to one side and busied himself with the monitor and lines.

"Please keep it to a few minutes; she hasn't as much strength as I would like."

Duffy quietened her voice as if frightened she could cause another heart attack just by talking to me.

"Emma, honey, I'm so sorry you were taken ill, but I have some good news." She plumped her bag on the wheeled tray next to her, the soft leather wilting in brown folds like the skin of an old bloodhound. She held up some pieces of paper in front of me. "Don't try to talk now, hun, but the judge called me and Horatio to her chambers. It seems that, after his little outburst in court, she has ruled that Staahl has to be reassessed. Best of all, Dr Lynes – Dr Margaret Lynes, that is..." she darted a look at Matthew, but he studied a long printout, apparently absorbed in the task and oblivious to her comments, "... withdrew her evidence and issued a statement saying she is standing by her original report. Now, since it..."

"Why?" I asked, desperate to know the details so that I interrupted her a little more forcefully than I meant to. Matthew flashed a cautionary look. "Why did she do that?" I whispered weakly.

"Hush, you save your strength now." She squeezed my arm lightly. "It seems that Dr Lynes thinks she might have been too quick to make a judgment of Staahl's state of mind. She says she made a mistake."

Matthew made a sort of choking noise, which he turned into a cough and Duffy's forehead puckered. "Anyhow, Kort Staahl is in a state institution for the foreseeable future and until fit to stand further assessment. He was just hollering as they took him away, a-wailing and moaning as if the devil'd taken his wits. He bit one of the sergeants on the chin. Poor man needed stitches, and he wasn't that pretty to look at in the first place."

"What does it mean for the trial?"

"It's over, hun, that's what I've been saying. The case against you has been dropped. Seems Horatio doesn't think Staahl's evidence would stand up to scrutiny and all, given his state of mind. Staahl's not competent to stand trial and it looks like he never may be, in which case he will be put away indefinitely. It means we won't get the trial and conviction we wanted against him, but nor will he be able to press his case against you…"

I closed my eyes as the significance made itself known like a reassuring clout to the back of my head. He would probably never be free to hurt anyone ever again: not me, or some random stranger, not Matthew. Anything he claimed would be discounted, nullified by madness.

"Emma, are you all right? Dr Lynes!" Her voice rose so I opened them again and smiled just enough to reassure her.

Matthew put the printout down. "I think that's just about as much as she can handle for now. I take it there will be no more demands from the court on Dr D'Eresby from now on?"

"No, not on *either* of you." She smiled sweetly as she looked first at Matthew and then at me. "You're both free to get on with your lives."

The door closed behind her. Leaning against it, Matthew surveyed me, lost in thought.

"Are you all right, Matthew, after all this, after everything?"

He smiled briefly. "I'm always all right, Emma."

He came and sat beside me, still miles away, and then I did what I wished I could have done a long time ago. Locating the well of his emotion, I placed my hand over his heart where the depth of his sadness stained his life mulberry, and drew the wound as if drawing venom. I watched as his colours changed perceptibly from dark to light, pulsed momentarily, then settled to a rich mid-blue.

He gave a short laugh of disbelief. "That's quite a remarkable gift you have there, Dr D'Eresby," he said, kissing my palm before leaning over, flicking a switch, and removing the monitor from my hand. The machine remained soundless.

He threw back the bedcovers and, picking me up, took me to the window. He placed me on my feet and we cradled together watching the snow fall, his cheek against mine, both hearts beating in time.

He looked down at our clasped hands, turning his so that the light caught the gold of the two rings he wore. His smile seemed poignant at first, then resolute, as he eased the band from his wedding finger. He held it for a second more, then reached out and placed it carefully on the table in front of us, a circle of gold on the dark wood. He breathed deeply – a long breath – letting go.

"Look," he murmured. Outside, a lone tree braved bitter winds. Pale pink flowers clung to every bough, each blossom crowned in delicate snow. "It won't be long now; winter will soon be over and we will breathe the sun again.

> *'As blown brown buds of death's decay*
> *In winter's empty grip shall lie,*
> *Till warm-beamed sun will fill the day*
> *And spring shall come again.'"*

"That's beautiful," I whispered. "Who wrote it?"

"A seventeenth-century gentleman," he said.

"That wouldn't happen to be you, would it?" I asked.

He raised his eyes to mine, and the light in them shone for me, and for me alone.

"It might," he replied.

Author Notes

BY LOYALTY DIVIDED

To that storm of blood that is now falling upon
this kingdom and all those fears and confusions
that petitions daily show to be in the thoughts
and apprehensions, both of the city and the whole
kingdom, we might add such circumstances that
are of late discovered and broken out concerning
His Majesty's person, and likewise a confused and
levelling undertaking to overthrow monarchy,
and to turn order, that preserves all our lives and
fortunes, into a wild and unlimited confusion.
BL E451(33)
Royalist proclamation for support, 1648

As the relationship between king and Parliament deteriorated in the early 1640s, the conflict we know as the English Civil War presented an opportunity for families to settle old slights and scores, and stories of internecine strife pepper the history of the period. The tiny county of Rutland was not immune. Families came to blows; just one of the numerous accounts where simmering tensions erupted into bloodshed was that of Edward Noel and his son, Baptist – fighting for the king – against their cousins, Sir Edward Harington and his son, James, who fought for Parliament.

Material held in the National Archives, Kew, in family records, crumbling parish accounts, local oral traditions – all hold clues to the personal conflicts bubbling beneath the surface of the greater, national one. Bullet holes in the stone arcading of a church, axe marks on a banister rail, ghosts of lovers wandering the manor gardens in which they were killed, together they bear witness to the minor tragedies that left a legacy of bitterness.

Relationships, in the broadest sense, lie at the heart of many dramas, and their power to heal or divide form the basis from which stories often spring. Littering the history of the period, such incidents provide the backbone to the emerging tale in *The Secret of the Journal*. When faced with the disfigured tomb of the knight lying in a little English church all those years ago, it was a simple step for me to imagine a story in which the jealousy of a younger brother led to conflict – with devastating results.

"For what can war, but endless war, still breed?" (John Milton, 1608–74.) As a historian, my protagonist, Emma D'Eresby, is acutely aware that events do not exist in isolation, but cast long shadows that shape the future. In *Rope of Sand*, Emma meets Matthew's family for the first time and, while she suspects that not everyone welcomes her, she is unaware of the lingering malevolence of historic conflicts that drove the family apart many years before she was born, sowing the seeds of disunity for the future. What goes around comes around.

REALM OF DARKNESS

The past is never far behind, and in *Realm of Darkness* – the fourth book in *The Secret of the Journal* series – as Emma begins a new life with Matthew, history catches up with terrifying results.